The Beach at Summerly

A Novel

Beatriz Williams

HARPER LARGE PRINT

An Imprint of HarperCollinsPublishers

THE BEACH AT SUMMERLY. Copyright © 2023 by Beatriz Williams. All rights reserved. Printed in the United States of America. No part of this book may be used or reproduced in any manner whatsoever without written permission except in the case of brief quotations embodied in critical articles and reviews. For information, address HarperCollins Publishers, 195 Broadway, New York, NY 10007.

HarperCollins books may be purchased for educational, business, or sales promotional use. For information, please e-mail the Special Markets Department at SPsales@harpercollins.com.

FIRST HARPER LARGE PRINT EDITION

ISBN: 978-0-06-332291-2

Library of Congress Cataloging-in-Publication Data is available upon request.

23 24 25 26 27 LBC 5 4 3 2 1

To the men and women who quietly gave their lives
in a war of unknown battles

The Beach at Summerly

I.

APRIL 1954
Wellesley, Massachusetts

Aunt Benedita telephones long-distance just as I'm rushing out the door. She's one of those people who has a knack for it.

"I can't talk right now," I tell her. "I'm late for class."

"You'll want to hear this. Your father told me that Tom Donnelly and his boys started to work on a new job."

"Gee, that's terrific. You know how I love hearing all the little tidbits from back home."

"Don't you want to know whose house they're working on?"

"Look, Auntie, I know you don't believe it, but a mile away from where I stand at this telephone, there's a lecture hall filled with undergraduates *desperate* to hear me speak about the Salem witch trials. Could you put them out of their misery?"

Aunt Benedita disregards my pique. That's how we've remained on speaking terms, all these years.

"They're fixing up Summerly," she says.

Lucky for me, an armchair sits next to the table where we keep the telephone. I land on it hard and notice that the telephone cord has somehow gotten twisted around the table leg. I unwind the cord while Aunt Benedita's voice leaks out of the earpiece, repeating my name. When I put the receiver back to my ear, the darn thing shakes in my hand, all by itself.

"Good for them," I tell her.

Outside, the air smells green. The temperature is positively balmy. The blossoms are popping out at last in their pinks and whites. Even after all these years on the mainland, I can't look on a blossoming tree without my throat feeling sore. You simply don't get blossoming trees on Winthrop Island. It seems so extravagant. The sky has turned an ultramarine shade of blue and the blossoms nod and waft against this exemplary field. I hurry across the quadrangle toward Founders Hall and try not to mind all the beauty, but it hits my gut all the same.

I wasn't exactly lying to Aunt Benedita about the lecture hall, but you might say I was stretching the truth. I still have time to hurry up the steps, deposit my belongings in the fourth-floor telephone booth known as my office, and drink a cup of muddy coffee before presenting myself in the classroom two minutes before the lecture's due to begin. It's the end of April and the air is green and balmy, as I said, and most of my students have given up trying to arrive early, if at all. "Women in Early Colonial America" is a brand-new course in the history department curriculum—a course I designed myself, if you must know—but I'm afraid nobody seems to care much about colonial history in these days of hydrogen bombs and Jackson Pollock, even though I try to present the subject with a certain amount of panache.

Still, a few young ladies have managed to drag themselves through the dreaming blossoms and into the classroom, and that's all that matters, really. To reach a few fresh minds, to plant some germ of inspiration. That girl in the second row, for example. The light, curling brown hair and the sharp chin; the dark, narrow eyes like a young fox. She sets that inquisitive chin into her palm and loses herself in the parable and I say to myself, in a thought that floats in parallel to my words and my theatrical gestures, *That's it, honey, just sink yourself into the past, so you don't have to spend so much time in the awful present.*

Later, when I retire to my telephone booth office in the fourth-floor attic, there is the newspaper to distract me. Sure, maybe it describes the awful present, but at least it isn't *my* awful present. I light a cigarette, pour myself another cup of muddy coffee, and add a splash of cognac from the flask in my desk drawer. If you're going to drink in your office, I always say, make sure it's worth the trouble.

The news is even more rotten than usual—same old mess in Indochina, the Red Sox lose another one, that chump McCarthy's starting in on the Army now—but I read on regardless. If nothing else, I know the trick of mental discipline. Close your mind to the unwanted thought. Throw yourself a nice, noisy party of the head so you don't hear it knocking.

Still, now that I'm sitting down to read the newspaper instead of lecturing, drinking this miraculous coffee instead of standing cold sober in front of a room full of dewy coeds, that damned word keeps streaking across my mind from wherever it is you hold your memories.

Summerly.

Why in God's name did Aunt Benedita have to

go and telephone me about a thing like that? Long-distance, no less. She might have put it in a letter—she writes plenty of those, too. Always trying to smooth things over, Aunt Benedita, always having the exact opposite effect. *I bicycled to Summerly the other day,* she might write, *and it's an awful shame how they've let it go to seed. The roof shingles are falling out by the dozen and the grass is up to the front window. Do you remember that old rhododendron bush? It's taking over the hedge.*

Does she not understand how these details hurt? Does she think they'll make me feel better? Now she wants to tell me that Tom Donnelly's crew is fixing up the place again so the Peabodys can return for the summer season like old times. What am I supposed to think about that? Am I supposed to want to join them?

Well, now I've done it. You see what I mean? You open your mind a crack, just a *crack* to allow a single dumb word like *Summerly* into the party, and the rest of that thought shoves through uninvited and eats up all the canapés. I lay down the newspaper and open the desk drawer, and this time when I uncork my bottle of cognac, I really let the coffee have it. I do like cognac. It's like brandy, only . . . more. A professor of mine made the introduction, junior year, and we've been friends ever since. The cognac, I mean, not the professor. No,

Professor Pete and I had the briefest possible affair before his wife found out and reported him to the department head. He accepted a research position at some progressive-minded college in the Midwest somewhere and I haven't heard from him since. The cognac was the best part of our friendship, to be perfectly honest. I prop my feet on the corner of the desk and slide the newspaper into my lap. The aqua vitae gives off its perfume inside my skull. I turn the page.

"RED BRAHMIN" PAROLE HEARING
CANCELED, SOURCES SAY

And I guess it speaks to the old adage about trouble coming in threes that my phone rings the exact instant I've absorbed that headline. The coffee spills in my lap. I swear savagely and reach for the receiver.

Emilia Winthrop, I growl.

The voice on the other end is a courtly Southern baritone. "Miss Winthrop. I hope I haven't called at a bad time."

When I arrive home at a quarter past five, Susana's making dinner. Lizbit sits nearby on the kitchen counter, stirring something inside a large metal mixing bowl.

"Emmie," she says sternly, "have you been hitting

the bottle at work again?" Lizbit calls us both by our first names, to the delight of visitors. They think it's so amusing and precocious in a seven-year-old.

"Hell, no." I swoop her into my arms and deliver a boozy kiss to her cheek. "I've been a saint. What's for dinner?"

"Pork chops," says Susana. "What's the matter with you?"

"You'll never guess."

"Not Cato again."

"No, not Cato. Believe it or not."

My kid sister's a terrific cook. I'm going to miss her terribly when she gets married in June. When I try to picture the aftermath—Susana and Harvey on their honeymoon in Key West, me and Lizbit sitting around the living room in our underwear—I get this sinister feeling of bleakness and hunger. I can only hope Lizbit takes over the cooking.

Susana flips the pork chops in the skillet. "So what gives? Poor Lizbit's going to get sauced just standing downwind of you."

"I can hold my breath," says Lizbit.

I snap my fingers. "*Witches*. That's it."

"Witches?"

"*Witches*, not *Women*. 'Witches of Early Colonial America.' That'll turn out the kids next semester."

"For God's sake," says Susana, "just go set the table, will you?"

Now, I don't mean to impugn the good Harvey. He's a real prince and I'm grateful he's taking my sister off my hands. It's a sad story, really. He's only twenty-six and a widower. Graduated Harvard Law and married his sweetheart, a girl from Brookline, nice girl by all accounts, then six months later she's dead of cancer. They didn't catch the tumor until it was too late. Terrible story. We don't know the details, actually—just that it was a female type of cancer. Harvey's too embarrassed to go into the specifics. Harvey's embarrassed about a lot of things. Honestly, I don't think they've even reached second base, Susana and Harvey. He came into the bookstore the Christmas before last to buy a present for his ex-mother-in-law. The Serenity Bookshop, right here in Wellesley, Mass.—ever heard of it? It's a nice cozy spot packed with armchairs and atmosphere. We keep some dirty novels in the back for people with real imagination. Susana opened it when she moved up here with me seven and a half years ago. She had to do *something*, and she didn't want to start college, like me. So she started a bookstore instead. I usually pitch in on weekends and holidays, but when Harvey Reed, Esquire, walked into the store late that Christmas Eve (well, he's a man, after all) I happened fatefully to be four streets away in our living room with Lizbit, trimming the tree and skimming the eggnog, and the next thing you know, Susana leads the widower Harvey home for the holidays like a stray puppy. *Can we keep him*, that was what I saw in her eyes that night, and it turned out we could. He's a lawyer at some nice Boston firm. Always a good idea to have a lawyer in the family, don't you think? Just in case? They'll be happy together, I'm sure.

Anyway, I once asked Harvey sort of a legal question. I asked him why the newspapers insist on making up catchy names for notorious criminals—the so-called Red Brahmin, to take a random example. He said he disapproved of the practice, that it mocked the sacred principle of innocence presumed until guilty proved, without which our democracy could not stand. (All right, so Harvey can be a bit of a prig.) But he conceded that democracy also required the freedom of the press to make asses of themselves, so what could you do?

And it was true that this Red Brahmin, though she had the privilege of belonging to one of Boston's oldest families, had betrayed our country's most vital secrets to the Soviet Union. So even if the moniker was a little crude, you couldn't deny it was apt.

One thing I love about Susana, she can take a hint. She refrains from questioning me about my day at work until after Lizbit is scrubbed clean and passed out cold in her pink canopy bed, so remarkably like an angel it chokes your throat.

Early on, we made a deal in our house, which is Susana shops for groceries and does the cooking, while I do the baking—the doctor says it's good for my nerves—and the washing up. Accordingly, I yank on the rubber gloves and plunge my arms into the hot water. Susana sits down at the kitchen table and lights a cigarette. *Well?* she says.

"Sumner Fox rang me up after class today."

She almost spits out the cigarette. "Fox? *Our* Sumner Fox?"

"Is there another one?"

"So what for did he call you?"

"He wants me to come to prison and talk to our mutual friend."

"Our mutual friend?"

"You know."

"Talk to Mrs. Rainsford? *Our* Mrs. Rainsford?"

"I wouldn't exactly call her *our* Mrs. Rainsford, dear. Not in public. People might get the wrong idea."

Susana drags thoughtfully on her cigarette. "Why does Fox want you to talk to Olive Rainsford?"

"He wouldn't say. She wants to speak to me, that's all. It is apparently of the utmost urgency, according to Fox."

"Well," Susana says.

"*Well* what?"

"Well, it's about time, I guess."

"What do you mean, it's about time?"

"Honey," she says soothingly, "any shrink could tell you that it would do you a world of good to sit down with that woman and—well, get some answers."

"You're absolutely right. Any shrink."

Susana rises from the kitchen table and snatches a towel from the hook. Susana's the only person I know who can smoke a cigarette and dry a plate at the same time. "Just because Cato's a psychologist doesn't mean the whole science is wrong."

"It might, though."

"All right," she says. "Let me correct myself. *First* you should end things with Cato, then you should visit that prison and talk to Olive."

"*First*, I don't see any reason to end things with

Cato. I think it's the most satisfactory relationship I've ever had. Second, nuts to Olive."

"Why not, though? Give me *one good reason* why you can't just sit down with her for half an hour."

I hand Susana a water glass. "You didn't happen to read the papers today, did you?"

"Sort of," she says. "Not really."

"You know Olive's been coming up for her first chance at parole, right? Well, the parole hearing's been canceled. Right there in the *Globe*, page four or something. And then—at that exact moment I'm reading about it—Fox rings up."

"So?"

"So you don't smell a rat? Because I smell a rat."

Susana turns to me all round—round face, round mouth, round eyes. "Oh! You don't think they've found out something else she's done? Or she's been spying from prison?"

"I just think it's funny, that's all. At this particular moment in time, Olive sticks up her hand and says she wants to have a nice friendly chat with the woman who put her in prison. No hard feelings."

"I would say you've got plenty of hard feelings."

I hand Susana the last fork, pull the plug from the drain, and peel off the gloves. The pipes bubble and gasp. A hint of putrescence drifts up with the bubbles.

I make a mental note to call the plumber. "I agree," I tell her. "Which is why I told Mr. Fox to go to hell."

When Susana and I moved to Wellesley seven and a half years ago, just in time for the start of term, we got this bungalow for a steal. Maybe the G.I. Bill was sending battalions of young men into college in the autumn of 1946, but you couldn't say the same for girls—especially the kind of upscale girl who went to Wellesley College to further her education. Those girls were mostly getting married. But not us. We needed a place to live, and this was the first place we saw. It was twenty years old and needed a lick or two of paint, to say nothing of a working icebox, but it had three nice-sized bedrooms and a modern bathroom and plenty of bookshelves left behind by a previous occupant, and it was only a mile from the center of campus. *We'll take it*, I said.

Since then, Susana has done wonders to make our place the kind of place you'd want to come home to. By the time Lizbit was born, she'd repainted all the rooms and lined all the drawers and made these nifty patch-work curtains out of fabric ends from the dry goods on Main Street. For mine she selected various patterns in green, because green's my favorite color. I'm looking at those curtains now, except the room is too dark to tell what color they are. You'll have to trust me. They're green. Green, the color of new life, the color of spring, the color of fecundity. I close my eyes and try to throw a party in my head, but nobody comes. Just the past.

Olive Rainsford.

Absolutely not, I told Sumner Fox over the telephone, and by God I meant it. I didn't want to see Olive again. I didn't want her treacherous eyes meeting my treacherous eyes, to determine which of us was the greater traitor. I didn't need to speak to Olive. I speak to her every day! All the time, we have these imaginary conversations.

My goodness, how you've changed, she'll say. *You're nothing like the Emilia I used to know.*

I'll light a mental cigarette and pour myself a mental Scotch. *Well, whose fault is* that, I'll tell her. And so on.

Fox was persistent, I'll give him that. He explained to me how this might be my last-ever chance to sit across the table from Olive Rainsford. How Olive had specially requested the meeting. She'd insisted, in fact.

What do you mean, insisted? I asked.

There was a long silence down the line, the kind you might expect from Sumner Fox while he picks his thoughts. I hadn't seen him in years, nor heard his voice—not since that final day in the courtroom when I gave my testimony and he thanked me afterward for what he called my courage. But time hadn't changed him, except to make his throat raspier and his words even more measured. I would almost say weary. I guess espionage is nearly as brutal a business as academics.

She has a request to make of you, he said. I'm afraid I can't disclose any further information over the telephone. But I urge you to think it over, Miss Winthrop. You'd be doing your country a great service.

That's when I told him I have already done my country more than enough service, thank you very much, putting her in jail in the first place. I'm not going to waste my time helping you get her out again.

Eventually I fall asleep. I know this because I wake to an immense pressure crushing my chest. This happens to me from time to time. Cato says it's a response to repressed trauma. He thinks I need analysis, a lot of analysis. I roll my eyes and tell him he *would* say that, wouldn't he? Personally, I think he's just miffed because I won't tell him about what happened before I moved to Wellesley. Why should I? I don't speak to anybody about what happened that summer, about what I lost. Even Susana knows better than to speak his name. The pressure grows on my chest, like a booted foot stands on the center of the sternum. My ribs crack under its weight. The room is still black, the color of longing. Tears leak out from the corners of my eyes and run down to the pillowcase, so badly do I want it all back—the summer, the man who loved me, the Emilia that was. In the distance, a telephone rings. I tell myself Pop will get it. He'll be downstairs by now.

Then I remember there is no downstairs, and there is no Pop. Not here with me, anyway. I'm a mainlander now, and I answer the telephone at dawn all by myself, before the noise wakes up Lizbit.

I cup my hand over the receiver. "Hello?"

"Emmie? Is that you?"

"Aunt Benedita? What's the matter? Is something wrong?"

Of course something's wrong. Aunt Benedita doesn't call you at five in the morning to tell you the sun is about to rise. Already my heart knows what's coming. My heart beats itself senseless, anticipating the blow.

"It's your father," Aunt Benedita whispers. "He's gone, Emmie."

MAY 1946
Winthrop Island

That was the summer the boys came home—those who were still alive, anyway. I guess some girls came home, too, the ones who went off to do war work or nursing work, joined the WAACs or the WAVES or the what have you, drove ambulances and flew airplanes and parachuted into France. I wasn't one of those girls. I spent the war right here on Winthrop Island, where I grew up. I listened to the war on the radio and read about the war in the newspaper. I grew vegetables and raised chickens and milked the cow and the goats. I wrote encouraging letters to the boys at the front. I wrote comforting letters to the families of the boys who died. Now the war was over. Even the rationing had ended. The bill had been totaled and paid and everything was going back to the way it was.

Well, except for the boys who died, and the people who loved them.

On a nice sunny day at the end of May, the Wednesday before Memorial Day, we didn't have all that many visitors at the Winthrop Island Library and Historical Society. The year-rounders couldn't be bothered, what with the weather turning so nice, and the summer folk had only just started trickling in with their trunks and boxes. At around three thirty that afternoon, Mrs. Collins stretched her arms above her head, so she resembled a chintz cushion about to attempt a dive. She glanced at the clock and smiled at me kindly.

"I guess you might as well go home and help your sister start supper."

"But I haven't finished cataloging this new shipment of books."

"Oh, I don't mind. Mr. Winthrop will be so tired after getting the big house all ready for the Peabodys."

"That's true."

"When is the family due in?"

"Tomorrow afternoon," I told her. "According to the latest telegram, anyway."

I was sure Mrs. Collins already knew this, on account of her younger sister worked at the post office and was therefore privy to all the Western Union traffic to and from the island. But it was nice of her to ask, anyway. I thanked her for letting me off early and gathered my hat and pocketbook and white cotton gloves from the desk drawer.

Just as I made my way around the counter, the little

bell on the door went *jing-a-ling* and a woman walked in, baby braced on one hip and a child clinging to the other hand, besides an older one trailing behind. She wore a flowery dress and a straw hat, kind of a striking woman with curling dark hair, real slender, red lipstick, about forty years old, smelled of rose petal soap.

I glanced back at Mrs. Collins, as if to say, *You want me to take care of this?* Mrs. Collins just waved me out the door.

The last thing I heard was this woman asking, in a fine educated Boston voice, whether she might trouble Mrs. Collins for some books to keep her children entertained while she worked.

Because we only had one car, the old Ford truck Pop used for work, I pedaled my way up and down Winthrop Island on this bicycle that used to belong to my aunt Hannah, before the island winters drove her crazy and she divorced Uncle Petey and moved out west to St. Louis or someplace. It wasn't much, but it got me around. Pop kept it shipshape for me, gears and chains all nicely oiled and everything, straw basket hanging from the handlebars to carry my pocketbook and lunch and Thermos of coffee, maybe a ragged novel or two. Of course, the library was in town, and home lay five miles down the main road to

the other end of the island, but I've always liked a little exercise and anyway the views along the way were
million dollar, even in winter. First you cycled up
West Cliff Road, which was hard work, but then you
breathlessly reached the top of the cliffs and the long
grass burnt against the horizon. As the pedals relaxed
beneath your feet and your breath caught up with
your chest, you discovered the sea and the green tip
of Long Island. The Fleet Rock Lighthouse, the tide
that flew into the sound from the giant Atlantic. The
tidy sails and the lobster boats and the lethargic ferry
to Orient Point. You passed the driveway to Greyfriars, brooding alone where the cliffs come down into
a little cove across from the lighthouse. The Fishers
spent their summers there—they'd be arriving in a
week or two. But today the house was empty and still.

The road turned around a bend after that, and the
sea dodged out of view. A public beach nestled underneath these cliffs, where the villagers and the day-
trippers and the renters went to swim and sunbathe and
picnic—regular people who didn't belong to the Club
at the private end of the island, where I was headed
on that May afternoon. The road wound this way and
that, following the general line of the island's southeast-
ern shore. Horseshoe Cove, where the kids lit bonfires
sometimes, away from their parents dining oblivious at

the Club. Eventually I came to the modest clapboard hut that marked the boundary of the Winthrop Island Association, the private side of the island. Stan poked his head out of the window and sent me along with a cheerful wave. I waved back. On either side of me unrolled the land my family had farmed for centuries. I passed the Lowell place, the Dana place, the Dumonts and the Monks. The big pond, where all the kids learned to sail, and then the little pond. Past the entrance to the Club, the sharp Tudorbethan roof peaks of the clubhouse, the shaved tees overlooking the water, the plush greens, the immaculate sand traps. Everything empty and waiting. Holding its breath. Finally Crystal Pool—that's Yankee irony, see, because the pond's so brackish—where at last you turned down Serenity Lane.

There are old-timers who will tell you that the arrival of the Families on Winthrop Island each summer resembles an invasion of starving locusts, that the purchase and development of the eastern chunk of Winthrop into a seasonal resort for rich folks ruined the island altogether. But I had never known anything different. When I turned down Serenity Lane that particular afternoon and saw the building asleep on the horizon, my heart swelled against my ribs. Summerly, the Peabodys called it. There must have been a dozen bedrooms, each with its own gable or tower or sleeping porch. It was made of fieldstone and gray shingle and white clapboard trim, topped by a slate roof to ward off the afternoon thunderstorms you got here during the hot spells. The bicycle tires jigged over the gravel. The limpid afternoon sun cast my shadow over the handlebars. Behind me stretched the bare and lifeless months of winter. Ahead of me, the house grew against the blue sky, ready to wake. I remember I stopped pedaling and braced my toes on the drive so I could get a hold of myself, so I could catch my breath and contemplate what was due to arrive tomorrow on the midday ferry—the end of the war, the return of summer, the return of the Peabodys. A giant new world gaping before me, packed with possibility and also with a dread I couldn't name, waiting for me to step inside.

Into this trance pierced the rattle of a car engine and a strangled *beep-beep* from a constipated horn. The noise startled me into the grass. I set my toe back down and twisted around to see what was coming. Some dusty black car about ten years old. It rolled to a stop right next to me and a woman poked her head out. Dark hair, red lipstick—the woman from the library.

"Hello there!" she called out cheerfully. "You must be Emilia!"

"That's right. Can I help you?"

"We're here for the summer! Just arrived today! The

guest cottage! Olive Rainsford!" She had to yell above the car engine, turning over in vast wheezy chugs. In the back seat, a couple of children squabbled over candy or something. I thought I glimpsed the baby sitting upright in the middle. She pointed her thumb at them. "My kids!"

"It's nice to meet you! We're the caretakers!"

"Yes, I know! Edwina Peabody's my sister!"

"Oh! You're *Aunt* Olive!"

"That's right! Will you children be *quiet*?" She turned her head to address the nippers. I couldn't make out what else she said to them, but they shut up quick.

"I've heard so much about you!" I called.

"What's that?"

"Heard a lot about you!"

"Don't believe a word of it!" She winked and yanked the car back into gear. She had nice arms, lean and already tanned apricot. "I'll be off now! Nice to meet you, Emilia!"

I stood for a moment, balanced atop my bicycle, one toe pressed into the short spring grass. The car rumbled away. An arm snaked from the window and waggled its hand. The fingers were long, the nails short and unpainted. The horn belched again. Inside the patch of rear window, two small, white faces appeared and stared at me like a pair of ghosts, unblinking, until the car disappeared around a hedge on its way to the Summerly guest cottage.

Once the dust settled, I pushed off with my toe and cycled right, onto the dirt track that led off the main drive. At the end of this track sat the caretaker's lodge, a fine old clapboard house dating back before the Revolution, all slanting floors and warped roof beams, picturesquely put to rights by the Peabodys when they built Summerly thirty years before. It had plumbing and electricity and central heating now, a modern kitchen and a hygienic upstairs bathroom with piped hot water and everything, so it was much more comfortable than when Pop grew up inside its walls, scrubbing himself once a week inside a wooden tub next to the coal stove—so he claimed, anyway, when I was a kid. But if you approached it as I did that afternoon, pedaling a bicycle down the middle of the track until the center chimney popped up from behind the profuse beach plum and then the whole house slid into view from around a bend, it looked just like it might have done when the Winthrops first settled here in the middle of the seventeenth century and gave the island its name.

I put my bicycle in the shed and ducked through the lean-to entrance on the side, where we kept our boots and things in the mud season. "Mama! I'm home!"

I sang out, as I always did, even though she couldn't answer me. Susana replied instead, from the dining room where she sat at the table, surrounded by homework. The school year was nearly over and she was studying for final exams. Next to her, Mama sat in her chair and laboriously folded squares of colored paper into flowers. I kissed the top of Mama's head on my way to look over Susana's shoulder.

"Tangents," I said approvingly.

"I hate 'em."

"Math is just logic, Susana. Everyone needs to learn logic."

"Says you."

"Where's Pop?" I asked her.

"He's still at the big house, helping Aunt Benedita air all the beds. Auntie said not to hold supper for him, he'll be late."

"Did Aunt Benedita say anything about somebody staying in the cottage this summer?"

"The *guest* cottage? Somebody's in the guest cottage? *Who?*"

She said this like you might ask about rats in the basement. I looked up from Mama's chair, where I was conducting my habitual inspection of her color and pulse and breathing, the dilation of her pupils and that kind of thing, which Dr. Pradelli taught me after Mama had the stroke, two years ago. (I was the one who discovered her, you know, on the immaculate white tiles of the new bathroom. She had fallen on her face and I'd had to roll her over to see if she was dead.) Susana stared back at me with a horrified expression. She had wide cheekbones and a small, pointed chin, so her face reminded you of a heart.

I gave Mama's shoulder a pat and plopped on the chair next to her. "Oh, just Aunt Olive and her kids, that's who."

"Aunt *Olive*? *The* Aunt Olive?"

"I don't know another one."

Susana clapped a hand over her mouth. A second later, she lifted it away and primped her hair, like she expected Olive Rainsford to sweep into the room *that very instant.*

I turned to Mama. "You've heard about Mrs. Peabody's sister, haven't you, Mama? The one who went to finishing school in Switzerland and never came home?"

"Are you *sure*?" Susana demanded. "Did you *see* her?"

"I saw her twice. Once at the library and again on the way home. She stopped the car and said hello."

"What did she look like? What did she say?"

"She said hello, that's all. She had a couple of kids in the back seat. I think there was a baby, too. She was getting some books for them at the library."

"What kind of books?"

"I don't know. Children's books, I guess. Mrs. Collins helped her."

"You let Mrs. *Collins* help her?"

"Well, I didn't know she was Olive Rainsford, did I? I thought she was just another summer renter."

Susana sat back in her chair. "*You're* no help."

"What do you want? She looked like a housewife, that's all. Kind of a stylish housewife, you know the type. She wore lipstick and a nice dress." I ran my palm down the grain of the wooden table and called up details to my memory. "I thought her hair was a little short, under her hat, just dark and waving naturally? Like she doesn't like to bother with it much."

"Of *course* she doesn't. She's too adventurous to think about her *coiffure*." Susana laid a French accent on the word.

"You don't even know her."

"But all the *stories*, Cricket! You remember the stories the boys had about her. How she lived in China and used to send them all those funny souvenirs."

"A lot of people travel to China."

"She's had two husbands, at least."

I stood up. "I'm going to see about supper."

"I'll help you."

"No, you finish studying. Exams start in two days."

Susana shifted her feet under the table and fiddled with the ends of her hair. "Mary says they're looking for more waitresses at the Club this summer."

"Not in a million years."

She threw back the curl she was fingering. "*You* wait tables at the Club!"

"I'm older than you."

"Besides, we could use the money, right? You're always worried about money."

"We'll manage. Now go back to your tangents. You have to pass your exams before you can even think about summer."

"Sure I do. But the last I heard, I don't have homework during the *summer.*"

Well, she had a point. I looked down at the top of Mama's head. Her nose pointed in Susana's direction. The doctor told us Mama couldn't understand everything we said to her anymore, that the stroke had shut off oxygen to various segments of her brain, so that Mama was left with the intellect of a small child. People used to come up to me and pat my arm and say—in that slow, condescending voice by which you convey comfort to grief-stricken people—that it was a mercy, really. Just think about it! If the circuits in her brain had plain shorted out, so to speak, upon receiving the news that her only son and favorite child had been killed the previous week on some mountain slope in Italy, maybe she was better off like this—like a child who didn't understand what was happening around her.

A mercy, really, people repeated. Patting my hand.

I told Susana, "All right. I'll see if Mrs. Collins needs any more help at the library."

By the time we finished the soup and washed the dishes, Pop still hadn't arrived back from the main house. Susana wanted to make up some excuse to go visit Mrs. Rainsford, bring her a neighborly food hamper or something, but I insisted it could wait for another day. Mrs. Rainsford would be getting the kids their supper right now, getting them bathed and in bed, and she wouldn't appreciate neighbors stopping by with their hampers of curiosity. Besides, Susana had school in the morning.

So Susana stomped upstairs to run her bath and I stepped outside for a breath of air. The sun had only just fallen and a sheen of orange still rimmed the horizon. The air was blue and cool and clear enough to see for miles. Between the birches—planted by the Peabodys thirty years earlier, likely for privacy—the shingles of the big house rambled on forever. Somewhere to the north, hidden by the sprawl of Summerly, the guest cottage perched right near the edge of the rocks—hardly a place you wanted to bring small children, now that I thought about it, but maybe Mrs. Rainsford was the type of mother who felt kids should learn to fend for themselves and have proper adventures. The Peabodys were like that.

I wandered to the edge of the lawn, a thick stubble grass that lapsed into scrub meadow before disappearing altogether into the rocks that tumbled down to the beach. Once I overheard Mr. Peabody pronounce that the island reminded him of Scotland—or was it Ireland? Never having visited either one—never having traveled farther from Winthrop Island than Boston, Massachusetts—I couldn't say. Certainly my ancestors didn't farm this land with much success. Only the hardiest survived around here, things that could stand the salt and wind and soil, the dark and bitter winters. All the timber came down in the great gale of 1815, according to my granddad, whose granddad told *him* the stories about that storm from when he was a boy. What's left was brush and scrub and meadow, like this. Some trees planted in by the summer people on the new summer estates. I brought together the edges of my cardigan and crossed my arms over my chest. In May, the air turned chill as soon as the sun stopped warming it. To my left, Summerly shone salmon pink along the white trim that reflected the dying sun, and it seemed to me that this light faded right before my eyes as the last beam fell behind the earth.

"They're not going to get here any sooner just because you're watching," said Susana at my elbow.

I turned my head. She wore her worn old dressing gown and her hair was already in pins. In the fading light she looked somehow old and wise.

"I wasn't thinking about the Peabodys," I said. "I was thinking about Eli. How strange it's going to be. I mean, it hasn't seemed real, has it? All the boys were away. Everybody was gone. Eli getting killed, it was just words on a telegram. But now that Shep and Amory'll be home again . . . all the boys who made it . . ."

Susana lifted my arm and slung it over her shoulders. Her sweet soap smell made me think of Mama's voice, reading bedtime stories. "At least they'll be back, though," she said. "Shep and Amory. They're almost like brothers, aren't they?"

"Almost," I said. "Now get to bed."

She kissed me on the cheek and scurried to the house. I folded my arms around my waist and stared a moment longer at the blue-shadowed house in front of me.

As I turned away, my eye caught on a small object just visible inside the attic window on the third floor. I stopped to squint—shaded my eyes, as if that would help. I couldn't be certain in the gloaming, and the lights in the attic weren't lit, but it seemed to me that an old rag doll slumped against the window frame.

It's funny how your body can understand a thing before your brain does. For a minute or two, I stood there absolutely numb in the head, while my heart clunked and my breath came short and my fingertips tingled, the way they did in the driveway a couple of hours ago.

I couldn't recall the first time a Peabody boy set the rag doll in the window, visible between the birch leaves to the bedroom I shared with Susana. When six kids play together daily, the rules and customs will develop naturally, growing like vines, sprouting off shoots—a wild, invented landscape mapped forever inside their heads.

But if I rummaged around the attics of memory, I did remember pedaling madly home from some adventure at the other end of the island, sun sinking, air gold with promise, supper wafting from the Peabody kitchen, Arthur and Amory and my brother followed by Shep and me, followed by Susana calling desperately to *wait up*, and it seemed to me that Arthur was the one who skidded to a stop, spraying gravel everywhere, and said, *Let's meet on the beach tonight*, and I said, *Sure, when?* because Arthur was our captain and we would have done anything he asked us to do, anything.

When the coast is clear, he said, so I asked him how I would know when the coast was clear, and he squinted up at the attic window, where the six of us played on rainy days—just exactly the way I squinted up there now—and said, *Why, I'll just stick something in that window there.* So that must have been it, the first time. Over the summers of our childhood, I had obeyed that signal on so many occasions I couldn't begin to remember them all, and the absence of that doll, the emptiness of that attic window over the past five years, was maybe just as painful as the absence of the Peabody boys themselves.

And now it was back, like it had never been away at all.

By the time I'd scrambled over the rocks to the little cove we kids used to call Pirate Bay, the last minutes of sunset had drained away. Blue shadow everywhere. I called out the password—no, I can't tell you what it was, I was lucky to remember it myself after so many years—and the next thing I knew, a meaty pair of arms had hoisted me off the final rock and whirled me in a circle to set me in the sand.

"Cricket! I was about to write you off."

"You're supposed to be in Boston!"

"Says who?"

"Last I heard!"

"Well, I decided I couldn't wait another minute and sailed over early on the *Esmeralda*. Holy moly, Cricket! Let a fellow breathe!"

He was kidding. Nobody alive on Winthrop Island could have obstructed the flow of air to those lungs. That's why we used to call him Shep, see—his size and his shaggy appearance. Short for *sheepdog*. Me, I've always been Cricket to the Peabodys, on account of my green eyes and olive skin and spindly stature. But shaggy, lumbering Nathaniel Peabody—Arthur called his kid brother Shep, so we did, too. He spun me around in a few more circles before we staggered, dizzy and laughing, into the sand.

Looking back, everything was so obvious. Sometimes I want to shake that girl on the beach that night, it was so obvious. But then everything looks inevitable in hindsight.

"Because there was nothing to tell," he said, when I wanted to know why he hadn't written in months.

"Baloney. You were right in the middle of Berlin, and you couldn't think of anything to tell me?"

"Maybe I was busy."

"Sure you were."

"What's that supposed to mean?"

"Some girl."

He folded his arms behind his head. "What makes you say that?"

"Isn't it always?" I turned on my side and poked his ribs. "Well? What about her?"

"There's nothing to tell."

"Well, if you don't want to talk about it—"

"I said what I mean. There's nothing to tell."

The moon hung in a bright, solitary quarter above our heads. I propped myself up on an elbow and stared at the side of his silvery face until he smiled and wanted to know what I was looking at.

"Your face, that's all. I can't believe it's you."

He rubbed a hand along his chin. "How so?"

"I don't know. It's been—how long? Since you joined up."

"Four years. May of 1942, right after graduation. But we last saw each other Labor Day the year before. Five years ago, almost."

"You were just eighteen. You were off to war and you were only eighteen."

"Well, almost nineteen," he said. "I was nineteen in July. I remember you sent me a birthday card. I was six or seven weeks into basic training. I nearly cried."

"No, you didn't."

"I did, I swear. I hadn't seen you since the summer before, when I left for school. And you were on Winthrop taking in the sea breeze, and I was sweating through my shirt at goddamn Fort Bragg in North Carolina."

"Poor you."

"Well," he said, after a second or two, "it meant a lot to me, anyway. It meant the world."

I traced a circle in the sand next to my leg. "Five years."

"Four years and nine months."

"Golly, was I only just sixteen the last time you saw me."

"Only just. Your birthday's three days after mine."

"You didn't send *me* a card when I turned seventeen."

"They don't sell birthday cards in the PX at basic training, Cricket."

"And now you're—what, twenty-two?"

"Hot dog. You've passed arithmetic."

"Oh, stop. I just mean you've—well, you've lost your baby fat, for one thing—"

"*Baby* fat—"

"And sprouted an awful beard—"

"This old thing? You should see it when I *don't* shave."

I nestled back in the cool sand and tried to think of something funny. Truth to tell, there *was* no humor to explain the difference—how the clumsy, rawboned, mumbling boy had disappeared under the serious skin of a man I didn't know. Or no, maybe the man had burst through the awkward skin of the boy, that's how to describe it. Well, that was life. That's what war did. Turned a boy into a man. Even his laugh was different. There was nothing silly left about it, nothing carefree.

"We were just kids," I said instead.

"Babies."

"You were supposed to be headed off to college."

"I guess I figured college could wait when there was a war on."

"Poor old Harvard. Losing all of you in one fell swoop."

He laughed. "Lucky break, if you ask me."

"But you're going back now, aren't you? In the fall."

"What, a college freshman? Wouldn't that be a gas, at my age. No, I'm thinking on something else."

"Oh? What's that?"

"Buddy of mine from the service. His family's got some land out near San Francisco, used to make wine before Prohibition put them in the cattle business. He wants somebody to help him sell the cattle and start up the vineyard again."

"California? You want to move to *California*?"

"Why not? It's a big country out there, Cricket. I've been figuring I might want to see some of it. Do some things I never used to think I might do."

"And just what do *you* know about making wine?"

He turned his head toward me. "I know a lot more than you think, Cricket."

"I'll bet."

"Anyway, he's got a real live Frenchwoman to help us, this girl from Bordeaux; she's worked the family vineyard all her life. Until the war, I mean."

"Is *that* the girl?"

"What girl?"

"The reason you didn't write much."

He turned back to face the sky. "No, Cricket. She's my buddy's girl. They got married last month in Paris. I was the best man. Geez, what makes you so sure I've got a girl somewhere?"

"I don't know. I just figured."

Above our heads, the stars popped out. I thought about the time I last saw Shep, a night like this one, stars popping out, except it was Labor Day and the fireworks had just started on the strip of sand at the edge of the golf course that people called a beach. The day after Labor Day, the Peabodys would pack up Summerly and head home, and the boys would

head back to their schools—Arthur and Amory to
Harvard, Shep to boarding school, his senior year.
I remembered that terrible adolescent ache I felt,
thinking of the empty days of autumn and winter
ahead, how it would be nine whole months before the
Peabodys returned to Summerly. Nine whole months!

"What are you thinking about, Cricket?" Shep
asked.

"Me? Nothing."

"Come on."

"Nothing special, anyway. Just how much time's
gone by. Everything that's happened to us both since I
saw you last."

Shep unfolded one arm like the wing of a condor and
slung me against his side. "Remember that time you
covered for me when I ran my bicycle into Mrs. Pinkerton's flowerbed?"

"I can think fast when I have to."

He laughed. "Thank God one of us can."

"It's a shame, what happened to Mrs. Pinkerton.
Poor Tippy."

"Yeah, poor kid. First her fiancé gets killed, now
her mother dies."

"They were so close. Tippy and her mother."

Shep made a noise of agreement. He wore an old
woolen sweater that scratched my cheek. You had to

wonder how many sheep must have given their all to knit a sweater big enough to cover Shep. It smelled of mothballs, like he'd dragged it out of a trunk from before the war. *Thank God*, I thought. Thank God it was Shep here tonight instead of Amory. Shep settled your nerves. Made you feel like everything was going to be all right.

He said softly, "What about you, Cricket?"

"Me?"

"Eli. When I heard the news—you know he was like a brother to us—"

"I know."

"It tore me up, when I heard. And you. I figured it must have crushed you. I couldn't sleep, I was so worried for you."

"I appreciated your letter."

"It was a terrible letter. I don't even remember what it said."

"It was a *beautiful* letter."

"I'm no good with words, you know that. I didn't know what to say that would help. I wasn't trying to make you feel better. I mean nobody should think she has to feel better about a thing like that, losing your brother, but I wanted you to know that—well, how much I cared about him."

The truth was, I didn't really remember the incident in Mrs. Pinkerton's flowerbed. We got into so many scrapes when we were kids, the six of us, you couldn't keep them all straight. Arthur and Eli always raced ahead together, because they were the oldest, and Amory went along with them because he wanted to be just like his big brother. Susana usually stayed behind because she was the littlest and didn't like to play rough games, so that left Shep and me, together in the wake of the older boys. It was funny, really. When I thought about summers before the war, I didn't think of the thrill of those final weeks of that final August—the prickly awakening, the infatuation, the last dizzying night. I thought of *this*, right now. I thought of some beach or dune with Shep, some sailboat, some bicycle. That slow, lumbering laugh. That voice. You could say anything to a voice like that. You could say anything to Shep and he would understand. You didn't have to think about how you looked or sounded. You could just exist.

Meathead, his brothers used to call him. *Gorilla*. But there is something permanent about a human body that size, something that can't be shifted, like a boulder. The substance of all my summers.

Anyway, maybe I can't help smiling when I remember how Shep came to ride his clumsy bicycle into Mrs. Pinkerton's beloved flowerbed—it's the kind of thing you expected from him—but I also recall how he spent the next day replanting them all under the hot sun. Not because this was his punishment, but because he felt so sorry for the flowers.

He poked me in the ribs. "Cricket? You all right?"

"You know something, Shep?" I said. "You've got a heart of gold."

The cold quarter moon peered down from the giant sky. The incoming tide crashed against the rocks. In the scant half hour since the sun disappeared, the air had chilled enough to make me grateful for Shep's arm and shoulder and ribs, like a woolen nest. How funny, five years had passed. Same arm, same shoulder and ribs as before, same sweater probably.

"How's your mama doing these days?" he asked.

"Oh, she carries on. You'll understand when you see her."

"I saw your dad when I came in. He looks well."

"No, he doesn't. He's miserable. Stoically miserable. Miserably stoic. Something like that."

"What about you? Miserable?"

"I don't know. I don't have much time to think about how I'm feeling, most days. Anyway, what good would it do?"

He stood up in a sudden, athletic move. You wouldn't think such a beast could lift himself so effortlessly. He stretched out his paw and drew me to my feet next to him. "We're having a party Friday night," he said. "Celebrate the start of summer and everything. You could stop by and raise a glass."

"Who, me?"

"Yes, you. Since we're neighbors and all." Shep shoved his hands in his trouser pockets. "Wouldn't be the same without you."

"I'll think about it," I said. "Turn around."

He turned obediently. In brusque strokes I brushed away the sand that stuck to the wool of his sweater. His shoulders were like the blades of a plow. I could smell the sea on him, salt and fish and weed. It was the scent of my own bones, the smell I was born with. I was just thinking that Shep was a little too quiet, like he was holding something back from me, when he spoke.

"Say, I almost forgot. We've got a surprise for you."

"I don't like surprises."

"It's my aunt Olive. You remember. Crazy Aunt Olive, we used to talk about her all the time—"

"And she's staying in the guest cottage this summer with her three unruly children?"

He turned around. "You've met already?"

"Don't look so disappointed. She stopped the car today while I was riding down the drive and introduced herself to me."

"So what did you think?"

"I think it'll be nice having a little intelligent conversation around here, for a change."

He punched my arm. I punched him back.

"That's what I was hoping, anyway," he said. "I was hoping you and Aunt Olive would hit it off. You always reminded me of her."

"Did I? How's that?"

"Because you're the smartest girl I know, Cricket. Because I always saw you traveling the world, having adventures."

"I guess you were wrong about that," I said.

"I'm not wrong at all. The war's over. The whole world is out there for you. You just have to leap on it, Cricket."

"I wouldn't know where to start anymore. Besides, there's my mother. I can't leave Pop to take care of her."

Shep set his hands on his hips and looked out to sea. I thought how funny it was that the two of us could stand here like this, on the old familiar beach, not having seen each other in five years, nothing but letters passed between us in all that time, and he seemed so different and I suppose I did, too, both of us grown up, like a pair of strangers almost, anguish and bloodshed staining the years of our separation—yet he was the same old Shep and I was Cricket. The territory of childhood remained between us. That landscape mapped in my head was mapped in his head, too. He'd carried it with him to Europe and back, how about that.

"I don't know," he said. "Maybe we can figure something out."

"Sure we can. You, me, and the pie in the sky."

Shep grinned and turned back to me. Before I could gasp, he grabbed me by the waist and heaved me around in a giant circle. I held on to his shoulders for dear life. When he set me back on my feet, I stayed where I was. It just felt so good, to lean against Shep. I told him so. I said it was good to have him back again, safe and sound.

"But you're coming to the party, at least," he said. "Right?"

I leaned back and looked up at his face. The stubble on his chin glittered in the moonlight. I thought I'd see the old mischief in his eyes, but they squinted down at me like a man's gaze, serious.

"Wouldn't miss it for the world," I told him.

II.

The last time I went to a funeral, I stood in the back and wore a wide-brimmed black hat and a pair of sunglasses, so nobody would recognize me. This time I sit in the front pew, in between Lizbit and Aunt Benedita. Susana sits on Lizbit's other side, Harvey sits next to Susana, and Pop's brother, Uncle Petey, sits next to Harvey. That's all of us in the front pew. There used to be a lot of Winthrops on the island but we're all that remain. And Aunt Benedita's not even one of us, really. She's Mama's sister and this might be the first time she's ever set foot in a Protestant church, God forgive her.

May has a habit of dithering back and forth in this

corner of the world, and this is one of those raw, blustery days that might as well be March. The minister drones on about the inevitability of death and the hope of salvation. Lizbit sits perfectly still and concentrates on his words. My mind, on the other hand, can't seem to focus on the matter at hand. I keep thinking of that other funeral, the last funeral I attended. It was in Boston, at a large Episcopal church in the Back Bay somewhere. It was almost a cathedral, really. I sat alone with my terrible guilt and stared at the grieving family in the front pew, knowing I would never see any of them again. I left before the service was over, before anybody turned toward the back and thought maybe he recognized the shape of my shoulders or something. Outside, the sun hurtled down on my black clothes. It was August and the cool air inside the church had been a relief, but now I thought I was going to die of heatstroke. Eventually I found my way to a bar—they're not all that hard to find in Boston, after all—and ordered myself whiskey after whiskey until Sumner Fox tracked me down and dragged me back to the hotel to dry out.

So you see why I try to avoid funerals unless absolutely necessary.

After the service and the interment, a hasty, drizzly affair at the burying ground behind the church, there is a very nice reception in the church hall. We spent the previous day baking, Susana and Lizbit and Aunt Benedita and I, at Aunt Benedita's house near the main harbor, and the minister's wife made a large bowl of punch that could knock out a sailor. Mrs. Collins brings her scallop pie. She tells me it's a very sad day, the last of the Winthrops on Winthrop Island. She aims a gimlet eye at mine as she says this, because whose fault is it, really, that no more Winthrops make their home on Winthrop Island?

I turn to the punch bowl and ladle my cup to the brim. "You could always change the name of the island."

"I doubt it," she says. "You know when Hugh Fisher's father put up the money to rescue the association after the crash, he tried to have them rename the island after him. Can you imagine? The nerve of that man. The motion was voted down, naturally, and he died shortly thereafter." She takes a satisfied slurp of punch. "You heard about poor Hugh, of course."

"It was all over the Boston papers. Terrible."

"Oh, it was gruesome."

"I can't believe that sweet kid killed him."

"The Vargas boy? Oh, I can believe it. A crime of passion. These Portuguese, they're so passionate. Well, he's off to prison now, and good riddance. The poor widow." Mrs. Collins's voice drops to a whisper. "Hugh left her penniless. It turns out Greyfriars was mortgaged to the hilt."

I glance about the room to signal somebody for help, but the crowd's sparse. It's the beginning of May, after all, and the Families haven't yet arrived. Instead they sent wreaths, which Lizbit and I carried from the altar after the service, so the air inside the church hall smells like a fog of lilies. Aunt Benedita and the Medeiro sisters confer in the corner. Tom Donnelly and Uncle Petey are having a chat over plates of scallop pie. Lizbit stands next to the plate of cookies, guilty as hell.

"She's growing up into such a little lady," says Mrs. Collins. "Your Elizabeth."

"You think so? Harvey says we spoil her."

"Oh! Well, he's just a man, isn't he. I think she's delightful. She and your father were so close. He just lived for her visits."

"Is that so?" The punch cup is made of cut glass. I imagine the minister and his wife received the set as a wedding present from some aunt. I run my thumbnail along one of the diamond grooves. "I wish I could take the credit, but it was all Susana's idea. Taking Lizbit to Winthrop every summer to stay with Pop."

"I wish you'd come too, Emmie," she says. "We miss you."

All this time, I've been looking anywhere but Mrs. Collins's face. She's wearing an old black dress that's witnessed so many island funerals, it could make its own way to the church. Her black hat might have done duty in the Hoover administration, by the shape of it. Still, she clings to a threadbare dignity as she clings to her pocketbook. When I raise my eyes to hers, I'm surprised to see an expression of fond longing. "That's funny," I say. "I don't remember anybody speaking up to defend me before I left."

"Nobody knew what to think. We couldn't believe something like that could happen here. On the island. You know, Communists among us. Soviet spies. Of course, now we know they're *everywhere*. But back then we thought it was some kind of awful mistake."

"It seems to me there was no mistake about the dead rat somebody left on my doorstep."

Her eyes widen behind her glasses. "A dead rat? *I* never heard anything about that. Are you sure?"

"There was a note attached that said *All rats die*. Or something of that nature. I don't remember exactly. It was a long time ago and I've got a busy life these days."

She straightens her back. "Well, it wasn't one of *us*, I can tell you that. It was likely one of the Families."

"It hardly seems their style."

Mrs. Collins sucks in her cheeks and moves her jaw

as if she's chewing something indigestible. She turns her attention to the portrait of Dwight Eisenhower hanging in the center of the wall to our right. "Do you know what your trouble is, Emmie?" she says. "You don't know who your friends are. You've always wanted to be one of *them*. You think you're too smart for us. You and your *busy life*. Well, I can tell you we would have defended you to the death that summer, if you'd let us. We still would. Why, we're proud of you. Standing up for what was right."

My eyes fix on her red lips. I can't remember Mrs. Collins except with that exact shade of lipstick, which she used to touch up after every meal or cup of coffee, fixing earnestly on her reflection in the compact mirror she carried in her pocketbook. So far as I could tell, she didn't wear any other type of cosmetics. When I asked why she took the trouble with her lips, she would heave this sigh and say it was good grooming. They don't wear a lot of makeup, the year-rounders. To stick it out through the winter takes a particular kind of no-nonsense orneriness that doesn't leave much room for frivolities, although I guess it's also the kind of orneriness that keeps you swiping the same damn lipstick on your lips, every day of your life.

"You shouldn't believe everything you hear on the radio, Mrs. Collins," I tell her. "McCarthy's a chump.

Why, my own lover's a Communist, and while I can't speak for his good sense, I'm not about to denounce him to the FBI for it."

"Don't mind Mrs. Collins," Susana tells me afterward. "Didn't her own kids move away when the war started? She's one to talk."

"But her scallop pie is delicious," chirps Lizbit.

We're sitting at the table in Aunt Benedita's spotless kitchen, picking at the remains of the funeral meats. Susana moves her fork around a slice of Mrs. Medeiro's currant loaf. In the years since we moved away, Susana's kept in better touch with Pop—telephone calls every week, snapshots of Lizbit, summer visits to Winthrop. I used to think they were conspiring, but it seems Susana has a gentler heart than I do. You can see it on her face. She's thinking about Pop as she excavates a single currant with the tines of the fork. Some memory of happier days, maybe, when we were kids and Pop took us into the barn and showed us patiently how to milk the cow. He would put his hands over ours on the teats and we would relish the closeness of his chest and his warm arms, the soft hiss of milk into the tin bucket. Why, you can almost smell the hay and the sweet new cream, just watching her.

She looks up bravely. "Did you notice that the Pinkertons sent a wreath?"

"Well, that's nice of them," I say.

Aunt Benedita stands up. "Emilia, would you come upstairs with me for a minute?"

It's funny, I don't think I've ever stood inside Aunt Benedita's bedroom, even when I was a kid. It's the house she grew up in, the house my mother grew up in, and she's the only one left of a noisy, seafaring Portuguese family. As physical specimens go, she and Mama couldn't have been more different. Mama was slight and refined. She curved out only where necessary to bear her children, and then she shrank back into herself when those curves were no longer required. Aunt Benedita, on the other hand, is like a bunch of pillows all stitched together, soft and delicious when you embrace her, although I haven't done so in years. Not since I was a kid. She lifts a milk crate from the floor and sets it in the middle of the bed. When she turns to me, her brown eyes reflect the light from the lamp on her bedside table.

"Your mother's things," she says. "I found them when I was clearing out your father's closet." She always describes them like that—*your mother, your father*—as if they bear no relation to her.

I pull the crate toward me and sift through the objects inside. They're mostly baby clothes. A silver rattle. A beautiful silk christening gown, the color of old butter. I peel away the tissue and dangle it in the air before me.

"This would have come in handy for Lizbit," I say.

"I know. I'm sorry I didn't find it sooner, or I would have sent it to you."

"I know you would."

I fold the dress back into its tissue and lay it on the counterpane. Aunt Benedita reaches out and fingers the lace.

"I remember we made this together, when your mother was going to have Eli," she says. "We took the ferry to New London and picked out the material. I knit the lace and your mother stitched all the smocking."

"Share and share alike, I always say."

"Emilia."

I pull out a photograph album from the bottom of the crate. "What's this?"

"All your baby photographs," she says. "And from her wedding."

"I don't remember seeing it at home."

Aunt Benedita shrugs. "I think she kept it tucked away, you know? To keep it safe. When kids are little they get into things."

The cover is plain brown leather. The words PRE-
CIOUS MEMORIES are stamped in loopy gold letters, so
sentimental it gives you a toothache just to look at it.
On the first page Mama's careful, familiar handwriting
sets out the captions, each one numbered, the subjects
named, the date noted. Mama was always orderly that
way. The first photograph shows my parents on their
wedding day. Mama wears a white dress and a frozen
smile. Next to her, holding her arm secure in the crook
of his elbow, Pop makes this grin wide enough to split
his face in two. I don't recall ever seeing him grin like
that. I don't recall ever seeing this photograph, either,
though it's nicer than the one Mama kept in an old
silver frame on the whatnot in the corner of the drawing room, in which her face is blurred like she was
turning away from the camera at the instant the shutter
opened. I flip through the pages—lots of snapshots of
Eli, smiling a gummy baby smile, a couple each of me
and Susana. I close the album and set it back in the
bottom of the milk crate.

"Keep it," I say.

"What, me?"

"She was your sister. You should have something to
remember her by."

"Emilia, don't be silly. You're her daughter. These
are *your* things, not mine."

I stare at my hands on the edges of the milk crate. I have exceptional hands, if you will allow me to brag. My mother's hands, slender and long-fingered. I'm proud of them. Sometimes I admire their elegance, as I do now—but always from a detached perspective, as if they don't belong to me at all, because it's vain to admire yourself, isn't it? People frown on that, especially other women. Next to me, Aunt Benedita quivers. Poor woman, she tries so hard to take care of me—she's got a knack for that, too—but I won't have it. There is a barrier between us that I can't quite bring myself to cross. I console myself that she's had Susana and Lizbit and, until last week, Pop to lavish her instincts on, although I know it's not enough. She wants me, too. She wants something from me that I can't ever give her.

"Anyway," she says, when the silence has stretched on far enough, "what am I going to do with a bunch of baby clothes?"

"Well, God knows I don't need them anymore."

Aunt Benedita places her hand on one of mine. The fingers are shorter, the palm wider. My aunt has workaday hands, practical hands. "You will someday, Emmie. I know you will. You have so much love inside you, so much kindness."

For a while, after the trial, after I left Winthrop

Island for good, I saw this doctor for my nerves. I didn't want to go but Susana made me. She said she was going crazy listening to my nightmares and it was going to have a terrible effect on Lizbit, babies being so sensitive. Susana did a lot of reading about such things before Lizbit was born. She went through stacks of books about babies, all of which left her with the conviction that an infant was a kind of blank slate on which each tiny vibration of the universe around her left some mark. So I went to this doctor who tried to get me to take some pills, which I refused, and to go in for analysis, which I also refused, and finally—in despair—taught me some exercises to control my breath and my pulse when one of these little attacks came on, *panic attacks*, he called them, which in my view was a gross exaggeration. I never panic. Anyway, it's now second nature to close my eyes and count off the seconds as I breathe in through my nostrils—*one Mississippi, two Mississippi, three Mississippi*—and then hold this breath in my lungs for another few beats, and then breathe it all out between my lips at the same measured pace, whenever the adrenaline starts in my veins, as it does now.

As I finish the second round, Aunt Benedita starts to draw her hand away. I place my other hand on top, holding her fingers between mine, and turn to her.

"I want to say that I appreciate all you've done, Auntie," I tell her. "For Susana and Lizbit and especially Pop."

For the first time in more than seven years, we look each other eye to eye. She has large eyes like my mother, light brown with a touch of green, and thick black lashes that are the same as my own. Some tears gather at the corners.

"Thank you, Emmie," she says.

Downstairs, Lizbit offers us tea. Lizbit is what you might call a proselyte when it comes to tea. She will offer it to you for every ill. She takes hers with a gigantic amount of milk, but she knows I like mine plain and strong with only a squeeze of lemon, if you've got it. The four of us sit around the kitchen table, drinking tea. Lizbit slurps hers from the rim of the mug.

"Just like when we were kids," says Susana. "Remember, Cricket? Cake and milk in Auntie's kitchen before we bicycled home from school."

Aunt Benedita smiles at me. "Emilia always had her nose stuck in some book. The bigger, the better. Scrawny little girl, great big book."

"I wasn't *that* scrawny."

"Yes, you were," says Lizbit. "I've seen pictures."

Harvey comes to the doorway from the living

room, where he's been listening to the Red Sox on the radio. He's a pleasant-looking man, about six feet tall, brown hair, fresh round pink face. He looks even younger than his twenty-six years. He shrugs on his jacket and taps his watch. "Emilia," he says, "we're going to have to hurry in order to make the last ferry."

I look at Susana. "Aren't you coming?"

She sets down her fork and turns her attention to Lizbit's hair, which has come undone from its bow. "I thought Lizbit and I might stay behind and start going through Pop's things. You've always got so much work to do before the end of term. We'll be out of your way."

"You know what a nuisance I can be when you're trying to work," says Lizbit.

"This is starting to sound like a conspiracy."

From the doorway, Harvey says impatiently, "Emilia, *please*? I've got an important meeting in the morning."

Lizbit slides out of her chair and comes around behind to take my shoulders. "We just want what's best for you, Emmie. Now hurry up and catch your ferry before Harvey blows a gasket."

Harvey and I don't say much on the ferry. It's May and the sky isn't quite dark by the time we drive onto the dock at New London and head up the highway toward Boston. Frankly, with all the excitement, I find myself dozing off around Providence, and it's only when we reach the outer suburbs that Harvey clears his throat like he's got something important to say. I call it his lawyerly scratch and gird myself.

He holds the wheel with one hand and lights a cigarette with the other. I'd offer to help but Harvey's the kind of man who likes to light his cigarette by himself.

"Emilia," he says. "Emmie."

"Yes, Harv?"

"You know how fond I am of you. You're like a sister to me. The sister I never had."

"That's sweet. I'm fond of you too, Harvey."

A drizzle starts to flick against the windshield. Harvey reaches for the switch and the wipers whisk the drops away. I turn my head to watch the lamps stream past in the darkness. A flash catches my eye in the rearview mirror. I turn my head to observe the pair of headlights directly behind us and it seems to me—thought I can't say for certain—it's the same black sedan that pulled onto the highway right behind us, back in New London.

"The thing is," Harvey continues, "when two people start a new life together—"

"You want me to move out, don't you?"

"Certainly not. I certainly wouldn't ask *you* to move on *our* account. I was thinking we'd get a place of our own, in fact."

"Of course you were. I'd expect nothing less. A nice roomy brick colonial in Brookline, maybe? Near your mother's place?"

"I— Well, that would be ideal, of course—"

"Swell place to start a new family. Does Lizbit know?"

"We haven't spoken to Lizbit. I thought I'd discuss the idea with you first."

"You don't think she'll want to have her own say in the matter?"

"Lizbit," he says, with a little bite to his voice, "should learn to do as she's told."

I don't reply to that, and maybe Harvey considers whether he's overstepped because he doesn't venture anything else. He rolls down the window an inch or so to let out the smoke. I glance back again through the rear windshield. The same pair of determined head-lights. We ride in silence for another half hour, when at last I speak up and tell him he can drop me off at Cato's place in Cambridge.

MAY 1946
Winthrop Island

Two nights later, Susana sat on the edge of the bed and watched me stroke on some lipstick. I'd bought the tube at the Medeiros' general store and it took me at least a quarter of an hour to decide among the four or five colors they kept on the narrow column of shelf grudgingly allocated to personal vanity. Finally Mrs. Medeiro had marched over and said, *Here, take this one. It's new.*

"It's a little bright, isn't it?" Susana said.

I rubbed my lips together and leaned closer to the mirror. "It's *supposed* to be bright."

Susana rose and snatched the tube from my hand. "Fatal *Apple*? Are they trying to be funny?"

"Give that back."

She relinquished the lipstick and sat back down on the bed. "Your dress is all wrong, too."

"My dress is fine."

"It's old. Drab. A little short, too."

"Golly," I said, "thanks for the pep talk. Are you jealous or something?"

"Maybe."

I blotted the Fatal Apple with a tissue, applied another coat, and examined the result. The bright red lips in the mirror didn't belong to me—didn't belong to any sensible woman—but that was the point, wasn't it? I turned around and pressed a kiss on the part of Susana's hair. "It'll be boring, probably. All those rich people droning on about government bonds."

"Your hair is too long. Everyone's wearing it shorter now."

"Nuts to them. Don't stay up late, all right?"

"Oh, go have your fun. Don't even think about little me sitting here at home."

"Don't you ever get tired of being so sweet to me?"

"Get lost."

I wobbled downstairs in my sandals with the three-inch heels, which had spent the last three years since graduation in a cardboard box in the back of the closet. Mama sat in the keeping room with her mending basket. Pop sat in the armchair next to her with his after-supper whiskey in the tin mug. Outside, the sun still hung gold above the west, and the cars had begun to rumble up the long Summerly driveway to toast the end of the war, the start of a brand-new summer.

"You're wearing lipstick," Pop said.

"Yes, I am. It's a party, remember?"

Pop cast his eyes down to the mug in his hand. "Just don't expect too much, okay?"

"What do you mean, too much? I don't expect anything. I'm just going to have a good time with some old friends."

Pop gave his head a small shake and mumbled something into the whiskey.

"What's that?"

"Nothing."

"Are you saying you don't want me to go?"

He looked up. "I'm saying the Peabodys are not your friends, Emilia."

"Oh, for Pete's sake, Pop. It's *Shep*. Shep and Amory. We grew up together."

"That was a long time ago. You were kids."

"Pop," I said, "you're so old-fashioned."

"And you're so smart, Em? Is that it? You think that because the war's over, it's going to be just like before? Boys and girls playing together?"

"Why, you're afraid, aren't you? You're afraid I *will* have a good time."

Pop stood up and went to turn on the radio. An instant of static, then the familiar men's voices filled the room, the baseball announcers, I could never remember their names, discussing some pitcher's elbow in the same keen, serious notes you might discuss General Eisenhower's right flank at Normandy. "I'm just saying you need to use your head, that's all."

"I'm not stupid, Pop."

He sat back down on the chair. "You think you're so damned clever, don't you? Smartest kid on the island."

Mama let out a slow hiss from between her teeth. I knelt next to her and took her hand. "I'll tell you all about it when I get back. Okay, Mama? What everybody wore and said."

Mama made one of her slow, lopsided smiles. I picked up a yellow paper flower from the tray at her elbow. It was folded like a rose with twelve petals. "Can I wear this?"

She nodded. I rummaged in the mending basket for a safety pin and fixed the flower to my dress, above the heart.

As I left the room, Pop's voice called out to follow me. *Don't come crying to me afterward, Em.*

Outside, the air was cool and fine, aged to a delicate gold. I walked behind the beach plum and the birches and crossed the lawn toward the big house. From here you could see the entire point, the grassy dunes and the sea roses and the rocks and the beach. Summerly sprawled in the middle, shimmering in the dying sun. Pop had repainted the white trim a few weeks ago and it looked mighty nice, crisp and bright. It's funny how a house can appear so gray and lifeless for nine months of the year, and then you throw open the doors and windows and slap a little fresh paint on the trim, fill the flowerboxes and start a record on the record player and pour a few drinks for a few people, and all of a sudden Summerly became a lively old joint again, the centermost point of the world, war and grief and the atom bomb all banished.

A car whisked up the drive, a turquoise convertible coupe, joining the others parked on the grass outside the house. Already the laughter poured through the windows. A man got out of the coupe and walked around the hood to open the door for the woman in the passenger seat. I squinted to make them out. The man was tall and trim, dressed in a sport coat and tan slacks; the woman had short, dark, glossy hair and wore a dress the color of limes. I paused on the gravel and watched the woman wobble up the steps in a pair of heeled shoes, like a cat on stilts, and disappear with her escort through the open doorway into the foyer.

When I was about twelve or thirteen, the Peabodys had a party just like this one—just like any of their parties, I guess. They are social creatures, the Families. They like to gather amongst their kind for luncheons or cocktails or dinners or bridge, any excuse will do.

Because they generally prefer their dogs to their children, the three of us Winthrops used to sneak away and join Amory and Shep to watch the grown-ups at play the way you watched animals at a zoo, from the banister if the party were indoors, and if it were out on the terrace, we'd hide among the rocks. I remember the smell of perfume and cigarettes, how the women wore these colorful gowns, how their hair frizzled from their hairdos in the salt air, how they dangled their cocktail glasses between their fingers and smoked their cigarettes, stained with lipstick. I used to practice with rolled-up paper squares in the mirror at home.

Anyway, this time back when I was twelve, it was just Shep and me among the rocks. Amory and Eli had gone off somewhere—they were teenagers now, easily bored—and Susana must have been in bed already. Shep had gotten his hands on an ashtray filled with half-finished butts and we sat smoking them, pretending we liked it. The Peabodys had hired a few musicians and cleared the living room for dancing. The sun had fallen and the air was blue with twilight, and through the wall of French windows we watched the dancers cavort inside that box of radiance. The dresses swirled and the jewels glittered and the women stretched their necks like swans. Now that Amory was gone and it was just Shep and me, I could drop my air of indifference. I said something about how wonderful it all was, how I wished I could dance in a dress like that, in a room like that.

Aw, you will someday, Shep had said.

I sat down with my back to the rocks and dragged tragically on my fugitive cigarette. I wore a plain yellow dress from the Sears, Roebuck catalog and a pair of beaten-up espadrilles from the general store, both too small and tight. I had never given much thought to what I wore, but now the shabbiness of my clothes shamed me. I saw the line that divided me from the people in the Peabodys' living room overlooking the ocean. Of course, I had always known it was there. But until this moment, it never seemed to matter.

Shep had elbowed my ribs. What's eating you, Cricket?

Nothing, I said.

You want to dance or something? We could dance right here.

Says who.

Says me.

Dance with *you*? Shep, you can't hardly stay upright on a bicycle.

You're saying I can't dance?

He took my hand. I shook it off and tossed my cigarette butt in a small pool left behind by the tide, shiny with moonlight.

Someone will see us, I said.

Aw, who cares. They're all sauced anyway. Why, I'll bet—

I put my hand over his mouth. *Shhh!*

Say, what's the big—

Someone's coming.

We went still as a pair of stones. From the direction of the lawn, just on the other side of the ridge of rocks, I heard a low chuckle. A throaty voice asking a question.

I turned my head a few inches to Shep's saucer ear. Who is it?

He shrugged. In the silence I heard the slow, rough noise of his breath under his ribs.

Now the voices came clearer, a man and a woman. She said something about the moon—how bright it was, though just half. Her words slurred gracefully into each other. A waft of cigarette smoke. *Bright enough to see your beautiful face*, the man answered her.

Shep and I looked at each other, eyes equally panicked and mirthful, mirroring the same thought—wasn't that Ben Monk? The oldest of the Monk boys, just finished his freshman year at Harvard. Curling hair the color of maple syrup, hazel eyes, six feet tall, football—the kind of kid who always seemed a year or two older than his actual age. I didn't know if Ben Monk had spoken five words to me, my whole entire life. Still, I knew his voice. He had a voice like a politician, all warm vowels and self-assured consonants. He put them to good effect now. He told this woman—whoever she was, her voice was too soft to make out, just those graceful murmurs—how beautiful she looked, how nobody could see them. Pretty soon he said nothing at all. I lay inches away from Shep, not daring to breathe, while the two of them kissed and groaned and sighed. A thump, a giggle, a gasp. The grunts took on a rhythm, counterposed with tiny cries like a kitten. I figured they couldn't have been more than twenty feet away. I remember the smell of salt, the way my eyelids hurt because I squeezed them shut with so much force. I wanted to put my fingers in my ears, but I couldn't move. GRUNT and GRUNT and GRUNT and GRUNT. The woman mewled, *Oh Ben, oh Ben, oh Ben.*

What's he doing to her? I whispered to Shep.

Shep made a noise in his throat and shrugged his big shoulders.

The rhythm picked up, like some kind of excruciating mazurka. I wanted to shut my ears, I wanted to get up and run away, but I was trapped there between the damp, barnacle-crusted rock and Shep's clumsy body prone alongside mine. When would it stop? It had to stop sometime!

Oh Ben, oh Ben. She was getting louder, shrieking

almost. I dug my fingers into the gravel. *Ben! Ben! Ben! Ben!*

Ben Monk ground out this shout that slid into a groan and faded to nothing. I opened my eyes. Blissful absence of human noise. The waves slapped sheepishly against the rocks.

Twenty feet away on the lawn, Ben spoke in this husky voice. *You all right?*

The woman answered with a murmur. Next to me, Shep's chest trembled. His foot moved in a spasm, sending a stone or a seashell or something down the rocks.

What was that? the woman gasped.

Ben asked what was wrong.

I thought I heard something!

Now my own chest started to shudder. Shep grabbed my hand and pressed his fingers into the palm. The human touch was like a jolt of electricity. Kind of shocked me quiet.

Aw, it was just a bird or something, said Ben. *Come on.*

I counted off the seconds. One Mississippi, two Mississippi. I think I made it to fifteen or so before the laughter exploded from Shep's chest. Mine, too. We laughed until our sides hurt, until the tears rolled down our cheeks. Just as we started to pull ourselves together,

Shep chanted, *Oh Ben, oh Ben,* in this soft, ridiculous falsetto, and we fell back laughing all over again.

I wiped the tears from my eyes. Who do you think she was? I asked.

I don't know. Somebody's wife.

Whose?

Shep was a couple of years older than me, and what's more, he knew everybody, all the husbands and wives, because the Families dined at the Club three or four times a week, not being especially inclined to use their own kitchens. So in retrospect, I think he probably knew exactly who she was, this woman who snuck out of a party in the company of strapping nineteen-year-old Ben Monk and committed adultery right there in the grass near the rocks, not that I really understood what was happening at the time.

But all Shep said was, Aw, I couldn't tell you, Cricket.

Anyway, I stared at that open front door of Summerly and I thought about Ben Monk, who was shot down over Europe around the same time as Arthur, so maybe it was just as well he got his kicks while he could. The breeze knocked my navy-blue skirt around my knees. Susana was right, I was dressed for a funeral. So who cared. Shep wouldn't care, he wasn't the kind of guy who read fashion magazines. Amory probably wouldn't even come. Shep hadn't said anything about Amory. Still, I wished I'd smoked a cigarette beforehand, from the pack of Lucky Strikes I kept behind the breadbox, because you never knew.

Mrs. Peabody stood at the entrance, greeting everybody in a bright yellow dress that said the war is behind us, you can't resurrect the dead but you can toast the living. The sight of it gave me courage. I bounded up the steps and looked over her shoulder for Shep. Inside, somebody let out a long bray of laughter. The record player in the living room sang out the "Chattanooga Choo Choo," which by coincidence was the exact same song Shep and I sang all summer that last summer before Pearl Harbor. I remember he'd tried to make me dance but I never would. *You'd break my feet*, I told him.

Mrs. Peabody turned from the couple ahead of me and her face brightened.

I stretched out my hand. "Mrs. Peabody, how lovely to—"

"Cricket, thank goodness! So nice of you to help us this evening. Mary's been waiting for you in the kitchen."

I stared at the narrow, powdery channel between Mrs. Peabody's two eyebrows, which were knit toward each other as if to point me forward and to the right, down the hall to the kitchen, where Mary had been making up trays of her famous cheese-and-onion puffs all afternoon, you could smell them in the air. For a second or two, I entertained a brief vision of me—or rather another version of myself, a Cricket with moxie— telling Mrs. Peabody this is a terrible mistake, I have no intention of serving cheese puffs to her guests all evening, where in the hell did she get such a crazy idea.

In the kitchen, Mary leaned against the enamel Hotpoint range and smoked a cigarette. She came down from Boston each summer and kept to herself. She didn't look at me but nudged her eyebrow toward the trays arranged on the large wooden table. I removed my cardigan sweater and folded it on a chair. The trays were made of silver and might have come over on the *Mayflower* or something. I lifted one with both hands and followed the noise out of the kitchen and down the hall to the drawing room that overlooked the ocean from a wall of tall French doors, which my aunt Benedita had cleaned yesterday with vinegar and rags.

What I'd do is I'd find Shep and have a good laugh about this. He'd see it for the joke it was. Set Mrs. Peabody straight and everything, in such a way as not to embarrass her too much. I mean, I *did* wait tables at the Club, remember, so you couldn't necessarily blame her for jumping to conclusions. Everyone was so happy about the cheese puffs. They really were delicious, kind of melted to this rich, oniony puddle in your mouth. Mary served them at every damn party because people loved them so much and didn't want to try anything new, in case it wasn't as good. I sneaked one into my mouth when nobody was looking. The trick was not to make eye contact. These people, they didn't want to know who you were, didn't want to go to all the tiresome effort of interrupting conversation to remember your name and politely ask after your family and whatnot. They wanted their cheese puffs, that's all.

In the drawing room people were already halfway loaded. Some shrill laughter rose from the corner. Long female claws reached out to pluck my tray clean. I veered back to the kitchen and clattered the empty tray on the kitchen table and picked up another. This time I made a survey of the drawing room—no sign of Shep, just sport coats and Easter egg dresses and the whirl of conversation above the record player— and turned the corner into the giant, wood-beamed library where Mr. Peabody stood next to the cocktail cart, mixing drinks with a chemist's concentration. He was a large-framed, shambling man—not quite as big as Shep, but the same air of clumsy distraction, like an overfed bear. As I staggered past under the weight of the silver tray he peered at me from behind a pair of powerful glasses.

"Miss Winthrop? Is that you?"

"Yes, Mr. Peabody. Cheese puff?"

"Why, I don't mind if I do. Can I pour you something? Lime rickey? Glass of fizz?"

"Maybe later, thanks."

Everybody looked the same, more or less, like the long months of autumn and winter and spring were just a series of rooms we'd walked through on the way back to summer. Mrs. Monk's hair was nearly white. She'd gone gray suddenly after Ben's death—brunette on Labor Day, silver by Memorial Day—and now she stood there by the bookshelf clutching a martini while she listened to Dr. Huxley go on about ornithology, probably, like he always did, and I couldn't find a single dark strand in that entire ball of floss on top of her head. She made the mistake of looking up as I held the tray in her direction and had to fumble for my name, even though I used to race screaming through her kitchen when I was eleven or twelve, pursued by Ben's kid brother Clay who had a worm farm and liked to drop the big night crawlers down the back of your shirt when you weren't looking. Dr. Huxley ate three swift, silent cheese puffs while we traded our stiff words, one after another.

Then he swallowed and said, "How's your mother these days, Cricket? Make it through the winter all right?"

"She's just fine," I told him. "Same as always."

Still I hadn't caught sight of Shep. It used to be you couldn't miss his shaggy head above the crowd, and even if you did, you just followed the disturbance caused by his shambling frame, knocking over drinks and priceless vases and maybe a cello or two. And his voice—big and chesty, like a baseball announcer or an opera singer. Then I considered he might be outside on the terrace. It was a mild evening, after all, and the sea breeze was so delicious. By now the tray was clear and I whisked out of the library like I was headed back to the kitchen, but instead I laid that tray on top of a Chippendale highboy and made for the sunroom, figuring I'd take the side door out into the garden and around to the terrace.

The door to the sunroom was closed but the bronze knob turned easily in my hand. Inside, the air was dusky. The sun had mostly set and the lamps hadn't been lit. I made my way around the furniture and had nearly reached one of the French doors when I stubbed my toe on the corner of the wicker sofa and swore.

A head stuck up from the cushions. "Who goes there?"

I stared at that head. The hair was dark, the face was shadowed. The voice was so familiar, I thought I was dreaming.

"*Cricket?* Is that you?"

"*Amory?*" I gasped. "What are you *doing* here?"

Sometimes, when I tried to conjure up Amory Peabody's face in my head, I couldn't do it. I read somewhere that there was a scientific explanation for this phenomenon. Apparently, the tiny electric impulses that make up your memory can get so overloaded with associated emotions, the brain cells are forced to jettison less important things like the shape of the eyes or the angle of the cheekbones in order to make room.

Anyway, the last time I saw Amory's face was like this—too dark to make out. It was Labor Day and the fireworks were shooting off from the beach—analyze *that*, Cato—and Amory had leaned over as we sat there on the Club lawn, watching the show, and whispered in a voice that smelled of booze, *Meet me in the gazebo in five minutes.* Then he swung to his feet and sauntered off.

I remember looking around me. Everybody was watching the fireworks. Susana sat between Pop and Mama. Arthur sat at a little distance, one arm holding Tippy Pinkerton to his side. Even the Club's manager

Mr. Finch had come to join us, jacket neatly buttoned. He sat with the Monks. Mrs. Monk bent her head to his ear and murmured earnestly. Only Shep didn't seem interested in the fireworks. He lay on the grass with his arms behind his head and appeared to have fallen asleep.

By then, we'd been flirting for weeks, Amory and I, though I had secretly pined for him for years. Of course I had! Amory was sleek and handsome, he had the look of a young god. I couldn't remember a time when I hadn't dreamed of kissing Amory Peabody, marrying Amory Peabody. Now a certain spark struck from the end of my birthday party had shimmered into flame and I was walking among the stars. Every dream had become real. We would steal off to the beach at midnight and the last two times he had kissed me. His lips had found mine and sent shivers down my back and over my chest, all those things you read about in books. By the time Labor Day arrived, I was ready to do whatever Amory asked of me.

After a minute or two, I rose and stole across the lawn toward the gazebo. The grass was already damp and my sandals were wet through by the time I stepped under the dainty white roof that reflected the flashes of light behind me in brilliant staccato. Amory called my name from the bench. I sat down next to him. He had brought a bucket of champagne and a pair of glasses, already full. He handed one to me. I don't remember what we drank to, but I do remember feeling grown up and terribly sophisticated, like the summer girls. I held out my glass for more champagne and said, *But you're leaving tomorrow.* He asked if I would miss him, and I said of course I would. Then I boldly asked him if he'd miss me, too. Amory sat back and reflected. I didn't know enough about men back then to realize he was just teasing me. *I don't know*, he said, *maybe you should show me what I'm missing.* For courage I drank back the rest of the champagne and leaned forward to kiss him. It was the first time I'd kissed him instead of the other way around, and I liked how it made me feel. When I pulled back, I couldn't see his expression but I did notice the gleam of moonlight in his eyes. We finished the champagne bottle and got to kissing again, and because I didn't know enough to realize how tipsy I was, I didn't notice that he had unzipped my dress until it was already down around my waist. He unfastened my brassiere and dropped it on the floor next to his feet. I tried to cover up with my hands but he said no, let me see you, you're so beautiful, Cricket, why didn't I ever see how beautiful you are? Then his hands were on my breasts, then his mouth. He pulled me on his lap so I was straddling him. I was frightened and excited, I was afraid of what was to come but desperate to please Amory, to show him how much I loved him, to show him I was the kind of girl he could spend his life with. Underneath my spread legs his hips moved against my underpants. His hands squeezed my breasts and his tongue stroked against my tongue. His hips moved faster and faster. I felt I was being carried away on some riptide into the ocean, and what you were supposed to do when a riptide got you was not swim against it. Just let it sweep you out to the open ocean until you could swim back to shore. So I did. I clung to Amory's shoulders while his hips carried us both to sea. Amory made these rhythmic grunts in his throat that sounded familiar, though I couldn't remember where I'd heard them before. All of a sudden he cried out and his hips stopped moving. To stop myself from falling off the bench, I slid my other leg to the floor and knocked over the champagne bottle, which then knocked over a glass and shattered it. The noise made me jump. Amory swore. Somebody called out from the darkness. Finch, I thought. I shoved my arms into my dress and ran out of the gazebo, across the lawn, into the path that led through the brush that led to the small pasture where we kept the cow. I ran along the fence until I came to the gate and ducked between the bars. I came in through the kitchen door and ran upstairs to lie on the bed in the darkness. Between my legs I felt every nerve as if somebody had scraped me with a knife. I stared at the ceiling and listened to my heart thunk in my ears.

The next day, after the Peabodys had packed up and left Summerly for the mainland, I walked over to the gazebo and stared at the section of bench I had shared with Amory and tried to remember everything that had happened. I tried to remember the shape of his face. How he had looked as he sat beneath me, shoving his hips against my underpants; where he had put his hands and his mouth, how I had felt and whether I liked it. But the memories were too slippery. I couldn't grasp them. Every sign of our presence there was gone. Not a shard of glass or a drop of champagne remained on the wooden boards, and neither did my brassiere.

Now Amory was back, five years later. Somewhere inside that shadow was his face that I hadn't been able to remember. His hair that curved around his left temple. I wanted to turn and run but my legs were stuck into the rug, the way you sometimes can't move when you're in the middle of a dream.

"Say, it *is* you!" he exclaimed. "Look at that. You're a sight for sore eyes."

"You scared me to *death*!"

"Jesus Christ, Cricket. It's *my* goddamn sunroom."

"But there's a *party* going on!"

"I'm taking a nap, if you must know," he said.

"A nap?"

"Not anymore, obviously."

Now that my eyes were growing used to the dark, I could make out the loft of his cheekbones, the tarnished glow on his hair, the familiar lazy droop of his eyelids. *Oh, right*, I thought. *That's how you look.* He climbed to his feet and stretched his arms.

"Can I get you a drink?" he said. "Since I'm already up."

I still felt like I was dreaming. "Honestly, I was about to leave."

"Hell, no you don't. If I have to endure this baloney, so do you. Champagne all right?" He headed to the cocktail tray—the Peabodys kept one in just about every room—and examined the glasses on the bottom shelf until he found a champagne coupe. Around us, the room was empty and still warm from the sunshine trapped by three walls of French windows.

"What about your guests?" I asked.

"Oh, they don't miss me. Having a grand time. Shep'll cover for me, that's what brothers are for." He looked around like he'd forgotten something. "Where the hell did I put the bucket?"

"On the floor next to the sofa."

"Oh, right. There you are, my best beloved. Right where I left you." He grabbed the champagne bottle by the neck, lifted it out of the ice bucket, and kissed the label. A jacket hung from his shoulders and his necktie hung from his white collar. Faultlessly he poured the champagne and held out the brimming glass. "Look at that. Fine stuff, isn't it? Shep brought her back from France. Liberated from some German cellar, he tells me. Nothing but the best, those goddamn Nazis."

I took the glass and drank. I hadn't drunk champagne in ages—maybe not since Amory himself poured me a glass in the Club gazebo—and the bubbles and the iciness surprised me. Amory grinned at my expression—that cavalier grin he had, which had seemed so dashing in my memory and now seemed something else. I couldn't say what. My head reeled. I set down the glass on a lamp table. "I should go."

"What's the hurry?"

"I shouldn't be here, that's all. I'm not dressed for it."

"You look fine." He wasn't looking at me. He was looking at his champagne coupe, into which he was pouring the last of the liquid from the bottle. "Did you get a load of Shep?"

"Not yet. I mean, yes, I saw him the other day—the other night, actually—"

"What did you think?"

"What do you mean, what did I think? It was good to see him. It's good to see you, it's terrific the both of you came home all right—"

"Terrific. That's it, that's the word. Terrific the both of us came home. But not Arthur."

"No, not Arthur."

"Or your brother. Poor old Eli."

"Not Eli, no." I picked up my glass again and finished off the champagne. It wasn't so much of a shock this time. Actually, it went down pretty easy. I made a cradle of my two hands and dangled the empty glass from my fingers. "I'm sorry. I forgot to say hello. It's good to see you again."

"Well, hell. Where are my manners." He held out his hand and we shook. He squinted at me. "Good to see you too, Cricket. You haven't changed, so far as I can tell."

"I was going to say the same of you."

"Is that supposed to be a compliment or an insult?"

"Why would it be an insult?"

"I mean you probably think a fellow should have improved beyond all recognition after going to war. Like my brother, to take an example."

"What, *Shep*?"

"It's miraculous, really. From roly-poly to deb's delight."

I laughed. "Deb's delight? Be serious."

"Don't tell me it's escaped *your* notice. Of all people."

"Of all people? Me?"

"The two of you, I mean. Joined at the hip. I can't imagine you didn't notice the transformation, shall we say, in the kid's physique." Amory tilted his head back and drained off the champagne, then he swirled the glass around to gather in the last drop or two. He eyed the bucket, eyed the bottle in the bucket, cast about the room. "Got to be a stash in here somewhere, don't you think?"

"I wouldn't know."

"No, of course you wouldn't." He bent in front of one of the cabinets lining the fourth wall, the one with no windows, and rummaged inside. By now the twilight had gulped up the dregs of sunset and the room was practically black. I remembered there was a lamp on the table between the two wicker chairs on the other side of the room, overlooking the ocean, the ones with giant backs shaped like a pair of hot-air balloons. I felt my way along the back of the sofa and found the French doors, then the chair, then the lamp, and switched it on. The bulb cast a dull glow on the furniture and the side of Amory's head.

"It's no miracle, when you think about it," I said. "Just years of marching around on Army rations."

"Damn, I knew it!" Amory emerged from the shadow of the cabinet and held up a triumphant arm. "It's not Nazi plunder, nor is it properly chilled. But I'll bet we don't care."

"Honestly, I can't—"

He plopped down on the sofa and peeled back the foil. "Look at that, a 1936 Pol Roger. How in the hell did she end up in a cabinet in the sunroom?"

"I really—"

He eased out the cork, *pop-hiss*, and motioned me over. The champagne buzz had reached my head and I felt I wanted more of it before I went outside to find Shep—*deb's delight*, Amory had said, whatever *that* meant—so I sat down next to Amory on the wicker sofa and held out my glass.

"You know it's what Churchill drinks," he said as he poured.

"This?"

"Pol Roger. Bottle a day keeps the Nazis away. Now, what were you saying?"

I thought back. "Marching around on Army rations."

"Turns any chump into Tarzan. Any ordinary guy into a hero."

"So why aren't you in there raising a glass to all the heroes?"

Amory clinked his glass against mine. "Because I'm in here with you."

"But *you* were in here before *I* was in here."

"Well, then. Why are *you* in here, instead of out there?"

I waggled my finger at him. "It's not the same thing. Those are *your* people, not mine."

"Them? Aw, they're just a bunch of phonies." He swung an arm toward the door and the party on the other side. "But you're different, Cricket. That's why I've always liked you. You're sincere."

"I think most people are sincere, when you get to know them."

"Good old Cricket." Amory sighed and patted his jacket pocket, came up with a cigarette case. He took out a cigarette and offered it to me. Maybe I could've used a smoke, but I shook my head anyway. He lit it for himself, skillfully balancing the champagne coupe in one hand while he manipulated lighter and cigarette. "See, I had a lot on my mind last winter. All crammed in here." He tapped his temple with the finger clenching the cigarette. "The war, you know? Messes with your head."

"I'm sure it does. I'm sure it was awful."

He flicked some ash on the rug. "Shep with all his goddamn medals."

From the living room came a burst of synchronized laughter, like you hear on the radio. Amory stared at the closed door and smoked his cigarette. I stared at his profile and wondered how I had ever forgotten how he looked. That straight, sharp nose, that sleek cheekbone. Nothing had changed, except to harden in place, like the war was an oven that had baked him.

"What were you saying about Shep and his medals?" I asked.

He answered in a growl. "What about them?"

"You said he'd won a lot of them."

"Oh, they hung the ribbons on old Shep like he was a Christmas tree. Didn't you hear?"

"No. He didn't say anything about any medals."

"Of course not. Modesty being among his countless virtues. Funny, though, how somehow the word always gets out."

"But what did he do?"

Amory laughed at me. "Cricket, my God. I know you're living on an island, but don't you read a newspaper once in a while? Didn't he write you a letter or something?"

"Of course he wrote! More than you did, anyway."

The smile fell away from his face. "I meant to write, Cricket. Honest."

"Then why didn't you?"

He reached down for the bottle in the bucket at his feet. "Oh, I'm a heel, I guess."

"Amory," I said, "I don't blame you or anything. You were fighting a war."

"That's right. I was fighting a war, wasn't I? Still, that's no excuse not to be a gentleman. I should have had the guts to write. I should have had the guts to do a lot of things. Come to think of it, I should have the guts to leave this room right now and face all those well-wishers outside the door."

"Well-wishers?"

"What's that? Cricket, darling, haven't you heard the wonderful news? The very reason we're gathered here this evening?" Amory held the champagne bottle high above his glass so the liquid came down in a long, reckless stream. I watched the foam rise and rise.

"To celebrate the end of war, right?" I said. "The start of summer."

"My God. Don't tell me he didn't tell you. Don't tell me he didn't bother to mention the happy, happy news."

Amory raised his glass and poured the champagne down his throat in a series of gulps. I watched his

Adam's apple jump beneath the pink skin. When he had swallowed the last drop, he smiled at me, sheepish.

"I'm engaged to be married," he said.

I took the bottle from his hand and refilled my own glass. "Well, congratulations. Who's the lucky girl?"

"Tippy Pinkerton."

"Tippy Pinkerton! *Our* Tippy?"

"You have a funny way of taking ownership of people you hardly know, Cricket. If by *our Tippy* you mean Tippy Pinkerton whose family summers over on Meadow Lane, then yes." He paused to smoke his cigarette. "You know her mother died just before Christmas."

"I know."

"Well, I guess she needed a little comforting, and who better to comfort a girl than yours truly?"

I slugged down the rest of my champagne and held out my glass to Amory. The room seemed to be tilting to the left and for some reason I found this movement hilarious. Tippy Pinkerton! Poor, sweet Tippy, to be comforted in her grief by Amory Peabody, who happened to be the brother of her dead fiancé. I had to fight down a fit of giggles. I knew I was supposed to say something, so I croaked out, "I'm sure you'll be very happy."

"Hell, of course we'll be happy. Nice, square, attractive girl, Tippy. I'm sure we'll have a nice, square, happy life together." He reached for the ashtray and ground out the last of his cigarette. "You know, I remember you and I had a little fun together, once."

"Did we?"

"You remember. That last summer. Your sixteenth birthday, do you remember? Your mother threw a little party for you. A real swell little party. You wore a new dress, a little pink number. You looked terrific."

"Oh, that's right. I still have that dress. Didn't you take me for a walk along the beach afterward?"

"I did. And when I brought you home I gave you a kiss. I had the funny feeling, when I kissed you, that it was the first time you'd ever been kissed."

"I don't know where you got that idea. I've been kissed lots of times."

"Really? My mistake. Anyway, I remember I enjoyed it very much." He paused to drag on his cigarette. His eyes considered me. "Didn't we see each other the next night, too?"

"I think we did, now that you mention it."

"And a few more nights after that."

"Yes, probably. I don't really recall."

"That last night. Labor Day, after the fireworks. Didn't we—"

I stood up and brushed off my dress. "So when did you and Tippy reunite?"

"Tippy? Oh, some Christmas party. Both of us pretty sauced. She was all broken up over her mother and all that. And I'd just stepped off the boat, damned happy to be back home."

"I can imagine," I said.

"You know how it is," he said. "One thing led to another. We saw a lot of each other over the winter. Then Shep came home in April—you must've heard they kept him in Germany for a while, some kind of intelligence job, if you can stand the irony—and my parents threw this swell party for him, and it seemed to me—well, it was the spur of the moment, really, an impulse. I proposed, she accepted."

Amory leaned back against the sofa and stared at me thoughtfully, waiting for me to say something, and as I stared back, a peculiar feeling came over me, nothing to do with any champagne. It was the opposite of champagne, actually, the opposite of some chemical making you feel as if the person standing in front of you was a god. I stood there and realized Amory was mortal. An attractive, charming, inebriated man I had kissed once, a long time ago.

When I didn't say anything, he reached for my hand and pulled me back down on the sofa. "That last night. That Labor Day. Did we really . . . you know."

"Of course not. You were pretty drunk, if you'll recall."

"That's the trouble. I don't recall. I wish I did. I have this picture of you . . . it's been in my head . . . You forgive me, don't you? Please say you forgive me. I was just a kid."

"Forgive you?" I laughed. "I can hardly even remember it."

He leaned forward and kissed me. I was too shocked to pull away. The drink fell from my hand and crashed to the floor, but I hardly noticed because at the exact instant of impact, the door to the hall flew open and the light switched on, revealing Shep Peabody in a navy sport coat and a funny plaid bow tie that looked like it was going to burst from his neck.

"Amory! There you are! What the hell are you . . ." Shep looked from Amory to me and back again. His hair was cropped short and he was so sinewy and stern that for a moment I thought it couldn't be Shep, even though I already knew how the past five years had melted the boyhood from his bones. Now I stared at him in full light, across a room. He was dressed for a summer cocktail party but you could see he was a soldier, a grown man, a stranger.

"Shep, old boy," drawled Amory. He spread his arms and leaned back against the sofa cushions. "Just having a drink with old Cricket. You remember Cricket. Her family works for ours?"

For a second or two, Shep's eyes met mine. They were like chips of ice. I thought I was going to die of the cold but he spoke just in time. "Cricket," he said. "I was wondering where you were."

"I was just on my way out," I said. "And I ran into your brother."

"I can see that." He turned to Amory. "You're wanted out there. For the toast."

"Oh, right. The toast." Amory slapped my leg. "Come on, old Cricket. It's time to toast the happy future."

I leaned down and picked up the pieces of my champagne coupe. Lucky I'd drunk all the champagne, lucky it hadn't fallen far. "Thanks," I said, "but I'll be on my way."

"Suit yourself," said Amory.

I made it all the way to the beach roses before I started crying. Well, wouldn't you? I could still hear

Amory's Boston drawl—*You remember Cricket. Her family works for ours.* I could still see Shep's face when he saw the two of us—his own brother and me—on the wicker sofa, champagne and everything, for that split second before we scrambled apart. I scratched at my eyelids, trying to gouge away the image, but the more I scratched the deeper it went, like a splinter. I dropped to my knees in the sand and a voice floated from the gap in the shrubbery that led to the beach.

"Well, hello there. Friend or foe?"

I looked up. From the light pouring from the windows of the house and the tiki torches on the terrace, I could just make out her face. "Mrs. Rainsford?"

She peered down at me, interested. "My goodness, is it Miss Winthrop? What the devil are you doing there?"

"I'm—I've lost an earring."

"That's awful. Can I help?"

"I think it's gone."

She dropped gracefully into the dune next to me and brushed half-heartedly at the sand. "You're probably right. Was it valuable?"

"Not really."

"Well, never mind, then."

With a casual fist I wiped the last of the tears away

from my cheek and sat up. "You should probably go inside. They're starting the toasts."

Mrs. Rainsford had opaque, hooded, inquisitive eyes, slanted upward a degree or two, and she fixed them on me as she spoke. "The toasts?"

"You know, Amory and his fiancée. The end of the war and the happy future, I guess."

She took a cigarette case from the pocket of her dress and opened it to me. I took one and she took one and as she lit us both up, she asked why I wasn't in there, toasting the happy future.

"It's not really my kind of crowd," I told her.

"But you *live* here. Whose crowd *would* it be, other than yours?"

"Well, *yours*. The Peabodys. All their rich friends. The people who come here in the summer. The rest of us, we're just the help. Seen and not heard."

She drew in a lungful of smoke and purled it out again from the side of her mouth. "You're a Winthrop, aren't you? The oldest family in New England. The island's named after you, for God's sake."

I made myself laugh. "We don't own a square yard of it anymore. When my grandfather couldn't afford to farm anymore, he sold his land to *your* people."

"To amuse ourselves on with our ghastly mill fortunes. Still, you have every right to rub shoulders with the summer tourists. You were here first. So go on. Grab yourself a cocktail and drink to the happy couple."

"I can't."

"Why not?"

"I'm wearing the wrong dress, for one thing."

"What's wrong with your dress? I think it's lovely. Suits your figure."

"It's years old. Styles have changed."

"Still, you shouldn't need to dress like some kind of fashion doll to feel like you belong at a party. You seem like a clever girl. Where'd you go to college?"

"I didn't."

"Well, that's a shame. Why not?"

I scooped up a handful of sand and watched the grains slide between my fingers. "I always wanted to go. But my brother was killed in the war, and my mother had a stroke—"

"How awful."

"So I stayed home instead. To help my father take care of her."

"And you've been stuck on this island ever since? My God."

"I wouldn't say stuck."

She reached out and took my chin and moved my face from side to side, like she was examining a horse she wanted to buy. "Do you like children?" she asked.

"I guess so."

"I've been hoping to find somebody clever to manage them while I'm working. Not one of my sister's people, but not one of *these* girls, either."

"What girls?"

She jerked her head to the house. "Oh, those empty vessels in there, not a single original thought to share among them. My children need somebody *interesting*, someone inquisitive."

"How do you know I'm inquisitive?"

"I have a nose for people." She tapped it with her finger, the one holding the cigarette. Then she stuck the cigarette in her mouth and managed, somehow, to smile as she was smoking it. "But you'll come to the cottage and meet them, won't you? I'd pay you, of course."

"Oh, you don't need to do that—"

"Damn it! Don't ever say such a thing, Emilia. You don't mind if I call you Emilia, do you?"

"Everyone here calls me Cricket, actually."

"*Cricket?* What kind of a silly name is that for a grown woman?"

"I don't know. I'm just used to it."

"Well, Emilia. Listen to me. You should always expect payment for your work. A woman's time is just as valuable as a man's."

"I guess you're right."

"Of course I'm right."

Mrs. Rainsford stood up and shook the sand from her skirt and held out her hand to hoist me up. From the house came a round of applause and laughter. She turned her face to the terrace doors and so did I. Through the windowpanes you could the see the crowded, colorful bodies packed inside, doused in gold light. Everyone had turned toward the end of the room where the speeches were taking place and I thought I could hear Shep's baritone reverberating through all that air and wood and plaster and glass, though I couldn't hear what he said. It wasn't meant for me, anyway, was it?

"I should be getting home," I said.

"You're not joining the party?"

"I'd rather not."

"Well, suit yourself." She stuck out her hand. "Is tomorrow morning convenient? Ten o'clock?"

I shifted the cigarette to my left hand and shook Mrs. Rainsford's hand with my right. "Ten o'clock, why not."

"Very good. Thank you, Emilia. I've enjoyed our conversation very much."

She turned toward the house and made her way through the sand to the lawn, and from the lawn to the terrace and into the living room, just as everybody lifted their glasses and gave three cheers to Amory and Tippy. I watched her until she disappeared into the crowd and then I watched the crowd itself as the bright-colored bodies dispersed in search of more fun. Some of them spilled through the doors for some night air among the tiki torches. Nobody noticed me standing there alone next to the beach roses. I guess the darkness had swallowed me up, or maybe they weren't looking hard enough.

The guest cottage had been added on some years after Summerly was built. I don't know why, there were plenty of bedrooms inside the main house. Maybe the Peabodys just figured it was better for everyone concerned if guests had their own space.

Anyway, the Rainsfords looked to be about halfway settled in when I poked open the front door at five minutes past ten o'clock that last Saturday morning in May and called out Mrs. Rainsford's name through some cacophony of childish noise. The air still smelled of vinegar but also of something warm and sweet baking in an oven somewhere, and a dozen or so cardboard boxes covered the living room floor in between stacks of precarious books. A boy burst from the hall, dressed like a wild Indian and hollering like one, too. He stopped dead at the sight of me.

"Hello, there," I said. "I'm Emilia. Is your mother there?"

He stared at me with a pair of steady black eyes. "You're the lady in the driveway."

The word *lady* startled me. At that point in my life, I don't think anybody had called me anything other than a girl. I stepped through the doorway and straightened my back. "Yes, I am. What's your name?"

"My name is Sebastian Aaron Grossmeyer," he said with dignity, or about as much dignity as an eight-year-old boy can muster when he's got a feathered headdress hanging halfway down the side of his face. He pushed a few feathers out of his line of sight and looked at me like he expected a counterattack.

"That's a very distinguished name," I said. "Could you please tell your mother I've arrived? She's expecting—"

Mrs. Rainsford's voice cut through my words. "Good Lord, it's you! I'm sorry, I'd forgotten you were coming. Come in, come in. Sebastian, for God's sake, take off that ridiculous headdress and tell your brother and sister to pipe down. My God. You see what I mean."

"What you mean?"

"About needing help. The nanny refused to leave

England with me. Sick mother. I've been run off my feet. Coffee?"

I didn't have a chance to refuse, because Mrs. Rainsford was already halfway through the door from which she'd come. As I started forward to follow her, I noticed a pair of small, inquisitive white faces peering around the doorway from the hall. A burst of giggles chased me into the kitchen, where Mrs. Rainsford had just pulled a cake pan from the ancient cast-iron oven. She wore a green housedress speckled with tiny white flowers and a blue apron and a red headscarf to hold back her curling dark hair. She closed the oven door and folded the dishcloth. "I'm making a sponge," she said.

"A sponge cake?"

"A celebration of eggs and sugar and real butter. You can't imagine how strict the rationing was back in England. Still is."

"Really? Most everything's been lifted here. Except sugar, but even that you can get more than you used to."

"In England you can't draw a breath without your ration card." She pulled a toothpick from a jar and stuck it in the middle of the cake. When she pulled it out, she made a noise of satisfaction. "I do love to bake, don't you?"

"I don't know. It gets old when you have to do it every day."

"My sister says you keep cows and chickens. For the eggs and milk and—well, all those things. That sounds like an awful lot of trouble to me."

"Gosh, that's no trouble at all. We've always had them. That's the one good thing about living on an island. We were already pretty self-sufficient when the war started, and Mr. Peabody—your brother-in-law—he likes us to keep on working the land—*his* land, I guess—at least so long as we send in the produce to Boston every so often."

"I'm sure he does. Eggs and milk for everyone, and he doesn't have to lift a finger."

"Vegetables, too," I said proudly. "My sister and I work on the garden, and our uncle Pete, that's my pop's brother, he helps takes care of the livestock and the bees—"

"*Bees?* Edwina didn't say anything about bees! For the honey? Ingenious!"

"It came in pretty handy when the sugar ran low."

Mrs. Rainsford turned to face me. She was the kind of person who gave you her full, dazzling attention when you spoke to her. "How fascinating! That's absolutely marvelous! Where do you keep the hives?"

"Next to the apple orchard."

"What, apples too? I'm enchanted."

"It's just a few trees, really. There used to be more, but once my grandfather died we stopped replacing the ones that got old."

"What a shame." She tilted her head to one side. She seemed to be turning over everything I'd said to her, picking it apart, storing the pieces of information in their relevant places. I was about to say something to break the spell, but she roused herself and straightened away from the sink. "I said something about coffee, didn't I?"

"I'd love some."

"And cake. More cake! Not sponge—currant. It's my specialty. Just a moment." She held up one hand and cocked her head again. "Do you hear that? They've gone quiet."

"Is that so bad?"

"Yes. When they're quiet it means they're up to no good. Sebastian!" There was no answer. *"Sebastian!"* she called again, much louder, and a boy's high voice answered—*Yes, Mummy?* "What are you up to?" *Nothing.* "What kind of nothing is that?" A long pause, then *We're building something.* "Building what?" *A fort.* "How nice. With what?" Another pause—*Books.* "My books or your books?" Slowly—*Your books.* "I thought so. Can I come and see it?" *Not yet.* "Are you going to clean it up when you're done?" *Yes, Mummy.* "Why can't I hear your sister and brother?" You could almost hear the clicking now, the tumblers whirring in Sebastian's brain like one of those mechanical calculating devices. Carefully, reluctantly—*Because they're inside the fort.*

Mrs. Rainsford looked at me, eyebrows raised. It seemed to me she was asking me what I should do in this type of situation. How I weighed the various consequences—the risk of broken childish spirits versus the risk of broken bones.

Of course, at the time, I didn't realize how much hung on my response. I just wanted to show her I knew how to handle kids.

I turned to the doorway. "Sebastian, why don't you set your hostages free so they can help?"

"But they don't *help*!" he wailed back. "They *pull everything down!*"

Mrs. Rainsford and I looked at each other again.

"I've got a terrific idea," I said. "Let's all have some cake and then we'll go walking . . . we'll go *exploring* on the beach."

After yesterday's sunshine, the weather had turned gray and a little chill, but Mrs. Rainsford had brushed me off when I suggested sweaters. A little hardship was good for children, she said. So they swerved and scampered on the sand wearing nothing but worn swimsuits and bare pink skin, and I had to admit that nobody complained.

"Luckily, they were so young," Mrs. Rainsford said. "And then he'd been separated from us for so long, because of the war. When I told them the news, they hardly blinked."

We were talking about her first husband, Oskar Grossmeyer. She'd met him while she was still in finishing school in Switzerland and jumped at the chance—so she said—to stay in Europe instead of returning home to Boston. Europe was where everything was happening, she said. They lived in Berlin for a time, until things got untenable—Grossmeyer was a Jew—and they fled for Shanghai. Fascinating city, Mrs. Rainsford said. Absolutely mesmerizing. Squalor side by side with obscene wealth, and the Europeans at the top of the heap, plundering everything, naturally. She could have stayed there forever, she said, except she got pregnant and Grossmeyer insisted she have the baby in Switzerland.

"That was Sebastian," she said, shading her eyes to watch him scamper in the surf. He was still wearing his Indian headdress along with a pair of dark blue swimming trunks that hung from his bones. "I was so angry at him for existing at all, right up until the moment he was born. Then I fell in love and decided I wanted to have a dozen children."

"You've got a way to go," I said.

"If only my poor husbands would stay alive. Not that one *needs* a husband, strictly speaking. If one wants children badly enough . . . well, there are plenty of men willing to supply the raw materials."

I clapped a hand over my mouth. "You wouldn't!"

"Why not? It's *wonderful*, being pregnant. *Delicious*, that's the word."

"That's not what my mother said. She said to avoid having babies at all costs."

"Did she? Poor thing. I adored the whole experience, from beginning to end. This lovely *ripening* sensation, you know, this miraculous *creature* growing inside you." She laid a hand on her middle and stared out to sea. "Planted there by someone you adore."

I should have felt embarrassed. I hardly knew her at that point, and here she was talking about how you made babies. Saying frank, intimate words like *pregnant*. Well, maybe I *was* embarrassed, but I didn't care to show it. That was the thing about Mrs. Rainsford—she made you want to be like her. "At least you have something of them, now that they're gone," I said.

Mrs. Rainsford turned to look at the smaller ones, Charlotte and Matthew—both of them blond and spindly, unlike the compact and dark-haired Sebastian. She called them by their full names, not even shortened for convenience. "What about you?" she said.

"Me?"

"Have you been in love, I mean."

"Oh! No, not really. There aren't so many boys to choose from around here."

"You don't mean you never had a crush on one of my nephews?"

I was surprised to find I could answer her with total composure. "Gosh, no. They're like brothers."

"What about Arthur? *He* was a dish, wasn't he?"

"Arthur? Are you kidding? He was about a million years old to us. We idolized him, maybe."

"Yes," she said. "Yes, of course you would."

I had the feeling she was examining the color on the side of my face—I've always blushed too much—so I scampered forward to take Matthew by the hand before he pitched face-first into the wave about to roll up the sand. He was about a year and a half old and moved like a toy soldier. Nearby, Sebastian chased a screaming Charlotte, brandishing a wad of seaweed. I scooped Matthew into my arms and inhaled the salty puppy scent of his hair. When

I returned to Mrs. Rainsford, she hadn't moved at all. Her arms were crossed and she watched me narrowly.

I handed Matthew over to her and she rubbed her nose against the skin of his neck. "How did he die?" I asked.

"How did who die?"

"Your first husband. If you don't mind my asking."

"I don't know exactly," she said. "He was arrested in Germany and disappeared."

"Arrested? For what?"

"For espionage."

You can imagine this knocked me a little flat. But Mrs. Rainsford didn't even flinch, didn't invest these terrible words with so much as a tremor of emotion. She lifted a delicate blond curl from Matthew's forehead and kissed the skin underneath it.

"Espionage?" I said. "During the war, you mean?"

"They gave me the news in—oh, let's see—it was February of 1942, I think. The Germans claimed he'd been working for one of the British intelligence services."

"And you never knew what really happened? How he died?"

Mrs. Rainsford set Matthew back in the sand and watched him scamper off to join his brother and sister.

The morning sun glittered in his hair. "No," she said. "We never found out."

Back in the house, Mrs. Rainsford put me to work sorting books while she iced the cake and the younger ones took their naps. Sebastian helped me. The novels were supposed to go in the rickety white-painted shelves lining the south wall of the living room, while the children's books fit in the eaves of the bedroom designated as the nursery. As for Mrs. Rainsford's books on history and politics and economics, they had to be carried upstairs to the attic, where she was setting up her study. Sebastian and I decided to save this chore for last.

"Mummy says her books are like old friends," he explained, holding up a thick, battered volume with a torn dust jacket. "She likes to have them around her while she's working."

I took the book from his hand and examined the cover. *The Fallacy of Political Economy*, by Oskar Grossmeyer. "This one looks like it's seen better days, though."

"That's because she reads them over and over again." He made a movement with his hand and rolled his eyes. "Over and over."

"They must be very interesting, then."

"I think they're ruddy boring."

I opened the cover. On the flyleaf someone had written a note in faded purple ink, the kind that came in fountain pens—*meine Liebling Olive*, followed by a few lines of German and a signature at the bottom, *Oskar.*

A drizzle had begun to tap against the window. I stared at the long German words, stuffed with consonants, written in jags and swoops by an impatient male hand. A whiff of pipe smoke came to my nostrils. I held the pages to my face.

"Having a good look, are you?"

I startled and dropped the book in my lap. In the doorway stood Mrs. Rainsford, wearing the blue apron, which was now smeared with streaks of white icing. She dangled a wooden spoon from one hand and a little grin from one side of her mouth.

"Did your husband really write this?" I asked.

She walked forward and took the book from my hand. Examined the back and then the front. Her smile widened. "This book changed everything for me," she said. "It opened my mind to a brand-new world. I knew I had to meet the man who wrote it."

"What do you mean? Was he a Communist or something?"

She handed the book to me. "Why don't you take it back with you and decide for yourself?"

"Oh, I couldn't."

"Why not? It would save you the trouble of hauling it upstairs, for one thing." She checked her watch. "Which reminds me. Where the devil is our help?"

"Help? What help?"

"I've called for reinforcements getting those books to the attic. Books are damned heavy, don't you think? Whenever I move house it takes me by surprise, just how heavy a small box of books can be."

"I don't mind. I'm used to—"

A couple of sharp raps rattled the front door, then it swung open.

"Reporting for duty!" called out a cheerful baritone.

If I'm honest, I first noticed the change in Shep when he wrote me a letter after my brother was killed in Sicily, almost three years ago. We got word in August as the island slumped toward the end of another crestfallen wartime summer. I remember Abe from the post office cycled up the drive against a luminescent sunset to deliver the awful telegram. The knock on the door. Abe standing on the front step like the Grim Reaper. Pop with his jaw clenched, Mama in his arms. Mama on the bathroom floor the next morning. I don't remember much about the weeks that followed—how we got her to Boston on the Peabodys' own yacht, the blurred days and nights in Massachusetts General Hospital, the dazed walks around Beacon Hill and Boston Common for some gulps of fresh air, the slow journey back to Winthrop Island that revealed all the ways in which the habits of daily life had to be learned again. But I recall with perfect clarity the moment when, flipping through the bills and letters that had accumulated during our absence, I found a squarish white V-mail envelope addressed to me in Shep's familiar handwriting.

Even before the war, Shep was a pretty reliable correspondent. During our summers we were inseparable; once he left for school, we translated that comradeship into sentences. I knew more than most girls would ever know about boarding school. I knew which teachers shared their knowledge with passion and which ones got their jobs because their parents knew the trustees; I knew which ones you could confide in and which ones you were careful not to find yourself alone with. I knew which school won the football championship and the hockey championship and who scored all the points (Arthur, invariably). I knew that the Peabodys opened their presents on Christmas Eve instead of Christmas and threw a party on New Year's Eve that everybody went to, and that this party was where Shep had kissed a girl for the first time, the year he turned sixteen. Her name was Hoppy Appleton. That was her nickname, obviously. In my next letter I asked Shep what was her real name, and he didn't know, so I wasn't surprised that I didn't hear much about her as time went on. We had our private jokes and our confidences. I wrote about how the girls at school thought I was stuck-up because I liked to read novels and talk about the characters in those pages as if they were real, or to read history books and talk about kings and queens as if they were still alive. He wrote back *NUTS TO THEM*. He wrote that I would leave for college one day and meet girls who were also interested in books, girls who were interested in history and science and all kinds of things, who would have the good sense to *want* to be friends with me, and anyway he, Shep, would come home in the summer and we would talk all day and all night about novels or history or whatever I wanted. I could talk myself out. So you see, Shep's letters were like food to me, like daily bread.

Then the war arrived. At first, Shep wrote all the time. He sent me these short but funny notes from boot camp and basic training and then advanced officer training. Then he shipped off for Europe and the letters began to change. He wrote about English people and English villages and about their adventures on leave. He couldn't write about training, of course, because the censors would black it all out. It seemed even the most inconsequential details about what Second Lieutenant Nathaniel Peabody did in uniform could inadvertently reveal the Army's invasion plans, and God only knew what would happen if a librarian on a scrap of an island in Long Island Sound got her hands on *that*. Still, though he managed to fill a page or two, it wasn't the same. Some intimate note had gone missing. I couldn't put my finger on it, but I can say for certain that his letters arrived less frequently. A whole month might go by without a word, and then I would receive a single tissue-thin page of forced cheerfulness. It was more than I got from Amory, true. Amory sent me exactly two postcards and one letter of such breathtaking banality, you wouldn't think a grown man had written it. Still, by the time Eli was killed, I felt that Shep was slipping away from me along with my childhood, and I might never get him back.

So you can imagine how the sight of that white square of V-mail hit me bang in the solar plexus. I remember how it was the last straw. Until then, I hadn't cried one single tear for Eli or for Mama. I'd wept exclusively on the inside because poor old Pop was already wrecked to pieces and didn't need some limp violet of a daughter weeping all over him. I'd taken pride in my own stoic composure. But when I spotted that tissue-paper letter from Shep Peabody, my eyes glossed over and my nose filled with snot.

Dear Cricket, I am no longer much good at putting things into words for you, but I figure I have to find some way to tell you how sorry I am about Eli and how much it hurts me to think about you and how you're suffering. I have lost some good friends in this war but nobody like Eli. He was a prince all right. If I knew any way to wing myself back to Winthrop right now I would do so. I would hold you hard enough to squeeze the hurt right out of you. If I could change places with Eli so you wouldn't have to lose him, I'd do it. But I can't do any of those things. My arms just hang here useless when they ought to be holding you up. What is the point of anything when Cricket has to suffer. You see what I mean, how I can't write things the way I mean them. All I can tell you is I will do my best for his sake and yours, Cricket. I will do whatever is required because if there is anything in this sorry world that makes any sense to me anymore, it's you. With love always from your Shep.

I read this letter over and over. I tried to imagine Shep's meaty left fist holding a pen and forming those words. I could not. The man who wrote that letter was not my summer comrade, the shambling and clumsy Shep of bicycle rides and smuggled doughnuts. This was a man of passion and conviction, a man who knew something about hardship, a man who knew what it meant to love somebody else, a man I didn't know.

That was the last I heard of him for some time, until I was afraid to mention his name to anybody for fear of that person replying, in a voice of surprise—*Why, didn't you hear he was killed in that big attack last month? Awful news.* That would have done it for me. That would have finished me, to get a letter from Shep so beautiful it made me cry, and then to hear he was killed right after he sent it. So I didn't ask or even say his name, but I kept that letter on my person through every exhausting day that autumn and winter, in which my grief for Eli and for my mother and for the dead days of youth channeled themselves into the labor of caring for a parent who could not stand or speak or eat without help. In those months, it seemed to me that piece of paper represented the only joy left to me in the world.

So maybe that's why I thought of that letter when the door to Mrs. Rainsford's cottage opened and Shep walked through it. He was dressed for golf in loose slacks and an indigo sweater over a checkered shirt. His short hair was brushed back, sleek and neat. I tried to remember how we used to pedal our bicycles together over the damp summer gravel and I felt the same confusion, the same failure of imagination I had felt last night at the party.

"Cricket?" he said, amazed. "What're you doing here?"

"Oh, I like to turn up where you least expect me."

"*Well*, Nathaniel," said Mrs. Rainsford. "*Here* you are. Better late than never."

"I'm not late. Am I?" He checked his watch. "You said noon, it's noon."

"I said before noon. But never mind. If Emilia and Sebastian have finished sorting these books—have you, Emilia?"

"Just about," I said.

"Good. Then you can put those primeval muscles of yours to work and carry these stacks up to my office."

"All right. Where's your office?"

"In the attic."

Shep tilted back his head to squint at the ceiling. He seemed to be avoiding the sight of me. "I didn't know there was an attic in this place."

"There is. You have to pull down the stairs."

"Well, that's a pain in the neck. Isn't it?"

"To the contrary, it means I can't easily be disturbed."

"What about the kids?"

"Emilia's going to watch them for me in the evenings."

Shep's head swiveled to me at last. "Cricket?"

"But I can't come here in the evenings!" I said. "I wait tables at the Club."

"At the Club?" Mrs. Rainsford lowered the wooden spoon in her hand. "Why didn't you say so?"

"I just assumed—I didn't realize you worked at night."

"Naturally I work at night. So the children aren't disturbed." She tapped the spoon against the side of her leg. "Well. This is a predicament."

"I guess my sister could come over," I said. "She wants to earn some extra money."

"I don't want your sister. I want *you.*" Mrs. Rainsford snapped her fingers. "I've got it. Why doesn't your sister wait those tables?"

"Oh, gosh no. Pop would never allow that."

Mrs. Rainsford stared at me with her narrow eyes. Her brows made a pair of sharp arches. "Why not?" she said. "If your father allows *you* to do it."

"Excuse me," said Shep. "If you don't mind. Could you show me where to find those attic stairs? So I can get started."

Mrs. Rainsford turned to him like she'd forgotten he was there. "You're in some kind of hurry, are you?"

"Dad's got us a tee time at one."

"Oh, golf." She pointed her spoon in the direction of the back hallway. "Right there. See the rope pull?"

Shep arched his gigantic back and hoisted up a stack of about a dozen books. The weight didn't seem to trouble him at all. He carried them into the hallway and called back, "Got it!"

I heard a soft squeak of springs, a thud, the steady thump of Shep's feet on the wooden steps. Mrs. Rainsford looked at me without a word, the same speculative expression on her face. I pushed back a lock of hair from my forehead and scrambled to my feet.

"I guess I'll give him a hand," I said.

I made it up the attic steps just as Shep straightened from the pile of books he had set on the floor. "I've got some more!" I gasped.

He turned and stepped forward to snatch them from my arms. "For God's sake, Cricket, you'll hurt yourself!"

"I'm stronger than I look." I stepped free of the stair shaft and watched Shep set the stack of books next to the one he'd carried up himself. "I just wanted to explain about the party yesterday."

"No need. Amory spoke to me later."

"Oh, he did? What did he say?"

Shep turned back to face me and put his hands on his hips. There was one narrow window at the other end of the attic and the air was dusky, filled with spinning motes. "I'm sorry, Cricket," he said. "I didn't mean to be rude last night. Caught me by surprise, that's all."

"Why didn't you *tell* me? About Amory being engaged?"

He put a hand to the back of his neck and ducked his face a little. "Didn't I? I guess I just figured you already knew."

"Me? Why should I know?"

"You're friends, aren't you? You and Tippy."

"When we were kids, sure. We used to play together. But she's older now, she's a debutante and all that kind of thing."

"That makes a difference to you?"

"It makes a difference to *her*."

Shep frowned. "I wouldn't have believed that. She's a sweet girl."

"Oh, she's real sweet. We just don't have so much in common anymore. She's got her world and I've got mine, and—well, it's nobody's fault."

"It's the war, I guess," he said. "The war's changed everyone."

The dust spun around his cropped hair. Everything about him was cropped—his hair that used to be shaggy, his cheeks that used to be round, his grin that used to be wide. I wanted to reach out and pull the old Shep out of his skin—the Shep who had belonged to me, the Shep who was part of me.

"I was so sorry about Arthur," I said. "I should have said that before. I hope you got my letter."

"Yes. I appreciated that."

I scuffed my heel against the floor and turned around. "Anyhow, I'll go fetch that next stack of books. Don't want you to miss your tee time."

"Cricket, wait—"

I laid my foot on the top rung of the attic steps and climbed gingerly down. The staircase bounced on its springs, then groaned as Shep stepped behind me. From the kitchen came the sound of silverware clattering, kids giggling, Mrs. Rainsford's voice saying something about tomato soup. I went into the living room and heaved up a stack of about half a dozen books.

"Put those down," said Shep. "I'm the muscle around here."

"I can do it."

"Tell you what. You wait at the top of the steps and I'll hand them to you."

Shep held out his arms. I handed him the books and went back out of the room and up the stairs to the attic. I hadn't really looked around before and it seemed to me like a dark, uncomfortable place to work. The walls were just bare boards; the small window faced north and needed a good cleaning. Some old mismatched bookshelves took up the wall ahead of me and a massive desk had been crammed next to them, under the eaves. Several wooden boxes sat on top of it, lids still nailed on. Behind me, Shep came up the staircase. The springs protested so loudly, I thought it might break under his weight. When he got to the top, he handed me the books.

"One more thing," I said. "I don't appreciate your inviting me over to serve canapés at Amory's lousy engagement party."

"Canapés? What in the heck are you talking about?"

"I thought you were asking me as a friend, as a guest—"

"I was!"

"Well, your mother sent me to the kitchen to help out."

Shep's jaw swung down on its hinges. "I had no idea! I'm sorry, Cricket. I swear I never meant—I don't know what she was thinking."

"Don't worry about it."

"I'm sorry, I really am. It never occurred to me that she might have meant . . . that you were . . ."

"Don't worry about it," I said. "It was my mistake."

The manager of the Winthrop Island Club in those days was a man named Godfrey Finch. Yes, you heard that right. Rumor had it that he'd once belonged to some rich family, had gone to all the right schools and lived at all the right addresses, until one fair October morning in 1929 he lost everything in the Crash, down to the crisp monogrammed shirt off his back, so that one of his old friends had to pick him up off the street and dust him off and pry the bottle out of his hand and find him this position at the Winthrop Island Club to make ends meet. I still don't know whether that story's true. You know how it is with rumors. Certainly you couldn't ever imagine having to dust off Mr. Finch. He was about medium height and slender, perfectly proportioned like a tennis player, so that his immaculate navy-blue suit—he always wore a navy-blue suit, bearing the Club crest on the jacket pocket—seemed to have grown on him like a shell. Every morning he brushed back his fine brown hair in the same exact wave, from which it didn't dare move. I wouldn't say he was handsome but he had regular features, sharp bones, unflappable blue eyes. About his past, he never said a word. The only clue was his voice. He sounded exactly like Mr. Peabody—same vowels, same clipped consonants, same habit of never, ever raising his voice.

He just looked at you, as he looked at me now, with an air of disappointment.

"Miss Winthrop," he said, "I believe your shift is due to commence in seven minutes."

"Yes, Mr. Finch," I said, a little out of breath on account of having bicycled to the staff entrance at the absolute limit of my strength.

"You will want to spend that time refreshing your appearance, Miss Winthrop."

I ran a hand over the top of my head to smooth my hair. "Yes, sir."

"In future, you will arrange your affairs so as to arrive at least half an hour before the start of your shift. It is otherwise impossible to avoid giving the impression of one's being rushed."

"Of course, Mr. Finch."

I waited for his eyes to release me, but they didn't. He seemed to be studying the flush beneath my skin, the threads of damp hair on my temples.

"Is there something you wish to tell me, Miss Winthrop?" he asked gently.

Judging by the noise from the bar, the Families were having a good time getting to know each other all over again. The new girl came back to the kitchen wide-eyed. "Do they always drink so much before dinner?" she asked me.

I smiled at her. We got a new crop every year, these college kids hired on for the season as waitresses and caddies—the type of wet-eyed son or daughter of some farmer or policeman or teacher or shopkeeper in the middle of the country somewhere, first one in the family to try for college, summer job essential to pay next year's tuition bill. I didn't know exactly how we found them. Probably some discreet listing in the student newspaper. A lot of the Families hired their summer nannies that way, and you could see why when you laid eyes on this girl. Good looks, good grooming, good education. Someone you could trust around your precious children. "What's your name, honey?" I asked her.

"June," she said. "June Lindstrom."

I shook her hand. "June. Nice to meet you. I'm Emilia Winthrop. Most folks around here call me Cricket."

"Winthrop? As in the *island*? Do you *live* here?"

"That's right. My family put down our stakes generations ago. You can see how far we've come."

She creased her pink brow, like she wasn't sure if this was supposed to be a joke. She had blue eyes and pale blond hair and a delicate, twitching nose. She made me think of a white rabbit. "I'm from Minnesota," she said.

"College?"

"Yes. I mean, Wellesley. I'm at Wellesley College. Sophomore year, just finished."

"That's funny," I said. "I was all set to go to Wellesley."

"Oh, *were* you? So why not?"

"My pop needed me at home."

"Oh." Her face fell. "Oh, I'm sorry about that. Just think, we might have been friends."

I tied the apron around my waist and looked across the dining room to table nine, where the Peabodys usually sat. "So, June Lindstrom," I said. "Have you done this before?"

"Sure I have. Last summer I waited tables at the country club, back in Minnetonka."

At that moment, Edwina Peabody herself turned the corner from the lounge, holding a martini glass in her left hand and a cigarette in her right. She wore a china-blue dress with elbow-length sleeves and a full skirt, so you had the feeling she had treated herself to something new and colorful to celebrate the end of the war and the safe return of two of her three sons, at least. Right behind her came Amory in his dinner jacket and his brilliant hair like a sheet of gold, telling some joke that made her laugh. In his deft right hand he held a martini and a cigarette, and on his left arm floated Tippy Pinkerton in a dress the color of forget-me-nots.

"My goodness," said June. "Who's that?"

"The Peabodys. Table nine."

"Oh, that's my table! What are they like?"

I turned to her. "*Your* table? I always serve table nine."

"That's what Mr. Finch said. You don't mind, do you?"

She twitched her anxious nose and smoothed her apron with her hands, as if to dry her palms. I glanced again at Amory. Something about the movement must have caught his eye, because he swiveled his head to look in our direction and spilled his martini.

I turned back to June. "Don't mind at all," I said.

The wonderful thing about waiting tables was you kept busy. It was the first Saturday of the summer season, the first summer season after the end of the war, and the place was jammed tight. You could feel the relief, the abandonment wafting off them, and it smelled like booze. They ordered whatever they wanted. June said the Peabodys and the Pinkertons went through four bottles of champagne and I don't know how many lobsters. You have to understand that these were not people given to extravagance. They weren't like the Newport crowd, they didn't go in for gilding. But tonight they drank champagne and ate lobster until we ran out. Over at the Dumonts' table, Isobel Fisher looked up at me with her haughty eyes and demanded to know how this could happen on Winthrop Island of all places—run out of lobsters.

"Can't you have one of your brothers take out his boat or something?" she said. She must have been about fifteen years old, going on twenty-five. My mother used to say she needed a good spanking. Her parents divorced some years ago and Hugh Fisher treated her like some kind of high priestess, when he wasn't ignoring her—like now, seated at the other end of the dining room with the Monks.

"*Isobel,*" said her mother.

Isobel's face sank into a pout. "I was only saying."

Mrs. Fisher looked up at me. "She'll have the softshell, Cricket. Thank you."

"Of course."

"How is your family, Cricket? Your mother getting on all right?"

"Same as always, Mrs. Fisher."

She handed me the menu. "Do tell your father I said hello."

I glanced down at the other end of the dining room, where her ex-husband had the Monks in stitches over some story of his. Over at table nine, the Peabodys were hitting the sauce like it was the night before Prohibition. Even Shep had a glass of something in his hand. Two chairs to his left, Mrs. Peabody let out a peal of laughter. Her cheeks and forehead and the tip of her nose were the color of raspberries. I remembered how I once bitterly said to my mother that Mrs. Peabody seemed to have taken the news about her oldest son pretty well, all things considered, and my mother—who would soon howl like a wounded animal when she looked out the keeping room window and saw Abe from the post office pedaling toward the house with his War Office telegram—said to me sharply that just because the Families didn't make the noise of their grief heard by the world didn't mean they didn't feel it.

No, I thought. *They drowned it instead.*

I took the Dumonts' orders to the kitchen. On the way back I paused at the small rectangular mirror on the corridor wall to tuck a few loose strands of hair back into my cap. My eyes looked too large and so dark you couldn't see their color. As I watched them, those eyes filled with tears. I ducked around the corner to the vestibule at the service entrance and threw open the door. The mist still fell from the sky. I leaned back against the wall, blinking and swallowing.

The door creaked open. "Cricket?"

I jumped and whirled. Amory stepped through the doorway and crossed his arms. His eyes were blurred and his hair had been raked through. He took a drag from the stub of a cigarette while I rubbed away the damp from beneath my eyes and said, "What are you doing here? You'll get me in trouble."

"I came out to apologize, Cricket."

"Apologize for what?"

"Aw, don't be sore. About yesterday. I was a heel. I should've told you about Tippy."

"I don't know what you mean. I think it's terrific news. The two of you belong together."

He stepped forward and put his hand on my arm. "Look, could you give me another chance? Let me try to explain?"

"I have to get back to the dining room. Finch'll kill me."

"No, he won't. I'll speak to him."

I pulled my arm away. "Just leave it alone, all right? Leave *me* alone."

"When do I see you again?"

"I don't know. It's a small island, we're bound to run into each other eventually."

"Eleven o'clock."

"What, tonight? Are you kidding?"

"I'm serious, Cricket. Meet me at the gazebo. I swear I'll be a gentleman." He finished the cigarette and dropped it on the gravel. "No funny business. Just you and me, old friends."

Even then, I wasn't so dumb as to believe him. The light from the kitchen shone through the window to the left, so half his face was gold. The other half dark. He smelled of booze and cigarettes and laundry starch. I didn't want him. I felt sick with despair, just to look at the wreck of him. But you have to understand, I had known him all my life. There wasn't a day of my life the Peabodys hadn't owned the air I breathed. There wasn't a part of me that could say no to Amory, if he needed me.

I closed my eyes and thought, *Shep. Please, Shep. Come on out here and rescue your brother. Come on out here and rescue me.*

"Come on, Cricket," he said softly. "Give a fellow a break."

"Eleven o'clock," I said. "But no funny business."

In the corner of the dining room nearest the entrance to the cocktail lounge, the orchestra had made a nice background noise through the first and second courses, but once we started taking dessert orders, they got down to business with "Choo Choo Ch'Boogie." It was like a signal, like the clang of the bell as the starting gates opened. Clay Monk galloped across the room to take Isobel Fisher by the hand and drag her to the dance floor. Pretty soon the tables had cleared and the dancers could hardly even wiggle for want of dancing room. You could hardly believe these were the same well-bred ladies and gentlemen in the bridge room that afternoon. I delivered my last dessert order to the kitchen and snuck outside for a cigarette, around the corner where Finch couldn't find me.

By now, the drizzle had stopped, but the air was still cool and damp and the moon lurked behind the clouds somewhere. I wrapped one arm around my middle and propped my elbow on my fingertips while I dragged on the cigarette and stared across the golf course to the sea, or where the sea ought to be if I could see it through the darkness. The noise of the orchestra came through the glass, ruffled over with laughter. I checked my watch—nine thirty. About a hundred yards to my right, the gazebo perched near the edge of the cliffs, a terrific view on a nice day. I lifted my hand and saw that my fingers were trembling. I told them to stop. I whispered not to be silly, you can handle Amory Peabody. You can say no. He's just a man, he's got no power over you. Still they shook. The trembling spread down my arms to my belly until I was shivering altogether, and at the same moment my ears picked up a noise from the shadows in front of me, where the pool terrace met the grass. I wrapped my arms around my middle to stop the shivering and heard it again—a small, muffled sob.

I threw the cigarette on the gravel and started forward. On the bench huddled a small woman, knees tucked to her chest, arms embracing her legs. Her hair was dark and shiny, and if there had been enough light to see the color of her dress, I knew it would be the same deep blue as a bunch of forget-me-nots.

I turned back to the door, but I must have made too much noise because she called out, "Who's there?"

"It's me. Cricket."

"Oh, Cricket." Her voice sank with relief. "It's Tippy."

I stood there awkwardly, curling my apron around my knuckles. "Are you okay?"

"Fine, just fine."

"They're dancing in there. Looks like an awful lot of fun."

"*You* should be dancing," she said. "I think it's a shame that . . ."

"That I'm waiting tables instead?"

"I'm sorry. I didn't mean to be rude."

"I know you didn't." I uncurled the apron from my hand. "I'm awfully sorry about your mother."

"Thank you. I appreciated your letter. I *did* reply, didn't I? It's such a blur now."

"You did."

"Well, that's a relief. I'm always afraid I'll slip up somewhere." She set her chin on her knees. "Anyway, it was a kind letter. You said the nicest things about Mama."

"Do you want some company?"

"Not really."

"Are you sure?"

Tippy made this sad kind of chuckle. "I'm not exactly good company just now. Don't worry, it'll pass. I was in there talking and laughing with everybody, and all of a sudden it hit me. You know. She won't be here to see any of this."

"The wedding, you mean?"

"Oh, all of it. She's been planning my wedding since I was born and I just— I'm sorry, I don't mean to keep you. I know you have work to do."

"I don't mind. We used to be friends, remember?"

Her head moved. She uncurled herself from the bench and twisted to look at me. She didn't look anything like the other girls around here. She had this delicate, silent quality, like a butterfly. There was some story about her grandparents, how her grandfather had been a lieutenant in the Navy and gone to Japan, where he had a baby son with a geisha woman. Then the geisha woman had died and Tippy's grandfather and his American wife had taken the poor baby home to raise themselves. That was Tippy's father. If you looked at Tippy closely, you might notice the trace of her Japanese grandmother in the shape of her eyes, maybe, or her dark, straight hair. To be honest, I didn't think about Tippy's features—whether they were pretty or not pretty, how she came by them—because I'd known her all my life.

"We're *still* friends," she said. "Aren't we?"

"Of course."

She smiled. "Come and sit with me for a minute. If you have one, I mean."

I made my way around the bench and sat next to her. "I forgot to say congratulations. On your engagement, I mean."

"Oh, isn't he a darling? Honestly, I don't know how I would have gotten through the last few months without him."

"So you're happy?"

"Happy? My goodness. Yes. Why do you ask?"

"I don't mean to suggest— It's just that you're here on this bench—"

"Oh, nuts. Never mind me. I get the blues sometimes,

thinking about Mother and how much she—how I wish she— Oh, here I go again—"

I searched the pockets of my apron for a handkerchief, but all I came up with was a dish towel. By that time she'd already got hold of herself and apologized.

"Believe me, I was much worse before Amory came along," she said. "Feeling loved again—feeling like I belonged to someone—someone who needed me, too—it's meant everything."

"But what about your father? He loves you."

"Poor old Dad. He's just lost." She wadded her hanky and passed it back and forth between her two hands. "Isn't it funny, I don't think Amory Peabody and I shared two words together before the war. I was so in love with Arthur, I couldn't even look at anybody else."

"It was a terrible loss. I still can't believe he's gone."

"I used to tell myself he was too good to last in this world. He belonged to another age that wanted him back."

Her handkerchief was white and fine, edged with lace, the kind that crumpled easily and had to be washed and ironed by women like my mother, taking care of the monogram that would be embroidered beautifully in the corner. She had stopped passing it back and forth and it now wadded in the palm of her right hand.

"How did you and Amory find each other?" I asked.

"Oh. It was a party. The Peabodys threw a party, you know, after Amory came home. Everybody was there, it was a real crush. It was the first party I'd been to since my mother died. And everyone was so happy because the war was over, and I felt miserable. I looked around at all those smiling faces and I wanted to scream. What about all the people who didn't make it? What about everyone who died? Don't you care? How can you laugh and drink and pick up your lives again like nothing happened?"

Tippy's voice, which was naturally sweet and released words in round, perfect syllables, grew more and more fierce. By the time she reached *nothing happened* she was almost spitting. Her back had stiffened and her hand fisted around the kerchief.

"And then you saw Amory," I said.

Her shoulders relaxed. "Well, he found me, I guess. I'd gone into the study to—to sit by myself and he came in with a glass of punch—you know Mrs. Peabody's rum punch—and said he thought maybe I could use a drink. And he sat on the sofa next to me and we talked for hours, it seemed. He understood everything. He felt the same way about the party, all those jolly people. He loved Arthur, too."

"Yes, he did. He worshipped him."

"Everyone worshipped Arthur. I remember, when he first—when we first got engaged, I couldn't believe it. I used to pinch myself. I couldn't believe he'd chosen me, of all the girls in the world. I thought I wasn't worthy. I don't mean that he made me feel unworthy, he was marvelous, just that he was so—so perfect himself. I thought I had to look perfect, to be perfect, all the time. It's easier with Amory, he's so human."

"I'll say."

"It just feels so right, being with Amory. Do you know what I mean? It's like we share this memory, this shining memory, and that everything I used to grieve for has—has transformed into something that lives on in our love together."

By now it was too much work to reply. The lump in my throat had grown too sticky, and anyway I couldn't think of anything, not a word.

She dabbed once more at her left eye and stuffed the handkerchief back in her pocketbook. "Anyway, I'm sorry to bore you with all this."

"Not at all."

"You've probably got to get back to work."

"I really should."

She stood up and held out her hand. "We'll walk back together, how's that? Before they start missing me. Amory worries when I get the blues like this."

I took her palm and let her draw me up. I remember her grip was stronger than I figured, that she wasn't exactly fragile or delicate when you encountered the tensile energy in her fingers.

When I arrived home that night, a little past eleven o'clock, my mother and sister were still up listening to the radio. Some chirpy music sung in perfect harmony by a couple of women in front of a jazz orchestra. Susana looked up from her book and asked how everything went.

"Oh, just fine," I said, bending over Mama, "but I guess I'd rather take care of Mrs. Rainsford's kids in the evening, after all."

"Mrs. Rainsford! But what about the Club?"

I turned to my sister. "I was thinking you could take over for me. What do you think, Susana?"

She threw down her book, rose to her feet, and whirled me around the keeping room.

"Yes," she said.

III.

MAY 1954
Cambridge, Massachusetts

I met Cato at a mixer three years ago. I had just started a doctoral program in history and he had just divorced his second wife, so we each happened to be at a figurative crossroads and also at the bar ordering martinis at the exact same moment. Half an hour later we were having intercourse in the back seat of Cato's car, so you see on what basis the relationship was established. Yet here we are, three years later, still screwing each other, so I suppose we do meet some deeper need in the other. Cato is forty-six years old and nearly bald. He claims I'm attracted to him because of my unsatisfactory relationship with my father, but this doesn't seem to bother him in the least. The opposite, I suspect.

When I arrive at his house at a quarter to ten, he takes me in and pours me a drink. He lives in a beautiful town house on Franklin Street—his family has a great deal of money—and it's all been expensively redecorated in a style we'll call Early American Bachelor. He asks about the funeral and I tell him it was awful, really, returning to Winthrop Island after all that time and exposing myself to all those small-minded people. Cato sits back and studies me with his cool blue eyes as I describe Uncle Petey and his brown suit.

"Interesting," he says. "How would you characterize your relationship with your uncle?"

I set down the empty glass and stand up. "Let's go to bed."

As you can imagine, Cato is an accomplished lover, as attentive to your needs as to his own. When we're finished, he asks if I've eaten. I realize I'm famished, having been too irritated with Mrs. Collins to enjoy her scallop pie as I should have done. Cato stalks into the kitchen and returns with cold ham and sherry. He lights a cigarette and watches me eat the way a scientist watches a lab rat.

"You're upset," he announces.

"I'm not upset. I'm grieving."

"What are you grieving?"

"My father, of course. What else?"

"Exactly," he says. "What else?"

Maybe it's because we're both naked, and because my nerves are raw. The story about Olive Rainsford tumbles out, or most of it. I leave out the names and the love affair. Cato is not a practicing psychiatrist but he knows how to listen thoughtfully and not to interrupt with silly judgments. When I'm finished, he lights me a cigarette and says, in a pained voice, that he wishes I'd told him a little of this before. He would have better understood certain aspects of my personality that have puzzled him.

"Such as?"

"Such as your reluctance to attach any sentiment to the sexual act."

"Well, that's rich, coming from you."

He takes the cigarette from me and drags on it. "Your single-minded absorption in your chosen academic field. Your resistance to all forms of Marxist critique, despite your extensive examination of the historical process."

"Please. That's just common sense."

"Your suspicious and even hostile attitude toward other women, which I previously attributed to straight-forward sexual jealousy."

"I'm not hostile about other women. Only the ones you sleep with."

"Why should it matter if I'm sleeping with other women, if you're not sentimental about sex?"

"Because I'm complicated and contradictory and in desperate need of analysis, as you've pointed out repeatedly. Also you've got the libido of a pygmy ape." I take back the cigarette. "So is there any hope for me, Doctor?"

He sighs. "Emilia, I've explained again and again about the difference between a psychologist and a psychiatrist. I can't cure you. Besides, we have a sexual relationship. It would be unethical to try."

"I wouldn't listen to you, anyway. You've got me all wrong."

"Oh? In what way?"

I wag my finger in his face. "I'm not falling for that."

"For what?"

"Your lousy questions. Poking and prodding. I'm not some subject in one of your studies."

He reaches for the cigarette and finishes it. "You're staying the night, then?" he asks, stubbing out the end in the ashtray.

"If you're not expecting anyone else. I didn't bring a car."

He swings out of bed and takes the empty plate and

glass into the kitchen. When he returns, he sits on the edge of the bed and frowns at me. "I thought you said you didn't bring a car."

"I didn't."

"There's one parked outside. A large black sedan."

"Oh! That must be the FBI."

He lifts an eyebrow. "You're in some kind of trouble?"

"They want me to speak to her. The Soviet agent I told you about."

"Why?"

"I'm afraid that's confidential information. You'll have to torture me to hear it." I hold out an inviting arm. Cato climbs obediently into bed and reaches for the drawer in the bedside table, where he keeps condoms in a handsome box of inlaid walnut. He also insists I wear a diaphragm. He's not taking any chances, Cato, and I guess I'm not, either.

He settles between my legs and starts to work. "But you're not going?"

"Hell, no."

"Why not?"

"Because I don't want to see that woman ever again."

He makes a thoughtful grunt and continues what he's doing, only more so. Just as I'm arching my back and fisting the blankets, he pulls out and turns me on my stomach and starts again. Like I said, I have no complaints with Cato as a lover, it's the talking that drives me up the wall. We carry on until we're piled against each other like a pair of puppies, damp and panting. Cato lifts himself on his elbows and says, "Why don't you want to see this woman again?"

"None of your business."

"I think you should. The experience has had a traumatic effect on your development. Your repressed feelings of guilt manifest in all your interpersonal relationships."

"Oh, you think so?"

"You betrayed her. A woman of principle you admired deeply, a woman who trusted you. Of course you feel deep unconscious guilt."

"What do you know about it? You're just a shrink."

He rolls away. "For the last time, Emilia, I'm not a shrink. I'm your friend. I think you ought to confront the woman. You'll never progress until you do."

"What if I don't want to progress? I happen to like things the way they are."

"You don't want to marry? Have children?"

I stare at the ceiling. An electric fan rotates lazily above our heads. Cato lies next to me, one hand resting on his ribs. He's about medium height and quite thin, almost cadaverous. I like to tease him about that. I tell him he needs to stop fornicating so much and eat a little more. He reaches for the bedside lamp and switches it off, so we lie side by side in the darkness like a pair of saints. I'm about to ask whether that was some kind of proposal, but he speaks first.

"I suppose I should tell you, Emilia. I'm going to be married."

By the time I wake up the next morning, Cato's already left. He explained to me last night that he has an early departmental meeting and I have no reason to disbelieve him. He's never told me anything but the truth, whether or not I want to hear it.

The sun's already up. I stare at the shadows cast on the wall by the rotating fan. Cato's decided he wants children and he doesn't think I'm the right woman for settling down into domesticity. I'm sure he's right. I'm too devoted to my career and set in my ways, too reluctant to open myself up to the examination and judgment of others. He's marrying one of his students, a sophomore—she's actually rather brilliant, he told me, lighting a cigarette. Of course she'll quit school. He thinks she'll be able to help him in his work, sort of an unpaid research assistant who also sleeps with him, makes his breakfast, and raises his children, although he doesn't describe the bargain in quite those terms. They're getting married in two weeks because she's already pregnant and he can't have any trouble with the department. He's up for tenure next year.

So I guess this is goodbye, I said, and he replied yes, probably. He's going to make an effort to be faithful this time. It's important to her.

I said he must be in love with her. Very much, he said, perfectly serious.

I climb out of Cato's bed and pour myself some coffee from the percolator while the bath runs. When I've scrubbed myself clean, I dress and make the bed in neat hospital corners, the way my mother taught me. I wash out my coffee cup and set it to dry on the rack. Last night's rain has cleared to a spotless blue sky and the fellow on the radio promises it's going to be warm, seventy-one degrees by lunchtime.

I head out the door and down the steps. The black sedan waits by the curb; the guy in the suit in the passenger seat has fallen asleep. I rap on the window, startling him awake. He rolls down the glass and his partner leans over from the driver's seat to ask me what gives.

"I don't suppose you two fellows could give me a ride to the airport?" I inquire.

By two o'clock in the afternoon the rain had stopped and the library emptied out. I wheeled the cart of returned books down the aisles and replaced them on their shelves. Across the room, Mrs. Collins slammed open the window sashes to allow a little fresh air, such as it was.

"Did you hear the news?" she called out.

"What news?"

"The old Armstrong cottage! It's been let!"

"Oh?" I pushed the cart around the end of the aisle to where Mrs. Collins stood in her flowery dress, brushing back the damp hair at her temples. "By whom?"

"Some mainlander. A writer, I heard. He needs somewhere quiet to finish his *novel*." Mrs. Collins laid a kind of sarcastic emphasis on the word *novel*—you know how she gets when it comes to anyone with artistic pretensions.

"I guess he's come to the right place, then. Anyone I've heard of?"

"*Fox* is his name. That's what Mrs. Medeiro said, down at the general store? He stopped by yesterday to pick up some groceries. Canned soup and that kind of thing. She said he was real nice but he didn't look like a writer at all. Big fellow, dressed in a nice clean suit."

"Writers can't be clean?"

Mrs. Collins puffed out a haughty *hmph.* "Not the ones *I've* met."

I think it's worth pointing out that Mrs. Collins left the island exactly once every year, in order to visit her sister in Hartford, whose husband did something in insurance. Mrs. Collins was a very nice woman and I'd known her all my life, the kind of woman who brought you hampers of cold chicken and pickled beets when you were sick, she was absolutely *indispensable*, but I'm afraid most of her ideas about writers came from those pictorial spreads in *Life* magazine about people like Hemingway. Not that I myself knew any writers personally in those days, except for the editor of the *Winthrop Warbler*, a very pleasant man by the name of Chester Green, and all right—he was kind of slovenly in the nicest sort of way. But I imagined writers were like most people. Each one different.

"*Fox*, you said? What about his Christian name?" I still had some idea I might have heard of him.

"Oh, I can't think. Something to do with the seasons. *Summer* Fox? No, that can't be right."

I angled the cart back up the next aisle. The wheels squealed as they turned. "I guess we'll find out soon enough," I said.

The morning rain had dragged in a bank of warm, thick air. As I bicycled up West Cliff Road I might have been pedaling my way through a steam laundry. At the crest of the hill I stopped to catch what breath I could and turned my head not toward the sea, as usual, but down Little Bay Road toward the smaller harbor where the Families moored their sailboats. A cluster of clapboard and shingle houses nestled into the folds of the hills around Little Bay. They used to belong to the fishermen but had since been bought up as summer cottages by those who didn't like the cost and bother of some rambling shingled estate within the boundaries of the Winthrop Island Association. Among the lanes and byways of Little Bay stood the old cottage that the Armstrong family let out every summer, ever since the divorce. For most of the war there were no takers, so I guess Mrs. Armstrong must have been pleased to find a paying tenant at last—the writer, Mr. Fox.

I glanced down at my wristwatch—a quarter past

three, almost two hours until I was due at the Pea-bodys' guest cottage to watch the Rainsford kids.

With a push of my toe, I started off down Little Bay Road.

I had only the vaguest memory of meeting Mrs. Armstrong, when I was about five years old and Mama brought me along to return a basket of freshly washed diapers. I remember she seemed like a tall, substantial woman, but maybe that was because I was so small. There were three children, including the baby whose diapers my mother had just washed, and the cottage was bright and neat as a new pin. A blue parakeet tweeted incessantly from an old-fashioned cage in the front room, which fascinated me. By the next summer the Armstrongs had divorced. Mr. Armstrong was a salesman for the Eastman Kodak Company and the story goes that Mrs. Armstrong discovered he had a whole nother family in Des Moines, Iowa, which was both shocking and logical, when you thought about it, trains being as slow as they were, and men being as weak. I don't know what happened to those three kids. Sometimes I thought about them and whether they had ever met their half-siblings in Des Moines, Iowa, or not.

Not a thing moved in that drowsy air. The sailboats

dozed at their moorings, the cottages squatted in their green lawns. I coasted down Little Bay Road, taking care to steer around the pits and potholes, and turned right on Sill Lane. Still gravel, Sill Lane. I had to pedal hard. The Armstrong place was on the left, overlooking the harbor. I remembered its screened porch and peaked roof. An apple tree grew near the drive, planted there by Mrs. Armstrong in happier days. But the drive was empty, the house motionless. I rolled slowly past and stopped, pretending to check my shoelace while I swept my eyes over the front windows for signs of life. The curtains were drawn, the sashes shut tight. Maybe this Mr. Fox was taking a nap or something. Writers were supposed to keep strange hours. Eventually I ran out of shoelaces to tie and set my sweating palms back on the handlebars. Just as I pushed off, the noise of an engine rattled into my ears, and a second later an old green Ford truck barreled around the curve ahead, a truck I knew pretty well since it came from my own driveway.

I waved my arm as he went by. "Pop!" I called out.

His amazed face flashed by. Then he hit the brakes and the truck stopped in a skid of gravel. I turned the bike around and rolled right up to the open window.

"Hello there, Em," he said. "What the heck are you doing over here? Aren't you supposed to be at the library or something?"

"Just got off work a little while ago. Thought I might take the scenic route home."

"You're crazy. Too hot for that kind of thing."

"What about you?"

"Me?"

"What're you doing around here? Working on a house?"

"That's it. The Wright place, down the road a piece."

The engine rumbled and coughed. I shaded my eyes from the sun and looked obediently down Sill Lane toward the Wright place, hidden by the curve of the road and the ripples of landscape, which certainly needed fixing up, if memory served. The Wrights hadn't summered here in a couple of years, not since the war started. People said they might not come back at all, might sell the place or else rent it out for the season.

"Anyhow," I said, "I'd better head home before it gets any hotter."

"All right. If you see your sister, tell her the shirts want ironing before she heads for work."

"I will. See you tonight."

He said yup, see you around and banged the Ford back into gear. I set off down Sill Lane and heard the grumble of the engine fade behind me. About a half mile down the track I passed the Wright cottage, surrounded by piles of shingles and two-by-fours and boxes of plaster and a bathroom sink on the front porch. Something bothered me but I couldn't put my thumb on it until I had almost looped my way back up Spinnaker Lane to West Cliff Road and remembered the impression I got, when Pop's truck flashed past, that some other person sat inside the cab with him.

The first two days I came to work for Mrs. Rainsford, she had me unpack all those boxes of books, catalog them into some kind of order, and arrange them on the shelves in the living room. She said I was a librarian, I could do it much better than she could. There were six hundred and twelve volumes altogether, I'm not kidding. She said they belonged to her first husband and she kept them for sentimental reasons. All I could say was it must have been some kind of sentiment. How she dragged them around the world with her I couldn't imagine. The novels and plays I set on the shelves on the west wall, alphabetical by author, and the histories and biographies and political treatises I arranged by subject on the north wall. We had to bring in extra shelves from the main house to accommodate them all. As a result of this labor, there was nothing I loved more than to pluck some book from one of those rows I had organized so carefully and curl up in one of the squishy Peabody armchairs, shredded by generations of warrior cats, and read myself into another world. Mrs. Rainsford said to come anytime, whether or not I was scheduled to work. She said someone might as well read them.

Like I did most days, I cycled straight back from the library to Mrs. Rainsford's house, without stopping at home. I was supposed to take care of Mama in the morning, Susana took over in the afternoon, and Pop came home at five o'clock so Susana could hurry over to the Club for the dinner shift. If I stopped at home, I'd find myself drawn to the dirty dishes or the ironing or some labored, dutiful, one-sided conversation with Mama and there would be no time to read, no time to just *think*. Right now I was in the middle of this memoir of the Great War by an English nurse and it left me hot and enraged and restless for some reason. Still, I couldn't stop reading. There was nobody home when I arrived and leaned my bicycle against the stoop. Probably out on the beach with the rest of the family, enjoying the sunshine in their colorful bathing suits.

Inside the living room it was warm and stifling. I opened the window facing the sea and drew the book from its shelf. I'd marked my place with an old ration card I found in my pocketbook. I'd read about ten pages when the door banged open and the Rainsfords thundered in like a hurricane, smelling of salt and sand, dripping water from their hair—first Sebastian and Charlotte, swimming trunks dangling from their hips, then Mrs. Rainsford carrying a variety of bulging straw baskets, then Shep Peabody bearing little Matthew on his shoulders. He ducked almost in half as he passed under the lintel. The sight of him startled me. I'd done my best to avoid the Peabody brothers these past few weeks and they had pretty much obliged me. From time to time I would catch some glimpse of Amory, roaring down Serenity Lane in this new convertible he'd picked up, or heading down to the beach with Tippy Pinkerton in her polka-dot bathing suit, and you would have thought this would hurt but it didn't. I had released Amory Peabody from my heart like you might release a bird from your hands—a ruffle of feathers and he was gone. Sometimes I glanced up at the third-floor window of Summerly, just out of habit, but I never saw anything stir, not even a light.

Now Shep walked into Mrs. Rainsford's living room like an actor in a movie, familiar but remote. This stranger I had known all my life.

I stood up and laid the book on the lamp table. "Been at the beach?"

"Yes, it's the only tolerable thing for children in this heat," said Mrs. Rainsford. "Were you reading?"

I held up the book for her to inspect.

"Oh, look what you've found!" Mrs. Rainsford exclaimed. "Vera Brittain! *Such* a tragic story. Have you got to the part where Roland was killed?"

"It was horrible."

"Shot through the stomach by a sniper. I couldn't stop crying. But what do you think of Vera herself?"

On the other side of the room, Shep hoisted Matthew over his head and set him on his feet. Like the kids, Shep wore swimming trunks and nothing else. He didn't look at me. I might not have been inside the room at all. He didn't seem to hear his aunt speak about how Roland Leighton was killed by a sniper. Instead he bent over Matthew, who had turned and flung his arms around Shep's thick, hairy calf and started to cry. Charlotte and Sebastian had already scampered onward to the kitchen, where the remains of last night's chocolate cake probably sat under a glass dome.

"Vera?" I said. "I guess she makes me feel small."

Mrs. Rainsford turned around and bellowed something to the children about rinsing the sand off with the garden hose. *But Mama,* groaned Sebastian from the kitchen.

"Come on, I'll take you," said Shep. "First one clean gets a piece of cake."

Mournfully they trooped back to the front door and went outside. I heard the gurgle of the water pipes.

Mrs. Rainsford turned back to me. "Small about what, Emilia?"

"I don't know. I guess because I spent my war here on Winthrop, doing exactly nothing to help out."

"You were taking care of your mother. You were helping your father. You were growing vegetables and milking cows. Someone had to do those things. We can't all be combat nurses and pilots and ambulance drivers."

"She went to college," I said. "Vera went to Oxford. Even though her parents didn't want her to go, she found a way."

Mrs. Rainsford took off her straw hat and shook out her small, dark curls. "Yes, I see what you mean."

I realized I was clasping the book with both hands and set it back down on the lamp table. "But it makes me angry, too. All that waste. She gives you this beautiful glimpse of how it could have been, and then the war comes, and for what? And everything that happened after that—the slaughter, the Bolsheviks. The economic depression, fascism. The atom bomb."

"Some people say it was all inevitable," she said.

"Nothing's inevitable. At any point that summer—I mean the summer of 1914—one of those statesmen could have had the guts to stop what was happening. But nobody did. Nobody had the nerve. Aren't men supposed to have all the nerve? But they didn't."

Mrs. Rainsford had folded her arms. The hat dangled from between a thumb and forefinger. Her head leaned a little to one side as the words tumbled out of my mouth and it seemed to me that she was smiling, although her lips weren't turned up or anything.

I asked her what was the matter.

"Emilia," she said, "*why* have you never left this island and gone to college?"

"I already told you about that."

The door whipped open again and the children bounded inside, tracking puddles. Shep ambled after them. Water trickled from under his hair, down his neck.

"Towels, children!" she called. "Nathaniel! Fetch the towels, won't you?"

"Yes, ma'am," he said, following the children into the hall.

"My dear," said Mrs. Rainsford, meaning me, "a little extra work came in for me today. You wouldn't mind getting the children their supper, would you? There's a chicken in the icebox."

The kitchen had been sitting in the hazy sun all afternoon and the air was almost too thick to breathe. Shep was busy opening the windows. The kids sat around the table wrapped in white towels, eating chocolate cake. "So much for dinner," I said.

He swore at the window, which was stuck shut. "Sorry," he said.

"I've heard worse."

"I mean about the cake." At last the window came open and Shep turned to face me, wiping his palm on his swimming trunks. "Also about the shirt."

"What shirt?"

"I didn't realize you'd be here already or I'd have put one on."

I rolled my eyes back. "Shep, I've seen you in swim trunks my whole entire life. I'm not going to faint or anything."

"No, I guess not." He kissed the top of the baby's head and ruffled Charlotte's hair. "Anyway, I'll leave you to it."

"Gosh, thanks," I said.

"Anytime."

He started for the door. I contemplated Matthew's round, sunburned face, smeared with chocolate. His large blue eyes contemplated me right back.

"Shep," I said. "Wait."

Shep stopped in the doorway and rested his hand on the wall, though he didn't turn to face me. "Yep?"

I stared at the line where his swimming trunks met the small of his back. When we were kids we used to live in our bathing suits. Me and Shep digging sand all the way to China. Me and Shep chasing each other in the surf. That time he saved me when the swift tidal current caught me unaware, an incident so nearly and impossibly tragic we never spoke of it again. But that was a different Shep, a brother, a child. You could not chase this grown-up Shep in the surf. In my mind I dressed him in Army pants and boots and jacket, leather belt, steel helmet. I put a rifle in his hand and a pack on his back. What was it like, Shep. Were you scared. When you heard the artillery and the gunfire and the thud of bullets, when you saw the blood. Did you ever see a sniper shoot a man through the stomach. What did he look like when he lay there bleeding and dying in the cold mud. Did you pull your first-aid kit from your pack and try to stop the blood. Was he your friend, your buddy, did you love him. What was I doing when this terrible thing happened. Was I sitting in the keeping room mending Pop's socks.

I said, "Do you remember that summer we rode our bikes to the airfield and found those old bunkers from the war?"

"Sure I do."

"Remember how we used to go out there on rainy days? Sit in those bunkers for hours?"

"That's right," he said.

"Mama used to make us sandwiches to take along. I don't remember what we did in there, even."

"Talked, mostly. Played at soldiers."

That was the moment. That was the opening. If I had replied to him, if I had said, *Who would have thought you'd be playing soldiers for real a few years later*, or something like that, then he might have replied back, *Yeah, but the real thing was nothing like we pretended*, or something like that, and I might have said, *Well what was it like, then?*

Then we might have started to get somewhere. We might have started talking again, like we used to, and he would be Shep again and I would be Cricket.

I went on staring at the waistband of his trunks. They were navy blue, several inches too big around the waist. His old trunks he used to wear that last summer before the war. I could see how he had tied the drawstring to hold them up on his lean new waist. The groove of his spine sliced through the muscles of his back. That same back I used to pelt with sand when I was mad or playful. Same back turned up to the sun as we lay side by side, shivering and panting, after he hauled me in from the tidal current that awful afternoon. His hand fell away from the wall and he turned to face me. My eyes flew back to Matthew's chocolate-stained face.

"Cricket?" he said. "Something wrong?"

"Nothing."

He gave me another second or two and sighed. "I'll be going, then. See you around."

At about half past nine, the attic stairs creaked and Mrs. Rainsford came down to join me in the living room. I looked up in surprise from my book. Usually she kept on working right until midnight or so. Once I asked her what she did, and she said, *Oh, translation mostly. I've got a knack for languages, it's about the only thing I'm good for.*

I closed the book and set it on the table. "Finished already?"

"Not yet. I wanted to speak to you."

"About what?"

She sat down on the worn armchair next to me and arranged her skirt. "Emilia. I had a talk with my brother-in-law about you, the other day."

"With Mr. Peabody? What about?"

"Oh, nothing but good things, I promise. I said I thought you were a very bright girl with heaps of potential and was there anything we could do for you."

"Oh. Oh, Mrs. Rainsford, honestly I wish you

hadn't. The Peabodys've been so generous already. They let us stay on in the house after Mama's stroke, when Pop couldn't work—"

"Well, my goodness. What were they supposed to do? Kick you out?"

"—without even charging rent or anything—"

"Emilia. Emilia, stop and listen to me a moment. I want to explain something." She smoothed her skirt again. "You know how the Peabodys made their fortune, don't you?"

"Mills or something, wasn't it?"

"Textile mills. Thomas's grandfather built a factory and hired hundreds of women—it was mostly women—to run the weaving machines, and he made piles and piles of money selling the cloth all over the world. All on the backs of these women. So the Peabodys are very rich and my brother-in-law feels—as I feel, my own family having built a fortune making guns for the Union—that we have a responsibility to return this wealth wherever we can, wherever it can benefit someone worthy, like you."

"You mean charity."

"Don't be so proud. It makes him *happy*, really it does, to pay for your mother's medical expenses and so on—"

"What?"

"Didn't you know that? All those hospital bills. He was glad to do it. Beyond his obligation as your father's employer, he felt it was his patriotic duty, because of your sacrifice to the country. That's what he told me, his exact words. And then he told me another thing, Emilia, which I found very interesting. He agreed with me that you ought to further your education. He said that in fact—because they had made a promise to your parents to sponsor your brother's college education—he had offered, when—what was his name again? Your brother?"

"Eli," I said. "Elijah."

"When Elijah died, Tommy told your mother the offer of college still stood, that he would sponsor you girls instead. But your father refused."

At some point in the conversation, I had clasped my hands in my lap. Bit by bit the fingers clenched around each other, until the nails dug into the fleshy hollows between the bones on the backs of the hands, and I only discovered this later when I saw the red marks and the tiny dried curls of broken skin. "I don't understand," I said. "Pop said there was no money. Because of Mama's bills and because she couldn't work anymore."

"I'm sure he had his reasons," said Mrs. Rainsford, in a sympathetic voice, "but money wasn't one of them."

"Maybe it was a misunderstanding. Pop hates charity."

"But he'd already allowed Tommy to pay for the hospital bills, and the scholarship for your brother. No, it's something more than that, Emilia. I can't begin to guess—well, maybe I can—but really it doesn't matter. We must look ahead, not behind."

"Ahead to what?"

"To your future. With my help, the Peabodys would like to sponsor your college education."

"What?"

"To pay for college."

I rose from the chair. The sudden motion made me dizzy. "Oh, but I can't—I couldn't possibly—"

Mrs. Rainsford rose, too, and steadied me with her hands on my elbows. "Yes you can. I don't want any nonsense about being unable to accept charity. It isn't charity, it's a scholarship. It's an investment. It's putting our money where my heart is, which is the education of women."

"I'm too old. I'm nearly twenty-one. I should have graduated by now."

"There are thousands of men entering college right now who are even older. Because of the war."

I plopped down again. "I can't think—it's very generous—but my mother. I can't—what about my mother?"

"I've already taken the liberty of writing about

your case to a friend of mine at Wellesley. She's gone to the admissions office on your behalf and explained your circumstances. They've still got your file, your records. They're going to allow you to enter with the current freshman class, provided you can pass an entrance examination—"

"I haven't studied. I haven't prepared."

"But you will. You can study here. All these books." She waved her arm at the shelves on the wall. "She's sending me a list of materials. Everything you need."

"I don't understand," I said. "I don't understand why you're doing this."

By now Mrs. Rainsford was on her knees on the hard wooden floor, holding my hands steady in my own lap, between her palms. She looked at me earnestly. "I've already explained," she said. "The Peabodys feel a responsibility. Because of all those women in the mills, making them rich. Now it's our turn to provide for you."

I remember the first time I had the idea I might go to college. It was Shep who said so. I think we were about twelve or so. It might have been that same summer we lay among the rocks and overheard Ben Monk getting friendly with his lady companion, whoever she was. That was a hot summer, I recall, and we spent a

lot of time on the water in Shep's dinghy or else ex-
piring on the beach at Horseshoe Cove or the stretch
of shore near the airfield, because it was usually de-
serted. Shep turned brown under the sun and so did
I. We would go out swimming past the breakers and
then race each other back. We would collapse side by
side in the sand, wet and panting and laughing. When
we'd caught our breath we'd start talking. This one
afternoon it was the very last day of August. Labor
Day weekend loomed up before us and the Peabodys
had already started packing things up for the annual
migration back to Boston. I said it wasn't fair. I complained that once Shep was gone there was nobody left
to talk to, nobody to swim with. Shep said well, in six
more years you'll head off to college and then when
the summer ends, you can leave with us. Shep said he
figured I ought to go to Wellesley. He was probably
going to Harvard, like all the Peabodys, and Wellesley
was pretty close, so he could look out for me. On the
mainland you could watch any movie you wanted, you
could go to museums and restaurants and pretty much
anything. What do you think, Cricket? he said, when
he noticed I hadn't replied.

I don't know, I said. I never thought about college.

He turned his head and looked at me. It's funny, I
can still picture his thick, astonished eyebrows and his

squinting eyes, hazel turned kind of green in the face of all that blue sky and blue water. The freckles over his nose and broad cheeks. His splattered hair filled with sand.

Not go to college? he said, like I'd just told him I never intended to marry or something.

I shrugged my thin shoulders. Nobody around here goes to college, I told him.

We lay on our stomachs, backs scorched by the sun. Our cheeks nestled into the sand, my right cheek and his left cheek, so we stared at each other on the level, just a foot or two apart. It amazes me to think about it now—how close we were, how carelessly we took our proximity for granted, didn't think anything of sprawling next to each other and saying whatever we wanted. Shep seemed to consider what I said, turned over this bewildering idea in his head—not go to college! He crossed his arms and lifted his head to rest his chin on his hands and stare thoughtfully at the dunes.

Well, I guess you'll be the first, then, he pronounced, with so much decision that the matter seemed closed.

Even then, I was smart enough not to mention this conversation to Pop. I told Mama about it instead. Mama was kneading some dough at the kitchen table and she nodded in rhythm with her arms. He's right, she said. You should go to college near Shep. You won't

have been away from home before, you'll want someone to look out for you.

I stared at the muscles of her forearms, working away
at that dough. What are you talking about? I said. Since
when did you decide I was supposed to go to college?

Mama turned away from the dough and looked at
me. There was a smear of flour on her forehead, like
it was Ash Wednesday and they had run out of ash.
She spoke to me tenderly, wearily. Since you were three
years old, honey. Since you were three years old and
taught yourself to read, I said to myself, my daughter
must get off this little island and go to college and make
something of herself. So I started to set aside a little
money each month for you. I told your father it's for
your wedding but it's really for you to get out of here,
my clever duckling, to get off Winthrop Island and go
somewhere you can be a swan.

Before the war, when he'd drunk enough in the evening, Pop would sometimes talk about how he and
Mama fell in love and got married. *The prettiest girl
on Winthrop Island*, he used to say, beaming at her.
She'd arrived from Portugal with her parents and
sisters and brothers when she was still a child, the
youngest in the family, because they had heard from
cousins and friends that there was plenty of work for

fishermen, that the lobster beds were full of lobsters and the island was full of rich people who ate them. It was my mother's job to pedal her bicycle around the island during the summer and deliver lobsters to the houses of those who'd ordered them. The way Pop told the story, he had admired Mama for years but never dared to say hello because she was so beautiful with her dark gleaming hair and dark gleaming eyes and he was nothing but a shy, rough, plainspoken Yankee farmer boy, until one day her bicycle chain broke when she was delivering lobsters to Summerly and he had fixed it for her—fixing things being among his assets as a potential husband—and she was so grateful she'd given him a kiss in return. It must have been some kiss because they got married two months later and Eli was born seven months after that, not that Pop ever said such a thing right out. *She gave me a kiss and I never looked at another girl again,* he would say, gazing worshipfully at my mother where she sat with her mending or her kneading or her shelling of peas. The same small, quiet smile always fixed on her lips, and I remember she stared not at Pop but at her work, whatever it happened to be. Not that she didn't love him. Of course she loved him. All the time I saw her touch him with affection, look after his breakfast and his washing and make sure he wore warm-enough clothes in winter and sturdy-enough shoes in the mire of fall and spring. Still, as I heard Pop describe the scene for the thousandth time and watched Mama make her invariable small smile into her mending, I used to wonder what the story might have sounded like from her perspective. How this beautiful Portuguese girl with her dark gleaming hair came to be kissing the shy, rough, plainspoken Yankee farmer boy with no house of his own, no prospects and no ambition except to tend the gardens of others, and to marry him and bear his children.

But she never did say.

When I arrived home from Mrs. Rainsford's house, Pop had already bathed my mother and helped her into her nightgown. She liked to drink warm milk before bed but she couldn't be trusted to drink it unattended, so Pop sat by the armchair in the bedroom with a cloth and a spoon, which was where I found them.

"You're home early, Emmie," he said.

He did not turn toward me. I had grown up with this habit of his—not to look at you when he spoke to you, to keep his attention on whatever it was he was doing with his hands—so I only noticed it from time to time. Like now, when I'd just come from a conversation with Olive Rainsford, who always looked earnestly into my face when she spoke to me.

I walked around the bed to the armchair. Mama looked up and smiled with the left side of her mouth. A trickle of milk came from the other side. Pop wiped it away with the cloth. The armchair must have been two hundred years old and the stuffing seeped through the threads of damask on the arms. Mama wore her flannel robe over her nightgown, because even in summer she could not seem to get warm. Pop wore his undershirt untucked over his work trousers, patched at both knees.

I kissed the top of Mama's head. "You're looking beautiful, Mama."

The smile fell from the one side of her mouth. She tilted her head to look at my face, then to Pop, then back to me. Her lips moved like she wanted to say something but the words wouldn't take.

Pop set the mug of milk on the nightstand. "Time for bed."

"Pop," I said, "could I speak to you a minute?"

Of course he remembered Mr. Peabody's offer, Pop told me. But it was impossible to send me to college.

"Impossible? Why? If the Peabodys were going to pay for it?"

He picked up the newspaper from the kitchen table. Every day he brought home a copy from the Medeiros' general store, where the early ferry delivered two stacks each of the morning editions of the *Boston Globe*, the *New York Times*, and the *Providence Journal*. Pop preferred the *Journal*. He said he didn't need to know what was happening around the world, which was going to hell in a handbasket anyway. Just what was going on in New England. He fiddled through the pages, pretending to find something to read.

"Because of your mother," he said. "How was I supposed to work, if I had nobody to help me take care of your mother? There was a war on. Times were tough."

"You might have told me. We might have found a way. Susana could have helped you."

"Susana's at school during the day."

"Then maybe someone from the village."

"We'd have had to pay for that."

"I could have gotten a job or something. The Peabodys would have helped, if you told them."

He folded the newspaper and slapped it on the table. "Maybe I don't want to take the Peabodys' charity for every damned thing."

"Pop," I said, "would you look at me when you're talking to me?"

"What's that supposed to mean?"

"I just don't know why you don't look at people when you're talking to them. At me."

He threw up his hands and pulled back one of the chairs from the table. The leg scraped against the linoleum. In the middle of the table sat a bowl filled with a dozen or so oranges the Peabodys had sent over the other day. He took one and dug his thumbnail into the rind.

I pulled out another one of the chairs from the table and sat next to him while he peeled his orange. On the shelf by the window, the radio droned with static. "Mrs. Rainsford wants to send me to college."

His fingers went still. "Mrs. *Rainsford*?"

"Yes."

"What business is it of hers?"

"She thinks I have potential. She thinks women ought to be educated, the same as men. She thinks I have brains and curiosity and they're all wasted here on this island, doing nothing but—but—"

"But *what*, Emmie?"

"I was going to say serving. Serving the Families. Waiting for summer every year, waiting for this great white sun to shine on us, for the Families to arrive and bring us to life. I want to shine by myself. I want to live on my own power."

His hands resumed the swift peeling of the orange. "Is this what you and this Rainsford woman have been talking about? Is this what she's putting into your head?"

"It's been in my head for a while! It's always been there! Mama wanted me to go. You know that. She set aside money for me to go to college. I was all set to go, you remember."

"'Course I remember. Didn't mean I agreed with it."

"So now Mama can't stick up for me, I'm supposed to forget about it. Stay here in this old house forever, looking after everybody but myself."

"Well, hell. You just want to escape all this, do you? To leave this terrible home of yours and live among rich people? Have love affairs and dinner parties and never do a day's honest work?"

"That's not it at all."

"I knew I shouldn't have let you associate with her. I don't know why I agreed."

"I'm almost twenty-one. I don't need your permission to associate with anybody."

"Haven't you heard about her? The things she's done?"

"She's lived! That's all. She's gone out and made something of herself!"

"She's a whore. Those younger kids, she had them with her lover during the war, while her husband was in some kind of prison camp."

"But he was dead," I said. "Her husband died in prison. She told me about that."

"She tell you she'd already taken up with this fellow? Even before the husband was arrested."

"What's that supposed to mean? Where do you hear these things?"

He pulled out a section of orange and slid it into his mouth. "I hear things."

"Doesn't mean they're true."

"She's a bad influence, Em. I kept my peace until now because I figured you're a smart girl, you know what's right and wrong. But she's not the kind of woman you ought to aspire to."

I reached over and turned off the radio. The click of the knob echoed off the wall.

"You think leaving will make you happy," he said, "but you'll just be unhappy in a new place."

"I'm not unhappy. I just want to go to college."

"What for? Fill your head with ideas you don't need."

"That's exactly what I want. To fill my head with new ideas. To be around people—other women—who like to read and think and—and see the world."

"We're not smart enough for you around here, is that what you're saying?"

"That's not what I mean—"

"And who takes care of your mother while you

improve your mind at some fancy college? How do I go to work and put food on the table, Em? Or do I go to Tom Peabody and beg for crumbs from his table? Live on nothing but charity? Or do you care?"

"Of course I care! But I want to *live*, too! I want to *live*, that's all!"

Pop stood up. The chair crashed to the floor behind him. The half-eaten orange rolled on its side. He clenched his fists, open and shut.

"You'd have let Eli go," I said. "That was all fine by you. You wouldn't have minded your boy going to college, even though I've got twice his brains. But a daughter, oh no."

"Stop your bragging and show some respect," he said.

"It's not bragging. It's a fact."

"You want to be one of them, don't you? That's all this is. We're not good enough for you around here. You want to turn yourself into one of them."

"One of whom?"

"*Whom*," he said scathingly. "Jesus, Em. Listen to you."

The kitchen door swung open. Susana floated inside and twirled a circle that skidded into an unfinished arc at the sight of Pop and me, staring at each other in the lurid light from the bulb that hung from the ceiling.

"What's going on?" she said.

Pop reached over the table and grabbed the orange and clomped out of the kitchen. Susana looked at me, eyes wide. The orange peels curled in a pile on the red-and-white-checkered tablecloth. I scraped them into my palm and threw them in the bowl for the compost pile.

"Nothing you can help, pumpkin," I said.

After lunch the next day I took my bicycle out toward Little Bay. It was my day off from the library and I had a million chores I ought to have been catching up on, but I pedaled off anyway into the hazy afternoon. I felt I was hunting for something, though I couldn't say exactly what I meant to find. The sun beat down in wrath. The honeysuckle was out and the heat wrung all the scent into the air until you felt you were drunk with it, the perfume of honeysuckle. When I turned down Sill Lane I remembered I'd meant to ask my father about yesterday, how I thought I saw somebody else in the cab of the truck with him. The gravel pulled at my tires. You didn't realize Sill Lane made a slope against the land until you pedaled it uphill. The Wright place was untouched, same two-by-fours piled in the grass and the old kitchen sink on the front porch. A half mile later, I passed the Armstrong place, which showed no sign of life, either. The sweat popped from my temples and ran down my ribs. I reached Little Bay Road and decided I'd head down to the harbor where I might find a puff or two of breeze from the water, or a cool drink at the harbormaster's office.

Most people who visited Winthrop Island didn't know anything about Little Bay Harbor. The main harbor was where the ferry landed, where the lobster boats docked, where you found the general store and the fire station and the Catholic church. The school and the library and the Mohegan Inn all clustered in the streets around Winthrop Harbor. But Little Bay Harbor was like a placid, genteel secret. The Families moored their sailboats there. In those days, you couldn't buy a thing in Little Bay Harbor except an ice-cold soda from the machine at the harbormaster's office. No reason for anybody to visit except to mess around in his very own boat, and on a day like today—hot sun, mild breeze— Little Bay was full of boats. I bought a soda from the harbormaster's machine and collapsed on the warped wooden bench in the shade of the harbormaster's office to watch the sails inch across the water and out into the sound. The mainland floated in the haze. I tried to imagine the rest of America stretching out from that green, rocky, hazy strip of land—all the forests and mountains and deserts and cornfields, the people in their houses, the cities, the factories and hotels and sporting fields, the Pacific Ocean at the other end and then the rest of the world, everything I would never see.

"Cricket?"

I nearly jumped right off the bench and into the water. A hand touched my shoulder and a deep, gentle laugh steadied me.

"Take it easy," he said. "I was just being friendly."

I turned my head and shaded my eyes from the sun that shone right above Shep's head. The bubbles from the soda tickled my stomach. "You shouldn't sneak up on a girl like that."

"Didn't realize I was sneaking. What're you doing around here? I thought you spent afternoons at the library."

"Today's my day off."

"Is that so?" He looked away to squint at the water. He wore a pair of soft cotton trousers and a white shirt and cap, and the sun glowed around the curve of his pink jaw, newly shaved. In one hand he held a coil of rope; the other hand he shoved in his pocket. "As long as you're here. You wouldn't have time for a little sail, would you? Old times?"

As kids, we sailed all the time. You couldn't live on an island without learning how to make a boat go across the water, and the Families taught their children to sail around the same age you would teach your child to ride a bicycle. Sometimes it was all of us, Arthur and Amory and Eli and Shep and me and eventually Susana, and sometimes Shep took me out on his dinghy, just the two of us, because the older boys had other mischief to attend to and also because Shep didn't just *enjoy* sailing—he had this peculiar connection to boats the way some girls have this connection to horses. He'd come into our kitchen at seven in the morning while I was stirring the porridge for Pop's breakfast and tell me the water was perfect today, the wind was just right, let's go out in the boat, and I'd finish up that porridge and put on my shoes and grab an apple or something and off we'd go. Old times.

"Do you remember the time that squall caught us and we got stuck on Block Island?" I said.

"Do I. Dad gave me heck for that."

I lifted my head. "Really? But you saved our lives. Anybody else would have capsized or wrecked on the rocks. I still don't know how you brought her in without killing us."

"Couldn't exactly get my best girl killed out sailing, could I?"

"Me? Your best girl?"

He turned his head to me and grinned. "Didn't you figure?"

"You never said anything."

"Because you were crazy about my brother, that's why." He turned his head back to stare at the horizon. "Couldn't exactly hold a candle to old Amory, could I? So I figured I would just be grateful for what we had."

I lay on the bow deck of the *Esmeralda*, the Peabodys' graceful little racing sloop. They had ordered her from some shipyard in Providence when I was about seven or eight years old, and she was as nimble a craft as you could hope for. The breeze had settled to a steady thrust that filled the mainsail in a gentle arc and rippled the hem of my old sundress. The sun baked my skin. Shep sat with one long leg stretched out, one long arm attached to the tiller with the lightest possible touch. I felt my body soar along the water with the boat, and it was like all the nameless worries emptied out of my head and washed into the sea. What I was hunting for, I had found it.

"You were my best friend," I said, "and you're worth a hundred of Amory."

"Oh, so you figured that out, did you?"

I rolled over on my stomach and laid my chin on my hands. I felt Shep's stare on the balls of my feet. "Every day, I worried about you," I said. "Every day."

"Me? Or Amory?"

"Both of you. But it was mostly you. Amory, he's charmed by the gods, he was always going to make it through. You were the one who worried me."

Shep's chuckle drifted from the stern. "Well, thanks."

"Oh, don't be sore. I didn't mean it like that."

"Anyway, you had it all wrong. Don't you know what the Greeks say? Whom the gods favor, right? That's why I always aimed to just lie low, beneath their notice."

"I'm serious, Shep. Do you remember that letter you sent me, right before you left for England?"

There was a single beat before he answered. "Sure I do."

Ahead of us, a lobster boat cruised across the heavy water with the tide rushing past the Fleet Rock lighthouse to fill Long Island Sound. One of ours, probably, returning to harbor. I could just make out the two men inside in their thick yellow oilskin overalls and white cotton shirts and gloves but we were too far away to see their faces. One of them raised his hand to us and I didn't have the energy to wave back, not in this heat, didn't have the nerve. I rubbed my chin with my thumb and said, "The moment I read that letter—the moment I saw it on the kitchen table—I had this terrible feeling I'd never see you again."

"Aw, Cricket—"

"I don't know why. I was wrong, obviously. But every morning from that day until the end of the war—no, even after, when I heard you were headed to Berlin—I woke up and thought to myself, *What is Shep doing today? Is he marching or fighting? Is he scared to death? Is he dead yet?* And I would just pray you would live through the day."

He laughed. "When did you get so religious?"

"I wasn't. But I prayed anyway."

"Well, maybe it worked," he said. "Here I am again, all in one piece."

"Are you, really? All in one piece?"

"Mostly." He whistled a few bars, a tune I didn't recognize. "You want to know something? I almost didn't want to come home, at first."

"Why's that?"

"Because I wasn't the same fellow anymore. I didn't feel like I belonged here. And my buddies were dead, or maybe lost an arm or a leg, and I figured—I can't explain it so well, it's not something you can find the words for—I guess you could say I didn't figure I deserved to come home to all this."

"Is that why you stayed on in Berlin through the winter?"

"There were a lot of reasons," he said, "but that's one of them."

The *Esmeralda* started across the lobster boat's wake. I curled my fingers around the bow and felt the deck skip beneath me, felt Shep's sure hand on the tiller reaching through the lines of the boat and into my stomach, flat against the teak. "We used to know each other so well," I said. "You would land here at the beginning of June and we would just pick right up from Labor Day, like nothing at all had happened to us and changed us over the autumn and winter and spring. I knew you better than my own brother. I knew you better than anybody."

"Cricket, I know," he said.

"Anyway, it's nice to be out here sailing like this. Talking like we used to." I sat up and turned to face him, swinging my legs over the hatch, and smiled. "Maybe we'll start to get to know each other again."

Shep looked at me and knit his forehead together, like he was concentrating on something. "Sure we will," he said.

"What's the matter?"

"Cricket, I thought you knew. Didn't Aunt Olive tell you?"

My heels pressed against the hatch cover. My hands curled around the edge of the deck. I thought I might be drowning. "Tell me what?"

Shep removed his cap and ran a hand through his

hair, which was growing shaggy again like when we were kids. He replaced the cap and said, "I'm leaving for California the day after tomorrow."

Of course I'd forgotten all about California and the vineyard, his buddy's new French wife, the fresh start. When we were kids, we used to tell each other all kinds of pipe dreams like that. One day, we were going to sail around the world. One day, we were going to cross the Antarctic. One day, we were going to start a ranch in Montana or someplace like that and live like pioneers under the big sky. A vineyard in California sounded exactly like the stories we used to tell each other, a pipe dream.

But Shep's hazel eyes were earnest as they looked at me. He wanted me to say something, and I didn't know what. This thing I'd been hunting for, this thing I thought I'd just caught, it jumped from my hands and disappeared under the black water.

"California!" I squeaked. "Oh, of course! It must have—must have slipped right out of my mind."

"I did tell you about California, right? That first night."

"You did. But didn't you say—I thought you said you were leaving at the end of summer?"

"I was. But my buddy Frank, he's been trying to get

me out earlier, I guess there's a lot of old brush to clean up, hasn't been tended to in years—"

"I see. Well, that makes a lot of sense, then. Big strong fella like you ought to be out west clearing brush, not sailing around Long Island Sound."

"That's what I thought."

I swallowed back something bitter and tipped my head down to stare at my toes, so he wouldn't see the expression on my face, whatever it was. "You know, your aunt said I should go to college."

"I know."

"You know?"

"We've talked about it some. She thinks you're terrific. A terrific mind, she said." He cleared his throat. "Say, could you hand me that jacket over there?"

I reached for the jacket and rose to my feet to hand it to him. He thanked me and rummaged around the pockets for a pack of cigarettes. He offered them to me. I shook my head, though I wanted one badly.

"You don't mind, do you?" he asked.

"Of course not."

He balanced the tiller on his knee and lit the cigarette. I told him it was funny, seeing him smoke.

"Picked it up in basic training," he said. "Seemed like the social thing to do. You're sure?"

I stretched out my hand and he stretched out his,

holding the cigarette. I took a long drag and handed it back to him. With his thumb he gave the end a tiny stroke before he put it back in his mouth.

"Anyway," he said, "she told me she was going to get you into Wellesley. You know she went to Wellesley. Did she talk to you about it?"

"I assume you know she wants to pay my way?"

He glanced to the side. "Well? What do you think?"

"Me? I'd go in a heartbeat. My pop's not so crazy about the idea."

"What? Why not?"

"Because of my mother. He can't take care of her by himself."

"That's ridiculous. Can't your sister help out?"

"Not all by herself. For four whole years? It wouldn't be fair."

"Then hire somebody, for God's sake."

I laughed. "Oh, Shep. Listen to you. My family can't pay for help. We *are* the help."

"Don't say that." He finished the cigarette and tossed the stub in the water. "Listen, I'm sure my folks would—"

"No," I said. "No charity."

By now he'd begun to ready the helm, preparing to tack. I slid back down from the deck and unwound the mainsheet from its cleat. We didn't need to speak; we'd done this a thousand times before. The sail began to shiver and flap. The boat leaned on its side. I drew the mainsheet taut until the sail filled and wound the rope around the starboard cleat. By the time we'd finished the operation, the *Esmeralda* was back on an even keel and so was I. I turned to face Shep and hoisted myself back on the deck. Crossed my ankles together and asked him to tell me about California.

"A little town called Sonoma," he said. "North of San Francisco Bay, pretty as can be. That's what Frank says, anyway. I'm booked on the North Shore Limited from Boston to Chicago Friday afternoon. Then the Overland Limited from Chicago. Should be in San Francisco by Monday."

"I always wanted to travel across the country like that," I said. "Cross the Rockies and everything. You'll be sure to take pictures and send them to me, won't you?"

"I will."

The Fleet Rock Lighthouse passed to the right. We were tacking around the southwestern tip of Winthrop Island, past the airfield and the old bunkers where we used to hide out when we were kids and played at soldiers. I watched Shep look to the side and gaze at the crawling landscape. I wondered if he was recalling the same memories as I was, or if the war had drained the joy from them.

He turned back to me. "Listen, Cricket," he said. "We're getting together at the Club tonight. Kind of a farewell dinner. I'd like you to come, if you could."

"You mean as a guest?"

"I mean as my friend. My oldest, dearest friend. Our last hurrah."

"Hurrah," I said, raising my fist.

"So you'll come?"

How the afternoon light loved his solid, honest bones. Along his cheeks and jaw the tiny stubble hairs glittered in the sun. He'd rolled up the sleeves of his white shirt and his forearms were like hams. In the years to come I would savor every memory I had of him, but this one most of all—Shep at the tiller of a sailboat, drenched in hazy sunshine—because that was the moment I knew for certain I loved him, the way I should have loved him all along.

"I wish I could, Shep," I said. "But I'm taking care of the kids tonight."

Back on solid ground, my legs wobbled. Shep put his hand on my arm to steady me and laughed, said something about my sea legs. I said I hadn't been out sailing much the past few years, I wasn't used to it anymore.

He peered up at the sky and said it was mighty hot, let's ride over to the general store for ice cream.

"Ride?" I said. "You mean bicycles?"

"I left mine next to yours. Right where we used to park them. What are you smirking at?"

"*You*, you big lug. On a bicycle."

He shrugged. "Amory won't let me so much as breathe on that new machine of his. Come on. Let me buy you an ice cream cone for old times."

I looked at my watch and said why not. For old times.

We collected our bicycles from the alley behind the marine stores. He still rode the same old blue one he got for his sixteenth birthday. I followed his white shirt up Little Bay Road and thought we were kids again, heading to the harbor for ice cream, except his back was so broad, like a sail, and I couldn't take my eyes off the tender pink skin above his collar. I had to stand on the pedals to make it up the last rise to West Cliff Road, where we turned and coasted, laughing, all the way down to the main harbor. My hair flew out of its pins and bounced around my ears. I skidded to a halt next to Shep, right outside the door of the Medeiros' general store, and because I had eyes for Shep alone I nearly ran down some man as he walked out of the store and onto the strip of pavement that served as the only sidewalk on Winthrop Island.

"Oh, I'm so sorry!" I exclaimed.

"She just got her license," Shep said apologetically, "and anyway she's half blind."

I gave Shep a shove and the man said not to worry, he should have looked before he barged right out the door. He was a solid-looking fellow, just under six feet or so. He wore a light blue shirt and a pair of white linen pants and he carried a milk crate of groceries like it was nothing. His face was broad and scarred and hollow under the cheekbones, like he could use a good meal. He looked at me and at Shep and he set down the crate and held out his hand. "Sumner Fox," he said, with a hint of a courtly drawl, almost Southern. "Just rented a house for the season, over by Little Bay."

I clapped a hand over my mouth. "*Sumner!* So that's it."

"I beg your pardon?"

"Mrs. Collins, at the library. She couldn't remember your name." I reached out and shook his waiting palm. "I'm Emilia Winthrop. Welcome to the island."

"Excuse me," said Shep. "Did you say *Sumner Fox*?"

"That's right."

"*The* Sumner Fox? Yale fullback?"

"Aw, that's ancient history."

Shep seized Mr. Fox's hand with both of his own and pumped it vigorously. The bicycle fell to one side; I grabbed it just in time.

"Sir! It's an honor! My God, Sumner Fox! Right here on Winthrop Island! I can't believe it! Cricket, don't you know who this man *is*?"

"Now, then," Mr. Fox said modestly.

"*Only* the best fullback ever to play the college game, in my own humble opinion."

"Game of what?" I asked.

"Game of what, she says. I *idolized* this fellow, Cricket! Wait'll I tell Amory, he'll go nuts!" He turned back to Mr. Fox, whose hand he still pumped up and down. "Excuse her, sir. She's not much of a football fan."

"Smart girl," said Mr. Fox.

"Oh, *football*. How nice. *His* name is Nathaniel Peabody," I said to Mr. Fox, "but most people call him Shep."

"Nathaniel Peabody," said Mr. Fox. "Now hold on. That wouldn't be the same Nathaniel Peabody who cleared out a whole company of charging Germans at the Bulge, would it?"

"Not a whole company, sir, no. I was just giving the men some cover when— Say, where'd you hear about all that?"

"Oh, I've got some friends in the service. Distinguished Service Cross, do I have that right?"

"Heck, I'm just the fellow who got the credit, that's all."

"Shep?" I said. "Is that true? You're a hero?"

"It's all bull," Shep said. "Just Army bull. You know how it is, they have to hang a medal on somebody."

"True," said Mr. Fox.

"You didn't tell me," I said. "You didn't tell me about any of this."

Shep shifted his feet and looked down at the crate of groceries on the sidewalk. There were cans of soup and pineapple and green beans, a couple boxes of cornflakes, a small sack of flour, a small sack of rice, a bag of oranges, Morton Salt, some meat wrapped in brown butcher paper, that kind of thing. "At least let me give you a hand with these, sir. You've got a car nearby?"

"Around the corner on Elm. But I can handle it."

"Don't think of it." Shep bent down and hoisted the box in his arms. "You've got to tell me what in heck Sumner Fox is doing on old Winthrop for the summer."

I leaned both bicycles against the wall of the general store and scampered to catch up. "He's writing a book," I said.

"I'm writing a— Say, what do you know about it?"

"I don't know a thing about it. It's Mrs. Collins, the head librarian. I work there with her. She keeps up with all the gossip. Her sister works at the post office."

Mr. Fox turned to me and lifted a pair of bottlebrush eyebrows. He had a rugged face, battered almost, like somebody set it outside in a hurricane. "The library, is it? So you must be *the* Miss Winthrop. The one who catalogs the historical materials?"

"Why, yes."

"Then perhaps you could be so kind as to assist me with a little research. You see, I'm working on a book—a novel, that is—that takes place during a certain colonial weather phenomenon called the Great Snow. Have you heard of it?"

"A series of blizzards that set in during the late winter of 1717 and buried much of New England for weeks."

"I see I've come to the right historian."

"You sure have," said Shep. "What Cricket doesn't know about Winthrop history isn't worth knowing."

"Oh, don't listen to him. I'm just an amateur. But I should be able to dig up some local accounts in the library archives."

"I'm much obliged. Here's my car."

We stopped next to a handsome blue Dodge coupe, several years old. Mr. Fox gave the trunk a bang with his fist and the lid popped open obediently. Shep set the grocery box inside and straightened, wiping his palms on his trousers.

"A novel, huh?" he said. "That's swell. I'm not much of a writer myself."

"Trust him, he's not," I said.

Mr. Fox laughed. He had the kind of loose, rumbly laugh you couldn't help but smile to. We stood in the shade of one of the elm trees that gave the street its name. They had been planted thirty years ago by some beautification fanatic, you know the type. Everyone grumbles along until it's all done and people realize she was right. Shep set one hand on his hip and took his handkerchief from his pocket to wipe away the perspiration that trickled down his temples. Next to Mr. Fox, he looked awfully young. His skin was fresh, his smile abashed. Like old times. You never could have imagined he'd been to war.

"Well, I don't know that I'm much of a writer myself," said Mr. Fox. "I guess we'll find out. If I can find enough peace and quiet to get started, anyway."

"If it's peace and quiet you're looking for, you've come to the right place," I said.

"That's what I'm hoping."

"Well, if it gets lonely in front of that typewriter, I'd be happy to make some introductions," said Shep. "Why, we're having a dinner tonight at the Club, if you're interested. The fellas'd be delighted to meet you."

Mr. Fox drew his keys out of his pocket. "That's kind of you, but I'd prefer to lie low for now. I'm sure you understand. Still, I'll call for help if I start to hate the sound of my own breathing."

Shep smacked his forehead. "Geez, in all the excitement, I almost forgot! I'm off to California in a couple of days. But I'll leave your name with my father. Tom Peabody, down on Serenity Lane."

"California," said Mr. Fox. "Business or pleasure?"

"Both, you might say. I'm starting fresh out west."

Mr. Fox looked back and forth between us. "Starting fresh? By yourself? But I had the impression—you'll excuse me—the two of you—"

"Oh, we're just old friends," I said.

"Old friends," echoed Shep.

"I see," said Mr. Fox. "Well, good luck to you, Mr. Peabody."

"Why, thank you, sir."

They shook hands and Mr. Fox turned to me. "Miss Winthrop? When may I call on you at the library to begin our research?"

I felt Shep's gaze on the side of my face and stuck out my hand to Mr. Fox.

"Why, I'll be at my desk around noon tomorrow."

On the way home, Shep didn't say a word. I thought it was maybe because he was out of breath from cycling up the ridge. We pedaled past all the old landmarks, the landscape of our shared summers. This pond where we caught crayfish. That field where we tried to race each other on the two elderly donkeys left over from the farming days. The grand Dumont place, which had these elaborate formal gardens where we used to play hide-and-seek after dark and scare each other half to death. By the time we turned down Serenity Lane, my dress stuck to my back and Shep's wet hair was curling all over his head. I stopped my bicycle. Shep pedaled on a few more yards before he turned his head and stopped, too.

"Something wrong?" he said.

"We forgot about the ice cream."

"Well, damn. So we did. I guess I owe you an ice cream cone."

"So what happened at the Bulge?" I asked him.

He sighed and looked down the road, then at his bicycle tire. "It was a battle, Cricket. That's all. There were a lot of them."

"Mr. Fox seemed to think this one was a big deal."

"There was an ambush. I covered the retreat."

"So you saved their lives."

"That's what you do in war, Cricket. You take care of each other."

His head was bowed, studying the ruts of his bicycle tire. I waddled my bike forward until we were side by side. "What are you thinking about?"

"Nothing."

"You can tell me."

"Maybe I don't want to tell anyone, Cricket. Maybe I don't want to remember what happened that day."

"Why not?"

He raised his head and looked at me. "Because I don't, all right?"

I stared back at him and thought about his boyish enthusiasm for Sumner Fox, how his skin had flushed with delight. His skin was still flushed but it was the heat and the exercise. "Is this why you're moving to California?" I asked him.

"What kind of question is that? No. I'm not moving to California because of some damn ambush in some lousy Belgian forest, all right? Any more questions?"

"Yes. Is it true that your aunt had Charlotte and Matthew with her lover while her husband was still alive?"

Shep's eyes widened, then the laughter burst from his chest. "Golly, Cricket," he said. "You'll have to ask her that yourself. But hell, I wouldn't be surprised. Come on, I'll race you back."

I launched my bicycle forward and together we tore along Serenity Lane and swerved down the drive toward the old Winthrop house, just like when we were kids. Back then it was always a draw, a perfect match between my nimble limbs and natural endurance versus Shep's boy muscle. Now his legs churned like a pair of enormous pistons, and I knew he could have shot ahead of me and won by open yards, if he wanted. But he didn't. Side by side we raced down the gravel drive, a perfect match. We flashed past the rhododendron bush at exactly the same split second, me panting hard and Shep hardly panting. He set his foot on the gravel and grinned. Told me I still had it. I told him he was full of baloney.

"You're sure you can't come to dinner tonight?" he said.

"Not my kind of crowd."

"What kind of talk is that? Nobody gives a damn about that kind of thing anymore, what your dad does for a living. Besides, you're better than any of them."

I ran my thumb along the handlebar. "That Miss Winthrop, you know, she's awfully clever, for a girl of her background. Not altogether bad looking, either, when you look at her. But she lacks a certain something. Polish, what? *Finish*."

"Now who's full of baloney. You call this polished?" He waved a hand to his own chest.

"Tell you what," I said. "Why don't you let me know when you're back. I'll come out of the house and say goodbye."

"It'll be too late to telephone."

I smiled and pointed my thumb to the attic window. "You don't need to telephone, remember?"

When I entered the keeping room, Susana jumped from the armchair. "There you are! Don't you know what time it is?"

I looked at the clock. "Oh! Sorry, I must've lost track of time."

"I'll say." She bent to kiss Mama on the top of the head. "I have to get dressed for work. Soup's in the pot on the stove."

"What about Pop? He should be home by now."

"Haven't seen him."

"But I have to leave for Mrs. Rainsford's!"

But she'd already whirled out the door and up the stairs. I turned to Mama, who had turned up the side of her mouth in what would have been a fond smile, if she could have bent the other half. In her lap she held her knitting. I remembered when we brought her home from the hospital and asked the doctor what was she supposed to do all day, she couldn't just sit around and stare into space, and the doctor said well, what did she do before, and we looked at each other and figured *Everything* wasn't going to be an awfully helpful response in the circumstances. So Susana volunteered *Knitting*, in a quavering, question-mark kind of voice. To which the doctor said, *Then let her knit.* As you can imagine, the results weren't so terrific at first. Mama got frustrated, and a lot of yarn got tangled, which Susana and I patiently rewound into balls. But eventually the fingers of her left hand started to figure out how to help the fingers of her right hand do their work, and you'd be surprised just how nice her mittens turned out.

I nodded to the one emerging half-formed from the pair of needles in her hands. "Who are those for?"

She made a noise that meant *You.*

"I should have known. My favorite color." I sat in the armchair next to her. "Are you hungry yet?"

She shook her head. She still had the lopsided smile fixed on her mouth and her gaze pointed out the window, which offered a view of the entire driveway, including the rhododendron where Shep and I had finished our race. Mama had always had a soft spot for Shep. She used to sit him down at the kitchen table and feed him thick slices of her famous *pão de ló* and ask him about Boston and about boarding school, what he was studying, who were his friends. He would tell her everything she wanted to know and then he'd ask her about her family, about Portugal, about her brothers who kept lobster boats and used to make extra money landing crates of liquor during Prohibition. Got into all kinds of scrapes with the Coast Guard. All those stories she told Shep and he ate them up along with the cake. When he left, he always thanked her and her eyes shone for hours afterward. *That boy will make some girl a fine husband*, she used to tell me, and I would laugh and roll my eyes because I was just a kid, and Amory was the handsome one.

"Don't even think about it," I said. "He's leaving the island tomorrow. Moving to California to make wine."

"You . . . go," she said in her slow voice, and I couldn't tell if this was a question or a command.

"Don't be silly, Mama. I'm not going to California."

"No?"

"Because he hasn't asked me, for one thing. For another thing, I couldn't possibly leave this place, could I?"

The smile sank from the right side of her mouth. "Because . . . me."

"Because Pop needs me, and Susana." I reached out and patted her arm. "Because I love you and want to stay right here with you."

Mama just looked at me with her slack, lopsided face. In her grave brown eyes you could read anything you wanted, or nothing. Sometimes I thought she had all these ideas she wanted to communicate to us, that inside her fragile skin a whole world roiled that she ached to tell us about. Sometimes I thought the opposite, that the mother who had raised me, who had all these unspoken ambitions for me that I could only guess, had gone forever and it was only wishful thinking to imagine she could think and feel and advise me, if only I could understand her better.

"What's the matter?" I said. "Don't you believe me?"

Mama tilted her head and picked up her knitting needles and her eyes filled with tears.

"Mama, don't cry," I said. "Everything's going to be all right."

But the tears still tracked down her face and her back heaved, so I knelt in front of the armchair and gathered her hands between mine. Over the mantel the clock ticked. I was going to be late to Mrs. Rainsford's.

"What's wrong, Mama?" As if she could tell me. She was pulling her good right hand from mine, tangling her fingers in my hair and sobbing, and pretty soon I was sobbing, too, saying *Mama, I'm not going to leave you, I would never leave you*, but she only cried harder. I didn't even notice the sound of Pop's truck arriving at last in the driveway, the melancholy creak of the kitchen door. He burst into the keeping room and stopped in the middle of the rug.

"What the hell's going on in here?" he demanded.

I pried Mama's fingers from my hair and stood, wiping my eyes. "Nothing."

"What have you done to her, Em? What did you say to her?" He started forward and dropped to one knee in front of Mama, whose right hand stretched out—for me or Pop, who knew. "How many times have I said not to upset her, Em? You and that damn Rainsford woman."

"What's Mrs. Rainsford got to do with it?"

"Everything! Put ideas in your head. It's all right, sweetheart. Everything's all right."

I stood there helpless in the stuffy wood room that smelled of centuries while my father crooned to my mother, cradled her like a baby. I thought I was going to die of something, the pain in my ribs or the heat in the room. Without a word I turned for the door.

"Em? Where are you headed? *Emmie?*" called my father.

"Work," I said.

One thing I loved about the Peabodys' guest cottage, it was spic and span. Our house was old and musty and crammed with the remains of generations, old embroidery samplers and china figurines and amateur paintings collected by nameless ancestors, which you couldn't throw away because of the pull of sentiment. To step into the Peabody cottage was to make a fresh start. The walls were bare and white, the shelves stacked with nothing but books. The furniture matched and the kitchen gleamed and each evening, once the kids were made to pick up their toys and pencils and other childish objects, the floor was like the wide ocean. You could breathe. I stood in the middle of it and called out Mrs. Rainsford's name.

She called back that she was in the kitchen.

Nobody loved to cook more than Mrs. Rainsford. I could smell the kids' dinner from here in the living room—one of those meat pies she learned to make in England during the war. I followed the scent down the hall to the kitchen and stood in the doorway while she hustled and bustled at the stovetop, kids all lined up at the kitchen table, scrubbed and hungry. They pointed their inquisitive faces at me. Mrs. Rainsford turned.

"Why, Emilia! What's the matter?"

"Nothing."

She wiped her hands on her apron and looked at Sebastian. "Could you keep an eye on your brother and sister for just a moment, darling? And don't let the rice boil over."

In the living room, Mrs. Rainsford sat me on the best armchair and pushed back a wave of dark hair behind her ear. "Now talk," she said.

"Mrs. Rainsford, you've been so kind, and I want to thank you for—"

"This is nonsense. Are you trying to tell me you're not going?"

"It's just not possible."

"Why not, in God's name? Because of your family? Your father doesn't want his precious daughter to set foot off this puny island and see the world?"

I stood up. "It's because of my mother. She needs me."

"You mean your father needs you to take care of her so he can do what he likes."

"That's not fair! He's devoted his life to her."

"Oh, is that what—" She bit off the rest of the sentence and pressed her red lips together. Even in the kitchen she wore lipstick. She exhaled a ribbon of breath and went on in a conciliatory voice, "Of course I see his point. Who wants to look after an invalid all by yourself?"

"She's not an invalid. She's my mother."

"She's still an invalid, and you have your life in front of you, you have heaps of potential, and if you were a *boy*, Emilia, if you were only a boy instead of a girl, with your brains and your class, you'd be off to college with your father's blessing, believe me."

"Don't be angry for me."

"Angry? I'm furious." She stalked across the room

and back. "We have to think of something, that's all. We have to find a way."

"Look, I appreciate your good intentions, I really do. But I don't want you to put yourself to this kind of trouble. You're only here for the summer. Winthrop's just a landing place for you. Come September you'll pack up and get on with your life and I'll get on with mine, and there's no reason for you to concern yourself with me."

"But I *do*, Emilia. I *am* concerned."

"Why?"

"Because you interest me. Because I see a little of myself in you."

I smiled. "That's funny."

"Funny? How?"

"Because Pop says you're a loose woman."

"Does he? Well, maybe he's right. I don't let little things like convention get in the way of doing what's right. If that's loose behavior, well, he's got plenty of grounds to throw me in the stocks. But then, doesn't everybody?"

"Doesn't everybody what?"

"Do awful things. And he who complains the loudest usually has the most to hide. Psychology, you know. Projection."

"What's that supposed to mean?"

"It means we human beings have a habit of accusing others of the sins we've committed ourselves. But that's for another day. Right now we have to find a solution to your little dilemma."

"It's not a dilemma. It's just the way things are."

"You can't simply accept this, Emilia. You can't give up. You can't be satisfied with what somebody else decides you're allowed to have."

"You don't understand. You're a Peabody, you've grown up thinking you can shape the world to your own desires. Where I come from, the world shapes you."

"Then change," she said. "Fight. Take the world by the throat and make it bend for you."

From the kitchen came a crash, followed by a scream. I started for the hall and Mrs. Rainsford took my arm. We stood so close I could smell the cigarettes on her breath. Her eyes startled me, a fierce blue.

"Emilia, I won't give up," she said. "I am *determined.*"

By night, Summerly reminded me of a castle. All those roof peaks, all the shadows and the moonlight that gilded the oily slate tiles. As a child I sometimes snuck out at twilight just to stare at the main house and weave stories, which I didn't remember now, except that there were princes and knights and humble maidens who fought alongside them, and sometimes ghosts from deeply tragic incidents buried in the building's history. I hadn't thought about those stories in years but for some reason they returned to me in slight, magical pieces as I walked home through the warm night, like leaves that whirled past your head but slipped out of reach when you tried to catch them. To the left, Summerly loomed. Light glowed from certain windows—the library, a couple of rooms upstairs. Mrs. Peabody hated to waste electricity, so they must have returned home from the Club by now. Out of habit my eyes went to the windows on the northeast corner, second story, which belonged to Amory's room. Still dark. I imagined he was downstairs in the library enjoying a nightcap with Mr. Peabody and Shep and maybe Mrs. Peabody, if she wasn't busy in her small study off the main landing writing thank-you letters and that kind of thing. My feet crunched on the gravel. In another moment the attic window would come into view. I still wore the same dress I'd put on that morning, years old, a little short, drenched with sweat and salt water and dried on my skin. Probably I should change into something fresh before I said goodbye to Shep. He deserved that much, a clean dress. The beat of my steps quickened on the gravel. I was hurrying now, running almost. Now a birch tree blocked my view; now the beach plum. When had the beach plum grown so high? I broke into a run and reached the top of the drive, where the beach plum ended at the giant, elderly rhododendron that had marked our finish line this afternoon, every afternoon since we were kids. The rhododendron was thick with waxy green leaves and the tiny new buds that would grow into next May's flowers. One year Susana and I picked all the buds within reach to whip up some kind of make-believe prairie stew. Did we get hell from Pop for *that* one, let me tell you. I stopped in the drive next to the rhododendron and looked up to the attic window, expecting to see the old doll staring through the glass with its button gaze.

The window was empty.

I stood there for about a minute and strained my eyes. I thought the doll must be hidden by the darkness or the shadow cast by the window frame. The thing about Shep was you could count on him. If he said he was going to do something, he'd find a way to do it. That was why I felt disappointed. That was why my chest felt like someone had pierced the sternum with a needle and let all the joy whoosh out through the hole. I checked my watch—five minutes to eleven. I should be in bed. In seven hours Pop's porridge must be on the table for breakfast, his coffee bubbling in the percolator. Mama's bowl and spoon laid out. I closed my eyes and opened them again and the window was still empty.

As I turned toward the house, a flash of light caught the corner of my eye. I peered down the hedgerow to the main driveway and saw a pair of beams from the headlamps of a car, which had stopped at the turnoff to our house. A small, sleek car. I couldn't make out the color but I knew it was red, the color of cherries. I heard the faint rumble of the engine now, voices, a sweet giggle. A door slammed. A pair of feet crunched rapidly along the gravel, the exact same noise I had made a moment earlier. The car roared off to the Summerly garage. I waited until Susana reached the rhododendron before I stepped out of the shadows and said her name.

How she jumped.

"Jeepers, Cricket! You scared me to death!"

"I hope I did. Maybe that'll shock some sense into you."

"What are you talking about?"

"You know exactly what I'm talking about. Or should I tell Pop you've been taking rides home from Amory Peabody?"

She shifted her feet and folded her arms. "I haven't been taking rides from Amory. It's just the one time."

"It's eleven o'clock at night. The rest of the family's been back for a while now."

"What's that supposed to mean?"

"*You* should have finished up by nine. Finch would never have kept you later than that. He has scruples about kids."

"It was busy tonight." Her chin tilted up. "And I'm not a kid."

The light from the house laid on the side of her face and made her eyes gleam. She wore her dark hair short and it curled around her ear. Pop said she looked cheap, but Pop had grown up disapproving of flappers and anything modern, really. But it was funny, how a haircut like that could make a girl look both older and more vulnerable. Maybe it was the way it exposed the tender skin of her neck. I thought of what Mrs. Rainsford had said before, how we accuse others of the sins we've committed ourselves.

"No, you're not a kid," I said. "You're old enough to know better."

A knock arrived on the kitchen door around eight o'clock the next morning, just as I finished giving Mama her breakfast.

"Hellooo!" called a female voice, much too cheerful. "Emilia?"

I pulled the napkin from Mama's collar and folded it on the table. "Come in!"

The next second the kitchen filled with rampaging kids and Mrs. Rainsford in a straw hat and plenty of lipstick. She held a picnic basket in one hand and a blanket under the other arm. "We held a vote," she announced, "and you're coming with us."

"Where?"

"To the beach, where else? It's too hot to stay indoors."

"I can't leave Mama."

Mrs. Rainsford turned her gaze to my mother, who sat upright in her chair at the kitchen table and watched Matthew methodically pull the canned vegetables from the larder shelf and stack them on the floor. "Can she walk?"

"With some help, but—"

"Well, then. Off we go."

When we were kids we had picnics on the beach practically every day. Mama used to pack sandwiches and jugs of fresh lemonade and set up an umbrella. She would sit under the umbrella reading a book from the library, smoking cigarette after cigarette while we dug in the sand and pushed each other into the surf, the Peabody boys and Eli and Susana and me. Sometimes

I wondered why Mrs. Peabody didn't join us. After all, the boys were hers. Only later did I come to understand—I don't remember whether Mama told me outright or whether I guessed—that this was one of my mother's jobs, to look after the children while Mrs. Peabody lunched at the Club or had her friends over for bridge.

Mrs. Rainsford didn't bring an umbrella, so we settled ourselves in the shade of the beach roses while the kids tumbled in the nearby sand. Mama sat in the beach chair Pop had built for her that first summer after her stroke. It was made of teak from some old sailboat and made her look like she was sitting on a throne. I told her that. I told her she looked like a queen. I asked Mrs. Rainsford when Shep was due to leave for Boston and tomorrow's train and she wrinkled her nose and said she was pretty sure he'd left already on the early ferry.

My heart turned to stone in my chest. I said I thought he wasn't supposed to leave until tomorrow.

Well, she'd heard that damned noisy sports car roaring down the drive at some ungodly hour, so she'd assumed it was Amory driving his brother to the harbor. It was a real shame, she said. Shep was so good with the children. She thought he meant to stay all summer before he left for California, but no.

"I'm sure he'll have a terrific time out there," I said. "It's a tremendous opportunity for a young man."

"Yes," Mrs. Rainsford said. She was staring at my mother, who had propped a book on her lap. She held the pages down against the breeze with her left fist and turned the pages with her right hand. Without turning her head, Mrs. Rainsford asked me if Mama was actually reading.

"I think so," I said. "The doctor said there's no reason to think her mind isn't working much the same as before."

"In other words, there's no reason to think it *is*, either."

"I think she is. I've always thought so. If you look at her eyes, they're moving across the page."

We spoke in low tones, so Mama wouldn't overhear us, or maybe she could. She gave no sign. She was reading a copy of *Rebecca* I'd brought back from the library the other day, a novel she'd loved when it first came out. She used to check it out over and over. Mrs. Collins once joked that someone ought to buy it for her at Christmas. The trouble was, we had no bookstore on Winthrop Island, just the few dime-store novels the Medeiros sometimes saw fit to stock when the Families arrived at the beginning of summer. I guess I could have bought a copy on the mainland during one of our occasional shopping trips, but I always forgot.

Mrs. Rainsford crushed out her cigarette in the sand and reached for the picnic basket. I thought she would pull out a sandwich or something, even though it was only half past eight in the morning, but instead she pulled out a bottle of gin and a can of tomato juice.

"Isn't it a little early for that kind of thing?" I asked.

"Darling, that's the beauty of a Bloody Mary. It's never too early."

"What's a Bloody Mary?"

"Exactly." Mrs. Rainsford poured gin into a glass tumbler and eyed it up critically. "You have got to get off this goddamn *island*, Emilia."

She mixed the drinks and lit another cigarette for herself and one for me, then we settled in the sand closer to the children, who were liable to do crazy things like run into waves. I took a sip and remarked that it was rather spicy.

"Yes, that's the point." Mrs. Rainsford tipped some ash into the sand. "I've been doing some thinking, Emilia."

"Listen, Mrs. Rainsford—"

"Oh, call me Olive, for God's sake. The truth is, Rainsford was never my choice."

"You can't choose whom you fall in love with, I guess."

"Fall in *love*?"

"Your husband. Mr. Rainsford."

She blew out a little smoke. "Emilia, darling. I wasn't in love with *him*. Didn't I make that clear? All I needed from Cecil Rainsford was his name, and a British passport. We had a nice bargain. But it wasn't love."

I swallowed back my drink. "I don't know if I ought to hear this story."

"Why do you think I asked you here this morning? It's been on my mind all night, that comment of your father's. I don't want you to think I'm lacking in morals, just because they aren't tidy little Puritan ones."

"I don't think you're lacking in morals."

"You must have worked out that Rainsford couldn't have fathered Charlotte and Matthew."

"I haven't really thought about it," I lied.

"Well, it's true. My first husband and I had drifted apart soon after Sebastian was born. I won't say more. Oskar was a very good man and I don't wish to sully his memory. The best I can explain is that our minds traveled in opposite directions. By the time the war started we were leading separate lives, and I was in love with someone else."

"Oh," I said. "Who?"

Mrs. Rainsford—Olive—leaned back on her elbows and smoked her cigarette. She'd already finished her drink. "His name was Jurgis. I met him in Switzerland, soon after we arrived. Smitten. Instantly. He was born in Lithuania and ran away to sea when he was fourteen. Thoroughly uneducated but the most brilliant man I ever met. I taught him how to read."

I stared across the beach, where Charlotte and Matthew cheerfully buried their brother in the sand. Matthew had a small red shovel that he dug into a nearby hole before trotting off dead serious to pour the contents over Sebastian's toes. His blond hair shone white in the sun and his long limbs were deeply tanned.

"He must have been handsome," I said.

"No. He wasn't handsome at all. That's much too civilized a word. A drawing-room word. *Amory* is handsome." She said this like *handsome* was a failing. Something to be ashamed of, something you had settled for. She was staring straight up at the hazy sky, smoking in long, dreamlike drags. "I'd never felt that way about anybody in my life. We were savagely in love. Savagely. If you saw him, you'd understand. If you saw us together. Don't you think there are certain people who speak to your soul? Who *inhabit* you. I can't explain it very well, I'm no good with words. We became lovers the night we met. I had Charlotte a year later. Oskar was very gracious about it, allowed his own name on the birth certificate. By then he was deeply involved in his antifascist networks. I don't know what he was doing but it was extremely dangerous. I guess being cuckolded by an illiterate Lithuanian must have seemed trivial." She chuckled around her cigarette. "Anyway, he was captured by the SS in Germany and sent into one of those prison camps and I never heard another word, though I wrote all these letters trying to find out what happened to him. Then Jurgis disappeared. I was expecting Matthew by then and marooned in Switzerland with two children already and no possible means of support."

"What about the Peabodys?"

"What could they do? You couldn't send money abroad because of the war. It was Cecil who saved me."

"Cecil Rainsford?"

"Yes. He worked for the British consulate in Bern. He offered to marry me and support the children, have me evacuated to England. The practicalities of life were solved, which was a relief. Once you have children, the practicalities are all that really count. Especially in wartime. But I still didn't know what had happened to Jurgis. He'd simply vanished. When the war ended, I thought he'd turn up. Like magic. He was like that. I imagined he would simply walk through the door one afternoon and set down his pack and call my name and carry me to bed. I asked Nathaniel to help me—he was in Germany, you remember, with the occupation force in Berlin. He was wonderful. Combed all the prisoner of war lists and put out the word at the displaced person camps, everything he could think of. Dear boy. But we never heard a word. Not a clue. Disappeared. Like so many. Into thin air. Or the mud of some battlefield, more likely." She stubbed out her cigarette and sat up, curling her arms around her knees, staring past the children and out to sea. Her nose was large and steep and sharp at the end, like a jib. "I gave up hope in the middle of April. Just gave up. I woke up one dreary morning and decided to come home. So here I am."

"Not a widow, after all."

"No, that part's true. Cecil had a heart attack last October. Terrible. He was a decent man. It was the strain of war, I think. It took him in the end." She reached for the gin bottle and unscrewed the lid. "The most decent thing of all was that he married me for love."

"He loved you?"

"Terribly. I do feel awful about that. He fell for me like a brick."

"Knowing you couldn't love him back." I sighed.

"Isn't it tragic?" She was mixing me another drink, the gin and tomato juice and the drops of sauce from a small bottle. "No doubt you're wondering why I'm telling you all this. These intimate details."

"To justify yourself. To explain yourself. Because of what my father said."

"Partly," she said. "But also because I want to open your eyes a little. To show you what's possible."

"Grief? I already know that."

"*Love*, you silly thing." She clinked her glass against mine. "Love comes first of all. Grief is only possible if you love."

To my wet ears this sounded profound and deeply courageous and certainly worth drinking to. Love! The necessary component to grief. I sucked down my Bloody Mary and never thought to examine the obvious fact that all three men who had loved Olive Grossmeyer Rainsford were now dead.

But when I rolled onto my stomach and looked toward the beach roses, I saw that Mama had dropped her book to the side and sat there simply staring at Olive, and for a second there I could have sworn she had heard every word.

The morning passed, the sun climbed in the sky. The heat built to a fever and the children dragged me out in the water. When we came back dripping, Olive had retreated to sit by my mother in the shade next to the beach roses. She was talking and Mama seemed to be listening. The kids collapsed like puppies on the blanket and Olive grinned up at me.

"I think your mother wouldn't mind a dip in the ocean. In this heat."

"Oh, but she couldn't," I said.

"Have you tried?"

"No, but—"

"You take one arm and I'll take another. What harm could possibly come to her?"

I looked at my mother's face. "Mama? What do you think? A little swim?"

Mama nodded.

We got her to her feet and helped her shuffle down the sand to the water's edge. She wore her old blue housedress with the little flowers on it and I figured a little salt water wouldn't hurt. Olive held her steady while I removed her sandals and set them above the line of high tide. In we waded. Because it was June the water was cool and felt cooler still against the hot air. Mama splashed with her leg and a laugh bubbled up from her chest. *Let's swing her*, said Olive. Carefully we braced her between us. She weighed hardly anything. Once she had been a comfortable plush motherly cushion but now she was all bones. Her dark hair had turned white but Pop refused to cut it short, so every morning I brushed it and gathered it in an old-fashioned knot at the back of her head. She was beautiful still, even though her face sagged to one side. Her eyes were lustrous with sun. She looked at the horizon like she expected Eli to step out of it and fold her frailty between his arms. After the morning calm the surf had begun to build. Olive pulled Mama forward, toward the breaking sea, but I held back. You seldom encountered the big waves around here, even though we faced the ocean on this part of the island, but sometimes they could knock you over if you weren't paying attention. Either Mama didn't care or she didn't remember. She shrugged off my hand and went ahead with Olive. Olive slung an arm around her waist and they laughed together as a wave rolled up their thighs and washed behind them. But Mama had never feared the ocean. She used to say that this water connected her to Portugal, that the Atlantic was home to her. I hung back and watched them together. Olive and Mama. All that cold, salty water licking them clean. An alcoholic peace settled over me, a nice Bloody Mary haze. I looked over my shoulder to check on the kids and saw them rolling across the sand—some kind of game. When I turned back a gigantic wave had built out of nowhere. I screamed at Olive to pull Mama back, pull her back, but the commotion of water swallowed my voice. The water drained from around my legs to join the gathering flood. I staggered forward and lost my balance and staggered forward again, but the wave was already cresting, already curling over itself to descend over Olive and Mama. You are supposed to dive in this situation. You are supposed to pierce the base of the mountain and let it crash harmlessly above and behind you, but Mama couldn't dive and Olive certainly couldn't dive for them both. Could she? I was too late. The water caught me up and knocked me flat, like when I was a kid and didn't know better. Sputtering I came up. Brine ran from my nose and mouth and ears. First I spotted Olive, picking herself up from the ocean floor, shrieking with shock or delight—I couldn't tell. I plunged forward and my hands found something solid. Mama popped up like a cork. I thought she was dead. I hauled her upward. She flailed against me— thank God. We sputtered together, dragged each other toward shore. We reached the foam and Olive came up from behind and slung an arm around Mama's other side, her good side. Dry sand and we tumbled into it, drunk, triumphant.

When I came inside with Mama half an hour later, Susana looked up from the kitchen table, where she was thumbing through a magazine, coffee at her elbow. "You're all wet," she said.

"We went swimming and rinsed off at the Peabodys' shower," I said.

She looked at her watch. "Don't you have to be at the library in fifteen minutes?"

"Good Lord," I said.

"I'll give you a lift," said Olive, who came in behind us with Mama's beach chair, which she rested against the wall. "I have to catch the noon ferry. Errands."

Susana rose from her chair and frowned at Mama's face. "She's got sunburn."

"Never mind, it's good for her," said Olive.

I ran upstairs to change clothes. When I came down again, Olive and Susana were laughing together at the kitchen table. Mama sat between them with a glass of water, watching the children play jacks on the kitchen floor.

Olive saw me and rose from her chair. "All set? Come along, children. Pick those up. And I mean all of them. Have you ever stepped on a jack?" She addressed this question to me and I shook my head. "Excruciating. Now kiss your mother goodbye."

I turned to Mama and bent down to kiss her cheek.

"Goodbye, Mama," I said.

When we reached the library, Olive asked if I needed anything from New London and I said no. I was still half-drunk and felt as if all the stuffing had been squeezed out of my muscles. Together we got the bicycle out of the back seat, wedged between the half-dressed children, and Olive hugged me goodbye.

"I feel as if we're sisters now," she said. "Say hello to that Mrs. Collins for me. She's such a dear."

To escape the heat, I spent the early afternoon in the library basement hunting through the historical archives for any documents relating to the Great Snow of 1717, or colonial blizzards of any year, or notable weather events in general. I knew the archives as well as anybody, I guess. In the months after Eli was killed, after we brought Mama home from the hospital in Boston, I set to work cataloging and cross-referencing every single document ever donated to the Winthrop Island Historical Society. There were boxes and boxes of them. New Englanders hate to throw anything out, especially anything related to their ancestors, but eventually you have to clean out the attic and if you haul those chests and drawers full of old letters and legal agreements and what have you down to the library and donate them to the historical society, which happens to be housed in the same building—why, you've done the right thing for your conscience and for posterity. So you can imagine how many busy hours I spent in that basement. As the autumn crawled into winter, day after day, I reviewed land sales and love letters, grocery bills and diaries. I cataloged it all and typed it up by subject on index cards, which I filed in alphabetic order in a drawer cabinet somebody had given to the library years ago.

It's funny, though. Ever after those dark, busy months, whenever I returned to that library basement I thought of my brother Eli. His ghost inhabited the stones for me. Sometimes I would catch myself speaking to him—not aloud, only in my head. Trivial things, mostly. I'd tell him about my day, about Mama, about the beans shooting up in the garden or Mrs. Menezes turning up drunk at carol service at the church. (Too much eggnog, her sister whispered, and we nodded like we didn't all of us know how many empty bottles were buried in the Menezeses' back garden.) Today, even as I rummaged through the cards and filled my head with thoughts of blizzards—with the idea of Winthrop Island a couple hundred years ago, sans Club, sans Families, sans everything but Winthrops—the back of my head kept up a patter of talk. Eli, remember that time we rode our bicycles to Horseshoe Cove at midnight and lit the bonfire? You were thirteen or fourteen and I must have been ten or so, and I worshipped the moon over your head, do you recall? Amory and Shep were with us. We roasted nuts and marshmallows and went swimming in the moonlight, and I cut my foot on the rock and Shep was the only one who noticed. Shep fished me out of the water and stopped the bleeding with his shirt. Then you carried me all the way home on your back, Eli, singing songs the whole way to keep my spirits up, and I remember smelling your neck and thinking it was worth getting my foot cut to find out that my big brother actually cared about me. I remember Shep, too. I remember how he tore off his shirt and wadded it around my foot and made some joke about how the sharks were coming for us now, they could smell a single drop of human blood from a quarter mile away. Did you know Shep's moving out to California? It's true. I never would have thought a boy like Shep would do a thing so dramatic, but there it is. Left behind his family and his friends, everybody who loves him, and went off this very morning to catch a train out west. He's going to run a vineyard with a friend of his. Sonoma, he said. That's where the vineyard is. An Army friend with a French wife who knows how to make wine, apparently. I never got a chance to say goodbye, either. Isn't that terrible? He must have forgotten. Maybe they had a lot of champagne last night. They had a dinner at the Club to send him off. That was it, too much champagne. So much champagne I guess he forgot all about his old pal Cricket. Maybe he'll write when he arrives. He used to write to me all the time. A short note, that would be okay, just to let me know he made it to California in one piece. Maybe tell me about the train journey, what it was like to cross the Rockies and look out your window and see mountains three miles into the sky. Just one little note, that's all I ask, his own handwriting on a sheet of ordinary white letter paper, maybe a photo. Or is that too much to ask of a fellow who's starting his life fresh, three thousand miles away? A fellow who wants to forget everything he left behind, apparently.

On and on the patter went, you get the idea. The nice thing about talking to Eli in my head, I could say whatever was on my mind and he wouldn't interrupt me. The dead, they don't judge you. They are beyond the petty jealousies of us mortals, I guess. I could say the truth. Upstairs, Mrs. Collins bustled about humming to herself. Every so often she made some exclamation about how hot it was, or wondered whether we would have any patrons at all in this heat. At one o'clock she left for lunch and a minute later the bell above the front door jingled. I hurried up the stairs.

"Why, Joan!" I exclaimed. "It's Joan, isn't it?"

She pushed back her hair over her ear, the pink new girl who had come to waitress at the Club for the summer. "June?" she said, like a question. "June Lind-strom."

"That's right. From Wisconsin."

"Minnesota?"

"Oops, sorry." I stuck out my hand. "I'm Cricket Winthrop, remember?"

"Of course I remember you, Cricket. Your sister and I, we get along real well. She's told me all about you."

"Golly," I said. "Were you looking for a book or something?"

"I was just returning this." She held out a thick volume. "Though I wouldn't mind picking up a new one."

I looked at the cover. "*Middlemarch*. My goodness, that's ambitious for summertime."

"I guess I'm a bit of a bookworm."

"I'll bet you are. Well, help yourself. Nobody here but us mice."

She giggled and wandered off toward the fiction shelves. Halfway there, she stopped and turned. "Oh! I saw your neighbor today."

"One of the Peabodys, you mean?"

"That tall, dark-haired one with all the kids? She sometimes comes to dinner with the rest of them."

"Oh! Mrs. Rainsford."

June snapped her fingers. "That's right. She was waiting for the ferry. She's such a *character*."

"She is."

"I hope she's all right? I mean, most people seem to leave the island only for emergencies."

June was right about that. The Families liked to settle in for the summer. You had to have an awfully pressing reason to leave, like a suspected tumor or a burglary back home in your empty main residence. Sometimes not even then. I thought about Olive's confessions today, the almost reckless way she'd thrown herself into the surf, and the whole morning took on a different color. I combed the ends of my hair with uneasy fingers. "Gosh," I said, "she seemed all right this morning. Said she had errands to run, that's all. She should be back tonight."

"Oh. Well, that's a relief. Just some shopping, I guess. Now that I think about it, she seems like the type to go a little stir-crazy, once in a while."

"True. I wouldn't worry."

She flashed me a radiant smile. "I won't now."

About four o'clock I looked with satisfaction at the neat stack of letters and newspaper clippings I had gathered together for Mr. Fox. There wasn't much, but it made for fascinating reading. "Mrs. Collins," I said, "did you know that by March of 1717, the snow had drifted so high that you had to climb out of your house from the second story?"

"That's nice, dear."

"Some houses were buried entirely. You could only tell there was a house there because of the chimney smoke coming out of the snowdrift."

"Dear me."

"Over on the mainland, almost all the deer died of starvation."

Mrs. Collins fanned herself with the June issue of *Yankee* magazine, which she'd been reading at her desk. "We don't have any deer here on the island, you know. Or I'm sure they would have died, too."

"Kind of hard to imagine snow like that on a day like today, don't you think?"

"Yes, it is."

"Anyway, it's all here in this envelope for Mr. Fox to borrow for his research."

"I'm sure he'll appreciate it, dear."

I looked at the clock. "He was supposed to stop by this afternoon. I don't suppose I missed him while I was down in the basement, do you?"

Mrs. Collins looked up and snapped her fingers. "*That's* what I was supposed to tell you. Mr. Fox telephoned. Said he couldn't make it to the library today after all. He was awfully apologetic."

I looked at the brown envelope in my hand. "Oh. I guess I'll just set this aside for him, then. What a shame, though. I dug up some really fascinating letters. Honestly, I was looking forward to talking it over with him. Did you know that—"

"Cricket, darling. I have a wonderful idea." Mrs. Collins lifted her bangs and fanned her forehead. "Why don't you just cycle out to his place and leave the envelope for him there?"

"Why, without making him sign it out first?"

"I'm sure we can trust a man of his reputation." Evidently Mrs. Collins had heard about the football.

"Well, if you're sure you don't need me."

"I'll find a way to manage," she assured me.

To say the truth, I didn't expect Mr. Fox to answer when I knocked on the door of the Armstrong cottage. As before, the place was quiet, the curtains drawn. A pot of geraniums had been set out near the doorstep; that was the only difference. I had the idea that he didn't want to be disturbed, that he was one of those writers who didn't think much of the outside world and preferred to sit with a typewriter or a notepad, magnificently alone. So I knocked softly. To my surprise, a voice called out and a moment later, the door swung open.

"Miss Winthrop," said Mr. Fox, with grave courtesy. "To what do I owe the pleasure?"

He wore a pair of tan trousers and a light blue shirt with no tie, collar unbuttoned. You got the feeling he had left off the tie and the button as a reluctant concession to the heat. What really shocked me was he was barefoot. Barefoot! Not even socks. He said the word *pleasure* like it was anything but.

"Mr. Fox, I hope I'm not disturbing you. I did some research for you, that's all, and I thought I'd bring it around."

"I'm sorry to have troubled you. Didn't Mrs. Collins give you my message?"

"She did. But I didn't have much else to do with myself, so I thought I'd have a look in the archives. See what I could turn up. I was curious about it, anyway."

He offered me a stiff smile. "Did you find anything interesting?"

"My goodness, yes. I'm afraid I bored Mrs. Collins to death. She's the one who suggested I take my research where it might be better appreciated." I held out the envelope. "So here you are. It's mostly letters that contain contemporaneous accounts, along with some passages I copied out of Hephzibah Winthrop's journal—that's one of our best sources, we have a lot of diaries in our collection, island life being what it is—but you'll find a few newspaper clippings from 1917. You know, the bicentennial year. Newspapers are always hungry for human interest copy, I guess."

He tucked the envelope under his arm. "I appreciate your efforts, Miss Winthrop. That's just what I need."

"Of course, I'd be happy to discuss it all with you. Once you've gone through the material. I'm sure there are plenty of additional directions we can take."

As I spoke, I tried to look past his ear and catch a glimpse of the room behind him. Well, wouldn't you? I couldn't see much because the curtains were drawn, as I said, and none of the lamps were lit. The room was the front parlor, which Mrs. Armstrong had filled with furniture that was both tasteful and lived-in. So far as I could tell, Mr. Fox hadn't changed a thing, except that the corner where the birdcage had stood was empty, and the children's toys were no longer scattered over the floor.

"Once I've had the opportunity to look things over, I'll be sure to let you know," said Mr. Fox. There was a note of finality in his voice. Likely I'd disturbed him in his work after all.

"All right, then," I said. "I'll be getting along. I hope you enjoy yourself."

His expression softened. "Thank you, Miss Winthrop. I do appreciate your kindness. I must admit, I wasn't expecting such efficiency."

"Well, we may not be as slick as you mainlanders around here," I said, "but we stumble along all right."

"Miss Winthrop, I—"

But I was already peeling my bicycle from the side of the porch. "See you around," I called back over my shoulder, and I pedaled my way out of his lawn and down Sill Lane as hard as the heat would allow.

I stayed good and mad for at least a quarter mile, pulling so hard and so fast that the cottages of Sill Lane blurred by in a haze of rage. Then the sun caught up with me. I couldn't breathe, I was so hot with anger and exercise and the sultry atmosphere. I rested my feet on the pedals and coasted for a bit, down to where Sill Lane hollowed out and started uphill again, toward Spinnaker Lane that led back to West Cliff Road. As I gulped the torrid air into my lungs I felt something nag me, some passing detail I had failed to take account of during my blind flight. I braked the tires and set my toe down in the gravel and twisted to look behind me.

That was it. Pop's old Ford truck, bottle green in the lawn outside the Wright place.

I checked my watch and saw it was half past four o'clock. Surely he should be on his way home by now. Maybe he'd lost track of time. I looked at the boiling sky. Some thunderclouds had begun to gather to the southwest, black and blue.

Just go home, Cricket. Pop won't thank you for barging in. Remember that time he nailed his thumb to the table because you scampered into his workshop at the wrong second? And for what—to say hello? Apologize?

I don't know why I turned my bicycle around and pedaled back to the Wright cottage, in the exact same direction as those thunderclouds. I think my spirit was a little bruised by Mr. Fox's ingratitude and wanted comfort. You couldn't talk to Pop about a lot of things but you could talk to him about the Great Snow of 1717 and he would come to life. He would stop everything and pull you up a chair and tell you what his great-grandmother had told him about her great-grandfather's stories about being a kid during the Great Snow. He would go outside and estimate how high the snow might have reached and what were the chances your livestock would survive. He could have gone on all day. In fact, what I should have done was bring Mr. Fox my father, not an envelope full of old letters. Although you'd have thought that a writer like Mr. Fox would be thrilled to death by a pile of old letters. *If* he were a real writer, that is, and not just some old football player trying to prove he had an intellect after all.

I reached the Wright place and dismounted. The air

was still, everything trapped in place by the heat. The two-by-fours in their stacks, the kitchen sink on the porch. A dog howled miserably from some distant lawn. I leaned the bicycle against Pop's truck and hopped up the porch steps. The door was ajar. I slipped inside and saw the familiar signs of renovation—furniture stacked to one side, walls stripped. I was about to call out *Hey, Pop* when I heard a woman's voice from the back of the house, asking a question. A man mumbled some reply.

I remember thinking, *That's funny.*

I stepped forward. A floorboard groaned under my foot. In the hot, delicate silence that followed, I couldn't seem to move or even breathe. I had never been inside the Wright place, but it seemed like most of the old cottages around here—high, peaked roof, single story, parlor and dining room and kitchen to one side, a bedroom or two at the back, maybe some stairs to an attic. In the old days it would have sheltered a fisherman and his family. I didn't know the Wrights personally, just that Mr. Wright was a professor at one of the Boston colleges and they started coming to Winthrop sometime in the twenties, after the Families had started building their summer estates on the private end of the island. They bought this place just about derelict and had it fixed up the same way the Peabodys fixed up our house—installed plumbing and electricity and a modern kitchen, patched all the holes and added fresh curtains and paint and a real bathroom. But a house needs to be lived in or nature takes over, and the Wrights hadn't summered on Winthrop since the war started. Now they'd hired Pop to clean up the damp and the missing roof shingles, to repair the leaky pipes and the rotted floorboards and the stains on the kitchen sink so they could either live in it or rent it to some nice young family for the summer. Or sell it. That was why Pop was here.

As for the woman—well, maybe she'd come to help.

Looking back, I think I should have left. I honestly do. When you live on an island with a permanent population of only two or three hundred souls, you grow up abiding by an unspoken pact as regards the boundaries of privacy. What somebody chooses to do indoors, out of sight of anybody else, is none of your damn business. Even—maybe especially—if that somebody is your own father.

But I didn't leave. I couldn't. Like a cat, I had to know.

I started forward past the dusty brown furniture that was pushed up against the wall, across the front parlor to the hall. I made my footsteps light as down, the way I learned when I was a kid. To my left was the dining room and the kitchen. I glanced inside but they were empty. The dining room chairs had been stacked along one wall; the table was missing, maybe under repair. The kitchen was white and forlorn without its sink. I continued down the hall and heard a fierce little noise that sounded like a whimper. On the right there were two doors. The first one stood open to a small room, empty except for the sunlight that poured through the window and lit the motes of dust to a shimmering, lazy incandescence. The second door had been left a few inches ajar. Through this narrow aperture I glimpsed some color, a slash of movement. I set my palm against the wall. I could hear my own breath whistle through my lungs, the sweat percolate from my armpits. I took a step, another step. My right hand dragged along the plaster. I was certain the floor would creak under the weight of me, but it didn't. I felt the edge of the door-frame under my fingertips. I realized I had closed my eyes. I opened them.

I have said before that I don't remember much about the weeks after Mama's stroke, but that's not quite true. Certain moments return to me in detail so sharp, it hurts the backs of my eyes.

One: I am sitting in a chair in a hygienic white hall-way, next to an open door. Inside the room, some nurses are discussing a patient. How beautiful she is, what a shame she'll never be the same. Some cases just hit you in the gut, don't they? Her poor kids. Her poor husband. The hallway smells like disinfectant and chicken broth and, somewhere, flowers. One of the nurses has a mellow, lilting accent from somewhere far to the south of Boston. *Well, I don't feel sorry for her husband at all*, she says. *What a cold fish. Never says a word. Face like a stone wall, bless his heart. I wonder if he loves her at all.* All of a sudden, the smell of that broth and Lysol and hothouse roses turns my stomach. I can't breathe. I need to vomit. I rise from my chair and the hygienic white hallway tilts to the left, so I sit back down, smack my bottom hard against that chair, and put my head between my knees. Another nurse says, *I don't know, I think that's just the way they are, these old swamp Yankees. They aren't much for hugging and kissing, if you know what I mean.* And the Southern one replies, *Then it's her I feel sorry for. Putting up with that cold fish all her life. No wonder she went and had a stroke.*

Two: the same hygienic white hallway, another day. I don't know if it's before or after that conversation among the nurses. These memories, they're like glass beads in a jar, all jumbled up. I am carrying two cups of hot, brackish coffee, trying not to spill any. A peal of laughter rings from one of the rooms, a guffaw rumbles underneath. Somebody's telling a joke. Mama's room is the second one from the end of the hall, on the left. There are two beds but the other patient was discharged this morning, having recovered nicely from her appendix operation. The doors are supposed to be kept open except during examinations, but as I approach I notice somebody has closed ours, or nearly so. I stop, undecided. Maybe the doctor is examining Mama, maybe the nurse is performing some intimate service. Should I interrupt? I sip from one of the cups of coffee. It tastes like boiled mud. A noise makes itself heard from the other side of the door, as if somebody inside is choking to death. I peer through the inch or two between door and doorframe. At first I don't see anything. I'm about to push the door open with my elbow when I catch sight of a human body hunched over in a chair, sobbing so hard that his back might break. In my shock, I spill half a cup of scalding-hot coffee on my hand. You can still see the scar if you look close enough.

This door was not the same door as the one in the hospital. This hallway was brown and coated in the dust and germs of ages, and the room was on the right, not the left. When I looked through the crack, I didn't see my father—not at first. I saw a woman on an old mattress upon the floor. She lay on her side and her naked back curved like a violin. Her dark hair spilled over her shoulders and pooled atop the mattress's thin blue stripes. She was saying something in a quiet, soothing voice I couldn't make out. Her arm stretched out to rest on something that lay outside the narrow range of my sight. If I pushed the door open another inch, I could see what it was she touched. I did not push that door. But while I couldn't see what she touched, I could hear it—the noise of someone choking to death, somebody sobbing so hard that his back might break.

I wanted to turn and run away but I could not. My legs and my arms were dead weight. I was scared to breathe. That damn dog took to barking again, *yap yap yap* right through the open windows. The woman sighed and fell back to face the ceiling, one knee raised to shield her crotch from me, thank God. Her breasts slid almost into her armpits. I thought she could see me there in the crack of the doorway—she must see me—those gigantic brown eyes could not fail to catch the slight figure poised in the hallway, a few scorching yards away. But she did not see me. Her mouth was small and her nose was a giant beak—a remarkable nose that could only belong to my aunt Benedita.

At some point I must have jolted into movement. I must have flown down the hall and across the front room to the door, I must have grabbed my bicycle and made my way along Sill Lane and up to West Cliff Road and turned down Serenity Lane, although I don't remember doing any of these things.

I did not return home. How could I look at Mama? What would I say to Susana? I don't remember thinking these things, but I must have known them. I stopped the bicycle at the bottom of the arc of neat gravel in front of Summerly and stared at the white portico and the gray shingles and the opaque windows—this I remember clearly. To my left down the path that led to the guest cottage, which was empty because Olive had taken the ferry to New London this afternoon, and the return ferry wouldn't dock for another hour. As I sat there on my bicycle seat, balanced on one toe, a long note of thunder rumbled over the air behind me. The sky took on an ochre wash. Though the air was as hot and still as ever, I began to shiver because my clothes were soaked with perspiration. The air rumbled again. I lifted my foot back to the pedal and pushed off to the left, down the track toward the guest cottage. Nobody ever locked their doors on Winthrop Island. It was a point of pride.

The storm came in fast. A gust of wind struck my back and whipped my hair across my face, so sudden and fierce I almost lost my balance. The bicycle veered off the track into the grass. I steered it back and a drop of rain plopped on my forehead. By the time I reached the cottage, the rain hammered down on my hair and shoulders. I jumped off the bicycle and bounded to the door—the house had no porch or any kind of sheltering overhang at all—but when I reached for the knob I couldn't turn it. It was locked.

A flash blinded me. Thunder cracked open the sky a second later, like the detonation of a bomb. Down came the rain, filling my ears and nose and mouth until I thought I was drowning. I kept rattling that doorknob, as if it might somehow relent and unlock itself. I think I called out, even though I knew nobody was inside. I don't remember what I shouted. Another flash, another explosion of noise. By now I was desperate. I had this irrational idea that I was in the middle of a battlefield, for some reason—that the thunder and lightning were actually shells exploding around me, that the rain was a barrage of bullets from a machine gun, and I had to find shelter or I would die.

The kitchen window, I thought. Olive kept the kitchen window cracked open. Ventilation, she said.

I ran around the corner to the back of the house. The rain was almost too thick to see through. With my hands I found the window frame. Sure enough, there were a couple inches of space between the sash and the base, through which the rain gleefully streamed. I got my palms underneath the sash and pushed. At first, the wood resisted me. I guess the heat and the wet had swollen the fibers just enough to wedge the sash fast in its groove. But I only pushed harder. I rocked that window back and forth until it gave way a quarter inch on one side, a quarter inch on the other, and finally slid up a foot or two so I could wriggle myself through and land like a fish on Olive Rainsford's kitchen floor.

They found me asleep in one of the armchairs in the living room. I don't know why it took so long to find me—I guess everybody was out looking for me, including Olive, and nobody thought to look inside the cottage. It was Sebastian who made the perfectly logical suggestion that I might be indoors waiting for them, since it was my job to look after the Rainsford kids at this time of evening. That's what Olive told me afterward, not without a touch of pride that Sebastian had figured out by himself what had stumped all the grown-ups.

I loved that armchair. Olive once mentioned that it had belonged to the library in the Peabodys' house on Commonwealth Avenue when she was growing up, and that Mrs. Peabody had brought it down to Winthrop one summer when the library paneling was being treated for woodworm or something and never got around to hauling it back. It was an overstuffed bear of a chair that stood on lion's paw feet, upholstered in dark plum paisley with a green velvet pillow. You could not have purposefully searched for a chair more out of place in its surroundings. I liked to curl up in it while I read books from Olive's shelves, and because it was so comfortable, so perfectly designed to cradle the human body, I sometimes fell asleep there with the book in my lap, and Olive had to wake me when she came down from the attic.

She shook me awake now, but more gently and less amused. Emilia, she said. Emilia, darling. Wake up.

I opened my eyes to her concerned face. I couldn't remember a thing, about the storm or the Wright place or even my own name, almost. I couldn't imagine what I was doing asleep in this chair in this room. I thought maybe I'd nodded off while I was supposed to be watching the kids and struggled to apologize. She shushed me and knelt by the side of the chair. Her skin was damp and pink, her eyes shone. I recall how she pushed back my hair from my forehead, like you do with a child.

"Emilia, darling," she said. "I'm afraid I have some dreadful news."

IV.

MAY 1954
Washington, DC

When I walk off the airplane and into the sunshine at National Airport, a couple of men in dark suits step forward from the hustle-bustle to meet me.

"Miss Winthrop?" asks one, in a voice that's higher than you might expect, like a choirboy.

"Yes, I'm Miss Winthrop."

"Come with us, please."

As we speed through the streets of our nation's capital in a black sedan remarkably similar to the one that hurried me to the airport in Boston, it occurs to me that maybe I should have asked for some form of identification. There was this time that a pair of sweet-looking girls came into the bookstore and one of them engaged Susana in a long discussion about Patricia Highsmith, and after they left Susana discovered the other one had been wandering about the store shoving books into her shopping bag. Susana was really upset about it. She said that's the trouble with growing up on an island like Winthrop—you're too trusting of other people. I don't know about that. I think I'm awfully suspicious of others. But maybe Cato's right, maybe it's just certain women who raise the hackles on the back of my neck. Bring me a man in a respectable suit and I'll walk away with him like a dog with a new owner.

The balmy weather in Boston this morning seems to be general down the Eastern Seaboard. I roll down the window an inch or two to allow a little breeze into the car's interior, and the man who's driving glances at me in the rearview mirror. He is not the smiling type. I turn my head to watch the buildings fly by. I've never been to Washington before. I've never flown in an airplane before, for that matter, and I wasn't so wrapped up in my own little problems that I couldn't stare amazed at the ground dropping away beneath us, the tiny ripples of the ocean as we winged over Boston Harbor, the dollhouses and quilted fields and toy cars on the model roads, the delicate rivers and furred forests. We flew right over Long Island Sound and there it plopped like a green pebble in the water, Winthrop Island, where Tom Donnelly's crew was busy fixing up Summerly so the Peabodys could return at last. I appreciated all that. I appreciated the perspective from which I viewed it. I appreciated the noise of the engines and the bumps of the air, all of which I pretended to ignore, like a seasoned passenger. Now the Capitol itself appears in the gap between buildings, marble white and perfectly formed, and this time I don't bother to hold back a gasp. The driver looks again in the rear-view mirror.

"I've never been to Washington," I tell him.

The war's been over for years and still this city has a boomtown feel. There's a whole world to rebuild, a fresh enemy to fight. Everywhere you look some ambitious new structure slashes the sky. Another minute, and we pull up in front of a cluster of modest buildings, the kind of flimsy clapboard shacks you see on a temporary Army base in time of war, painted in drab olive green. The door of the nearest building swings open and a man strides out in a dark suit with a fedora drawn low over his forehead. As he tries to shut the door it sticks and you can see him swear while he shoves it into place. "Where are we?" I ask.

"Headquarters of the Central Intelligence Agency, ma'am," says the man in the passenger seat.

"I thought you boys were from the FBI."

He sounds offended. "This is a CIA matter, ma'am."

I return my stare to the building nearest me. The door shudders, as if somebody's trying to force it back open. "You've got to be kidding me. We're going to outsmart the Russians from *here*?"

He gets out of the car and stands next to the rear door, so I can't see through the window. The driver remains at the wheel, eyeing me in the mirror. I ask what's going on. He checks his watch and peers at the building entrance through the passenger window.

"Ma'am," he says, "could you move to the middle seat, please?"

"Why am I supposed to—"

Both doors swing open on either side of me. A thick-shouldered man in a navy suit climbs into the seat on the far side. Next to me, another man stares down from beneath the brim of a gray fedora. He has a patrician, middle-aged face and a fringe of short white hair.

"You must be Miss Winthrop," he says. "Would you mind making room?"

"I beg your pardon. Who the hell are you?"

He laughs and holds out his hand. "Forgive my manners. Allen Dulles, director of central intelligence."

Of course I've heard of Allen Dulles, newly appointed director of the Central Intelligence Agency. His brother happens to be the current secretary of state, for one thing. You know the gentleman—John Foster Dulles, a man who isn't taking the Communist threat lying down. When you look at newspaper photographs of John Foster, you'd think he was some kind of Calvinist minister with all the humor of a frying pan, so it's a relief to find his brother climbing into the back seat of a government-issue sedan with a smile on his face, a pipe in his hand, a blue twinkle in his eye. As the car yanks away from the curb, he looks across me to address the man on my other side.

"Fox," he says, "you sly dog, you didn't tell me she was so pretty."

Sumner Fox removes his hat and brushes at some speck of dirt on the crown. "Miss Winthop's personal appearance is irrelevant to the operation."

Mr. Dulles settles back in his seat and confides in my ear, "I apologize. He's a newlywed."

I turn to Fox. "You're a newlywed?"

"I was married last year," Fox says in his gravelly voice.

"Baby on the way," adds Dulles. "Busy man, our Fox."

"Well, congratulations. Seems everybody's doing

it these days." I glance out the window at the blur of streets. "Can somebody tell me what's going on? Where you're taking me? Why the CIA's involved?"

"Fox?" says Mr. Dulles. "This is your circus."

Fox examines his hat. "First of all, Miss Winthrop, I'd like to thank you for agreeing to help us once more. I know we asked a lot of you eight years ago. I know the consequences were tragic for you."

"They were tragic for a lot of people."

"I can assure you, there's no physical danger involved today—"

"Nobody's going to die, you mean?"

His breath hitches. "No."

The car makes a sharp turn to the left. Mr. Dulles grabs the strap that hangs from the side. Fox grabs the door handle. I grab Fox's knee. When we straighten again, I steal a glance at Fox's face for the first time in over seven years—the first time since the conclusion of Olive Rainsford's trial—and I'm shocked to see how ravaged it looks. The eyelid droops, the nose is bent, a long scar runs over the bridge of his brow. And that's just the right side of his face.

"Say, what's happened to you?" I ask softly.

"Just a brief encounter with a KGB interrogator— what was it, a year ago?" says Dulles.

"A year and a half," says Fox.

I cry out, "You were in *Russia*?"

Fox turns to Mr. Dulles and stares across the tip of my nose. Dulles clears his throat.

"Fox, why don't you start from the beginning? I think Miss Winthrop ought to know how much is at stake here."

"Oh, terrific," I say.

"Very well. We don't have much time, so I'll try to be brief," says Fox. "As you know, thanks to some legal maneuvering on the part of counsel, and because there was certain evidence we couldn't submit in a public trial because it would compromise our own intelligence assets, Mrs. Rainsford was cleared of the most serious offenses. The charge of manslaughter was dismissed."

"Because of my testimony," I say.

"I understand your distress, Miss Winthrop," Fox says quietly. "Believe me."

"Do you really? Because I had the impression you didn't give a damn about the manslaughter. You were just happy to get your single lousy espionage conviction. Fifteen years, wasn't it? Eligible for parole after seven."

"I think we were lucky to get what we did. After what happened."

"I did my best, Fox. Don't you think I haven't gone

over the memory of that night a million times? Don't you think I haven't shredded myself to bits over what I might have done instead?"

Mr. Dulles lays a hand on my arm. "Miss Winthrop—"

"*You.* Butt out."

Dulles's hand darts back. He digs around in his pocket for a matchbook and fixes his attention on the bowl of his pipe. I turn back to Fox.

"I hope you haven't blamed yourself," he says. "It was my fault. My fault entirely. I had little field experience at the time. I underestimated the situation."

"You mean you underestimated *her.*"

"Yes. I underestimated Mrs. Rainsford."

"To be fair, Miss Winthrop—" Dulles begins.

"I said butt out, Mr. Dulles."

"—to be fair," he continues blandly, sucking his pipe, "we were all a little new at this, right after the war. We didn't really understand what we were dealing with. And a lot of people thought we shouldn't be going after Soviet agents to begin with. Didn't believe they existed, really. The Soviet Union was our ally, we'd just won a war side by side. What we didn't fully comprehend back then was that these men and women had been honing their tradecraft for years. Had gone for specialized training in Moscow. They were professionals. They had established networks, they had hundreds of agents in place. We were only just starting to catch up."

The anger dies out of me. I don't want to argue anymore. I don't want to fight. It's all ancient history, isn't it? You can't change the past and all that. The dead are still dead. I close my eyes. The car turns to the right and I sway into Dulles's shoulder. He smells of pipe tobacco and something else familiar, some soap I recognize from the old days. I don't know whether it comes from his clothes or his skin or his hair or what. He smells like *them*, like the Families. How funny to sit in this big black sedan with my old pal Sumner Fox— with Allen Dulles, of all people, director of the CIA, whom I just told to butt out—making our way through the streets of Washington, talking about Olive Rainsford. To think I woke up this morning in Cato's bed and stared at an electric fan. Maybe I doze off a second or two, I don't know. There's been a lot of excitement. The car brakes and thuds to a stop. I open my eyes. "Are we here?" I ask.

Fox opens his door. "Yes."

It seems I left my watch behind at Cato's house. This is probably a manifestation of some subconscious urge but for the life of me I can't imagine what. I don't particularly want to see him again. I don't bear him any ill will, either. Or maybe a forgotten watch is just that, a watch you left on the bedside table because you were thinking about something else. Someone else.

Anyway, though I don't have the time, I suspect it's around five o'clock. Cocktail hour. I suspect this because I badly want a drink right now. Fox has taken my elbow and led me inside a squat gray concrete building to a lobby the exact color and smell of wet clay. A receptionist speaks quietly into a green telephone. Dulles stands a few feet away, sucking his pipe. I have the feeling he's watching me, though I won't give him the satisfaction of my attention. The receptionist hangs up the telephone and smiles at Dulles.

"They're ready for you, Mr. Dulles," she says. "Second floor."

There is no elevator. The gentlemen motion me up the stairs in front of them. When we reach the landing, I turn. "What is this, a prison?" I ask, in a hushed voice. "Is Olive here?"

"Not exactly a prison," says Dulles. "We'll brief you upstairs."

I continue up the next flight. The noise of our shoes clatters off the walls of the stairwell. I realize I'm still wearing my funeral suit of black gabardine, nipped at the waist, pearls at the throat. At the top of the stairs we head down a cramped hallway to a door at the end. A man in a dark suit stands by the door, hands crossed below. He nods to Dulles and stands aside to open the door for us. Inside, the room is more comfortable than you would expect. The walls are painted a soft shade of green. A wooden table separates four wooden chairs, two on each side. In the middle of the table sits a pitcher of water and a few glasses, plus an ashtray. Another small round table hides in the corner. There is a black telephone on this table, like the one you have at home, and a cigarette box. Dulles scrapes back one of the chairs and invites me into it.

"Cigarette?" he asks, when I'm seated. I nod yes and he fetches one for me from the box on the round table. Lights it for me with his own silver lighter. Fox pours water and hands me a glass. I inspect the feeble contents with disappointment.

"By the way," I say to him, "how long have you worked for the CIA?"

Fox sits in the chair across from me. It seems to me he moves stiffly, like certain joints pain him. "Not *for* the CIA. *With* the CIA. Since I returned home from a case overseas, a year and a half ago."

"The one in Russia?"

"Yes." He glances at Dulles. "I'm afraid I can't disclose the details."

"That's all right. I don't particularly care."

In the meantime, Dulles has taken the chair next to mine. His blue suit is so impeccably tailored, it could stand up on its own. He crosses one leg over the other and caresses his pipe, like a professor deep in study. "What we *can* tell you," he says, "is that this country owes a debt to Mr. Fox that it can never possibly repay."

"I don't doubt it. But what does that have to do with Olive Rainsford?"

Sumner Fox, who has not taken a cigarette, being the kind of man who harbors no vices, knits his fingers together on the table and leans forward. "In the course of this operation," he says, in that voice like an unpaved country road, "we left a man behind in the hands of the KGB, a man named Sasha Digby."

I snap my fingers. "Digby! Wait just a minute. Wasn't he that diplomat who disappeared a while back? With his wife and kids. Big story, all over the papers."

"You have a good memory, Miss Winthrop."

"I remember people were saying he'd defected, that he was some kind of Soviet spy, on the point of being arrested. And you're saying he was your man? All that time?"

"I'm afraid the Digby case remains classified, Miss Winthrop. All I can tell you is that since my return, I've spent considerable effort trying to track him down. At first, I was afraid he'd been executed. But six months ago I was able to establish his location inside a labor rehabilitation camp in eastern Siberia."

"Brrr," I say.

"Fox brought this information to my attention immediately," said Dulles. "And I told him there wasn't anything the CIA could do about it. The Soviets believed him to be what's called a double agent—you know the term?"

I nod.

"So you understand this wasn't a man the Soviets intended to release. However, they hadn't executed him, either. We don't know whether this was because he's an American citizen with an American wife, or for some inscrutable reason of their own. The Soviets play the game like a chess match, you see. Several moves ahead."

I reach for the ashtray and drag it close to my elbow. Dulles looks to Fox; Fox shrugs.

"I consulted with Mrs. Digby, who now lives in England," Fox says. "It was her wish we should do our utmost to bring him to safety."

"And it was my wish, too," says Dulles. "A man like that is a gold mine of information about the KGB, about the Soviet Union, everything that interests us. *If* he's willing to talk."

"Why wouldn't he be willing to talk?"

Dulles examines the bowl of his pipe and taps the spent ash into the tray at my elbow. He reaches into his pocket for a silver case. "I asked my brother to look into the matter. You know my brother—"

"The secretary of state? Not personally, I'm afraid."

Dulles smiles. "Just as well. I don't think you'd get along. Particularly after you've told him to—what was it?"

"Butt out?"

"Yes." He points the stem of his pipe at me and chuckles. "I'd like to see it, though. Don't you, Mr. Fox? John Foster and Miss Winthrop?"

Fox smiles faintly.

"In any case," Dulles continues, "my brother had little success through diplomatic channels. He did, however, share with me a hint that came through one of the cables. Would the United States perhaps consider releasing a prisoner of its own, a naturalized Soviet citizen known to authorities by the name of Olive Rainsford?"

I look back and forth between them. Dulles holds his silver lighter to the bowl of his pipe and sucks on the stem. Fox stares intently at me. The lamp above his head casts unflattering shadows over the bumps and scars of his face.

I speak slowly. "Are you saying they want to swap this—this agent of yours, this Soviet prisoner—for *Olive?*"

Dulles leans back in his chair. "Yes, my dear. That's exactly what they're proposing."

I wasn't in the courtroom when the judge formally sentenced Olive Rainsford to fifteen years in the federal penitentiary. I had other things on my mind, like midterm exams and the imminent birth of Lizbit. Like everyone else, I'd read about the verdict in the newspaper. Guilty on a single count of espionage under hire of a foreign power. The sight of that paragraph made my stomach churn so violently I had to fold the newspaper back up and take it out to the trash.

As chance would have it, this sentence was handed down the day that Lizbit was born, so I didn't hear about it until a few days later, when Sumner Fox himself telephoned to see how we were doing. I remember I happened to be holding her in my arms when he called. He was surprised to hear I hadn't kept up with the case and filled me in on the details. Because of the nature of Olive's crimes, she would serve her sentence in a maximum-security women's prison in Kansas somewhere. There was no possibility of escape, he assured me. We were safe, Lizbit and me and Susana.

After I hung up, I looked down at Lizbit's tiny red wadded-up face and thought, *She will be seven years old when Olive comes up for parole, imagine that.* The distant future.

Now the seven years have nearly come due. Dulles and Fox are both staring at me, waiting to see how I'll absorb this turn of events. I don't wish to disappoint them. I lift the cigarette to my lips and think it over. This astounding idea. Olive traded to the Soviet Union for one of ours. Like when you were a kid, trading baseball cards. I'll give you my rookie Rainsford for your World Series Digby. This man whose life was equivalent to Olive's life. I tell them I have a question.

"I imagine you have several," says Fox.

"Where do I come in? I mean, she's your prisoner. You can do whatever you want with her."

"Ah. Not quite," says Dulles. "After all, Mrs. Rainsford must also agree to the arrangement."

"Well, hasn't she? Or has she decided she'd rather live in a capitalist prison than a socialist paradise after all? Am I supposed to talk her into it or something?"

"Mrs. Rainsford has stated that she's willing to make the exchange, on principle," says Fox. "But not until she's spoken to you first."

"But what for? What can she possibly have to say to me, after all this time?"

Dulles nods to Fox, who sets his fingers on the table and levers himself to his feet. As his knees straighten, a wince flashes across his face, so quick you'd almost miss it. He walks to the corner of the room and I notice the limp now, the kind of limp you make when you're studying not to limp. He reaches for the telephone and starts dialing. Dulles turns to me.

"Mrs. Rainsford has a proposal for you, Miss Winthrop. You're not required to accept it, of course. But we fervently hope you will."

Fox speaks quietly into the telephone. The old sick panic takes hold of my chest. I stub out my cigarette and reach for the water glass.

"What kind of proposal?" I ask.

Fox replaces the receiver. The click sounds monstrous in the small room.

"Mrs. Rainsford will tell you herself in a moment," he says. "She's on her way up."

We held Mama's funeral five days later, on a Tuesday. Pop said there was no reason to wait, it wasn't as if we had people coming in from all over. Everybody who mourned Mama lived right here on Winthrop Island.

Those storms that had thundered through the island on the day of Mama's death dragged in some lovely weather behind them. The days had been clear and warm, the nights cool. When we emerged from St. Mary's after the service around four o'clock in the afternoon, the sun shone in our faces and made the harbor sparkle. Aunt Benedita kissed both my cheeks and said it was fitting that the sun shone on the day we buried my mother, because the sun had shone from her heart as well.

Aunt Benedita had been so helpful in the days since Mama's death, the same way she'd helped us out when we brought Mama back from the hospital in Boston. She'd brought soup and bread and her succulent almond *pão de ló.* She'd cleaned the dishes and changed all the sheets and washed the clothes, all those things that Mama would have done if she'd been alive, or able to do them. All week I'd sat at the kitchen table with a pot of coffee and answered the letters of condolence. Just about everybody on Winthrop Island had written to express their shock and sorrow, from Mrs. Dumont and Godfrey Finch and Mrs. Medeiro at the general store to Mrs. Collins and June Lindstrom and even the great and mighty Sumner Fox himself. I remember thinking his letter was kindly expressed but unremarkable, which made me wonder whether he was wasting his time on this writing kick of his. Tippy Pinkerton sent the loveliest note written on correct black-bordered stationery, pink with empathy. Anyway, as I sat there with my coffee and my rote sentences of appreciation, Aunt Benedita stood elbows-deep in soap suds at the kitchen sink, humming to herself as she worked. The tune was a sad one and she kept repeating the same line of melody in its melancholy minor key, over and over, until I wanted to scream. Sometimes I glanced over at her soft dumpling figure and the apron cinched around her waist. I thought about when we were little and Aunt Benedita sat with my mother at this very kitchen table, drinking coffee from this very pot, laughing and talking in rapid Portuguese. You wouldn't have known

Mama was the same quiet, soft-edged person she was in Pop's company, or with us, or the Peabodys. Aunt Benedita was slenderer back then. She was supposed to marry some lobsterman, I forget the fellow's name, but it never came off. When the rum-running work ran dry, so to speak, he decided lobstering didn't pay enough to keep him living on this godforsaken island the rest of his life, each day exactly like the one before, and he up and ran off with some mainlander girl to Boston or someplace. Anyway, that's what I heard.

After the service and the interment in the small, square cemetery behind the church, everybody got in their cars or climbed on their bicycles and went to Summerly for the reception. Mrs. Peabody had insisted on holding a reception for Mama at the main house. You'll be happy to know that she didn't expect me to serve cheese puffs to the guests. In fact, Mrs. Peabody herself bustled about, making sure the sandwiches and the salads didn't run out or the punch run dry. She brought out the best silver and laid all the food on shining trays in the giant drawing room that overlooked the ocean. That punch tureen was a thing to behold. It could have held a good-sized tire. Mrs. Peabody—or more probably Mary in the kitchen—had set a big block of ice in the middle and the punch lapped the sides all afternoon long. It was painted with delicate blue-and-white scenes and had come all the way from Holland, Amory once told me when we were kids, from the town of Delft, which his parents had visited on their honeymoon. They had bought the tureen from a factory there and had it shipped back. I'd joked that they could have rigged a sail and shipped themselves back in it. Amory didn't think this was funny but Shep just about dropped dead laughing.

Of all the people who loved Mama, and all the people who knew her, the only one missing today was Shep. By the time the Peabodys thought to send him a telegram, he was already on the train. He'd been racketing down the middle of some cornfield, probably, or the mountains or the prairie, and by the time word caught up with him, it was Monday and he had reached San Francisco. He'd cabled me as soon as he heard.

DEAREST CRICKET DEVASTATED TO HEAR AWFUL NEWS STOP WILL CATCH EARLIEST FLIGHT HOME TO PAY RESPECTS STOP ALL LOVE SHEP.

That was Monday, like I said, and today was Tuesday. We couldn't exactly delay the funeral for the arrival of Shep Peabody and nobody had suggested we should, least of all me. I wanted the whole thing over with. I wanted the soonest possible end to this period of freezing my face into the appropriate expression of bereavement while I accepted the sympathies of all these people who didn't understand a thing. Mrs. Collins, for example, who had kindly given me the whole week off from the library. She thought it was for the best, really. An end to Mama's suffering. Went peacefully in her sleep. What she would have wanted.

"You're so kind, Mrs. Collins," I replied. "It's such a comfort to know she's in a better place now."

It was Olive Rainsford who quietly replaced the cup of punch in my hand with something stronger and asked how I was doing—not how I was grieving, mind you, but how I was coping with everybody asking about my grief.

"I'm all right, thanks," I said, "but I hope they go home soon."

"Won't be long now. Edwina brought out the petit fours ten minutes ago."

"Thank God."

"And don't bother about coming to watch the kids the rest of this week. You can return when you're ready."

"I don't mind. Honestly, I'd appreciate the distraction." I sipped the drink she'd handed me—a gin and tonic with a slice of lime, easy on the tonic. "It's funny, she never said much—I mean, even before the stroke, she wasn't much of a talker, at least around Pop—but the house seems so quiet now, I want to scream."

Olive was about three or four inches taller than me, and she bent her head to speak in my ear in a confidential way. "Whenever you're ready, dear. You have your whole future ahead of you now. There's no need to rush."

I patted the side of my leg for a pocket that wasn't there. A reflexive dive for a cigarette, I guess. In the absence of tobacco I lifted the other arm and swished back gin and tonic to quench the guilt. Because I'd had the same thought, you see.

My future ahead of me.

Wretched, culpable thought. Every time it tickled the back of my head, every time it whispered in my ear—like now, like Olive—I had swatted it away.

That didn't mean it wasn't still there.

"Nobody's rushing anything," I said.

The guests left one by one, then all at once. I looked around and realized I hadn't seen Susana in some time. Poor Susana, eyes pink from crying. She was always the tender one, always the one who couldn't stand it when we wrung the necks of the chickens or sold the heifers. I found Pop in the library with Mr. Peabody, who was pouring him a drink from a bottle of what looked like a tremendously old Scotch, reserved for special occasions like the death of somebody's wife.

"Where's Susana?" I asked.

Pop looked surprised, as if I'd asked him to knit me a pair of socks. He was wearing the stiff black suit he'd acquired for his wedding and the dark tie he'd acquired for Eli's funeral. I had cleaned and starched his white shirt myself, that very morning. The clothes made him look like a stumpy, crag-faced mannequin. "I haven't seen her," he said.

"Wasn't she out on the terrace?" said Mr. Peabody. "I'm sure I saw her out on the terrace, not long ago."

"Was anybody with her?"

"I'm afraid I don't recall. Can I pour you a drink?"

"No, thank you, Mr. Peabody. I appreciate all you've done. This was just lovely."

Mr. Peabody set the bottle back on its tray and took some time to arrange it among the other bottles, labels facing just so. "It was our pleasure, Cricket. Your mother was like family to us."

I fixed my gaze on Mr. Peabody's slender fingers, arranging the bottles of liquor until there was no possible further improvement. My nerves were so sharp, I heard the clink of glass. I smelled the Scotch in Pop's glass. "I'm sure the feeling was mutual," I said.

"Shep—" Mr. Peabody cleared his throat. "Shep wanted me to tell you he's sorry he was delayed and couldn't be present today."

"Oh, is Shep on his way?" I asked innocently.

"Yes, by air. He sent us a telegram from Buffalo. The airplane had to stop over because of weather. He should be home by tomorrow, I understand. He seems keen to pay his respects."

Mr. Peabody had turned his gaze to stare at my face when he said this. He had soft hazel eyes like Shep, or like some dogs you might know—all trust and feeling. Exactly *what* Mr. Peabody was feeling, I didn't have the foggiest. Somewhere to my left, Pop jiggled the ice in his Scotch. I guess he hadn't had the nerve to tell Mr. Peabody he didn't drink his whiskey on the rocks.

"That's very kind of him," I said. "He didn't need to take all that trouble, really. Fly all the way back across the country when he'd only just reached California."

"He's a good boy," said Mr. Peabody. "He looked on her as a second mother, I think."

We couldn't find Susana anywhere. Pop said maybe she wanted to be alone. Aunt Benedita shook her head and said no, she had probably gone off with her friends. Friends were so important to a girl her age. She'd turn up by suppertime.

We went home and Aunt Benedita heated up some soup. I couldn't stand to be in the room with her so I went upstairs and changed out of my best dress and my stockings to lie on the bed in my slip. The sun was low in the sky outside the window and the light was turning gold. I listened to the creaking house and the undertone of voices in the kitchen, where Pop had joined Aunt Benedita. Everything seemed distant, like it was happening in another dimension. Underneath me, a quilt spread across the bed. This quilt, I had been told, was stitched by Pop's mother when she was a child, because back then girls passed the long winter hours stitching quilts to cover the beds when they were married. It was made of pieces of red flannel and white flannel arranged in a geometric pattern. Over the years the red had faded to a rusty pink thanks to the sun streaming through the window onto the bed. If I closed my eyes I could imagine my grandmother's little hand working the pieces of flannel. I could almost feel the electricity of her flesh quivering beneath mine. She had died when Pop was about eight or nine, while giving birth to a baby that also died. According to Pop, when Grandmother went into labor, the island's only doctor was visiting friends on the mainland and by the time they got word to him, a gale had kicked up and it was too dark and too dangerous to cross the water. When he reached Grandmother's bedside the next day, she was dead and so was her baby. She left behind Pop and Uncle Pete and Grandfather and these quilts, under which we still slept.

I woke to the sound of rain hurling on the window. The sky was dark and the voices in the kitchen had gone quiet. The rain came in bursts, like bunches of gravel thrown against the glass. Then I listened some more and realized it *was* gravel.

I swung my legs over the side of the bed and staggered to the window. I couldn't see anything outside. I shoved the sash upward and poked my head out. A large, stocky figure stood below. The moonlight cradled his face.

"Shep! Is that you?"

"Cricket," he said. His arms hung down by his sides.

"I'll be right down," I said.

I almost forgot to put a dress on. Imagine that, me running outside in my slip and nothing else. My best dress had too many buttons so I threw on an old yellow housedress instead and hurried downstairs. All the lights were out. By the height of the moon I must have slept for hours. Out the kitchen door I flew.

Shep came around the corner of the house and we met where Mama's rosebushes tickled the bricks of the kitchen yard. He lifted me right off my feet. I couldn't breathe but I didn't care. He smelled of wool and stale cigarettes and his jaw rasped against the side of my head. I'm so sorry, he said. Cricket, Cricket. I'm so sorry.

Sorry for what? I gasped.

I shouldn't have left, he said.

His arms loosened and a cry scratched my throat. Without the grip of those arms I felt like I had no skin. I would rather not breathe at all than breathe outside of Shep. I was still half asleep, I guess, and not making sense.

What's the matter, honey? he said, stroking my hair. What do you want?

I said, Just get me away from here.

I have this scene in my head still. I am bicycling down West Cliff Road with Shep Peabody in the middle of the night. The damp salt air blows in my face. Ahead, Shep's pale blue shirt guides me through the dark. Every so often he looks over his shoulder to make sure I'm still there. His face catches the moonlight and the shape of his silvery nose and chin makes my heart rip underneath my ribs. In my head, the scene goes on forever. The shadows of the houses pass by without end. Shep is always there, pedaling his bicycle a yard ahead of me, just out of reach.

We cycled all the way down to the main harbor and veered left, toward the airfield and the dunes behind it where the old bunkers were dug into the slopes of the hills. At the far edge of the airfield, Shep stopped his bicycle. I coasted to a halt next to him. He dismounted and set his bicycle against the side of the hill and set my bicycle against his. When he took my hand to lead me up the path it was the most natural thing in the world.

I thought I knew this corner of the island like I knew my own bedroom. Hadn't I spent hours exploring the dunes and the bunkers with Shep and Amory and Eli? Hadn't we tumbled to rest in the sand on this remote stretch of beach where nobody else came to bother us? It was our territory, the territory of our childhood, but when I climbed up the dark hill with Shep that night, I felt that I was crossing the threshold of a new world. Nothing looked the same. The moon was cool and bright above our heads. The tide rushed gently up the sand. Shep found us a spot against the dunes and pulled me down to sit with him. I burrowed into his side like a barnacle. I have heard scientists talk about the physical comfort of human touch and whenever I consider this phenomenon I think about how I cleaved myself to Shep that night, how the bulk and the warmth of him brimmed over my bones like some kind of liquor, so that you wanted more and more, you couldn't get enough, you wanted to stay drunk like this for the rest of your life and never feel pain again. Probably any animal body would have had the same effect. But Shep's animal body was the one that lay against mine that night.

We didn't speak at first. There was something so new and intimate in the mood between us, I couldn't risk shattering it with words so we'd have to start all over again. The moon crept across the black sky. Shep's arm held me snug. His shoulder cradled my head. I asked if I could tell him something.

Sure, he said.

"The day Mama died, I saw Pop with my aunt Benedita. I mean *with* her. You know."

Shep took some time to consider this. "Where?" he asked.

"The old Wright cottage, near Little Bay. He's supposed to be fixing it up. They were alone together in the bedroom. I saw his truck so I went in to talk to him. I was—I was mad about something. And I heard a woman's voice so I peeked through the door and Aunt

Benedita was lying on the bed. Naked. I didn't see him but I could hear him."

"The day your mother died, you said?"

"That afternoon. He was crying. That's what I heard, I heard him crying. I didn't know she was dead. I thought he was crying because he felt guilty, doing that with Aunt Benedita."

"You're saying you think he knew she was dead already?"

"I don't know." My voice choked. "I don't know. It's been torturing me. And I couldn't say a word to anyone, nobody knows I was there, Pop and Aunt Benedita have no idea I saw them together—"

"Oh, Cricket." He circled his other arm around me. "Oh, Cricket."

There was nothing in the world but the thump of Shep's heart. It was like being in a womb—no light, no air, just warm human flesh and heartbeat. I had to turn my head to the side so I could speak.

"How could he do it? How could he do that with Aunt Benedita? Her own sister? When he loved her so much? You *know* how much he loved her, Shep. He didn't talk much but you could see it. Remember that story he used to tell about how they met?"

"I remember."

"So how could he do it? With another woman?"

"Honey, people do it all the time. When the person you love is—is gone."

"She wasn't gone. Mama was still there, she was alive, she was the same person."

"Cricket."

"Don't you dare say it was all right. Don't you dare say that he was right."

"I'm not saying it was right. I'm saying we're all human, aren't we? Everyone's got something to bear on his back. Sometimes we break."

"Even you?" I asked.

"Cricket, I said before. I'm no hero."

My hand lay flat on his chest. He moved his arm so that his pinky finger brushed my pinky finger and then somehow we were holding hands, my hand tucked into the palm of his hand. I liked how we talked to each other in the dark like this. It was like talking to yourself.

"I guess that's not what you wanted to hear," he said.

"No, you're right. We all do things we wish we hadn't."

"You want to be mad at him. You should be mad at him."

"I'm not mad."

"You're mad as hell, Cricket."

"All right, sure. I'm mad."

"And now you're mad at me."

"I'm mad at everything. I'm mad at myself."

"At yourself? Why?"

"Because I'm a coward," I said.

With his thumb he fiddled the backs of my fingers. *Ker-thud*, went his heart in my ear, through his muscle and bone, skin and shirt. *Ker-thud*. Measured and slow. I was afraid each beat was the last one of all. "Cricket, honey," he said, "what's happened has happened, that's all. You have to find a way to live with it."

"Says the fellow who's running off to California."

Maybe he didn't hear me. My voice was very soft when I said this—I almost couldn't hear myself. If I shut my eyes we might have been floating somewhere together, Shep and me. In a blue-and-white punch tureen in the middle of the ocean in the middle of the night. A thought came to me.

"How did you get back so soon, anyway? Your father said you were stuck in Buffalo. He said you'd be home tomorrow."

"Oh. Well, I caught the train. Rolled into South Station a few hours ago, then I talked a buddy of mine into letting me use his motorboat."

"His motorboat? At night?"

"I didn't want to wait around. I had to see you."

"You didn't miss me, did you? Your old pal Cricket?"

He squeezed my hand. "Not so much, I guess. Only as much as you miss your own heart when somebody rips it out of your chest."

"Ouch," I said.

"I'll say," he said.

"Then why'd you leave in the first place? Why didn't you say something?"

"Because I'm used to missing you, Cricket. That's all I've done my whole life. All autumn and all winter, every year I can remember. Every minute I have ever been away from you."

I lifted my head to rest my chin on his sternum. "That's the truth?"

"That's God's honest truth. The only truth I know."

I remember I stared at his mouth. Shep's mouth. I'd never studied it before, I couldn't even have said what kind of lips he had, thick or thin. It turned out the bottom lip was round but the top lip was a straight, narrow line. I kissed the bottom lip first, then I pushed myself a little higher and kissed his whole mouth.

When the first gray streaks appeared in the eastern sky, Shep kissed me awake. I hadn't slept much for the past five days and I was so groggy I had to cling to his hand as we stumbled over the dunes to our bicycles.

We pedaled back slowly while a damp pink dawn overtook the horizon. Get some sleep, he said to me as we clung together next to the kitchen door, but he didn't let me go. It was too awful to contemplate, letting go of each other. What if we never found our way back?

Finally he drew away a few inches. He rested his forehead against mine and told me he'd promised his buddy he'd return the borrowed boat back to Plymouth Harbor today but he would come back. I'll be back by evening, Cricket, he'd said. Evening seemed like an impossible distance but I nodded and lifted my mouth so we could kiss goodbye. We had done a lot of kissing in the past few hours but that was our first goodbye kiss, long and hard, and it hurt so much that when he let me go I ran into the kitchen and shut the door hard behind me. I crept up the stairs to my room, avoiding all the squeaky floorboards, and took off my clothes so that when I lay in bed, window propped open to cool the air, I felt the sheets against my bare skin and imagined they were Shep's hands, touching every inch of me.

Ever since that War Department telegram arrived like a torpedo to blow my life apart, I had been tethered to the care of my mother. I had sometimes strained against that rope but I couldn't imagine existing without it—the structure of the hours, the daily tedium, the tasks that must be performed, over and over, into infinity. Now my life had blown apart again, my earth had groaned on its axis, except that this time, when I opened my eyes to the midmorning sun, I had nobody to take care of except myself.

The house lay quiet. By now Pop would have finished his chores and left to work. I crawled out of bed and shrugged my worn dressing gown over my shoulders. I went to the window. On the other side of the hedge, Summerly dozed in the sun, each white point catching the glare. I couldn't see Shep's bedroom from this angle but I knew it was empty. Over in the rose garden I saw Mrs. Peabody's straw hat bob from bush to bush, clipping flowers to fill the Summerly vases. I stepped away from the window and tiptoed to the bathroom to draw a bath. Along the way I peeked into Susana's room. She lay on her stomach, arms and legs splayed like a starfish. Because her window faced west, the room was dusky, but I could make out her clothes scattered over the furniture and the rug. I breathed out a sigh of relief and closed the door so I wouldn't disturb her with the noise of my washing.

When I was clean and dressed, I went downstairs and poured myself the cold dregs of the coffee. I made some toast and stared at the merry pink-cheeked apples dancing across a yellow field of wallpaper, chosen during the house's redecoration because—I can only assume—it suited the older Mrs. Peabody's ideas of a New England country vernacular. I should have been exhausted but I was awake in every nerve. I was so alive I wanted to sing, even though I was supposed to be grieving. I wanted to dance. I wanted to live! I stared at the apple-strewn wallpaper but in my head I was searching each memory of the night before for some new detail to add to my cup of joy. When I came to the instant Shep's hand lay flat against the small of my back, I closed my eyes. His heavy, gentle hand like a magnet. Yes, that was it. If I felt nothing else the rest of my life, I had felt that. I had felt his hand on the small of my back, I had felt the weight of his arms around me as he kissed me goodbye. I couldn't recall the exact instant I had ripped my skin from his but I had done it. Somehow I had run inside and shut the door behind me. In my head I heard the slam of that door over and over so it took me a moment or two to realize that the noise now coming from the kitchen door was real—a couple of sharp knocks, repeated at intervals. I swallowed back the rest of the cold coffee and rose. My heart went *bam-bam*. My fingers shook. I hurried across the kitchen floor and threw the door open.

"There you are!" exclaimed June Lindstrom, cute as a button in a dress of sunflower yellow and white

lace-up oxford shoes. Her lipstick was the color of geraniums. "I hope I didn't wake you up?"

"Why, no. Is something wrong?"

"Wrong?" She laughed. "Goodness, no. I just came
by to see if you'd go out on the water with me today.
And I won't take no for an answer."

"Sailing? I didn't know you could sail."

"I can't." She leaned forward. "Somebody's asked
me out on his motorboat and I have a feeling I'll need a
chaperone."

"Who?"

June put a single scarlet-tipped finger against her
lips. "I'm not telling. Not unless you come with me."

"That's not fair."

"All's fair in love and boats."

"I think you mean war," I said. "Love and war."

She reached for my arm and pulled me out the door.
"Oh, just come along. You have to pass the time somehow, don't you?"

To my surprise, June Lindstrom had a car—a nifty
Lincoln-Zephyr convertible, about the same sunflower
color as her dress. I'd seen it parked at the Club and
figured it belonged to one of the Families. Somebody's
spoiled son. June aimed it around the curves of West
Cliff Road in a way that made me think she did a lot

of driving back home in Minnesota. When I told her so she laughed and patted the curving dash.

"We've had some good times, Ginger and me. Daddy let me drive her out here for the summer. Isn't she a doll?"

"If you like them fast, I guess."

Immediately she let up on the gas. "Oh, I'm sorry! I didn't mean to scare you. I'm used to our nice straight Midwestern roads."

"No, I like it. Fun."

"Well, that's it, isn't it? I sort of thought you could use a little fun right now." She shifted gears and sent me a quick, graceful glance. "When my mother died, everybody was scared to speak to me. Like it was contagious or something. I sat all by myself for a couple of weeks before a friend of mine finally got up the nerve to take me out for a laugh. Did me a world of good."

"I didn't know you lost your mother."

"When I was fifteen. It was awful. Pneumonia. You know how cold it gets in Minnesota during the winter. She had a bad case of flu and it went to her lungs."

"I'm sorry."

"Anyway, I said to myself, *That poor girl, she needs someone to take her out for a laugh.* And I've been hoping to make better friends with you anyway. I was awfully low when you quit waiting tables."

"You mean you haven't hit it off with my sister?"

"Your *sister*," June said, "seems to have other things on her mind."

I looked out the window. We were about to pass the guardhouse at the entrance to the private association and June slowed the car to wave at the guard. She had put on a pair of dark sunglasses with tortoiseshell frames and they made her look like a film star. When we turned right onto Spinnaker Lane toward Little Bay, I angled my head to examine the sharp tip of her nose and the sly little smile at the corner of her mouth.

"So tell me about this friend of yours," I said. "Is he one of the summer caddies?"

"God, no. They're such infants. I like them a little older."

"How much older?"

"That depends on the boy. This one's a real man. A soldier."

"Do I know him?"

"Of course you know him, Cricket. You know everybody. It's really remarkable. Everywhere I go, people have an opinion about you."

"They don't."

"They do." She removed one hand from the steering wheel and rummaged in the pocketbook at her side. "Aren't you going to ask me what it is?"

"Only if you mean to tell me."

"Oh, it's no secret." With that one nimble hand she extracted a cigarette from a pack or possibly a case—all of a sudden she seemed like the type to own a cigarette case with her initials engraved on the front—and lit the end from a silver lighter exactly like the one Amory Peabody used. "Most people—the locals, anyway—think you're a snob."

"A snob?"

"Let's see. Emilia Winthrop thinks she's too smart for us. She thinks she's too clever and too pretty and too high-class for the nice folks of Winthrop Island, even though she's lived here all her life. Likes to brag about all the books she's read and the history she knows and especially about how the Winthrops were the first settlers on the island. Keeps to herself and only makes friends with the summer crowd." June turned her head and blew smoke into the slipstream. "With the Peabodys."

"That's ridiculous."

"That's what people told me. I said to myself, *She sounds like my kind of girl.* Oops, here we are!"

I was so busy working myself into a high state of indignation, I hadn't even noticed the turn onto Little Bay Road. June heeled left in a shriek of rubber. I grabbed the door handle and dug the balls of my feet into the floorboards. The clear, pleasant weather of the past few days had given way to a dull warmth, and the harbor smell hung in the air, salt and fish and gasoline. June squealed to a stop next to the marine store building and set the brake. She turned to me, grinning, and took off her sunglasses. I hadn't much noticed her eyes before but here in the glare of the hazy sun I saw they were a remarkable sparkling blue.

"What are you waiting for?" she said. "An engraved invitation?"

For a girl who was just one of the summer help, June seemed to know her way around the marina. Full of surprises, June Lindstrom. I had to skip to keep up with her purposeful, long-legged stride. She turned down one of the docks and marched toward the slip at the end, where a Gar Wood runabout bobbed on its rope. Near the stern a man in a striped knit shirt and ivory pants bent over the engine. He must have spotted us from the side of his gaze because he straightened and waved one heavy arm and called out a greeting. When he stepped onto the dock, I saw his stocky build and cragged face. I stopped short in disbelief. June took his outstretched hand and leaped into the boat.

"Good morning, Mr. Fox," she said. "You see? I

warned you I'd bring a chaperone. This is Miss Emilia Winthrop, although from the looks of it I'd guess you've met already."

Sumner Fox turned to me and held out his hand. "Miss Winthrop," he said gravely. "Welcome aboard."

For the first half hour or so I stretched out on the rear seat and let the two of them chatter up front. I didn't know much about motorboats anyway. The runabout had a big, throaty engine that chugged irritably at the slow journey out of Little Bay. Once we left the harbor Fox let the throttle go and pretty soon we were cruising along in open water to a thunderous draft. I heard the two of them conspiring together and closed my eyes. The spray flew over my hair. The sun was just warm enough. June called out to ask whether I wanted a bottle of lemonade.

I sat up and turned to face them. "Sure."

June handed me the bottle and I eyed them both as I drank. Sumner sat at the wheel, one hand gripping the top. He wore a straw boater that shaded his face but the glare still emphasized the ridges of his face and the way his nose angled a hair or two to one side. In spite of his stocky frame there was something a little spare about him, a little starved. It came to me that maybe he'd had a tough war. Hadn't June said he was a soldier? He'd never mentioned fighting but that usually meant it was too awful to talk about. His eyes squinted at the water ahead, but I knew he was looking at me, too. Sizing me up. I set the bottle in my lap and asked if there was anything to eat. Fox looked at June and eased back the throttle. Our momentum ebbed away until we just edged across the water. June ducked into the cabin and emerged almost immediately with a picnic basket, from which she took three sandwiches wrapped in paper and handed one to me. In all this time nobody said a word. I unwrapped my sandwich.

"Chicken salad all right for you?" said June.

"How'd you know it was chicken salad?" I said.

She looked at Fox, who nodded his head. She looked back at me and pushed her sunglasses on top of her head.

"Come sit over here," she said, patting the leather next to her.

"I'll stay here, if you don't mind."

Again the two of them exchanged a look. Fox shrugged his wide, spare shoulders. June settled back with her sandwich and said, "I suppose you've realized by now that I haven't just asked you to join me on an innocent afternoon cruise."

"If you're going to murder me, I hope you'll allow me to finish my sandwich first."

Fox cracked a smile. "Naturally."

"Certainly we're not going to *murder* you," June said, turning brusque, "but the situation isn't without some danger, to be perfectly frank."

I ripped off a large bite of chicken salad sandwich and chewed it thoroughly. "What kind of danger?"

June glanced at Fox. The water slapped the sides of the boat. Fox studied some object past my left ear— Block Island, possibly, which lay behind me at approximately that point on the compass. We used to sail to Block Island all the time when we were teenagers, me and Shep and Amory and Eli. You might have said it was a rite of passage. On Block Island nobody knew us. We could stretch out on the beach in our swimsuits and eat ice cream and wander through town and play pranks without danger of running into our parents or their friends, who had grown up in another time. True, you had to watch your tides. You had to glide out with the tide and back in with the tide, because the stretch of water between Block Island and Winthrop Island funneled right from the Atlantic Ocean into Long Island Sound and the resulting current was like a running river in certain places, especially during spring tides when the moon was full. That was how Shep and I got stuck on Block Island overnight one time, but that's another story. The point is, between the tidal current and the constant run of ferries and fishing boats and sporting yachts, these waters can turn pretty treacherous, and it occurred to me that Sumner Fox, not being native and possibly not even a natural-born sailor, might be ignorant of that fact.

Still, I had to admit he handled the wheel with the right kind of unconscious grace. He squinted over the glinting water like a man concentrating on its whims. His mandible jutted at a stubborn angle, which was as necessary to sailors as to soldiers. Above the wheel, the muscles of his forearm flexed. He turned his face to me.

"Miss Winthrop," he said, "perhaps you could start things off by telling us a little more about your friendship with Olive Rainsford."

It was a stupid thing, that night I spent with Shep Peabody on Block Island. The four of us were supposed to go out sailing that afternoon but Amory decided to play tennis instead—mixed doubles alongside one of the Dumont girls, the prettier one. Once Amory dropped out, Eli decided he'd rather make a dollar or two caddying that afternoon. *Anyway,* he said, peering at the sky, *I'll bet a gale kicks up around five o'clock.*

Shep and I rolled our eyes at each other—Eli was

always predicting five o'clock gales. Like a stopped clock, he was sometimes right. But the sky was perfectly blue, perfectly hot, not a single cloud anywhere you looked. And I was mad at Amory for picking tennis with Mimi Dumont over a sailing date with yours truly. I thought I'd show him how much I cared. Shep and I cast off around one o'clock. It was July and there was plenty of time to sail out to Block Island and return before sundown on the incoming tide. We horsed around a little. We were young and full of beans, and Shep had grown taller and broader over the previous winter and was beginning to lose some of his baby fat. I suppose, looking back, I was aware of this transformation on some subconscious level—that Shep was growing out of his soft, shaggy puppyhood and into something a girl might covet, though I certainly didn't realize it out loud. Anyway, we were heeling into harbor, horsing around with each other, wind filling the spinnaker from the southwest quarter, when I happened to get this electric sizzle on the back of my neck just before a mighty gust of cool, damp air swirled in from the northeast. The boom swung, the spinnaker flapped, the boat nearly capsized. By the time we got her right again, the squall had overtaken us. I won't go into the details, but we just managed to skim clear of the lee shore and out to sea. Once the squall passed, we brought her around and limped into this cove on the eastern shore. The sky was darkening and we'd missed the tide, so we figured we'd just hunker down and wait until sunrise to sail back to Winthrop. In the ignorance of youth, we never imagined the folks back home might worry. We pictured them at dinner, at bridge, at cocktails, passed out cold with sleeping pills. We just hoped we could sneak home early enough tomorrow morning that we wouldn't be missed. Shep got some blankets out of the deckhouse and we made a kind of nest in the sand and dropped off to sleep like puppies. Around dawn somebody prodded us awake. It was a policeman. And while you know this story ended happily, other than the fact that Amory Peabody first took notice of me only after I spent the night with his brother, I will never forget that harrowing hour in the police station on Block Island. They thought we were criminals, you see. Apparently a pair of burglars had been terrorizing the wealthy enclaves of the Eastern Seaboard all summer and the Block Island police thought we were Bonnie and Clyde or something. They put us in separate rooms and interrogated us. I could hear Shep shouting through the walls that they had better release us this minute, that if a single hair on that girl's head was hurt he would personally knock the lights out of the fellow who did it. Until somebody finally called over with the news that two kids from Winthrop Island had been reported missing at sea the night before, that sergeant thought he'd finally hooked the whale of his career, and he wasn't going to let us get away.

So I have some experience with that moment when you realize that shadow casting over you is the shadow of the law. That the question laid before you, ever so innocently phrased, is a trap. We were surrounded by open water, not a lawyer in sight. That bitch June Lindstrom, she'd played me like a round of golf.

I set the chicken salad sandwich in my lap and wrapped it back in its paper. There was too much celery anyway. "Who wants to know?" I asked, brushing the crumbs from my fingers.

"The Federal Bureau of Investigation, Miss Winthrop. Counterintelligence division."

"Counterintelligence?" I sputtered. "You mean *spies*?"

"Yes."

"*Olive?*"

"Yes," he said.

I started to laugh. "Boy, are you barking up the wrong tree. Olive Rainsford is a housewife. Well, a housewidow, to be exact. She's a mother of three children who translates documents for a living. She bakes sponge cakes, for God's sake."

"She's also operating an illegal radio set from her attic, transmitting information of the most sensitive nature in a cipher known to be employed by the military intelligence service of the Soviet Union."

I stared at Fox's striped shirt, his casual hand on the wheel, his expressionless face, his nose tilted a couple of hairs to one side. I turned to take in June's dark sunglasses, her geranium lips, her hair ruffled by the wind. I unwrapped my sandwich again and stuffed it in my mouth, celery and all. "Sure, and I'm the Queen of Sheba," I said, around the sandwich.

"I'm sorry," said June. "I realize this is a shock. And I ought to apologize for the way I brought you out here today. It's just that we thought it best to conduct this interview where there wasn't the slightest chance of anybody overhearing us. As you know better than anybody, Winthrop Island is what you might call an insular environment. Everybody protects each other. Outsiders like us are looked on with a certain amount of suspicion."

"I can't imagine why."

June hopped from her seat and reached for her pocketbook. I thought she was hunting for a cigarette—at least, I hoped she was hunting for a cigarette and not something more fearsome—but instead she pulled out a leather wallet, which she unfolded to display a thing that looked like a badge. Well, it *was* a badge. I pretended to inspect it carefully. My hand clenched the remains of my sandwich. My insides had turned to porridge. I turned my gaze to June and saw my own face reflected in each of her dark lenses. My eyes were twice as big as they should have been. I hoped to God I didn't look that scared in reality.

"I didn't know the FBI hired girls," I said.

"They don't, as a rule. Fox insisted." She stuck the wallet back in her pocketbook and returned to her seat. "I don't suppose the name Gouzenko rings a bell, does it? Igor Gouzenko?"

"Not even a chime. Should it?"

"Only if you've been reading the papers closely. Last September, a Russian clerk inside the Soviet Embassy in Ottawa decided he wanted to defect to the West. He went to the police with a stack of classified information that revealed the existence of extensive Soviet espionage networks within Canada and the United States."

"A couple of months later," said Fox, "a woman named Elizabeth Bentley walked into an FBI field office in New Haven, Connecticut, and revealed the existence of two more Soviet espionage networks operating in the United States, turning over the kind of intelligence that would make your eyes burn."

I looked at Fox and back to June. "You're saying the Soviets have been spying on us?"

"In February, the Canadian government indicted twenty-two Communist agents," she said. "Trials to take place over the coming months. There are hundreds more names we're still investigating."

"I don't understand. The Soviets are our allies."

Fox answered, "We threw in our lot with the Soviet Union in order to defeat a common enemy, Miss Winthrop. Now that the war's over, I don't think I'd characterize the Soviets as our allies at all. For one thing, some would say Stalin's as bad a thug as Hitler ever was. Between the famines, the purges, the gulag, he's probably responsible for just as many deaths, if not more."

"But we knew all that going in. Didn't we?"

"Of course we did," said June, "which is why a lot of our military intelligence was kept strictly classified between the Western Allies—the United States, Great Britain, Canada. The trouble was, a lot of people involved in the war effort didn't exactly view things the same way. They'd swallowed the Marxist gospel hook, line, and sinker. They saw what they wanted to see. And they thought it was an outrage that the Western nations were keeping information secret from our Soviet allies."

"That's terrible," I said. "But if you're trying to tell

me Olive Rainsford is one of those Communists, I can tell you right now you're wasting your time. She hardly says a word about politics, for one thing."

"Well, she wouldn't, would she?" June said.

"Besides, she was in England for most of the war. She lived in a house outside of London. She only moved back here in the spring. How's she supposed to be gathering classified information in the United States?"

"She isn't out in the field, gathering information," said June. "But she operates a radio transmitter somewhere inside the Peabody estate on Winthrop Island, which she uses to communicate coded messages to Soviet receivers offshore. Probably from the cottage itself."

"That's ridiculous. A radio transmitter? I've never seen a radio in that house."

"I assure you it's there," said Fox. "We've located the signal. She transmits twice a week, at ten minutes past eleven o'clock, for twelve minutes at a time."

"It might be anything. All kinds of people use radio transmitters. Anyway, how do you know what kind of information it is when it's in code?"

"We don't," said Fox. "That's the trouble. We think we know what it is, but we can't prove it."

I threw up my hands. "You see? It might be anything. I'm telling you, you're barking up the wrong tree. Anyway, what makes you think Olive Rainsford is behind all this? It might be anybody. Mr. Peabody's always been a tinkerer. I'll bet he likes to fool around with radios. Amory Peabody, he was involved in all kinds of things during the war. Olive is the last person to go involving herself with radio sets. She's a translator, she's got three kids. She doesn't have the *time*!"

I said these last words in a fury. I really was mad. The reason I was mad is because a tiny, doubtful lobe at the back of my brain considered that maybe they had a point, that Olive Rainsford was a damn clever woman with a lot of mysterious characters in her past, a lot of places she had lived and ideas she had harbored and roles she had played, and maybe the role of Soviet intelligence agent was one of them. I mean, naturally the whole idea was ridiculous. Of course it was! But nothing makes you madder than when somebody offers you some nugget of truth you don't want to admit.

Fox was smart enough not to tell me to calm down. That would've been the last straw. Instead he turned to June. "Can you take her for a minute?" he said.

At first I thought he meant me, but June hopped up from her seat and took the wheel from his hand. Fox ducked into the cabin. June tilted her head so she was looking away to the east, toward the tip of Long Island. Her hand was light on the wheel and to my mind didn't look as if it belonged there at all, with those elegant fingers and the immaculate scarlet lacquer coloring the tips. The sun was above our heads now and the sky was growing hazier, the breeze dying. We ambled slowly across the water. Fox emerged from the cabin, carrying a brown envelope. I thought I saw him wince as he straightened. He handed me the envelope and June rose to give him her place at the wheel.

"What's this?" I said.

"I don't know what Mrs. Rainsford has told you about herself," said Fox, "but we've been able to piece together a few facts from our counterparts in Britain, where she's been under surveillance for some time."

I examined the envelope in my lap. It bore no markings of any kind, just a plain envelope like you see in offices, like the one I filled with old documents about the Great Snow of 1717 and handed to Sumner Fox a week or so ago. "Why was she under surveillance?" I asked, in a voice as tiny and bewildered as I felt.

He answered me in a warm, sympathetic voice. "She's a remarkable woman, Olive Rainsford. I expect you know that already. Left her Swiss finishing school in the spring of 1930 and moved to Berlin, where she fell in with an intellectual crowd that happened to be firmly committed to Marxist ideology. Married her first husband a year later. Twenty years older, almost twice her age, a professor of political science."

"You mean Grossmeyer," I said.

"That's right. Oskar Grossmeyer. They moved to Shanghai in 1933, after the Nazis took power. We believe that's where she became radicalized. There was an active ring of Soviet agents in Shanghai during those years, providing support to the Chinese Communists, who were brutally repressed by the government. Dangerous work. Led by a man named Richard Sorge, a known agent of the GRU—that's the Soviet military intelligence—who happened to be a friend of the Grossmeyers. We suspect he recruited Mrs. Rainsford."

"How do you know this?" I snapped.

Fox shrugged. "The ring was eventually cracked. British intelligence was able to figure out who was involved, based on known associations and the like."

"Maybe it wasn't her," I said. "Maybe it was her husband. Grossmeyer. He was the Communist, right?"

"They were both Communists, Miss Winthrop. And this seems to be one of those cases in which the pupil is more devout than the teacher. Grossmeyer might have subscribed to Marxist theory, but he was no admirer of the Soviet Union. Too many friends caught up in the purges. He wasn't blinded by his faith, you might say. But his wife—well, you know how it is when you're young. You want to believe in something. You don't want doubt, you want answers. You want black and white. You want a system of thought that explains everything, some universal truth that gives your life meaning and purpose. Something you can fight for. Anyway, Olive Grossmeyer found her crusade in Soviet Communism, and nothing was going to stop her from fighting for it. Certainly not her husband."

I heard Olive's voice in my head—*Our minds traveled in opposite directions.*

"All right," I said, "maybe she did have Communist sympathies. I mean, a lot of people did, right? But she must have outgrown them. We've never once discussed politics. She's no radical. She's not even a dabbler. All she cares about are her kids."

"In the spring of 1937," Fox continued, as if he didn't hear me, "the Grossmeyers returned to Europe. To Switzerland—they didn't want to live in Germany anymore. Mrs. Grossmeyer gave birth to her first child in a hospital in Zurich. By that point her husband was alarmed about the direction of Nazi politics. Got involved with a ring of what you might call internationalist Germans who opposed Hitler. His wife, on the other hand, left her husband and baby in Zurich and lived in Russia for five months. Her story was she was studying Russian literature at Moscow State University. In fact, we suspect she underwent an intense training program with the GRU designed first of all to confirm her loyalty to the Soviet Union, and second of all to learn advanced espionage techniques."

I stood up. "I'm not going to listen to this. It's just impossible. If you met Olive, if you *knew* her—"

"For God's sake," said June, "what do you think? She's going to walk around wearing a sign from her neck? Of *course* she's going to make everybody think she's just a dumb housewife with her kids and her sponge cakes. It's the perfect cover."

Fox went on in the same comforting baritone. "While in Moscow, she met another GRU agent, also there for advanced training. A Lithuanian."

A wave rocked the boat. I came down hard on the seat. "That's not true. She met him in Switzerland. I'm sure she said she met him in Switzerland."

"They met in Moscow, Miss Winthrop. He was from Vilnius, the son of a dockworker. They fell in love. After finishing the training course, they were posted to Switzerland together. They were supposed to infiltrate German diplomatic circles and bring the Soviets information about Nazi intentions. Remember, at this point, everybody else was appeasing Hitler. The Soviets were the only nation standing against fascism, the only ones protesting the Munich Agreement, the annex of the Sudetenland. You could feel you were on the right side, working for the Soviets. You could feel like Communism was the way forward, the good guys, the ones standing up to Hitler."

"Until they didn't," I said. "Until Stalin signed a treaty with the Germans."

"Right. And Hitler invaded Poland a few days later. The GRU dropped all contact with its Western agents. And for most of those agents, that was it. The most shocking betrayal you could imagine. A treaty with the fascists! It was like an earthquake, like everything you believed in turned to dust. Some of them disappeared. Some of them offered their services to the British."

"What about Grossmeyer? Olive said he was captured and sent to prison."

"That's correct. Unlike his wife, he hadn't received any training. They were all amateurs, these early German antifascist rings, and the Gestapo broke them up without too much trouble. Grossmeyer made the mistake of traveling across the border. He was captured, sent to prison to await trial. Then he disappeared."

"What about Jurgis? Her Lithuanian."

"Yes. By then, they were living together openly, in a village outside Bern. She had a child by him. But then he disappeared, probably captured, and with her husband in prison, Mrs. Grossmeyer couldn't afford to stay in Switzerland. The Gestapo was everywhere. She got involved with a diplomat at the British embassy—Cecil Rainsford—and he agreed to marry her. She wound up in a nice detached villa outside London where she ran into an old friend of hers from her Berlin years, a fellow traveler who was busy carrying out work for the GRU. Mrs. Rainsford was happy to help. She used her training to set up a radio transmitter on top of her roof, and in no time she was sending off coded messages to a relay station in Norway, and from there to Moscow Center."

By now I couldn't look at either of them. Those earnest, unblinking eyes. I stared at the weathered teak boards along the bottom of the boat, ending at Fox's feet. He wore large white rubber-soled oxford shoes. They reminded me of flippers. I mumbled about how there must be some mistake. It was all I could think of, that there was some mistake. Things like this didn't happen on Winthrop Island. People didn't take you out on a boat and tell you, in the middle of the salty breeze, that your employer was a Soviet spy. I mean, the war was over. All these exciting intrigues were supposed to be finished, and anyway she was Olive Rainsford, she was a Peabody, she was a New Englander, she was a patriot.

"How did she end up here?" I said. "In America. On Winthrop."

"Two reasons, we think. Firstly, she may have suspected she was under surveillance in England. Secondly, the Soviets somehow got wind that certain North American networks had been compromised by Gouzenko and Bentley and shut them down. So they needed a replacement. A GRU agent seemed ideal because she wouldn't be implicated in these compromised networks, which were run by the KGB."

June said, "You do understand, by the way, that this is secret information. All of it. If you reveal anything to anybody, you could be prosecuted for sedition."

"For the love of God," I said.

"I suppose you're wondering why you're here. Why we're telling you this."

Now I looked up. "Oh, I *know* why you've told me all this. I'm not stupid."

"Well?"

"You said yourself you needed proof. You want me to snoop around her house and find it for you."

"Obviously we need somebody she trusts," said June. "Somebody who can come and go from her house at will."

"Not exactly at *will*."

Neither of them replied. I turned my head west,

toward Winthrop. You couldn't quite make out the Peabody house from here, but I knew the exact spot where
it lay. The gray dot that was Summerly. The guest cottage behind it. My own house, the old Winthrop farm,
obscured by vegetation. Everything I knew, everything
that was familiar and loving. So what if my father was
sleeping around with my dead mother's sister? That
seemed small now, a human failing, like eating all the
fudge in one sitting. I set my elbows on my knees and
leaned my face into my open palms. A few hours ago
I was tucked into Shep's arms. I wanted them back. A
few hours ago everything had been right.

My God, what was I supposed to say to Shep?

I raised my head. "Well, you can just find yourself
another dummy. I want no part of this."

June swore. Fox made a movement with his left hand
and she crossed her legs and looked out to sea.

"Miss Winthrop," he said, in that same grave voice,
"I urge you to think carefully. Think of what might
happen if the secrets to our most sophisticated tech-
nology should fall into the hands of a man like Josef
Stalin."

"It sounds like they already have."

"Maybe so. All we can do is try to stem the tide. Do
what we can to keep any more vital information from
escaping the borders of liberal democracy, which might

have its failings, sure, but at least it has the rule of law. At least it has elected governments with some degree of accountability to citizens. Not a totalitarian state with a proven record of killing its own people, killing anybody with even a shadow of a suspicion of opposing its power."

"Olive would never. She would never."

"Then prove it. Clear her name. If she's innocent, you won't find anything, will you?"

"And if I do?"

He shrugged. "You said yourself she would never."

I turned my head back to the island. It was the middle of the day and behind that warm haze people were golfing, they were having lunch and playing bridge and pouring themselves gin and tonics with a twist of lime. They were watching the kids frolic on the beach and exchanging nibbles of gossip.

Another memory slipped behind my eyes, another glass bead from the jar of those weeks after Mama's stroke. I don't know how it got there, don't recall remembering it before that day. Maybe it was a dream, who knows. I am asleep in a chair in Mama's hospital room. Neck stiff, back stiff. I wake to some hushed male voices conversing near the door. One belongs to Pop. He says it's too generous, I can't ever repay you for this. The other man says, Nonsense, Winthrop, you're family to us, and anyway it's done, the bills are coming to us, it's the least we can do. Pop says it's more than that, it's more than any man can expect from another. And this other man—it's Mr. Peabody, of course, I recognize his voice now, his neat patrician vowels—the other man says no, on the contrary, loyalty is the least you can expect from your fellow man, I depend on your loyalty just as you should depend on mine. My eyes are open now. I peek over the edge of the chair and watch my stump of a pop shake hands with tall, shambling Mr. Peabody. Their hands remain linked for several seconds, a long time for two men to hold hands, and even in my disordered state I recognize what I'm witnessing—a sacred pact, an oath between men, a vassal swearing fealty to his baron.

Mr. Peabody will take care of us. In return, we are bound to the Peabodys.

Underneath the boat, the slack tide had begun to turn. If you live by the sea, you learn to notice how the water tugs you in the direction it wants to go, and God help you if you wish to travel against it. Maybe Fox felt the tide, too. He said something to June and reached for the throttle. I waited until we were underway, heeling gently to port as we skimmed toward the southern point of Winthrop Island, where Shep and I had spent last night among the dunes, before I spoke.

"So what exactly happens to people caught passing along secrets to another country?"

"Well, that depends on a lot of things," he said. "But I'm sure you're aware that treason is a capital crime."

"You mean she could be executed."

"If she were found guilty, yes."

June said, "Unless she cooperates, of course. If she cooperates she'll get a prison sentence."

"You're assuming she's guilty."

"Sweetheart, I *know* she's guilty."

"This is America, isn't it? She's presumed innocent."

"Does this mean you're going to help us?"

"Of course not," I said. "I have my faults, but I don't snitch on my friends."

June opened her geranium mouth, looked at Fox, and closed it again. I sat with my arms crossed over my belly to keep myself from shaking. The boat skipped over a wake. *Shep*, I thought. Was he on the train by now? He would take the train from Boston to New London and then one of the afternoon ferries, the early one or the late one. Probably the late one. He would be home around suppertime. Dinner, the Families called it, but here on the island we still called it supper, like our parents and grandparents before us. As for Olive, she would have taken the kids to the beach after breakfast. Today was Wednesday, which meant Sebastian and Charlotte had their tennis lessons at three o'clock on the Club's aristocratic grass courts. They had tennis on Mondays, Wednesdays, and Fridays because a good tennis game was an essential accomplishment for a young lady or gentleman who summered on places like Winthrop Island. Sometimes Olive stayed for a drink by the pool with the other mothers, sometimes she took the kids straight home. I always thought it was funny, how she sipped her gin and tonic and gossiped like any ordinary person, but she seemed to enjoy it and I figured that maybe human beings are meant to take an interest in each other's intimate affairs—it was part of our nature.

June drove me home in her yellow Lincoln convertible. We hadn't said much, cruising back to Little Bay, and it was nearly three o'clock by the time we reached the dock. To our right, the early afternoon ferry was already crawling into Winthrop Harbor. I could see that June was angry with me, angry and impatient that all her plans had come to nothing, but that Fox played a longer game and figured he would bide his time with me.

Well, let him bide, I'd thought. He could bide all summer if he wanted, and then he could find somebody else to spy on Olive Rainsford.

Not that they'd discover anything. This was all a giant misunderstanding. Maybe out in the middle of the water my imagination had gotten the better of me, listening to Fox spin his tall tales in circles around my head, but as we'd rounded the point and angled toward the harbor, the familiar contours of the island had pulled me back to reality. Olive Rainsford, a Soviet agent! It was ridiculous. Advanced espionage training in Moscow! Tell that to the Marines.

I didn't speak as we wound our way up from Little Bay and neither did June. At the entrance to the association, the guard poked his head out of the booth and waved us right through. June hardly slowed. Her irritation crackled the air and gave me no little satisfaction, because June Lindstrom was the type of woman who was used to getting her own way. When we reached my house she took off her sunglasses and looked me straight in the eye. Her skin was speckled pink from the wind and sun and her blond hair danced around her ears. How had I ever thought of her as a shy, trembling Minnesota mouse? She'd had me there, for sure.

All right, June said to me. We can't force you to cooperate with our investigation. But if you tip off Mrs. Rainsford you'll be in big trouble. If you say a word to anybody about what happened on that boat, the

FBI will prosecute you to kingdom come. Do you understand?

Sure I understand, I said, and got out of the car.

I watched her turn the Lincoln around, rumble back up the drive, swing left onto Serenity Lane. When the roar of that V-8 engine disappeared on the breeze, I lurched forward and ran toward the cottage. It was half past three and the driveway was empty. Olive's car was at the Club, Olive and the kids would be on the tennis courts under the hazy sun. The front door was locked but I shimmied in through the kitchen window, the way I'd done the day Mama died.

The stairs to Olive Rainsford's attic made a long, despairing groan when you drew them down, no matter how slowly you pulled on the rope. I thought the whole island could hear me and closed my eyes, as if that would stop the noise, until the bottom section rested on the floor and the house went still around me. Unlike my own house, which had settled where it stood for a quarter of a millennium, the cottage was only twenty years old and it didn't squeak and moan for no reason. All I heard was the distant hum of the electric icebox in the kitchen.

I set my hands on the edges of the attic stairs and climbed upward.

To be clear, I wasn't spying on Olive Rainsford. I

wanted to prove them wrong, that was all. I wanted to set my mind at ease. I wanted to discover nothing at all, and even if I did discover something peculiar—which I wouldn't—I meant to keep that discovery to myself. What Olive got up to in her spare time was none of my business. She'd seen more of the world than I had and I figured she had her reasons. I reached the top of the attic stairs and contemplated the dusky quiet of Olive's office. There were two small windows, one at either end. Both were shut tight. The air was so hot and stuffy, I had to remember to breathe. I'd only been up here a couple of times since the afternoon in late May when Shep had helped me carry up Olive's boxes, and even then I'd only stayed briefly. Long enough to hand her a book she wanted, say, or to allow her to adjudicate some dispute between the children. Each time I'd experienced a vivid impression of Shep. Because of our conversation that day, I guess, he seemed to live in this cramped, triangular space for me, like a ghost. I couldn't start up the stairs without thinking of Shep. Now that impression was so strong as to weaken my bones. I felt his wide smile and his arms and I wanted to pillow my face on that shoulder of his, that shoulder that possessed the magical power to shrink all your troubles into nothing, but instead I stepped forward and turned my attention to the surface of Olive's desk.

Like the rest of the house, Olive's office was in perfect order. Everything in its place, that was her motto. Her kitchen was a marvel. Flour and sugar and rice and coffee beans and so on, all contained in a row of blue tins, neatly labeled. Canned fruits and vegetables lined up in soldierly fashion—alphabetical order, I'm not kidding. Utensils tidy in their drawers. Olive used to laugh away my awe. *I spend a lot less time putting things away where they belong*, she liked to say, *than I'd waste running around trying to find them later*. Once, in a rush of determined energy, I'd tried to put our own kitchen at home in streamlined Rainsford order, but I'd given up after an hour. There was too much stuff accumulated over the decades. Olive had moved to a new country every couple of years so she wasn't bogged down by this junkyard of items that were of no possible use to man or maid but you didn't have the heart to throw away.

On Olive's office desk, three pens and two pencils stood in a jar. I didn't inspect the pencils but I knew they would be sharpened to ready points. Two books lay on their sides next to the wall—a French dictionary and a German dictionary, such as you might expect a translator to keep handy. In the corner sat one of those green-shaded lamps a bookkeeper might switch on to illuminate his accounts. That was all. The desk was made of wood and bore the scars of a second- or even thirdhand history. One wide drawer in the middle contained additional pens and pencils and several pink erasers and a slide rule. The file drawer on the right side was locked. I jiggled it a few times to be sure, because—as I've said before—we don't lock a lot of things on the island, even things of a confidential or valuable nature. It just wasn't done. Locks are for people who don't trust each other. But Olive had only arrived on the island seven weeks ago. She'd lived all over the world, in bustling and amoral cities where neighbors didn't know each other's names. She probably locked her desk as a habit.

I straightened from the desk and looked down the attic to the window. It offered a small square view of the ocean, or else it would have done if it wasn't obscured by a layer of salt. To be honest, I hadn't thought much about what Olive did during all those hours she spent in this attic. She was translating documents. What kinds of documents? I had no idea. How did she receive the originals and send them back with their translations? The post office, I assumed. Where did she keep them while she was working on them? Beats me. If I looked around the room, I didn't see any papers. On one of the shelves in the bookshelf sat an object draped with a fitted cloth cover in the shape of a typewriter. I couldn't remember having heard any typewriter racket during all those hours I sat reading downstairs, but I wasn't listening for a typewriter, was I? In fact, I hadn't heard a thing. Obviously, the sound didn't carry, that was all.

I walked to the bookshelf and lifted a corner of the typewriter cover. It was clean of dust and so was the machine underneath, a standard model like the one we had at the library. The typewriter occupied its own shelf. Above and below it were more books, all of which had foreign titles. I pulled out one of them and spread it open. The smell of old paper and old ink and mildew drifted from the pages and hung in the stuffy atmosphere. On the flyleaf someone had inscribed *Dr. Oskar Grossmeyer* in old-fashioned, purpling handwriting. The book was in German and printed in that alarming Gothic script that made you think of Nazi edicts. I closed it with a bang and slid it back in its place. I noticed that my fingers had left damp prints on the cover, that the perspiration had begun to trickle from my temples and run down my spine. I consulted my wristwatch. It was almost four o'clock. Tennis lessons were over at four. Like I said, Olive usually collected the kids from the courts and herded them to the pool terrace to play with the other children while she finished her gin and tonic, but sometimes she didn't. Sometimes she put her offspring in the car and drove straight home. You couldn't predict which. It depended on her mood, maybe, or the company at the pool. Either way, it was time for me to leave. I hadn't found anything suspicious or even interesting. Books and pens and a typewriter. At the other end of the attic stood an old bureau, about five feet high. It was made of dark, paneled wood with elaborate decorations carved into the corners of the panels, a Victorian thing that looked as if somebody had forgotten it there. An ancient desk clock stood on top of it. The needle-thin hands were stopped at just short of half past six o'clock.

For some reason, I had never taken any notice of this bureau before. It stood by itself, on the opposite side of the room, right in the middle of the triangle formed by the roof, so that the small, dusty window hovered just above the top, partly blocked by the clock. It was so old and unassuming that it seemed to be part of the wall itself, nothing you would actually make use of.

I wiped my damp hands on my skirt and walked toward the bureau. A floorboard creaked under my shoe and my heart jumped from its place to knock against my ribs. I stopped and listened to the house. Having grown up in a building older than the republic, I knew how to separate the inanimate sounds from the living ones. But the only noise in Olive's house was the dust drifting through the air. The absence of sound was like a sound itself. I started forward again. The floorboards creaked twice but this time I didn't flinch. I reached the bureau and up close it was really a beautiful thing, just neglected. I imagined it had arrived here like the chair downstairs, the one I liked to read in, from some corner of the Peabodys' grand house on Commonwealth Avenue. When Mama was in the hospital we had stayed there, or rather slept there, and while I didn't remember much about the place, I remembered there were a lot of corners. You got lost in them. I reached out and ran my hand along the thick, carved molding at the top. My thumb dragged over the edges. Like on any bureau, the door to the top cabinet swung down to make a desk. There was a key stuck in the keyhole. The handle was in the shape of a clover and a green tassel dangled from one leaf. I turned the key and the door swung down. The inside face was lined with soft green felt. I held it steady with my hand and bent to peer inside the cabinet. It was fitted with lots of little drawers and shelves for your stationery and your bills and letters and whatnot, but they were all empty. Not a single forgotten object lay inside. I poked a few of them with my finger to make sure. They were inlaid beautifully in delicate geometric patterns the color of honey. A couple of the tiny knobs had broken off their drawers; nothing my pop couldn't fix. I straightened and swung the door shut. Underneath the top cabinet was a smaller cabinet with two doors. An empty keyhole locked it shut. I ran my finger along the seam but the cabinet doors wouldn't open. Probably the key was in one of those dainty bureau drawers. I swung the top door back down and pulled open a drawer. There was nothing inside. I closed it and reached for the drawer below. As my fingers grasped the tiny knob, somebody's voice drifted up the open hatch from the floor below.

I am a liar. It pains me to say so, but it's true—well, unless I'm lying about that, too, but I guess that's a circular argument and gets us nowhere. Let me illustrate. That time when Shep ran his bicycle into Mrs. Pinkerton's prized impatiens, I didn't even have to think about it. I told Mrs. Pinkerton those flowers must have been trampled by the Websters' pig Suey—I swore I saw that pig trotting down West Cliff Road just a minute ago, it was forever escaping its pen—and spun an elaborate tale around poor Suey's supposed adventures while on the lam. That doesn't mean I'm any *good* at lying. I couldn't even look Mrs. Pinkerton in the eye when I told her all this. I pointed down the road and mimicked a pig burrowing under its fence and oinked and did just about anything else I could think of to avoid giving Mrs. Pinkerton the opportunity to notice the dilation of my pupils and the blood throbbing beneath my skin. No, I hate to lie. It makes my heart thump and my skin heat. Lying causes the perspiration to pour from my armpits as if I've run a marathon. I only do it when the trouble in question is even worse, like poor, clumsy Shep getting belted for destroying those flowers when it was Amory who drove his brother off the road and into the flowerbed in the first place.

Now, Mrs. Pinkerton was a tough woman, may she rest in peace. That's what Mama used to say, shaking her head—*That Mrs. Pinkerton, she's a tough woman.* I sometimes think that's why Tippy's such a sweet little soul, because she had to bend to that woman's wishes one after another, day after day in order to survive. Anyway, it took all the nerve I possessed to stand there lying through my teeth to tough Mrs. Pinkerton, making those stupid pig noises to disguise my own panic, and to be perfectly honest I don't think she even believed me. When I finished, she didn't say a word, so I stole a kind of sideways glance at her face to appraise what effect my absurd story had had on her. Her cheeks were purple and her eyes were bright. She had pressed her lips so tight together that they had practically disappeared inside her mouth. *Well, that's about it*, I said, and I scampered away thinking she was purple with rage, you see, about to blow her stack like the tough woman she was.

It was only later that I figured she might have been fighting the impulse to laugh.

I was no longer a child as I stood in Olive Rainsford's attic, listening to the sound of her arriving home, but I felt all the old panic. I couldn't even move. My fingers had stuck to the tiny knob of that beautifully inlaid drawer inside the bureau. Downstairs, Olive told the children to wash their hands and faces and change out of their tennis clothes. The house was compact and I heard every word as it whooshed up the attic stairs. I heard the hoofbeats of Sebastian and Charlotte on the living room floor and out into the hall. Until they stopped short.

"Mummy," said Sebastian, in his peculiarly unchild-like voice, "is somebody in the attic?"

Olive didn't answer right away. In retrospect, I should have examined this detail more closely. I mean, any ordinary woman would have said something like, *Good heavens, why do you say that?* or even laughed and said, *Of course not, silly goose.* But Olive said nothing. Olive considered Sebastian's question for what must have been several seconds, while upstairs my heart pounded and my armpits gathered sweat almost directly above her, and I tried to extract my paralyzed fingers from their compromising position.

At last she spoke. "Sebastian, darling. Why don't you and Charlotte go into your bedroom and help Matthew change for his bath?"

The hoofbeats resumed, down the short hallway to the children's bedroom. I heard their little voices squabbling over shirts or something. My fingers fell free of the knob. I swung the cabinet door back up and turned the key in its lock. The tassel swung back and forth. I grabbed it with my fist. I had some irrational idea that the swinging tassel was going to give me away. The tassel stopped and my gaze found something else.

A thin black wire that emerged behind the bureau, along the wall to the right of the clock, and traveled a couple of inches to disappear out the corner of the window.

The attic stairs groaned softly, hardly more than a sigh. Olive had had more practice going up and down them, I guess, trying not to wake the children. I heard the click of her shoes on the stairs. The top of her curly dark hair appeared in the shaft, then her white forehead, turned in my direction where I now stood, next to the bookshelf, clutching a book.

Then her eyes, wide with shock.

"Why, Emilia!"

The words tumbled out of me. I always spoke too fast when I was lying. "I'm so sorry to disturb you! It's just that there was this book I wanted, I remembered seeing it up here, I thought you'd be home by now, I forgot about the tennis but I didn't want to go home again, I can't bear to be alone there anymore, and I—"

"Emilia. Emilia." She pressed a hand to her heart. She'd climbed the rest of the stairs and now stood at the top in her white tennis clothes and white tennis hat. "It's all right. Of course you're welcome here. Whenever you like. You just startled me, that's all. How did you get inside?"

"I—I climbed through the kitchen window."

Her eyebrows made a pair of high, round arches. "I see."

"I remembered how you left it open. For ventilation. Like the time it was raining, when I took shelter here, and you found me and told me about Mama. For some reason that stuck in my head. The kitchen window."

She looked at the book in my hands. "I didn't know you read German."

"Oh—this. Yes. I—I studied it in high school, on my own. I wanted to know more about the Germans, how they got to where they were, how they arrived at National Socialism. You know, to understand."

"I see," she said again. Her eyes wandered around the room—to the bookshelf behind me, to the desk, along the wall to the bureau and the window behind it. Then they returned to me. She wiped her forehead with the back of her hand. "My goodness, it's hot up here. Hot and stuffy. Your face is all red, Emilia, you're just *dripping*. How about we head downstairs for a cool drink?"

"That sounds wonderful."

"All right, then."

She turned to step down the stairs. There was no railing, just the hole cut in the attic floor and the stairs that folded up, so you had to be careful and watch your step. At the last second, she swung back to me, so swiftly I startled a step or two.

"Oh! I'm sorry, Emilia. I just wanted to see what book you've picked out. What book is so irresistible to have brought you all the way over here and through my kitchen window in the middle of a fine summer afternoon."

I looked at the cover and handed it to her. She held it with both hands in front of her face, the way my pop did when he forgot to put on his reading glasses.

"Good gracious. Heady stuff for a girl your age." She handed it back to me and smiled. Her lipstick was all smudged away and her teeth were white and perfectly even. "You're going to *love* college, Emilia. Maybe you can further your German studies while you're there."

I stayed in Olive Rainsford's kitchen only long enough to swallow a glass of iced lemonade. Honest, I don't know how I did it. My stomach revolted at the first sip but somehow I kept it all down while I chatted and smiled and helped the kids into their chairs for cake. Then I looked at the clock and said—like I was surprised at the time—*Oh, my goodness, I really must be going*. I couldn't possibly go home so I headed around the corner of Summerly toward the beach. I made it all the way to the beach roses before I vomited that ice-cold lemonade into the sand, every drop.

When my stomach stopped heaving, I sat up and gathered my knees to my chest. My head spun woozily. *If I could just take a nap*, I thought. I needed to sleep. How heavenly it had felt last night, to fall asleep inside the ring of Shep's arms. I hadn't slept so deeply in ages, that velvety drunk sleep that was the nearest thing to oblivion. I wanted it now. Summerly sprawled out lazily before me in the golden afternoon light. I could see the attic window from here. It was empty. The late ferry docked at half past six, two hours away.

That was the trouble with the attic window, I

thought. The Peabodys could signal when they wanted me, but I couldn't signal them.

I let go of my legs and stretched my arms. I felt as weak and unbalanced as a baby, but I forced myself to stand, limb by limb. The house was so quiet, it might have been asleep. Mr. Peabody liked to golf in the afternoons, when the sun shone. Mrs. Peabody usually went to the Club with him on Wednesdays, because of the weekly bridge tournament. Amory had his own amusements, golf or sailing or spending time with Tippy, who knew. Mary, now. At this time of day, their housekeeper Mary might be in the kitchen or she might be in her room, listening to the radio.

I slipped off my shoes and made my way up the beach. The sand was soft and still warm from the day's sunshine. I went around the side of the terrace and opened the door to the Peabodys' sunroom. Like I said, we don't lock things up on the island. The sunroom was hot, as you might expect, but when I slipped through the door to the hallway the air was cooler. I was afraid I might encounter Mary on the back stairs so I climbed the main staircase instead, dragging my hand along the banister as I went. Once we took the dinner trays from the kitchen and sledded down that banister until Shep broke his arm stopping me from flying off the side. Mr. Peabody about tanned our hides for that. I remembered in the house on

Commonwealth Avenue the staircase was lined with portraits of dyspeptic ancestors, but here at Summerly the Peabodys had hung old photographs of the beach, shell collections labeled and framed under glass, that kind of thing. The sun poured through the windows upstairs and laid the walls and floors with gold. I knew exactly where to find Shep's room, even though I hadn't been upstairs at Summerly in years. They hadn't changed a thing except the fresh flowers. Same Chippendale highboy halfway down the hallway, containing probably the same linens, if I cared to open the drawers. Same wedding photograph of Mr. and Mrs. Peabody, surrounded by bridesmaids and groomsmen. They looked laughably young. It was 1918 and Mrs. Peabody's gown had a square neck and a hemline above her ankles. She wore white stockings and white low-heeled shoes and a circlet of white flowers around her head that secured her veil, in a style that always reminded me of a medieval princess. She looked a little too serious, in my opinion, for a woman who'd just married a kind, rich, handsome prince like Mr. Peabody and was about to head off on a European honeymoon where she was destined to fall in love with an enormous Delft punch bowl, but maybe she was just overwhelmed by it all. They must have been happy with each other because Arthur was born the following spring.

I reached the end of the hallway and turned right. There were three doors—one at the end of the corridor, which was Arthur's old room, and two on the left, one to Shep's bedroom and one that opened to the bathroom he shared with his brother, or used to share. The bathroom door was ajar but Shep's door was shut tight. The knob turned under my hand. Inside, everything was exactly as I remembered it, except neat as a pin. The same blue-striped drapes covered the window that overlooked Mrs. Peabody's hydrangeas. The same brown rolltop desk sat along the wall, the same mirror on the same chest of drawers reflected the same single bed, covered by the red-and-white quilt in a geometric pattern not unlike the quilt on my own bed. If I examined the objects littered on top of that chest of drawers, I knew I would find the same silver-backed hairbrush and the swimming medals I had teased him about when he was eleven. Shep had always been a strong swimmer—it was the one sport at which he could lick anybody as a kid. I guess his gigantic wingspan conferred some advantage in the water, or maybe the water was kinder to his over-grown body than the air. Honestly, I was too tired to think about it. I dropped my shoes by the side of Shep's bed and crawled on top of the quilt. The pillow gave up his smell. I wrapped my arms around it and fell asleep on my side, facing the wall.

V.

MAY 1954
Washington, DC

The last time I saw Olive Rainsford, I was inside the witness box in a marble courtroom. I had just concluded my testimony and rose to leave, escorted by the bailiff. I was grateful for the bailiff's tall frame and large belly because it sheltered me from Olive's gaze, which I had felt on my skin throughout the day, though I never looked her in the eye.

Still, as I'd waited for the bailiff to free me from my cage—it was an old-fashioned courtroom and the witness box was a real box with a door cut seamlessly into the wooden side—my eyes found her anyway. The temptation was irresistible. I knew this would be the last chance, that we would never exist in the same room together, ever again. So I looked.

At that moment, Olive had turned to her lawyer. They were conferring over something, I guess, or sharing some observation on my testimony. What startled me was she looked the same. She wore a demure dress in a dainty floral pattern and her short, dark hair curled around her ears, styled with maybe a little more polish than during the summer, when most people tended to let their hair go wild. You would have thought she was any old housewife, any old patriotic suburban mother who had bought Victory bonds and donated her sons to the Army. She looked pretty. She wore cheerful red lipstick. Honestly, I'm not surprised those jurors found her guilty only on a single charge. I myself had felt a sick, cold dread as I locked my gaze on that wholesome profile. Maybe I'd made a mistake. Maybe I'd hallucinated the whole thing. Worse—maybe she was right and I was wrong, and her historical purpose was greater than my grubby allegiance.

Then she turned her head and our eyes met. I won't say her expression changed, exactly, just that her eyes cooled and her cherry mouth thinned. I felt her inside my head, ransacking my soul. The bailiff yanked at my elbow. "Come along, ma'am," he said. I walked away. That was the last time.

Now I'm in a different kind of box, a small, airless room somewhere in the middle of Washington. The door squeaks open. In my head Olive Rainsford is the same as she was before. I stand with my fingers pressed against the wooden table. The chair nudges the backs of my legs. My cigarette burns in the ashtray, half finished. Fox stands next to me. His elbow brushes my sleeve and I think he does it on purpose, to remind me he's there. Dulles stands on the other side of the table, head turned curiously to the door.

I hear her footsteps first, clacking on the linoleum in a syncopated rhythm with the heavier thud of a man's shoes. The sound of their walking gets louder and clearer until it might as well come from the same room. At that instant the door opens wide and she appears. Wearing a plain, shapeless dress the color of cement. Her hair's gone gray. Her face is colorless, her skin slack. The cheerful lipstick is gone, leaving her lips invisible. Her eyes are as cool as ever, pointed toward me, then to Dulles. Her hands are cuffed behind her back. A guard stands behind her, holding her elbow.

"I want to speak to her alone. That's what I said, alone."

Dulles looks at me. "Miss Winthrop?"

"Be my guest." I motion to the chair across the table and pick up my cigarette before I resume my seat. The guard looks at Dulles, who gestures back. He unlocks the handcuffs and steps from the room. Olive shakes her arms a little, rubs her wrists.

"Very well," says Fox. "We'll be in the foyer down the hall. If you require any assistance, the guard's outside the door."

"Oh, for God's sake," Olive says scornfully. She pulls out the chair and sits in it. Fox and Dulles leave the room. I wait until the door clicks shut before I speak.

"Cigarette?"

"Have you got one?"

I rise and fetch the box of cigarettes from the table in the corner. She selects a cigarette; I light it. Would she like a glass of water? *Yes, please.* I wonder if a pair of men would so scrupulously obey the laws of hospitality. I take my seat and retrieve my own cigarette from the edge of the ashtray.

"You look well, Emilia," she says.

"You look like hell. Don't they have lipstick in prison?"

"This *cigarette*." She exhales luxuriously. "You can't imagine how hideous they are, the cigarettes they sell in the prison canteen."

"I hear Soviet smokes are nothing to write home about."

Olive sits back in her chair and crosses her legs. Her wrists are pink where the handcuffs rubbed against the skin. "So what have you been doing with yourself, Emilia? I hear you're at Wellesley."

"Yes. A doctoral course in early American history."

"Good. Good. It's what you were meant for. I'm very pleased, Emilia."

"Am I supposed to care?"

She looks surprised. "I have only ever wanted the best for you. I have only ever had your best interests at heart."

I stub out the remains of my cigarette and reach for the water glass. How peculiar, talking to this waxy, bloated Olive. I have to remind myself it's her. Her voice isn't so different, I guess. A little more salt in her throat, but if I close my eyes I might be sitting in her kitchen on Winthrop Island, listening to her talk about the luau party last night at the Club.

"Well?" she says. "Don't you have anything you want to ask me?"

"I thought you had something you wanted to ask *me*. A favor, they said. Isn't that why we're here?"

She shrugs. "I thought we might get to know each other a little first. Warm the air."

"Talk about the weather, you mean? The latest movie? Or do you watch any movies in prison?"

"They bring in movies to watch. *The Glenn Miller Story*, that was very good."

"Kind of sentimental, I thought."

She taps some ash and nods at my neck. "Your pearls are very attractive, Emilia. You have good taste."

"They're imitation." I finger the necklace anyway. "And don't be flattered. I wore them for my father's funeral yesterday. I haven't had a chance to change."

"Oh, I'm sorry to hear that. Was it sudden?"

I examine my fingers. A speck of polish has chipped from my right thumb. I tap my fingernail against the side of the water glass. Olive's fingernails are bare and short now. Her hair is short, too. The curls aren't entirely gray but streaked with dark brown. There is no vanity in prison, I guess. Nobody who cares how you look.

I ask, "Why am I here, Olive?"

"Because I thought you might want a little redemption, Emilia. Before I'm gone."

"Redemption?" My voice skids up an octave. "Redemption? For what?"

"For betraying me. For betraying the trust I placed in you."

"You were operating an illegal radio set from your

attic. Broadcasting classified information to the Soviet military intelligence agency. You betrayed your *country*, Olive."

"I would much rather betray my country than betray my principles. It takes guts to betray your country. To betray your principles is a moral failing."

"Are you calling me a coward?"

"Of course not. I understand pressure was brought to bear on you. You were young, you were easily manipulated." She drags on her cigarette and smiles. "I forgive you. I forgave you long ago."

Her eyebrows are like soft gray wings. Above the right one is a small scar I never noticed before. I fix my attention on this short white line and say, "It's funny."

"What's funny?"

"What you said. It reminds me of something you said to me that summer. How we accuse others of the sins we don't admit to ourselves." I smile. "*Projection.* Remember? I had a psychologist friend explain it to me once."

"Oh, Emilia. I'm so glad that you remember the things I taught you. I had such hopes for you."

"Did you think you were going to radicalize me? Just by paying for my college education and making me feel like I was somebody?"

Olive shakes her head and turns her attention to her

cigarette, which she's tapping into the ashtray. "You reminded me of myself, that's all."

Shep's voice in my head, a thousand summers old: *You always reminded me of her.*

I sit back in my chair and reach for another cigarette. Olive watches me lift the lid of the box and extract one. I light it with a match from the matchbook in my pocket. I don't carry one of those silver lighters. It seems dishonest for a girl of my pedigree.

"Let me tell you a story, Emilia. You've heard a little of it already, but I couldn't tell you everything back then. I think it might help you understand."

"Go on," I tell her. "I love stories."

"A long time ago, I moved from Berlin to Shanghai with my first husband. And I hated it. I remember telling you that, how much I hated Shanghai at first. Packed with Europeans out to make their fortunes. Bourgeois types, everything I disliked, boring, complacent, bigots to the core. And there was nothing for me to do. You want to know what it is about these expatriate wives, they don't *do* anything. It's remarkable, really, their complete and utter dedication to accomplishing nothing of any purpose. They've moved to this strange country because of their husbands and all they can do is redecorate their flats and get stoned on imported liquor while the kids are at school. Prattling on about things they know nothing about, about how dirty the local people are and how you can't trust your housekeeper. I was bored out of my skull."

"I'll bet you were," I said.

"Then I met someone. The most extraordinary man. A German, about the same age as my husband. His name was Richard Sorge. Maybe you've heard of him. He worked for one of the German news services in Shanghai. He knew everybody. The most fascinating man I ever met. Clever and complicated and full of life. He was magnetic." She drags on the last of her cigarette and crushes the stub into the ashtray. "Mesmerizing."

"Except he was a spy, wasn't he? He worked for Soviet military intelligence. Supporting—what was it? The underground Communist movement or something."

"How do you know all this?"

"Fox told me, long ago. He said this man recruited you."

"He did more than that. He *awakened* me."

"That's nice of him."

"He's also Sebastian's father."

"Oh, for God's sake. Who cares."

She reaches out like a snake and takes my wrist. "Listen to me. He was the first man I ever met who was willing to die for his principles. For what he believed in, for the Communist cause. I would have followed him anywhere. I would have followed him into hell."

"It seems to me you did."

"*This?* This isn't hell. Hell is what the Chinese did to the Communists. What the Nazis did to the Jews, to anybody who opposed them."

"What about what Stalin did to the kulaks? To the White Russians? To anyone who opposed *him*?"

She releases my wrist. "Those were counterrevolutionaries, Emilia. People who tried to thwart progress."

"Oh, never mind. Fox was right, it's like trying to argue with a religious fanatic. Why does everybody have to think he's on the right side of history?"

Olive settles back in her chair and lights another cigarette from the box nearby. She takes her time about it, strikes the match with precision, closes her eyes as she inhales. "Let's not argue, Emilia. That's not why you're here, to argue with me."

"Then why *am* I here, Olive? I don't understand. I really don't. Why don't you just accept their lousy offer and go to live in utopia? This ought to be a dream come true, right?"

"Yes, of course," she says.

"I mean, personally speaking, I think you should have the guts to put your money where your mouth is. As we dirty capitalists say. If you think the Soviet

Union's such a paradise. Why, they'll treat you like a hero, won't they?"

She doesn't reply. I study the weary lines at the corners of mouth, the pillows beneath her eyes. I remember Fox's voice over the telephone when he told me about her prison sentence. Fifteen years with chance of parole after seven, if the prisoner demonstrated remorse and rehabilitation. I remember he said these words in a voice even lower than usual, a voice of apology. I asked him did he think she would get parole. He said he didn't think so. She hadn't shown *him* a shred of remorse. In fact, it was his opinion she would do the same thing again, if she could.

Well, I laughed at that. Fox asked me what was so funny. I said she didn't need to *feel* any remorse. She didn't need to rehabilitate herself. She just had to demonstrate these fine things to some parole board, and believe me, there was no parole board in the entire United States of America that Olive Rainsford couldn't bamboozle with her eyes closed. Then she would be free. She would walk scot-free.

Maybe so, Fox said, just before he hung up. But remember she'll never really be free. She'll always be looking over her shoulder.

Why's that? I asked.

Because the only way you leave the GRU is when you're dead, he said.

Olive looks up to catch me staring at her. "Of course I'm going to accept the offer. I'm a colonel in the Soviet Army, dear. I do as I'm ordered. But I have one necessary condition."

"What's that?"

"My children," she says.

The Rainsford children were not in the courtroom that last day, the day I gave my testimony. They had been put under the care of the Peabodys following Olive's arrest, and none of the Peabodys had attended the trial. They were still grieving, after all, and anyway the kids were too young to watch their mother stand trial for betraying her country.

I hadn't forgotten them, though. After she was convicted and sentenced to prison, I'd asked Fox what was to become of them, and he said they would remain with the Peabodys. Maybe they would ease the Peabodys' loss, the way Lizbit eased mine. Sometimes I would think about them. Determined Sebastian and clever Charlotte and Matthew like a miniature kamikaze. You can't care for children the way I had, you can't put them to bed most nights and listen to their secrets, feed them cake and hold their hands as they learned the rhythm of the surf, without falling a little in love with them. I wondered how they were coping with the loss of their mother, on top of everything else they had lost. I wondered whether they missed me at all. I still wonder if anybody told them what had happened on the beach that night, and how it was my fault that the ground had fallen away beneath them. Probably the Peabodys had taught them to hate me. Well, I couldn't blame them for that.

The one vector of this relationship I hadn't wondered about was Olive. For some reason, it never occurred to me to wonder how she felt about being separated from her children, unable to watch them grow, unable to feel their small young stomachs pressed against her and their wiry young arms slung around her neck. If you had asked me, I would have said she deserved it.

Not because she was a spy, but because she'd always known what would happen if she got caught. And she did it anyway.

"Your children," I repeat.

"Yes, my children. Don't you remember? I have three."

"And you want to take them with you, I guess? You want me to intervene with the Peabodys so you can take those poor kids to Russia? I mean, you do realize the family blames me for what happened, don't you? I haven't met them in eight years, I wouldn't even—"

"Emilia, stop. You're misunderstanding me. I don't want to take the children with me to the Soviet Union. It would be unspeakably cruel. They hardly know me, they can't just leave their home and move to another country, a country they've been taught to hate, where they don't know the language or the customs. Why, Sebastian will be seventeen now. No, no. That's not what I meant."

"Then what do you mean?"

Olive stubs out her cigarette carefully in the ashtray and starts to cough. She waves away my gesture of concern. Lifts her glass to her lips and gulps down the water. All this time I'm trying not to think. My head whirls a little. She coughs again and clears her throat and apologizes.

"Emilia," she says. "You must understand how much I trust you, despite everything. Your character, your ambition, your imagination. You remind me of myself. My younger self."

"You've got to be kidding me."

"You love them. I remember how you cared for them. There's nobody I'd rather—"

"You've *got* to be kidding me."

"Listen to me. Just listen to what I'm proposing."

I stand up so quickly, the chair tips back behind me. I grab it just in time. "You're nuts, you know that? They're happy with the Peabodys, for one thing. That's one thing I'm sure of. Happy as clams, I'll bet. And the Peabodys would never allow it, for another thing. And for thirds, I don't want your lousy kids. I don't. I've got enough trouble raising just one."

Olive rises, too. "If you don't take them, I won't go, Emilia. I won't agree to the exchange."

"So what?"

"I'll let that traitor they're trading me for rot away in his labor camp, like he deserves. What will your precious Mr. Fox think about *that*?"

She stands there blazing. Her eyes flare open. Her fingers spread like claws on the wooden table. It's a vivid thing, her passion. For her children, of all things—the children she had with her dead lovers—all she has left of the men she adored. It almost makes her beautiful again.

I pick up my pocketbook and sling it over my elbow. "Well, guess what, sister? I don't happen to give a good goddamn."

AUGUST 1946
Winthrop Island

I woke in Shep's room in the middle of some dream.
The light had grown old and yellow but the blue of
twilight hadn't set in. I couldn't remember the dream
exactly but it left me anxious—something to do with
Olive in the middle of the ocean, calling my name, and
me on shore trying to put on my swimsuit and bathing cap and so on, but I couldn't get anything fastened.
When I opened my eyes I didn't know where I was.
Then I felt the pillow in my arms and smelled Shep's
smell. I heard a voice through the walls and realized
what had woken me up—the noise of a car engine.
Some swift footsteps thumped in the hallway outside
the room. I sat up and turned to the door just as it
swung open. Shep's grinning face turned to shock.

"Cricket!"

I laid a finger over my lips. He stepped forward and
shut the door behind him. I sprang out of the bed and
we met in the middle of the room in a tremendous col-
lision of arms and chest and lips. He lifted me in the

air. I wrapped my legs around his waist and my arms around his neck. "What are you doing here?" he whispered fiercely into my hair.

"I got sick of waiting around. I can't stand it at home."

"Aw, I'm sorry, Cricket. I just got back. I was about to put that stupid doll in the window—"

"That's the trouble," I said. "That's the trouble right there, Shep Peabody. I don't have a doll in my attic, for when *I* need *you.*"

"Why, what's wrong, Cricket?"

"I had the most awful day. *Everything* goes wrong when you're not around." I stuck my nose in the side of his neck and drew his sweaty smell into my lungs. "Since we were kids."

"My girl," he said. "My girl."

"Don't go away again, all right?"

"I'm not going anywhere without you, honey. I swear I won't."

"I've been such an idiot. Do you really love me when I'm such an idiot?"

He laughed and loosened his arms just enough so I slid down his front to stand between his feet. My face ended up somewhere along his sternum. "Cricket Winthrop, I have loved the bones of you since I was five years old. You could be an idiot or a drooling imbecile or plain senile. Do you know I've been waiting all day to stand here right now with your arms around me? All day, I've been thinking about this."

"Shh! Your mother will hear!"

"No, she won't. They're at the Club, having dinner."

"What about you? Aren't you hungry?"

"I told them I already ate." He tapped his finger to his temple and grinned. "All part of my dastardly plan, Miss Winthrop."

"What dastardly plan?"

Shep took my hand and kissed the knuckles. "Come along and I'll show you."

Shep set me on top of the kitchen table and said I wasn't supposed to move, he was going to show me something that would knock my socks off.

"Do I have to close my eyes?" I asked.

"Absolutely not. I want you to watch this. I want you to see just what your old Shep can do for you."

So I crossed my legs and watched while he fetched the eggs and butter from the icebox and the pan from the shelf. He tied one of Mary's aprons around his waist. I told him it looked more like a loincloth than an apron. He said that was enough of my sass or else.

Or else what? I asked.

Or else I'll put a stopper in that gob of yours, he said, waggling his eyebrows so I understood exactly what he meant.

I told him he could put a stopper in my gob anytime. He set down the mixing bowl, walked to the kitchen table, and did just that, for a good minute or two, until the smell of browning butter hit us both at the exact same second. Then he swore and hurried back to the old Hotpoint range while I licked my lips to savor the taste of his kiss, which happened at the time to be whiskey. (He had poured us both glasses of his father's favorite single-malt Scotch.)

To hell with Olive. To hell with June Lindstrom. To hell with Sumner Fox. This was all I needed. Shep was all I needed.

"So where did you learn to make an omelet?" I asked him later, as I scraped up the last crumbs with my fork and licked them off the tines.

"Germany," he said.

"They had eggs left in Germany by the end of the war?"

"I was billeted at this farmhouse in Bavaria for a while. They hadn't had much fighting around there. The woman there had a flock of chickens out back, she'd somehow kept them alive. A couple of cows, too." A pair of pink stains appeared on the apples of his cheeks. He made a show of chewing his omelet and washing it back with some whiskey. "Sad story, really. Her husband was killed outside Moscow in the winter of 1941. Her son, he was sent out to man the Atlantic line, he got blown up during the Normandy invasion. He was just sixteen, she said. Real sad story."

I stared at the pink spot on his left cheek. "She must have been lonely."

"Yeah. Yeah, I guess so. She had her daughter living with her, too. Her daughter and son-in-law. The daughter'd gotten married a couple of years into the war—they were just kids, the two of them, younger than me—but her husband's legs got blown off at Stalingrad. Boy, did he hate me. Being American, of course, but just being whole. Having my two good legs under me. Poor guy, I didn't get the idea he was any kind of Nazi or anything, he just had to fight. I think—" He coughed and reached for his whiskey.

"Think what?"

"Well, I got the idea it wasn't just his legs blown off, if you get my meaning. There weren't any babies around, for one thing."

"That's terrible."

"In the beginning, I couldn't give a damn, to be honest. I thought to myself, *Hell, you get what you ask for, buddy.* I'd seen one of their damn camps, I knew what those bastards did. But how could you not feel a little bit sorry for a family like that? They were just ordinary Germans. They couldn't care less about politics. They woke up one day in a dictatorship. Sure, they never spoke up. But who's going to speak up and find himself in a Gestapo prison the next morning? Not a lot of people. Not a lot of people have that kind of nerve. Most people just want to stay alive." He swished the whiskey around and finished it, avoiding my gaze. "Anyway, I lived there about a month and they showed me how to make an omelet, the widow and her daughter. The right way, you know? So I'm grateful for that."

I laid my fork diagonally across my plate. "They taught you well. That's a fine omelet."

Shep rose and took my plate. When I protested, he told me to sit down and put my feet up, I was in mourning, after all. He gave the dishes all his concentration. I gave him all my concentration. I loved the way his old clumsiness had given way to this loose, long-shanked grace. He moved around the sink, washing and drying, humming a little to himself. I imagined him lying naked with his German widow, or her daughter, or possibly both of them. I should have burned with jealousy but I didn't. Maybe it was the whiskey. All I felt was gratitude that somebody in that bleak, deadly continent had taken him into shelter for a little while, had shown him something like love. Also, this widow was thousands of miles away in her tragic farmhouse, and I was right here in the same kitchen.

When he was almost finished, I shook off my stupor and snatched one of the clean white towels from the stack Mary kept by the sink. He tried to shoo me away but I dried the forks anyway and laid them in the drawer while Shep returned the plates to the cabinet. I folded the towel over the edge of the sink and walked to the kitchen door.

Where are you going, he wanted to know.

I said over my shoulder, To the beach.

The sun had almost disappeared and a warm twilight settled over the sea. The air was blue and thick enough to drink. I toed off my shoes and reached behind to yank down the zipper of my dress. From the other side of the beach roses I heard Shep calling my name.

Over here, I called back.

I stepped out of the dress. I wasn't wearing stockings or a girdle or anything, because it was August. I unfastened my brassiere and shimmied out of my underpants. The water was colder than I expected and I yipped when I ran into the surf. Shep called out a question but I couldn't hear what it was, so I just yelled back that I was going for a swim and dove into a wave.

I used to go swimming naked all the time during the war. Why not? The boys were gone and the grown-ups were in bed by nine or ten. I waited until the sun was down. Because of the blackouts the sky was like velvet and if you floated on your back you could see all the stars in a dazzling array. I would think of what Mama had said, how the Atlantic Ocean connected her to her home in Portugal. I stared at those millions of stars and imagined all the ships afloat on this sea and the sailors inside them, the submarines and the deadly peril, all connected to my peaceful bare skin by an infinity of water. Never in a thousand years would I have swum naked on a public beach in daylight, but I loved my own nakedness in the night ocean. I loved how intimate it felt, how primal. All day I had to be a smiling, faithful, dutiful daughter and sister and neighbor, and for this one hour I was just Cricket.

Tonight the surf was frisky but once you got out past the line of breaking waves you got used to the chill and the calm overtook you. I stroked a few yards to stretch my muscles and then rolled on my back. I had picked out the Big Dipper and my old constant friend Polaris when Shep caught up with me, breathless.

"You're nuts!" he said.

"Just look at those stars, will you?"

"Tell me you haven't been skinny-dipping out here alone all summer. Just tell me that."

"Not *this* summer, no. The boys are back and the lights are on."

"I think I'm going to have a heart attack."

I splashed upright and turned to face him. "Not really!"

"Just a figure of speech," he said. "I think."

"Don't scare me like that."

"Well, that's rich. Who's scaring who?"

"Whom," I said.

"La-di-da."

A roller carried us up and down. "You're not scared for me, are you? You know I can swim all right. I've been swimming here all my life. We used to swim together, remember?"

"Not like this, we didn't."

Another wave came through. This time I let it carry me into Shep. He reached out and caught me and for a moment we floated like that, tangled together. He kissed my neck and my ear. I kissed his shoulder. We floated in a circle. Shep's legs waved back and forth, keeping us above the surface.

"I've had dreams like this before," he said, "but then I woke up."

"Well, you're awake now."

"I don't know. Sure feels like a dream, floating like this with you in the middle of the night. Holding you right between my two hands."

"Don't I feel real enough to you?"

"Cricket, I've been dreaming of this so long, I can't tell what's real and what's not. All I know is I could die right here. I could die happy. I don't know, maybe I'm already dead. Maybe I'm in— Say! What was that for?"

I pinched him again. "See? You're not dreaming." I pinched his ribs. "Not dead, either."

"Cricket Winthrop, you come back here."

He chased me through the water, back over the breaking waves and up the surf. I think he could have caught me sooner but he waited until we reached the line of high tide before he snaked an arm around my waist and tumbled me into the sand. We laughed and wrestled and rolled together like a pair of kids, until suddenly we grew up and started kissing. He kissed my mouth and my neck and tenderly kissed each breast. Down my stomach and back up again. I wound my arms around his neck.

"Honey," he said, "are you sure about this?"

"Yes."

"You're not just feeling blue about your mother?"

"I'm feeling blue about my mother," I said, "but that's not why I'm here."

He buried his face in my neck. "Cricket. Cricket."

"I want this so badly. I want to be yours. Don't you see? So we can't ever go back."

All this time I was touching him, his back and his round buttocks, his shoulders, his shaggy hair, his throat, his ears. I didn't really know how you touched a lover, whether I was doing it right, whether he liked it. I just had to know what Shep felt like. His skin was wet and salty. He lay still under my hands except for these tremors that rose from his middle, like earthquakes. He raised his head and said, "You've never done this before, have you?"

"No."

He started to lift himself away but I grabbed his shoulders. "I want it to be you. I need it to be now, like this. You and me together. Don't you want it, too?"

"*Want* it? Are you kidding me? I'm like the petri-fied forest down here. I'm scared to touch you."

I laughed. "Scared? Why?"

"You're so little."

"I'm not that little. To most people I'm really quite a normal size."

"You're perfect." He kissed each breast. "You're perfect and I'm a big lummox."

I took his hand and dragged it between my legs.

"Oh my God," he said. "I'm going to die."

"No, you're not."

Shep raised himself on his elbows. "I don't want to hurt you."

"I don't care if it hurts me. Maybe I want it to hurt. I want to feel something, I want to feel—" My fingers dug into his shoulders. "*That.*"

"You want me to stop?"

"Don't you *dare* stop now, Shep Peabody."

He made a gentle shove with his hips. I strangled another gasp in my throat. For a long time he kissed me, velvet dark night holding its breath around us, and when he lifted his head he was smiling. "I could die right here. I could die happy."

"You keep saying that."

"Because it's true."

"Nobody's going to die," I said. "We're just beginning."

I can't say how long we lay there afterward. I remember feeling this deep peace. I remember the soft, pleasant ache between my legs, like after a long day at sea. I remember smelling the beach roses and the drying salt on his skin. Every so often I stuck out my tongue and licked it, like a deer.

"What are you thinking?" I asked.

"A lot of things."

"Like what?"

"I don't know. Berlin."

"Berlin?"

"I'm thinking about how close I was to giving it all up, back then. Now here I am, lying here with you like I dreamed. But it was close. It was so damned close. And I had no idea. No hope at all."

I nestled my head back in the crook of his shoulder and asked him what was so awful about Berlin. The war was over, wasn't it?

He lay like a brick next to me, under my head and my arm. The tide swished toward our feet. "Forget it," he said. "Forget I said anything."

"No, tell me. I want to know."

"Cricket, it's done. I don't want to think about all that anymore."

I lifted my head. His eyes were shut tight and the lashes lay against his skin. I brushed my fingertip across one eyelid, then the other. "But you *are* thinking about it."

"So kiss me until I forget."

"Oh, is that how it works?"

"Every time."

I ran my fingertip along the top lip, the full bottom lip. "Or you could tell me about it first. You could tell me why it bothers you so much."

"Cricket, you don't need to hear this. I'm okay, honest."

I slid my finger upward to cross his forehead, temple to temple and back again. The bone was so thick, the forehead so broad. It was a real journey. I said softly, "Do you want to know what I missed most, when you were gone? How we used to tell each other everything. I could say anything and you would understand. You could say anything to me. Those letters we used to write, remember?"

"I remember."

"You knew me better than anyone in the world. I knew you. Just two pieces of the same puzzle, you and me."

Shep lifted his hand to tangle his fingers in the ends of my hair. He opened his eyes but he didn't look at me. He looked at the sky behind my head, the wash of stars. "You know how Berlin fell, right?" he said.

"Just what was in the newspapers."

"Well, you know the Soviets got there first. All that spring we bombed the hell out of the city, turned the place to rubble, but the Red Army, they were the ones who marched in and took Berlin. By the time we rolled in, they had control of everything. Streets, buildings. They were looting everything that was left, they made the Berlin women take apart the machines in the factories and put every last bolt on trains for Moscow. God, the women. The things they did to the women. Girls, even. Little twelve-year-old girls! I mean, how was Hitler *their* fault? I can't tell you, Cricket, I can't ever tell you what I saw. There was this woman we hired to translate for us, she told me—well, never mind. You could see it in their eyes. Like they were dead inside. I mean, sure, it was war. And God knows the Germans did terrible things, evil things, raped *their* women to the bone. I guess the Soviets figured it was their turn. Revenge. But for some reason, even after all I'd seen by then, it was the last straw. The war was supposed to be over. The Allies, we were supposed to be the good guys. And these Red Army bastards—excuse me—these damn thugs, they're acting no better than the stinking Nazis. So I'm asking myself, what's the point? What the hell were we fighting for? For this?"

"But it won't be like that forever," I said. "The Soviets will go back home. People will get on with their lives."

"I don't know, Cricket. That's the trouble. When I left, they were setting up barricades. East from West. I just don't know. You heard about Churchill's speech, didn't you? Last spring? In Indiana someplace, I think. An iron curtain, he said, right down the middle of Europe. That's what it was, Cricket. That's exactly what it was, an iron curtain. And I sure as hell wouldn't want to be on the other side of that curtain. Not after what I saw."

I disentangled myself from his arm and sat up. "Well, you're not in Europe anymore. You're with me."

"I sure am," he said. "Not going anywhere."

"Oh, yes, you are. Remember? We're going to California together, as far away as we can get."

Shep propped himself on his elbows and stared at me. "Hold on a second. *California?*"

"Yes, California. That's what you planned, isn't it?"

"Well, yeah. But that was when I thought you— that was before we—I mean, this is your *home*, I wasn't thinking that *you* would want to—hell, I guess I don't know what I was thinking. I haven't thought straight since you kissed me last night."

"Tomorrow. We'll leave tomorrow."

"Are you serious? Tomorrow?"

"Don't you want to?"

"Sure, I do, but— Hold on, you mean just *elope?*"

"Whatever you want to call it."

"What about your pop? Your sister?"

"I don't care. I don't care about anything anymore except you. All I want in the world is a cabin in the middle of a vineyard, just you and me, starting our own little family. What do you think?"

He laughed and pulled me onto his chest. "Is that a proposal?"

Before I could answer, his arms stiffened. His head shot up.

"What's wrong?" I said.

"Jiminy Cricket, Cricket. My pants!"

"What?"

He sprang up and cast around us. The moon was just a sliver and the only light came from a couple of windows still illuminated at Summerly, a hundred yards away. I sat up and watched his limbs flash about in the night air. *He's mine*, I thought. The beauty of his big, shambling body crushed my chest. I rose to my knees. He made a cry of discovery and lifted something from the sand, rummaged around the pockets, exclaimed, *Ah! Thank God!*

"Thank God for what?"

He crashed back into the sand next to me and held something up to the glow from the Summerly windows. "I have to confess something to you, Cricket."

"Confess what?"

"My buddy didn't really need his boat back so soon. The truth is, I went into town this morning to fetch something."

My heart was thumping so hard, I almost couldn't hear him. "Fetch what?" I whispered.

Shep turned on his side to face me. "My mother gave me this when I turned eighteen. Belonged to her mother, oh, fifty years ago. She gave it to me to give to the girl I wanted to marry, someday. And as far as I'm concerned, there's only ever been one girl it was meant for."

I dropped my forehead against his furry chest. "You big lug," I gasped.

"Do you want it, Crick? Can I give it to you?"

I couldn't really speak. I just nodded against his ribs while he wriggled that old ring onto my finger. For a minute or two we just lay there quietly, breathing against each other. Then I slid my arms back up around his neck. He rolled me on my back and kissed me all the way down and back up again. He had grown his hair out again and I loved the shaggy feel of it under my fingers. He asked me if I was sure about all this. Was I sure I wanted to marry him and start a whole new life with him in California, away from our folks, away from everything familiar. I don't remember saying anything back. I don't remember being able to say anything at all. I just slid my hands around him and held on for dear life.

We must have fallen asleep after that because Shep kissed me awake sometime after the moon had slipped over the side of the earth. I remember I didn't want to wake up. I kept my eyes screwed shut so he had to kiss each eyelid to open them. Even then I burrowed myself into his shoulder and told him just a few more minutes.

"A few more minutes and your dad will be out here with a shotgun," he said.

"So what? He can't stop us. We're eloping."

"Now just hold on a second about this eloping business. What about a wedding? In a church with our families behind us? Flowers and cake and you in a white dress? My folks'll want a wedding."

"I don't care about a wedding. Do you? I couldn't care less about a dress and cake. All I want is you. If we wait around for a wedding, it'll be weeks or even months. You can't just leave your buddy hanging around out west with all that brush to clear by himself. And I won't let you go without me. I'm not going to let you get on that train and leave me behind. Think about it. Besides, what if I'm—you know. After what we did."

"All right," he said. "All right. Let me think."

"You don't need to think. All you need to think about is a nice little house in the middle of a vineyard and the sunshine on our heads and kisses all day long."

"Honey, we can't just hop on board a train together. We'd have to get married first."

"Who says we have to get married to ride a train? We'll get married in California."

Shep started to laugh. I asked him what was so funny.

"You," he said. "Trapping me into marriage."

I climbed into his lap and cradled his face with my hands. He rolled me into the sand and kissed me everywhere. I still remember how we laughed in sheer joy as we rocked together, just laughed at this newfound miracle. How our hands clasped in the sand, how he arched his back and hollered, how we lay panting in some impossible configuration of arms and legs, sweating into each other.

All right, he said, when he could speak. You win.

I stole back home through the kitchen door just before dawn, singing in every nerve. The smell of new coffee brought me up short. I spun to face the kitchen table.

"Good morning, Em," said Pop.

It's funny, I didn't even think to lie. No jumbled, improbable stories bubbled up from my throat. I just folded my arms and said, "Good morning, Pop."

"I've been waiting up all night for you."

"I'm sorry to have cost you any sleep. I didn't think you'd notice."

"Not notice my own daughter was out all night?"

"Seems to me you have your own company these days. Or did Aunt Benedita have other plans?"

He climbed stiffly to his feet, like an old man. "Don't you say a word against your aunt."

"I see you don't deny it. Not that there'd be any point. I saw the two of you together on Sill Lane."

Not a single lamp was lit in that kitchen. Pop had sat there all night in the dark, rising only to make more coffee, it seemed. His face was blue with shadow. But my eyes were used to the night and I caught the flash of movement as a muscle flinched in his cheek.

"How long?" I said. "Just that one time? Or has it been going on for a while, you and her?"

"That's none of your business."

"See, at first, when I saw the two of you on that mattress together, I thought you had just done it for the first time, and that's why you were crying. But I've been thinking. I've been thinking about how I thought I saw someone in the truck with you, a couple of days before. I've been thinking about how she's made herself helpful around here, ever since Mama had her stroke, kind of wormed her way in, and now I think you've been doing it with her for a while, haven't you? Sneaking around behind our backs."

Pop wore his work clothes, his bib overalls and a

flannel shirt underneath. Broad-shouldered and wiry. His short gray hair prickled from his head.

"Your aunt's a good woman, Em," he said quietly.

"So am I, Pop."

"What's that supposed to mean?"

"It means I've been out all night with someone. You might as well know. It's just as bad as you feared. I've been out all night and we're going to run off together."

He sighed and rubbed the top of his head. "You and the Peabody boy?"

"We're in love," I said.

"Oh, you're in love, are you?"

"Savagely."

Pop threw up his hands. "And what do you think Tom Peabody is going to think about that? What about the missus? Their son eloping with the caretaker's daughter?"

"They'll think it's romantic. They'll be glad he's happy."

"You know what? For a kid who's supposed to be the smartest thing on Winthrop Island, you don't understand much."

"I understand more than you do."

"You think so? I'll tell you what. You think the world's changed, and maybe it has. But people are the same. People don't change."

"You know what you are? You're—you're just—you're *antediluvian*."

"What in hell does that mean?"

"It means you're stuck in the past. Nobody cares about what family you come from anymore. Especially now. We just fought a war, people know what's important."

"Em, there's things people always care about, and blood's one of them. Nobody wants to see his son marrying beneath him."

"*Beneath* him? Are you kidding me? I'm no more beneath Shep than—"

"Shep? We're talking about *Shep*?"

"Why, what did you think?"

Pop set his hand at the top of his forehead like he meant to squash the two sides together. "I thought—I guess I thought you were sweet on the other one. The older one. Amory."

"When I was a *kid* I was sweet on Amory."

"Oh, when you were a *kid*. God almighty, Em. Don't you see what's happening here? You don't love either one of those boys. You love what they are, that's all. You want to be Mrs. Emilia Peabody, lady of the manor."

"That's not true. That's not what I want at all. I want Shep, I love Shep. He's always been my friend, my best friend, the best friend I ever had, and now that he's back from the war I've come to realize what a—what a terrific human being he is. How much I loved him all along. *You're* the one who thinks I'm beneath him—"

"*I* don't think you're beneath him, Em. I'm talking about them. The Peabodys. They may not admit it, but that's what they think. They want some nice Social Register girl for Shep, same as that Pinkerton girl for Amory. I know it and you know it."

"I don't either know it! What makes you think I know a thing that isn't true?"

"Because you're *eloping* with him, Em. If you thought the Peabodys'd like the idea of your marrying their son, you wouldn't be running away like this. And he wouldn't agree to it, either."

"You've got it all wrong, Pop. That's not why we're eloping at all. At *all*."

"Then you tell me why. You tell me why my daughter's sneaking off to marry some boy. You tell me what kind of fellow runs away with a girl instead of marrying her in a church in front of man and God."

I burst out, "Because I can't, all right? I can't wait that long. There's something else, something you don't know about, something that could—that could *destroy* them. Destroy the whole family. And I have to get away, that's all. I have to leave, before they—before the people who— Oh, forget it. I'm going to California with Shep, that's all. And we're going to be the happiest two people on the face of the earth."

Pop was staring at me like I was crazy. "What in God's name are you talking about? Destroy the Peabodys?"

"I said forget it, all right?"

Pop reached out one long arm and grabbed my shoulder. "What's going on, Em? Is it something to do with that Fox character?"

"I don't know what you're talking about."

"You went out on the water together yesterday afternoon. You and Fox and that waitress from the Club."

"Why, how do you know about that?"

He released my shoulder and set his hands on his hips. "People talk, Em. A couple of people saw you out there and thought it was funny, that's all. And maybe they were right. Were they right, Em?"

"I said forget it and I mean forget it."

"People say he got sent out to the Pacific. Doing God knows what."

"What's that got to do with anything?"

"You tell me, Em," he said.

When I didn't reply, he walked to the range and took the percolator off the stovetop. The smell of fresh coffee was driving me wild, but I wasn't going to tell him. He refilled his mug and gestured to me. I dug my nails into my palms and shook my head. Pop shrugged and set the percolator back on the range. He picked up the pack of cigarettes on the table, shook one out, lit it with a match from a crumpled paper matchbook. The mug came from the old enamelware set that was a wedding present for him and Mama. How many times had I watched him drink his coffee and smoke his cigarette before he left for work in the morning? I leaned back against the counter and asked if that was all, because I needed to pack my things.

"You're not packing anything," he said.

"I'm sorry. I don't think I heard you right. I think you just *forbade* me to marry Shep Peabody."

"Did I say that? I don't give a damn who you marry, Em, so long as he loves you. But I won't have you leaving this house before you tell me just exactly what is going on with you and the Peabodys. Because whatever it is, if it's got something to do with Fox, it's not going to stop just because you've left, all right? And I won't have it. I won't have some—some *mainlander* try to make trouble for this family."

"Just why do you care, anyway? It's not *your* family. This place doesn't belong to us Winthrops anymore. You're the *caretaker*, Pop. You don't own a thing."

The sun was rising now. Some watery new light

came through the eastern window, the one that offered a view of Summerly through the shrubbery. Pop's skin was creased deep. The flesh on his cheeks had worn away altogether. I hadn't taken much notice of his face lately and now he looked like an old man. He wore the same soft flannel shirt of blue plaid he wore in winter, even though the morning air was already foggy with warmth. He lifted the coffee mug to his lips and I saw that his hand trembled a little. When he set down the mug he seemed to compose himself. He said, "Because I don't want to lose my job, is all. New family moves in here, they might want to make some changes. We've got a nice situation here. The Peabodys take care of us."

"Because you let them take care of us."

Pop sat down on the chair and stared at the window, smoking to himself. "Let me ask you something, Em. Do you want to know how your mother came to marry me?"

"I've only heard the story a thousand times, Pop. She came to deliver some lobsters and you fell in love."

"That's right. *I* fell in love. But not her, Em. Not your mother."

"What are you saying?"

"I'm saying she didn't love me. She never loved me."

"That's not true. She *devoted* herself to you! To all of us."

Pop looked down at his left hand. His fingers were short, his palm wide. The gold wedding band still hugged the fourth digit. He lifted his fist and picked at the nails, one by one. "Em, I don't want to say a word against your mother. She was a good wife, all right. I ought to let it die with her. But the truth is, she thought I was one of them. One of the Families, I mean. She was from Portugal, she didn't know how things were around here. She heard my last name was Winthrop, what was she supposed to think? She thought I owned the whole island. She thought I lived at Summerly, not the damn caretaker's house. By the time she realized what was what, she was expecting your brother. Had no choice but to get hitched."

"She told you this?" I whispered.

"I figured it out, Em. Even a dumb Yankee like me can tell when his wife doesn't love him like a wife should."

I reached for the pack of cigarettes he'd left on the kitchen table and lit one. Pop gulped down his coffee and spent some time arranging the mug next to the little tin ashtray on the red-and-white oilcloth while his eyes blinked rapidly. At last the two were in perfect alignment. He raised his head to stare out the window again and said, "So you see, I owe the Peabodys everything. My work, my house, my goddamn wife. All those hospital bills. Little things down the years, things I never even told you about."

"Are you saying you don't like the deal anymore? You think they own you? They don't own you, Pop. You can leave. You can find another house to live in."

"What house?"

"I don't know. In the harbor or something."

"And do what? What else am I supposed to do, Em? What else am I good for? Taking care of rich people's houses, that's all. Taking care of rich people's lives."

"That's what you chose, Pop."

He examined the end of his cigarette. "Can't you just tell me? At least tell me what the hell's going on, so I don't take it on the blind side when everything breaks loose."

I pulled a mug from the cabinet and poured myself some coffee from the percolator on the range. "Tell you what, Pop," I said. "I'm going upstairs to pack my things. If you're so damn curious about what your Peabodys are up to, you can just drop by Sumner Fox's place on your way to knock around with Aunt Benedita and ask him yourself."

It didn't take long to pack. Honestly, it kind of shocked me to see how easily my earthly belongings fit into a medium-sized suitcase. Best and second-best dress.

A couple of sundresses, a couple of warmer woolen dresses for winter, brassieres and underpants and girdle and stockings, the fine corselet Mama and I had purchased in New London for my high school graduation. Hairbrush and pins, toothbrush and toothpaste and face cream. I left my few books on their shelves and my winter coat in the closet. It was California, after all. I'd save up and buy a different coat when I arrived there, a lighter and more stylish coat, such as a married woman might wear. Maybe a matching hat, if we could afford it. I didn't want to depend on Shep's parents for money.

A married woman, I thought. Shep's wife. Mr. and Mrs. Nathaniel Peabody.

I swallowed back a shiver of nerves and closed the suitcase.

When I came back downstairs, Pop was gone. I looked out the window and saw that the garage was empty. A note lay on the kitchen table inside a plain white envelope. I tore open the envelope and pulled out the paper, folded over once. At the top was a small black engraved monogram in plain lettering, *NBP.* In an instant of panic, I realized I had no idea what the *B* stood for. I was engaged to marry this man and I didn't even know his middle name!

The note was scribbled in an eager and untidy hand.

Cricket, honey,

Off to catch the early ferry and make all plans with Union Pacific and my pal Frank out in California who will arrange for wedding ceremony etc. Can you meet me at South Station at 4pm. If you have any trouble getting away leave a message at the USO waiting room. Otherwise in three days time you will be my lawful wife. But I will always mark the real date of our anniversary Aug 6th.

Your loving husband, S.

The last time I checked, Susana was still asleep. It was funny, how much time she spent abed these days. Until this summer she was always the first one up, even before Pop, singing and dancing around the kitchen while the rest of us stumbled in bleary-eyed. Mama used to call her a lark. Mama always adored Susana, her baby. She admired me but it was Susana she adored. Now Susana didn't rise until late in the morning and for some reason I hadn't thought about it much. Waiting tables was hard work and ran late. When you finally collapsed into bed, you wanted to sleep forever. And Mama's death was a terrible shock to her. She'd been devastated, she'd hardly spoken. I climbed the stairs in a state of awful guilt. How had

I allowed myself to become so distracted, so sunk in my own pain, I hadn't noticed the suffering of my own baby sister?

The staircase was narrow and dark, the steps worn. I came to the top and rested my hand on the newel post. *I might never climb these stairs again*, I thought. Never rest my hand on that old post. Another shimmer of panic went through my stomach so I closed my eyes and conjured Shep. Shep a few hours ago, saying a silent goodbye outside the kitchen door. The sun hasn't risen and his face is dark, so I see him with my skin and nose and ears. His large hands on either side of my face. The smell of salt on his skin. He whispers something. I whisper something back. My fingers brush the sand from his hair. I don't want to let him go. He laughs quietly into my mouth. I ask what's so funny. He says it isn't funny really, it's just that I can't seem to let go of you. I tell him he's being silly. We have our whole lives. He says, I know that. But he doesn't move. We stand there for another minute, another minute, because neither of us wants to be the one who pulls away.

I opened my eyes. Through the old wooden walls stuffed with horsehair and the desiccated bones of generations of mice, a sound reached my ears—a muffled human noise like a sob.

I hurried around the landing. I'd left the door to Susana's room ajar. Now I pushed it open, without knocking. From beneath the covers, Susana made a little cry and sat up.

"Sweetie, what's the matter?"

She turned away to face the wall and wiped frantically at her face. "Nothing!"

I rushed to the bed and laid my hand on her back. "You're sad about Mama?"

"Yes. *Yes*. I-I miss her, th-that's all."

The sobs still shuddered through her body, which was far too thin. I felt the bones of her ribcage through all the layers of nightgown and sheet and quilt.

"Me too," I said. "I miss her terribly."

We weren't much for talking, we Winthrops, even and maybe especially in times of sorrow. I couldn't think of a word of genuine comfort. I didn't think such words existed when you were stuck in new grief. Instead I went around the bottom of the bed and sat next to her. I put my arm around her thin shoulders and bundled her close to my side.

"Susana," I said, "how would you like to come to California with me?"

She jolted away. *"California?"*

"Yes, California." I tried to pull her back, but the more I reached for her, the farther she drew away. I returned my hands in my lap and said, "I'm— Susana, I'm going away with Shep."

"With Shep? To California? What are you, *eloping*?"

"I know it's a shock. I tried to tell you before, but you were asleep or away, or it wasn't—I just couldn't tell you. We've—well, I guess I was going to say we've fallen in love, but I think we've always loved each other, and now that—well, now that—"

"Now that's Mama's gone," she said in a dull voice, "you're free. Aren't you? Free as a bird to fly away."

"No! No, it's not *that*. Not at all. I just can't stay here any longer. All the memories and the—the walls, Susana, the *furniture*. You know what I mean. She's everywhere. I need to start fresh. Shep feels the same way. He feels—oh, what's the word. Claustro-phobic. He feels as claustrophobic here as I do. So we're leaving, before anyone can try to talk us out of it, and the only bad thing, the worst thing is leaving you behind, Susana. When you're miserable like this. You need to start fresh, too. You need to come with us. You—"

"Do you know something, Cricket? I can always tell when you're lying to me. You start to babble."

"Babble?"

She threw the quilt over her head and lay back on the pillow. "Go to California, Cricket. I'm sure you'll have a wonderful time there. It's what you've always wanted, anyway. Marrying a Peabody."

I jumped to my feet. "How *dare* you!"

"Go away," she said. "Just go."

I made it all the way to the landing before I burst into tears. I tried to sob softly so I wouldn't give Susana the satisfaction of hearing me, but how do you fall apart without making a noise? I braced my hands on the banister rail and ground my teeth into each other. In the hallway below stood the ancient grandfather clock that Pop wound each morning on his way to the kitchen. I watched the brass pendulum swing back and forth. Half past nine. Was that all? I should have told Shep I would leave with him on the early ferry. We could have left together, hand in hand. Now I had hours to wait. I'd thought I needed time to pack and gather my wits and explain everything to my sister. I'd thought I needed to go through each room in the house where I had spent my life, to say goodbye tenderly to the memories stuck in the walls and floorboards and furniture. It turned out that the old saying was right. You should make a clean break. You should just go.

A knock shook the old panels. I jumped away from the banister and ran down the stairs before I realized I'd moved at all. Nerves, I guess. The knock came again, from the front door in the center hall. I grasped the metal door latch and flung it open. I don't know whom I was expecting, but it wasn't the man who stood on the front step.

"Dr. Pradelli!" I exclaimed.

He took off his hat to expose his thick black hair. "Excuse me, Miss Winthrop. I'm awfully sorry to disturb you in your time of mourning. Do you mind if I come in?"

I stepped back. "Not at all."

Five or six years ago, old Dr. Smith had retired and this new fellow had taken over his practice on the island. It was a good thing for Mama—or maybe a bad thing, depending on how you looked at it—because Dr. Smith didn't know a cerebral hemorrhage from a cereal box, let alone how to treat one. People had loved him, though. He'd had a nice friendly bedside manner and he prescribed pills by the dozen, which always made you feel better even if they didn't. I didn't know if the summer families liked Dr. Smith as much. For most of their ailments they tended to call up Dr. Huxley, who had a practice among all the top-drawer types in the Back Bay and summered here on Winthrop in a sprawling shingle house overlooking

Little Bay. But Dr. Pradelli had been raised in Norwalk, Connecticut, by his Italian parents and gone to medical school on scholarship, so he couldn't afford to take over somebody's fancy metropolitan practice. He was stuck with Winthrop Island. When I found Mama on the bathroom floor I was all alone in the house and Dr. Pradelli had only started practicing the previous year, yet he had rushed over within minutes of my incoherent call. He had taken thirty seconds to examine her and used our telephone to ring up some old colleague from his residency at Massachusetts General—not forgetting to reverse the charges—and by evening Mama was inside a Boston hospital room surrounded by all the best brains in the brain repair business.

So I will always worship Dr. Pradelli and when he arrived at my door that morning, even though I was in the middle of eloping with Shep Peabody, I bustled him straight into the keeping room and asked if he would sit, if I could bring him some coffee or a slice of cake. (Our neighbors had brought us cake enough to last until Thanksgiving.) He said no thank you, he didn't want to intrude, he wouldn't have come at all if it weren't a matter of such concern. He spun his hat in a circle between his hands as he said this, looking at me earnestly through a pair of thick glasses. I felt a little cold in my fingertips and asked him what on earth could have caused him such concern.

"Miss Winthrop," he began—I had begged him once to call me Emilia but he was the kind of fellow who persevered with formality—"Miss Winthrop, I didn't want to burden you at the time, but when I first examined your mother—God rest her—when I first examined your mother at the time of the—er, the discovery of her body, it seemed to me that she had not died in such a way as you might expect a woman in her condition and of her general health to perish."

"I don't understand," I said.

"She died in her sleep, as you know. Her heart simply stopped beating. And this gave me some not inconsiderable concern because she had never manifested any previous heart trouble. I would say her heart was always robust, quite robust. I didn't imagine that it would simply give out, without prior symptoms of disease. Yet she hadn't experienced another brain hemorrhage. She had no other dangerous conditions of which I had become aware, in the years during which I had the honor of overseeing her care. In fact, she was hardly sick a day in all that time, other than the aftereffects of her stroke."

The windows of the keeping room faced west to catch the afternoon sun. As a result, the morning light

was shadowy, almost opaque, and it made Dr. Pradelli's smooth, young face look like it had been polished from sandstone. I put my hand on the back of
Mama's old armchair. Dr. Pradelli looked down at
the hat between his hands and turned it over. It was
a fedora made of straw, appropriate for the season, if
a little worn. He wasn't what you'd call a handsome
man, Dr. Pradelli. He was slight and soft of limb and
had terrible eyesight, judging by the thickness of his
eyeglasses. But he was also the kind of man who read
robust technical journals in the evening the way other
men listened to baseball. I always pictured him in his
humble childhood kitchen, turning the pages of some
volume of Kant or Carlyle he'd dragged home from the
library, while his brothers played stickball in the empty
lot next door. I wondered what Winthrop Island had
done to deserve him.

"But her death certificate said it was a heart attack,"
I said. "Your signature was on the paper. A heart
attack."

"Yes. But I also collected samples of her blood and
urine, as a matter of routine. I sent them to a laboratory
for analysis."

"You didn't mention that. A *laboratory*?"

"As I said, I had some questions. I don't like to leave
questions unanswered."

"But you said it was a heart attack." My voice rose. "A heart attack, right there on the death certificate."

"I never imagined—that is, as I said, I was puzzled, but there was no evidence of any other cause of death." He spun the hat around in the opposite direction. "Until the laboratory returned some unexpected results."

"Well," I said. "Well, that's just terrific."

"The laboratory found a very high level of pentobarbital in her blood. It is the chemical found in Nembutal, which is the sleeping pill I had previously prescribed for her."

"Mama took sleeping pills?"

"Your father told me she had trouble sleeping. I have always been reluctant to prescribe a pill for a condition whose root cause lies elsewhere, but in the case of your mother—well, she had never manifested any tendency to psychological depression."

"Are you saying—are you trying to tell me that Mama killed herself?"

"My goodness, no. I certainly couldn't speculate on the manner in which the drug was ingested. I can only tell you the result of the laboratory report." Dr. Pradelli looked to the doorway, for some reason, and then back to me. "I'm glad to have found you alone, Miss Winthrop. Ordinarily I would convey this kind of difficult information to the surviving spouse, but I have always felt that your father—well, that between the two of you, it was best to approach you first. It's up to you to decide whether to communicate this information to Mr. Winthrop. You know him best."

"Dr. Pradelli," I said, "are you going to change the official cause of death?"

Dr. Pradelli sighed and turned his head to look out the window. "Miss Winthrop, before I took over my duties here, I spent many hours with Dr. Smith discussing the practice of medicine in a small community—an island. He gave me some excellent advice. He told me—reminded me, really—that I'm here to serve the needs of the residents in a medical capacity. That is my first duty. And it doesn't seem to me that any particular need is served by revealing the exact means by which your mother's heart stopped beating." He put his hat on his head. "Of course, if you feel such a course is necessary, you'll let me know. Won't you?"

"Of course," I said.

Dr. Pradelli held out his hand. "I must return to my office, I'm afraid. I can only hope I haven't caused you any undue pain at a time of unimaginable grief. You will of course let me know if you have any further need of me."

I shook his hand and said I appreciated his taking the time to visit.

When he was gone, I sat in Mama's armchair next to the radio and stared at the wall. One of my great-grandfather's sisters had had a passion for oil painting, and an example of her efforts hung before me in its plain wooden frame. It was there on the keeping room wall all my life so I never really took much notice. The subject was a storm at sea and a small, helpless sailboat heeling to starboard at such a deep angle it seemed on the brink of capsizing. A curl of foam licked the bow deck. At the tiller sat a dim, futile figure, hunkered down to await his fate. That was all you could do, really. You did your best to survive but in the end you were no match for the ocean.

I hadn't asked for many details about Mama's death. It was late in the evening when Olive had woken me with the news, and the excitement was over by then. What I understood was Pop had found her in her bed when he came home from work—from sleeping with Aunt Benedita, I wanted to scream—and she wouldn't wake up. She was dead. It was Susana who had taken Mama upstairs for her nap after I'd left for the library with Olive and she was hysterical. She blamed herself. Apparently she thought she should have gone upstairs to check on Mama at some point that afternoon, but she'd just figured Mama was exhausted after her adventures on the beach that morning.

Don't kick yourself, I'd told Susana. *It wouldn't have made any difference. It was her time, that's all.*

I rose from the chair and went upstairs to the bathroom. On the wall hung an old cabinet where we kept Mama's medicines. I opened the door but it was empty, not a single tube or jar or bottle remaining, certainly nothing labeled *Nembutal* or that advertised itself as a sleeping pill. Pop had packed up all of Mama's things in the days after her death. Had put what was worth keeping in some cardboard boxes in the cellar and thrown everything else away. Susana and I had offered to help but he'd insisted on doing everything himself. It was only right, he said, the last thing a man could do for his wife.

I decided there was nothing for it but to strap my suitcase to the back of my bicycle and pedal down to the harbor. I couldn't ask Mrs. Peabody for a ride, after all, and God knew Olive Rainsford was out of the question. Then I remembered Tippy Pinkerton.

She was surprised to hear my voice on the line, all right. "Why, Cricket! Is something wrong?"

"I need a lift to the harbor this afternoon, is all. I'm going to town for a few days and I've got this old suitcase, and it seems everybody's out playing golf!" I made myself laugh, all lighthearted. "Would it be too much trouble? Just say the word if it's too much trouble."

"Why, of course it's not too much trouble. Honest, I'm glad you asked. I'll be there in a jiffy, Cricket."

She was, too. Tippy Pinkerton drove her family's station wagon, a venerable Buick woody. I couldn't remember the Pinkertons driving anything else. She jumped out and helped me hump my suitcase into the back. She wore a pink flowered dress and tortoise sunglasses and a headscarf over her short, dark hair that matched the dress. When she closed the door over the suitcase, she turned and wrapped me in a tight hug.

"I've been so worried about you, Cricket," she said. "Those first few weeks, you know, you're just in shock."

"I'm all right, really," I gasped. "She's out of her misery, anyway."

"She's with Eli now. You have to remember that."

"Yes, she's with Eli. He always was her favorite."

I said this in what I hoped was the kind of wry, sad voice that showed how well I was coping. Tippy made a wry, sad laugh in return and let me go. "You should come over for coffee or something. When you're back."

"Yes, I should. I really should."

We got in the car and Tippy started the engine again. The Buick had a nice throaty all-American chug that made you feel you were going places in a dignified way. She reached below to release the parking brake and we rolled down the drive. I tried not to think that this was the last time I would roll down my familiar driveway, the last time I would pass the giant rhododendron and catch sight of Summerly through the beach plum. Well, maybe not forever, but certainly for some time, certainly until everybody had forgotten the scandal of my leaving. We turned onto Serenity Lane and I looked deliberately away from the crisp white geometry of the guest cottage, though I couldn't help noticing that Olive's car sat in front of it.

Tippy was the type of driver who hunched over the steering wheel like she thought somebody was going to steal it from her. She didn't say anything. Most girls like her have the gift of chatter but not Tippy, at least not today. When I cast a sideways glance at her face, I saw she was wearing a stiff, wide smile beneath her sunglasses.

"How are the wedding plans going?" I asked.

"Oh, fine. Fine."

"I heard Mrs. Menezes is making your dress."

"Yes, she is."

"That's nice of you to have somebody local do the job. Instead of one of those fancy Boston shops, I mean."

"Oh, gosh. I didn't even think of that. I just like Mrs. Menezes," she said.

"Well, I'm sure she appreciates the extra dough. With her husband gone and all."

"She's such a talented seamstress. I wouldn't have wanted anyone else to—to make my wedding dress."

Her voice had caught on something that sounded like a sob. "Why, Tippy," I said.

"Don't mind me."

"But you're crying."

"I'm not! It's just—you know, wedding jitters—"

She pulled the car over to the side of the road and rummaged in her pocketbook. I thought she was going for a cigarette but instead she yanked out a pretty white handkerchief and blew her nose into it. "I'm sorry," she said.

"Don't be sorry."

"It's just that . . . I don't think there's going to be a wedding after all!"

"Oh, Tippy!"

"I think I've made a terrible mistake."

"What makes you think that?"

She folded the handkerchief and stuffed it into the pocket of her sundress. The day was warm and hazy and even with the windows rolled down, the air inside the Buick was turning hot. Tippy set her hands on the wheel and stared through the windshield. She had a dainty snub nose scattered with freckles, beneath which the skin was now pink to match her scarf and dress. I didn't know if it was the heat or what. She said, "You know Amory pretty well, don't you? Since you're neighbors."

"Pretty well, I guess. Not as well as you. I mean, I've only ever seen him on vacation."

"What do you think of him? His moral character?"

"His *moral* character?"

"Do you think he has one?"

Tippy's voice had turned cold and determined. You couldn't fudge around a voice like that. You couldn't babble some half-truths and call it a job well done.

"Not particularly, to say the truth," I said.

"That's what I thought." The engine had died. Tippy reached for the ignition switch and turned the key. The Buick made a couple of rheumy coughs and fell silent. She swore and pumped the gas pedal and tried again, and this time the engine chugged reluctantly to life. "Thanks for being honest with me, Cricket. Sometimes it seems to me that nobody on this island ever says what they really think. Not to your face, anyway. It makes me nuts. It's like some kind of pact. We'll protect each other to the death, even when it means somebody gets hurt. Don't you think?"

I opened my pocketbook and drew out a pair of cigarettes. "Ain't that the truth," I said.

———

The ferry was already loading when we pulled up at the dock. It was a Thursday and hardly anybody had a reason to leave the island, so the boat was mostly empty except for a couple of day-trippers headed home early. Well, I assumed they were day-trippers—I didn't recognize their cars. Tippy stubbed out her cigarette and jumped out of the station wagon to swing open the door at the back for my suitcase. She gave me a swift, hard hug.

"Have a lovely time," she said.

"Thanks for the ride. I hope everything works out."

"You're sweet. I think I know what I need to do."

I picked up my suitcase from the crumbled pavement. "Amory's a skunk, Tippy. He really is. You deserve somebody better. I mean you could really use a break."

She laughed. "You can say that again. Now go. You'll miss the ferry."

I jumped aboard just as the boys were starting to cast off the ropes. It was better this way, I thought. No time for second thoughts. The engine ground and the boat backed away from the dock. The black water swirled. I went inside the deckhouse and set down my suitcase next to a bench in the back. The air was stuffy in the midday heat so I ducked back out to stand by the port rail, away from the chattering day-trippers, and watch the sleepy buildings along the harbor. I caught a flash of Tippy's station wagon heading back up West Cliff Road before the ferry's prehistoric engines grumbled from reverse to forward and we turned to head out of the harbor and into the sound. A couple of lobster boats were returning from the morning catch. The gulls squawked and circled. All the old sights and sounds, driving me up the wall with their sameness but somehow precious at the same time. Each one sharp. I shut my eyes and thought about Shep. Thick shoulder under my cheek. Warm voice saying my name—*Cricket, honey.* Warm, shaggy, sandy hair. He would be waiting for me in Boston. He would be looking for me in the crowd walking off the train. He would see me and his broad, bony face would light up. He would grab my suitcase and hoist me off the ground with his delight and his artless strength. He would hurry me on board the train that would carry us across the country. Maybe he'd even booked us a private berth as Mr. and Mrs. Nathaniel Peabody. It was the kind of thing he would do, to surprise me. I would pretend to be surprised and a little scandalized. We would have dinner in the dining car and possibly a bottle of champagne to celebrate. I had never taken a sleeper train so I didn't know exactly how these things worked. I imagined the steward would make up the berths while we were having dinner, like they did in the movies. We would retire while the countryside blurred past the window, while the lights of the farmhouses glimmered like beacons in the dusk, and in the morning when we woke, we would be rolling into Chicago already and the steward would knock on our door with coffee. He would call us Mr. and Mrs. Peabody, and Shep, who would be smoking a morning cigarette, would look at me and wickedly wink.

"Miss Winthrop," said a voice at my elbow.

My eyes flashed open.

"I'm sorry to disturb you," said Sumner Fox, in his grave, courtly baritone. "I was hoping to have a private word, before we disembark."

We sat on a metal bench in the stern, so that everybody's back was turned. I didn't want to make a scene. Fox offered me a cigarette, which I accepted. The pack was new and he didn't light one for himself. "You don't smoke?" I asked, around the cigarette, as he held a steady match to the tip.

"No," he said.

"That's funny. I would have thought all you FBI men went through a pack of smokes like candy."

"I haven't been at the bureau that long. Maybe in a few years."

There were two cars on board the ferry, two groups of day-trippers. One was a family of five—lean, unsmiling husband and expectant wife and three children, two girls and a boy. The boy was the youngest, maybe three years old. I thought maybe the husband had been overseas in the war, he had that stare in his eyes. His wife looked like she might drop that baby any day now. The other passengers were a pair of teenage lovers, billing and cooing near the bow where the draft blew back the girl's brown hair so the boy could kiss her. They seemed very much in love. Out here on the water, the air was much cooler, but the perspiration still dripped down my sides. I turned my head to blow out some smoke and said, "You can say what you want, but I'm not changing my mind. I'm on my way out of town and nothing's going to stop me, least of all you."

"All right," said Fox. "But you'll hear me out, at least?"

"I don't have much choice, do I? Ambushed and all."

"I'm sorry about that."

"People noticed, you know. They saw us out on the

water together. You can't hide anything on Winthrop Island."

"I know." He leaned back against the railing and crossed one meaty leg over the other. He wore a pair of tan slacks and a blue knit shirt like a man trying to fit in with his surroundings. On top of his cropped brown hair sat a straw boater with a narrow navy-striped grosgrain ribbon around the crown. You didn't realize just how big his head was until you saw this hat, perched on top. The sun had tilted past noon and he squinted thoughtfully at the lumps and bumps of Bluff Point to the west, drowning in haze. He seemed in no hurry to speak.

I blurted out, "Pop—my father—he said he heard you were sent out to the Pacific somewhere."

"That's true."

"So what did you do there?"

"Not much, really. I spent most of the war in a Japanese prison camp."

He said the words so casually, the horror of them seemed somehow greater. "That's awful," I said. "I'm sorry."

"I'm luckier than most. I survived it."

"So how did you end up in the FBI?"

"I spent a few months in the hospital after I came home," he said. "A friend of mine came to visit and said he had a job for me, if I was interested. The bureau had been approached by a woman who claimed to be part of a Soviet spy ring that had penetrated the highest levels of the United States government—I told you about her yesterday. Elizabeth Bentley. They needed someone to chase those leads. I happen to have a knack for languages and—well, a few other skills. My friend thought I was the right person for the job."

"And you took it. Why?"

Fox uncrossed his legs and leaned forward to rest his forearms on his thighs. His straw hat cast a delicate pattern of shadow on the gray-painted deck. "There was this fellow I used to know, back home," he said. "Terrific guy. Not much of an athlete, more of a cerebral type. Mathematician, musician. He could play just about any instrument you wanted. He was funny, too. We used to have a lot of laughs, Bill and I. Then he got to college and he fell in with what you might call a political crowd. Smart young fellows, socialists to a man. There were a lot of them back then. It was the thirties, the Depression. People had turned away from capitalism, young people especially, and who could blame them? They wanted something new, something better. They looked to the Soviet Union and thought Communism was the wave of the future. I mean, whatever you think about Stalin, he's a terrific salesman.

And when you're young and clever, like this fellow, like his friends, and you've turned away from religion because it's a relic of the old superstitions, this old imperialism that drove millions of men into the trenches and all that—why, there's a certain appeal to an intellectual system that does everything a religion does, only without what Bill used to call the *mumbo-jumbo*. Here was this bright shining thing called Marxism, something you could believe in, a system that explained everything and wrapped it up in a neat little bow, original sin and repentance and salvation and everything, and so he believed in it. He believed in it passionately. We used to argue. I had my own ideas, he had his. At first those arguments were friendly, lighthearted even, but gradually he got to see me as—" Fox shook his head and pressed his thumbs together, as if he were squeezing out a word between them. "As a heretic, I guess. A nonbeliever. He didn't want to hear my arguments against this bright shining thing he believed in so deeply, this faith that he couldn't seem to separate from himself. I mean his *sense* of himself, as a man who cared about humanity. He stopped speaking to me at all. Eventually he left his own family here in the States and traveled to the Soviet Union, moved to Moscow, and for a while he seemed happy enough. He was living right in the middle of the city, studying at the university there. He sent a letter every so often, telling me about this heaven on earth, this workers' paradise that was Soviet Russia. It was everything he dreamed, he said."

Fox looked down at his hands and spread his palms. I had finished the cigarette and reached over the railing to drop it into our wake. I noticed the scars on his skin, these horny calluses that disfigured his fingers. Where had they come from? Blisters, maybe. God only knew what kind of torture went on in those prison camps.

"And then what?" I said.

"He disappeared. His letters just stopped coming. At one point I wrote to the university and tried to find out what had happened to him, but they returned all my inquiries. Finally there was this official reply that stated they had no administrative record of old Bill, that he had never registered with Moscow State University or even existed, apparently. That was in early 1941. I tried to arrange a visit, see what I could do to track him down. But Hitler invaded Russia that summer, as you know, so it came to nothing. Then Pearl Harbor. Wasn't until the end of the war that I finally got some word of him."

Fox's voice caught on itself. He raised his fist to his mouth and cleared his throat.

"Was he alive?" I asked.

"No. He'd been denounced by a colleague of his,

accused of counterrevolutionary activities, spying for the West. Executed at dawn in the basement at Lubyanka. Bullet through the head. The body was probably cremated, but there's no way to know for sure. Certainly not now."

"What's Lubyanka?" I asked.

"The KGB prison in Moscow."

We had reached the mouth of the Thames. Behind Fox's big head, the Groton shore edged past in dark, abundant green. The sun slanted down on his hat and the shadow of the brim cut a sharp diagonal line across his cheek and jaw to a point just below his ear.

"He seems to have meant a lot to you, this fellow," I said.

"He was my brother," said Fox. "My kid brother. William Fox."

"Oh, gosh. I'm sorry."

He straightened and recrossed his legs. Folded his arms across his chest and stared straight ahead to the deckhouse, where the teenagers necked frantically on a bench. The tip of his nose was pink, just like Tippy Pinkterton's nose as we drove down West Cliff Road toward the harbor.

"So you see, Miss Winthrop," he said, in the same gravelly drawl as before, "I take this whole business pretty seriously. If I go to my grave trying to fight that kind of system—the kind of system that denounces anybody who's got the nerve to disagree—why, I would count my life well spent."

"I'm sure you would."

"Look, I understand your point of view, believe me. You're loyal to the core, Miss Winthrop, and that's a quality I admire. You're loyal to the island and you're loyal to the family that's provided yours with a home and a living. They're people you love and admire. And I don't deny Mrs. Rainsford is an admirable woman. She's brilliant and brave and resourceful. She's like my brother. She believes in something with all her heart, and she's blind to the evil it does. Willfully blind, maybe, and that's what makes her dangerous. But you can't let your loyalty to some misguided individual blind *you*, Miss Winthrop."

I stood up. "That's not true. I'm not blind. I'm not blind at all, and I'm certainly not some kind of toady to the Peabodys. I'm leaving the island for good, if you want to know the truth. Washing my hands of this life. If you think Olive—if you think Mrs. Rainsford is a Soviet spy, why, go ahead and nab her. Be my guest. I'm not going to stop you."

Fox stood up and took my elbow. Firmly he guided me to the starboard rail and stood right next to me, blocking my view of the other passengers. Up close, his size dwarfed mine. He looked down on me with that same absence of expression as before, except his eyes had narrowed into fierce crescents. "Forgive me," he said, "but that's not what you told us yesterday."

"Yes, it is. Yesterday I washed my hands of the whole thing, and that's still true today."

"Today you're leaving Winthrop Island altogether. So what's forced your hand?"

"Nothing."

"You're hiding something."

"I'm not hiding a thing."

"Our meeting yesterday. Set off an alarm."

"Our meeting yesterday was an annoyance, that's all."

"You realize the FBI doesn't treat fugitives lightly."

"Well, I'm not a fugitive."

"How else am I to interpret this sudden flight?"

"There's nothing sudden about it. I'm getting married, if you must know."

"To whom?"

"None of your business."

Somehow I managed to keep my gaze steady with his. I didn't babble, either. It seemed I was getting used to this kind of thing. Fox went on scrutinizing me with his hard crescent eyes. He had an unnerving tendency not to blink but I held my nerve anyway. The ferry made a couple of short blasts of its horn. We were outside the shadow of the deckhouse now and the sun burned my arms. Fox's face settled into a frown. He turned his body away from me and leaned one elbow on the railing.

"You've heard about the atom bomb, of course," he said.

"Gosh, no," I replied. "What's an atom bomb?"

"All right. Maybe you've heard about the recent tests out on the Pacific? The Bikini Atoll?"

"I think it's outrageous. The war's over. The sooner we set aside these immorally destructive weapons, the better."

"You might say *any* weapon that can kill another human being is immorally destructive, Miss Winthrop. A single life or a thousand or a million lives, the loss is still irreplaceable. But that's not my point. My point isn't whether we were right or wrong to drop the bomb, or even to create it in the first place. That horse is out of the barn, this is the world we've got. The point is what we do with it next."

I looked at my watch, then toward shore. The New London docks were taking shape off the port bow. "Mr. Fox, honestly, I don't really have time for a discussion about the ethics of atomic research. In ten minutes I'll be walking off this boat and boarding a train for Boston."

The breath rushed out of Fox's lungs. He set his two hands on the rail and braced himself. He seemed to be in some kind of physical pain, though you wouldn't know it from his expression. He didn't wince or grimace or anything. It was just a feeling I had.

"You agree, don't you, that the atomic bomb is a weapon of immense destructive power. That such power should never fall into the hands of an undemocratic state. One with scant regard for the lives of its own citizens, let alone those of other countries."

"All right. I see where you're headed with this."

"Imagine for just a second what would happen if an airplane dropped an atomic bomb on Boston or New York."

"Oh, please."

"You don't think it's possible? You don't think Stalin might do such a thing, if he could?"

"Why would he, though? Even if he could? We'd just bomb him back, wouldn't we?"

"You're willing to stake the fate of the world on that? A paranoid psychopath like Stalin? The lives of everyone you know and love? Think of what would happen, Miss Winthrop. Think of Boston obliterated, of a cloud of radiation spreading across New England. You would feel the force of the blast here on this island. You would likely be in the evacua-

tion zone. Your father, your sister, your friends.
The Peabodys. Winthrop Island would have to be
abandoned. The effects of the radiation would cause
burns, cancers—"

"All right, all right!"

"You want that on your conscience? You want to
know in your heart that you could have done something, and instead you ran away?"

"That's not fair!"

He angled his head closer. "Listen to me. The
development of a working atomic weapon required
the cooperation of a vast number of scientists from
countries around the world. Not all of whom, it turns
out, were vetted as well as they could have been. Or
it might be better to say that we needed certain scientific knowledge and skills so badly, we didn't look
too closely at where they came from. People who held
not just Communist sympathies—I mean any man can
believe what he wants, that's his right—but outright
loyalty to the Communist Party. People who didn't
like the idea of the capitalist West having a monopoly
on atomic power. And some of those people—not all,
maybe, but some—seemed to think there was nothing
dangerous about giving away the recipe to a weapon
that could destroy entire countries in a single day to a
murderous dictatorship. That it was just fair play."

"You're saying scientific information about the atom bomb got into the hands of the Soviets?"

"Landed right on Stalin's desk," he said.

The ferry's horn blasted again. In spite of the heat I was shivering. My legs shook underneath me so I had to grip the railing, right next to Fox's gnarled hands. "So it's already too late," I said.

"It's not too late. They haven't built it yet. If we can stem the tide. If we can stop the flow of information."

The engines ground to maneuver into the dock. I could hear the shouts of the dockworkers, the answering calls of the ferry's deckhands. Tom and Steve, good island boys. Tom had lost a couple of fingers on his father's lobster boat when he was ten and Steve was blind in one eye, so they'd both been turned down by the Army and spent the war working the ferry, summer and winter. Now here they were, still at it. I followed Fox's gaze and realized he was observing Tom carefully, and it occurred to me that if you wanted to know who was coming and going from Winthrop Island, you couldn't find a better man.

Even as this thought struck me, Tom turned his head to take us in, and I'll be damned if he didn't move his head in the smallest nod you ever saw before he returned to his ropes.

In a steady voice like he was reporting on the

weather, Fox said, "I'm saying that two days ago, one of our field teams followed the automobile of a known Communist International member whom we suspect to have recruited several atomic scientists to gather classified information for the Soviets. We followed the car to New London, where we believe Mrs. Rainsford's dead letter drop site is located. That's how she collects and leaves communications for her sources. The team lost the subject before the drop occurred, unfortunately. But that very morning, Mrs. Rainsford was observed to board the early ferry to New London and return again in time for your mother's funeral."

The ferry banged into place. This is it, I thought. Your last chance. Now or never.

I picked up my suitcase. "You're nuts, you know that? This is out of my league. You're on your own."

As I turned away, his hand snared my right arm.

"One last detail, Miss Winthrop," he said softly, almost a whisper. "I don't mean to pry, but I understand you received a visit from your mother's physician this morning?"

I pulled back my arm, but he held on with a gentle, implacable grip. "I don't think that's any of your business, is it?" I said.

"Maybe not. But a man who's carrying on an affair with the sister of his recently deceased wife might not want the world to know that she died of an overdose of Nembutal, rather than some natural cause."

The ramp clanked down. From around us came the noise of a couple of car engines, roaring to life. "I—I don't know what you mean," I said.

Fox sighed and released my arm. "Let's not waste time we don't have, Miss Winthrop. The point isn't whether I would or would not make use of this information. The point is what I can do to help, should that information somehow make its way to the district attorney's office. If, for example, such a report could be considered classified material, due to its relevance to an espionage case before the FBI."

Around the handle of the suitcase, my fingers had gone numb. My head spun, like I might faint or something. I thought of Dr. Pradelli's earnest eyes, the expression on his face that now seemed to convey not sympathy, but something more like a warning.

I whispered, "You're actually trying to blackmail me?"

"I'm saying we all do what we must, when it's a matter of life and death."

"This isn't a matter of life and death, though. Is it?"

Fox reached for the suitcase and pulled it from my numb hand. "But that's what I've been trying to tell you," he said. "It is."

When we were kids, Shep and I used to get ice cream from Mrs. Medeiro and sit on the bench outside the general store to watch the comings and goings in the harbor. Shep liked to watch for the lobster boats but I wasn't much interested in the fishing trade. Just about every boy at Winthrop Island School worked on his pop's lobster boat during the summer and who cared about that? No, it was the ferry that fascinated me. During the summer season it carried in day-trippers for their picnics and beach afternoons and carried out islanders for their errands and their business trips. A lot of the men summering on Winthrop worked in the city during the week, New York or Boston or sometimes Hartford, and they would take the early morning ferry out on Mondays and the evening ferry back on Thursdays or Fridays. But every so often you got someone you couldn't figure out. Like that one summer when this attractive dark-haired man used to arrive on Tuesday or Wednesday morning, and Mrs. Nolan, whose husband was a lawyer in New York, picked him up in her little Nash Six. The Nash was a convertible but she always raised the top when she arrived at the ferry dock and waited for this man to climb in her car. I remember frantically licking my ice cream cone under the hot sun while I tried to puzzle it out. I poked Shep in the side and asked him what he thought, and he just shrugged and said it was none of our business. The Nolans divorced the following year and sold their house to a new family called Hughes, who became members of the Club last summer after years of maneuvering.

Anyway, in my eyes, the ferry glided across Winthrop Island Sound inside a cloud of magic. It was the gateway to the world beyond, the door through which you could escape and return. When I rode the ferry as a child, on some necessary shopping expedition or a rare visit to a relative, I looked forward to the journey as much as the trip itself. You would stare at the swirling water as the engines ground and the boat backed out of its dock. You would feel that instant of thrilled panic as the gap widened between the ferry and the island. Then you realized you had now actually *separated* from Winthrop, that this land on which you slept and ate and played and went to school was now somewhere else, apart from you, receding, and as you drew farther away you realized how small it was, just a lump of rock and bushes surrounded by tiny sailboats, and how big was the world outside it, waiting to be explored.

And then you returned. You boarded the ferry in New London, laden with your shopping bags, a little beaten up and frazzled by all the strangers and the traffic and the stores with their vast arrays of goods—things you'd never imagined—all the noises and hustle and the thousands of little decisions you had to make, instantly. You sank down on one of the metal benches in the deck-house, slippery with its dozen or so layers of paint, and you didn't even notice the moment you separated from the mainland. You were chugging out of the mouth of the Thames River before you even recovered from your stupor. You heard the bowel-like groan of the engines, you smelled the oily smoke. You roused yourself in time to spot Winthrop in the distance. Steadily the island grew in size and detail, more familiar by the second. You picked out all the sailboats clustered around Little Bay and the lobster boats moored in Winthrop Harbor. You recognized the houses perched on the sides, exactly the same as you'd left them. You didn't know whether you felt relief or despair.

But you couldn't imagine a world in which they no longer existed, the signposts to home.

On the ferry back to Winthrop Island with Sumner Fox, I didn't feel much at all. The shock had numbed me, I guess. Fox didn't try to make me speak, not until we were halfway back and I turned to him and said, "Before we do anything else, I have to make a telephone call."

"Why?" he said.

"To the fellow I was supposed to meet in Boston at four o'clock this afternoon."

He nodded. "Nathaniel Peabody."

"How did you— Oh, never mind."

"I knew he left the island on the early ferry this morning. And it doesn't take any particular investigative skill to understand that he's in love with you."

I rubbed the side of my shoe against my suitcase. We sat in the deckhouse now, staring straight ahead. The windows were thick with salt spray, so you couldn't see through them very well. It was like peering through a storm.

"If he's half the man I think he is, he'll understand you're doing the right thing," said Fox. "He'll be proud of you."

"Maybe," I said. "So how does this work? What am I supposed to do?"

"You go home, as usual. You make contact with Mrs. Rainsford, tell her you're ready to resume watching the children for her."

"What if she decides she doesn't need me after all?"

"Why would she do that?"

"Maybe she noticed me leaving with a suitcase. Maybe she's suspicious of you. A lot of reasons."

"Well, then it's up to you to regain her trust, as soon as possible."

"Terrific," I said.

"Once you're back in the house, I'll give you a camera. A miniature one you can hide on your body, so you can take photographs of anything you find," said Fox.

"Piece of cake."

"When she asks you to come over and watch the children, telephone me." He took a small notebook from his breast pocket and scribbled something on one of the pages with the delicate metal pen attached to the case. "Here's the number. If there's no answer, call the Club and tell Mr. Finch you need to speak to June Lindstrom about a compact Mrs. Peabody left at dinner the other night."

"Don't tell me Finch is on your payroll, too."

"I wish he were. No, June will know what the message means. I'll come over to your house with my receiving equipment around six. It's going to take some time to—"

"What? You're coming inside my *house*?"

"Yes. Didn't I make that clear? Your house is our listening post. It's within a hundred yards of the target, and what's more, we'll leave no outward indication of our presence inside. No one will know we're there."

"The heck someone won't. My pop, for one thing. He's never going to allow it."

"Then we'll get him away for the evening. He has a lady friend in the harbor, I'm sure it can be arranged."

I turned my head and stared at the side of Fox's face. He sat with his back straight and his arms crossed and his shoes laced, a real square. "You've got rocks for brains if you think Pop won't find out what's going on at the house. And when he realizes what I've done, he'll hit the roof. He stands to lose his job, his home, the house we've lived in for generations."

"You think the Peabodys will blame him?"

"Blame him? It's their own property!"

"Then you'll have to find a way to convince him. We need that house."

"In other words, you want me to blackmail my own father."

Sumner Fox went on staring straight ahead, as if he could see through those salt-crusted windows. The skin of his face was taut and flushed, though he didn't seem to be sweating even in the trapped heat of the deck-house. Maybe after living a few years in a prison camp somewhere near the equator, he didn't find our New England summers all that taxing. I couldn't tell if he was turning over this new development—my father's intransigence—in his head or what. *Rocks for brains*, I thought. That was what you might think, all right, just to encounter this hunk of brute meat and shake its paw, but it turned out he was as cunning as a snake under all that thick bone.

As if he could hear my thoughts, he stuck one hand out. The left hand, palm outward. He had big hands, large bones. The knuckles were like knobs; the joints stuck out at different angles, like they'd been broken and reassembled in the wrong places.

Ahead of us, Winthrop Island loomed so large, you could no longer see it all at once. The horn sounded, two short blasts. The engines pitched lower, the boat angled to starboard.

"I've been meaning to ask," I said. "What happened to your fingers? Football?"

He wiggled the digits. "Oh, that. No, that was during the war. Interrogation camp. The gentlemen there, they used to snap your fingers to make you talk."

"Did it work?"

"No," he said.

By chance—or maybe not—Mr. Medeiro was making a delivery to the Peabodys that very afternoon. He was happy to give me a lift. He didn't say anything as we trundled up West Cliff Road in the delivery van, and neither did I. I was thinking about Pop and how in

God's name I was supposed to convince him to allow the FBI to eavesdrop on Olive Rainsford from the comfort of our keeping room, the result being that his life would be ruined. I imagined myself saying, *It's either that or they prosecute you for murder, Pop. Your choice.*

Mr. Medeiro dropped me off at the end of the lane with a nod and a *So long, Emilia.* All the Portuguese on the island still called me Emilia. They didn't get this Cricket business. I humped my suitcase down the gravel track, past the rhododendron. The heat seemed to thicken with each step. I glanced at the garage and saw Pop's old green Ford parked halfway inside. I set down the suitcase and lifted my arm to look at my wristwatch. Three o'clock in the afternoon—why was he home? He was supposed to be out working right now.

The house dozed in front of me. Mama and I had planted geraniums at the start of summer but I had neglected to water them this week and the heads had turned brown and wilting. Mama would be appalled, I thought. She was only a week gone and already I had let her down. I picked up my suitcase and continued around the side of the house to the kitchen door. Just before I opened it, I heard a noise that made my hand freeze on the knob—like an animal keening for its dead.

Then my father's voice, honed sharp.

I turned the knob and burst into the kitchen.

Susana sat at the table in her old pink dressing gown. Her arms were crossed on the table's surface and her head was buried between them. Pop stood by the range, facing her. His cheeks were red and he seemed to have grown six inches. His head swiveled to greet me.

"Did you know anything about this?" he bellowed.

You have to understand that my father never bellowed. I couldn't even remember the last time he'd raised his voice—maybe back when Roosevelt was trying to pack the Supreme Court. Compared to my mother's sudden passions, his emotions ran the gamut from wooden to impassive. I shut the door behind me. Susana lifted her head. Her face was wet and blotched, her hair stuck to her temples. She looked at me like she was begging for something.

Oh, no, I thought. *Not this, too.*

The smell of cigarettes hung in the air. I looked from Susana back to Pop. The short gray hair stuck up straight from his scalp. His fists clenched. "Well, Em?" he yelled. "Did you?"

"I don't know what you're talking about."

"Of course you don't. You were too busy running around with the younger one."

Susana stood up. "Pop, stop it. It's not her fault."

"What's not my fault?" I said, even though I knew.

"That Peabody boy," Pop said. "I swear to God I'm going to kill him. I'm going to kill the bunch of them."

I opened my mouth to tell him no, he couldn't kill the Peabodys. To yell at him, *What about Mama, what did you do, did you make her swallow a bunch of pills, Pop, did you? Was it all for the best? Her best or yours?* But the telephone rang before I got the words out.

Susana cried, *I'll get it!*

The telephone was in the hallway. Susana scurried away while Pop and I stared at each other. I guess my face was as pink as his. I wanted to scream, I wanted to cry. I wanted to sink a kitchen knife into Amory Peabody. Pop's legs gave out and he crumpled into the chair.

"She's right," he said. "It's my fault. You were right. We should've left the island when that family bought us out. Clean break. On our own two feet, instead of living here for years on our hands and knees."

I sank to my knees in front of him and took his hands between mine. They were clenched into claws. "Pop, listen to me—"

Susana reappeared in the doorway. "Cricket? It's Mrs. Rainsford."

Olive's voice practically melted the line with sympathy. "Emilia, darling. How are you feeling?"

"Pretty well, all things considered."

"I wanted to apologize, first of all," she said.

"Apologize for what?"

"Well, I'm afraid I made it sound as if you weren't welcome, yesterday. You know you should consider my house the same as yours. I hope it isn't clumsy—so soon after your dreadful loss, I mean—I hope it isn't clumsy to say that I feel about you as I should feel about a daughter. I want you to feel as if you can turn to me."

"Of course—" I swallowed. "Of course I feel the same way. I shouldn't have taken you by surprise like that."

"That's it. I was surprised, that's all. I hope you'll forgive me."

"There's nothing to forgive, truly."

I felt somebody watching me and turned around. Pop stood in the kitchen doorway, arms crossed, frowning ferociously.

From down the line came the distant sound of screaming children. Olive's voice was muffled, like she'd put her hand over the mouthpiece of the telephone receiver. "Sebastian! Let go of your sister! No, I don't *care* if she took it first. Give it back. Oh, Emilia!" Olive released a frazzled laugh and her voice returned to clarity. "I admit it, I need you rather badly. They won't listen to me anymore. They keep asking for you."

"My goodness. Do you need me to report for duty?"

"Would you mind? I have an awful lot of work to catch up on, and I have the feeling that Tom and Edwina are sick and tired of playing babysitter. I'm afraid the children ride roughshod over them. Sebastian especially."

"I wouldn't mind at all. When do you need me?"

"Would tonight be too soon? There's this silly party at the Club, but I'll be straight back afterward to put my nose to the grindstone."

She spoke clearly enough that Pop must have heard her through the still, warm air of the hallway. His mouth opened and he took a step forward, as if to tear the receiver from my fingers. I turned away and shielded the mouthpiece with my other hand.

"Tonight's just fine," I said. "In fact, I think it would be a welcome distraction."

VI.

MAY 1954
Washington, DC

From his chair in the foyer, Fox shoots to his feet so quickly, he doesn't have time to wince.

"What's the matter?" he demands.

I stab my finger into his chest. "You *knew*. You knew what she was going to ask me for."

He hesitates. "Yes."

"Where's Dulles?"

"He's gone back to the office. I'll debrief him after you've made your decision."

"Well, you can tell that cunning little bastard the answer is no. *No!* Do you hear me? I'm not taking those kids. What am I, running some kind of an orphanage?

They don't remember me from Adam! And if they do, I'll bet they hate the sound of my name."

Fox takes me by the elbows. "All right, all right. Take it easy."

"Don't *tell* me to take it easy."

"You don't have to do it, all right? I know it's a lot to ask of anybody. Especially a woman who's got her own family. Her own career. I've already told Dulles, it's your decision."

My breath comes in panicked little spurts, like I've just sprinted the length of Boston Common. I seem to be leaning into Fox's hands, toward his chest. I straighten and push the strap of my pocketbook up my arm. Fox stares down at me, eyebrows knit in that concerned way he has.

"You're all right?" he says.

"Yes, I'm fine."

"Then I'll call for a taxi and take you to a hotel. You can't fly back to Boston tonight."

The rhythm of my breathing begins to slow. "You mean it? What about your deal? What about this Soviet prisoner you want to bring home?"

Fox shrugs his shoulders. "I guess we'll just have to find some way to bring her around."

In the taxi, Fox doesn't speak. Somehow the sun has fallen all the way down in the sky and a vivid sun-

set lingers on the horizon. I catch glimpses of it between the buildings and down the boulevards. There
is something so detached about riding in a taxi around
a city you don't know. You might be anywhere. You
feel as if you've slipped into another universe and left
your old life to carry on by itself. Why, only last night
I was flopping into bed with Cato. Now it seems like a
lifetime ago. A different woman.

After a while the silence gets on my nerves. I light
a cigarette and ask Fox about his wife. How did they
meet?

He's been looking out the window and turns to me
like he's forgotten I'm there. "My wife? I've known her
for years, though I'm afraid she didn't know I existed."

"That doesn't answer my question."

He smiles. "Let's just say she finally lost her senses
and agreed to marry me."

"And you've got a baby on the way. How nice."

"Due any day."

The taxi stops at a light. I crank down the window
to drop some ash on the pavement. "Can I ask you a
hypothetical question, Mr. Fox?"

"Certainly."

"If Mrs. Fox were to go into labor while you were at
some critical point in these negotiations—the prisoner
exchange, I mean, say the Soviets have some impossible

new demand and the clock is ticking to doomsday—would you drop everything and race to the hospital or merely send your wife an encouraging message over the telephone?"

Fox leans his head back against the seat and laughs from his belly. "Miss Winthrop, you're a national treasure."

"Well? You haven't answered."

"I'd go to the hospital, of course. If you'll pardon the crudity, my wife would have my balls off if I didn't."

"She sounds like my kind of girl. Is she the reason you left the FBI?"

The smile falls from his face. "No. I left the bureau years ago. Not long after the Rainsford trial, in fact."

"What for?"

He glances at the driver. "A special investigation. We had some leaks to plug."

"Top secret, I guess? Well, whatever it was, it's done a number on you."

"You think so?"

"The Fox I remember wouldn't give up so easily. The Fox I remember was all gung ho to save liberal democracy from the likes of Stalin. Hell-bent on rescuing us all from your poor brother's fate."

"Believe me, I still want to save liberal democracy."

He looks out the window again. "Maybe I'm just tired, that's all."

"We're all tired, I guess. The world knocks us around. You give your all to keep the atom bomb out of Stalin's hands, and what happens? You might as well have stayed home, that's all."

"Is that what you think? It was all for nothing?"

"Me? I don't give a damn anymore. That horse is out of the barn, as you said to me once. But I'll say this. Every time I see that clown McCarthy on the front page of the newspaper, I can't help wondering what my old friend Sumner Fox thinks about the state of things."

For a moment, it seems he's not going to take the bait. He stares out the window at the swift passage of streets and people, the incandescent sunset on the windows, like he's lost himself among them. Then he speaks, still staring. "George Bernard Shaw used to say you shouldn't wrestle with a pig, because you'll get dirty—"

"—and the pig likes it."

"Exactly," he says. "Exactly."

The taxi pulls up in front of a swanky brick building with three gold doors and a doorman in a red uniform. "The Mayflower," says Fox. "I hope it's to your liking."

"Oh, it'll do."

He jumps from the car with painful agility and opens the door for me. I guess a man of his breeding would rather cripple himself than allow a woman to climb out of a taxi unaided. We cross the lobby together and stop a few yards from the front desk.

"A suite has been reserved in your name," he tells me. "Stay as long as you like."

"That's a dangerous offer to make to a penniless doctoral student."

"You can charge your meals to the room, of course."

"Golly. To what do I owe all this generosity? The poor old American taxpayer, I guess."

"You've earned it. And it's fair to say the agency's budget has some flexibility."

"I can imagine." I stick out my hand. "I appreciate your understanding. Sorry I couldn't help you. I wish you the best of luck on this. And the new baby. God knows you'll need it."

He shakes my hand and draws a small white card out of the inside pocket of his jacket. "If you have second thoughts."

I pretend to examine the card and slip it into my pocketbook while I offer him this cheap, overbright smile I've learned since I moved to the mainland. "Of course."

The bellboy shows me every courtesy, even though I don't have any luggage. The suite is grand and empty, except for a pair of folded blue-striped pajamas on the bed and a tube of toothpaste perched on the edge of the bathroom sink, together with a toothbrush. I'm starving to death but I run a bath instead, give my skin a good hard scrub, wrap myself in the fluffy white robe and lounge on the sofa while I study the room service menu. The words blur together. The silence hurts my ears. The room, it's so big you can hear your own thoughts. You can hear the echoes of all the voices you heard today.

You remind me of myself.

I would much rather betray my country than betray my principles.

I remember how you cared for them.

I fling the menu to the floor and change back into my funeral suit and pearls. I brush my hair and color in some lipstick on my lips. The reflection in the mirror belongs to an exhausted woman whose eyes are too bright for her own good.

Downstairs, the after-work crowd seems to have boarded the trains for the wife and kids in the suburbs. I slide onto one of several empty stools at the bar and order a dry martini and a dinner menu. The bartender wears a red jacket and a flashy white smile. He delivers the martini with a flourish and asks what I'll have to eat. I order the sole meunière and sip the martini, which is beautifully made as you would expect from a high-class establishment like this. I feel only the littlest pang of guilt when I think of the American taxpayer.

I'm nibbling on a peanut when the second martini arrives. I look up from the peanut bowl in surprise. "But I didn't order another one," I tell the bartender.

The bartender nods to his left. "Compliments of the gentleman."

I turn to my right.

At the end of the bar stands a tall, plain, wide-shouldered man in a gray suit. He holds his hat in his hands. His face is even bonier than I remember, and his eyes, if I were close enough to see them, would be hazel. He seems to be waiting for permission to approach.

For some reason, I think I should stand. I turn a quarter-circle on the barstool and attempt to put my weight on my legs. But my legs are all of a sudden wobbly and my heel catches on the bar at the bottom of the stool, so instead of rising gracefully to my feet I lurch spectacularly to the ground like a drunk. The man darts forward to catch me, only he's too late to do anything except pick me off the floor.

Cricket, he says anxiously. Are you all right?

It's not fair to say I haven't heard from Shep Peabody in all this time. A year or so after the trial he sent me a letter all the way from California, which I keep in a file cabinet, tucked inside the folder of documents relating to the Great Snow of 1717. I figure nobody will ever find it there, not even Lizbit.

Dear Cricket,

Please excuse my taking the liberty of writing to you. I hope you'll do me the favor of reading this through, despite everything that has passed.

First let me say that I understand now why you chose not to speak to me after what happened that terrible evening. We were all in a state of great shock and my mother, as you know, was devastated by the outcome. Your father refused to forward my letters and the FBI would not disclose your address to me. All this is not to excuse why I gave up trying. I guess you could say I was mad. I felt as betrayed as anybody. From your silence I came to figure that my worst fears were true, that what happened between us wasn't real and you had been using my affection to win my trust and it was all part of the FBI operation against my aunt. What I didn't learn until recently was that my mother had found a way to reach you afterward. I don't know exactly what she said to you but I can guess. Cricket, I am sorrier than I can express. It is safe to say that Mama was not the same after that terrible night. She has required constant medical supervision for some time now. In order to cope with her grief she has focused all her anger and blame on you, and I know you don't deserve it. I know this because I know you. I know this because when I think over the sequence of events, it seems to me you didn't want to participate in this operation and felt you had no choice. I think you had second thoughts and went through with it anyway because you wanted to do what you felt was the right thing. And I know that never in a million years would you have done it if you had known what would happen that night.

Anyway, I'm writing this letter because I want to apologize for what my mother said to you that day, and to tell you that I have long since forgiven you for all of it. Now it is for you to forgive us for making a terrible experience even more painful

*for you. If you care to reply I would be grateful
for just a word. I have missed you every moment.
I have been walking around this beautiful country without my heart. I have been walking around
without my right arm, and my left, and pretty
much everything.*

Yours always,
Shep

As you know, I have never replied to that letter,
though I sometimes take it out and read it, when it's
very late and I've had too much to drink. So I really
don't know what I can possibly say to the man who
helps me to my feet right now. What excuse I can give.
He makes sure I'm not hurt and hands me my pocketbook, which somehow slipped to the floor with me. I
thank him and ask to what do I owe the pleasure.

Shep says, "I was told by a mutual friend where I
might find you."

"Mutual friend? You can't mean Fox."

"Yes. Fox."

"The man who put your aunt behind bars?"

"I got to know him later. He's a good man. Do you
mind if I sit down?" He gestures to the stool next to mine.

"Be my guest."

Shep waits for me to sit before he climbs onto the

stool. It's amazing, he has the exact same loose, shambling grace as before. The same movements I memorized long ago, come faithfully to life again. He sets his hat on the counter and the bartender brings him a dry martini, just like mine. My legs and arms feel as if someone has extracted the bones from them. My mouth is full of stones. Shep sips his martini and sets it down and stares earnestly at the olive. His profile is the same. Everything is the same, even his smell. The warm salt smell of man flesh.

"I'm sorry to ambush you like this," he says. "I never meant to bother you again."

"It's no bother."

"I wrote you a letter a while back. I don't know if you ever received it."

I run my finger around the rim of the martini glass and consider lying. But how can I lie to Shep? "It was a beautiful letter," I tell him. "It meant everything to me."

The silence falls like dust. Shep takes a long drink and plucks out the olive. He still hasn't looked me in the eye. I want to touch his chin with my fingertip and turn his face toward me, even though it would probably hurt me more than him.

He chews and swallows the olive. "Well, I meant every word," he says.

"I know you did. Believe me."

"Anyway, here I am again. I promise not to make a fool of myself this time."

"Shep, no. That's not what I thought, not at all."

"Well, you don't need to worry, that's all. I'm engaged to be married, as a matter of fact."

I am not prepared for the shaft of pain that slices through my vital organs, not at all. My God, what a hypocrite I am. I am pregnant with anguish. Shep married to some other girl? Shep going to bed with some other girl? Shep waking up in the morning next to some other girl?

"Congratulations," I say. "I hope she's a nice girl."

"She's very nice. She's out in California."

"Ah, yes. California. How's the wine business?"

Shep signals the bartender for another martini. "The wine business is booming, as a matter of fact. But I'm thinking of selling up."

"Oh?"

"My mother died last winter and—"

"Oh! Oh, I'm sorry, Shep. Really I am."

"Well, that's generous of you. I mean it."

"I don't blame her. It was enough to unhinge anybody. I'll always— Shep, you know I never meant to hurt anyone. I was just as devastated as anybody."

"I know that, honey."

The word slips out and stops us dead. I reach for

the peanut bowl. The bartender mercifully arrives to take away Shep's empty glass and set a nice new brimming martini in front of him. He sips from his. I sip from mine.

"Anyway," he continues, "as I said, with Mama gone, I was thinking of taking the kids back out to Winthrop for the summer, maybe even stay there for good."

As luck would have it, I'm in the middle of another drink. I choke out, "The kids?"

"Olive's kids, I mean." He turns to me at last. "You didn't know? I took them out to California with me. I've been—well, I've been *trying* to raise them. For a bachelor with no idea about kids."

I stare at my fingers, clenched around the martini glass. "No. I didn't know that."

"It was pretty obvious that my parents—well, it wasn't going to work, that's all, so I figured they were better off away from everything. Out in the sunshine, working the land. Frank and Marie—that's my Army buddy, you remember—"

"With the French wife."

"That's right. They couldn't have been nicer about it. They had a baby coming along themselves. Marie, she's a terrific cook, you know, being from France and all. Real motherly type. Kind of feisty, too, like you. So you might say we've been one big happy family out there."

"I—I'm glad, Shep. I'm so glad. I've thought about those kids a lot, I've been worried. Guilty, I guess—"

"Guilty? No, Crick. It was *her*. It was their mother. It was what *she* did."

I shake my head because I don't trust my voice to behave itself. Shep wraps his fingers around the stem of his glass and waits for me with an air of unending sympathy. I reach for my pocketbook and shake out the pack of cigarettes. To my horror, it's empty.

"I don't suppose you have a smoke," I whisper.

"I'm sorry, no. Gave them up. Do you want me to—"

"No, it's all right. I'll manage."

"I didn't mean to upset you. Honest, Cricket. I wouldn't have come here at all if it wasn't for this—this thing that's come up. This proposal of Aunt Olive's."

I lift my head to the sight of Shep's face. Not his profile—his *face*, his plain, beloved face, his warm hazel eyes fixed on mine, his tanned California skin, all grown up, steady mature bones. I speak in a wobbly voice. "Fox told you?"

"Yes, he told me. Because of the kids. Because he knows how much I—how much they mean to me."

"Oh, Shep. Is that what you're worried about? Is that why you're here? Losing the kids?"

He turns away. "I just—we've grown kind of attached to each other, that's all. We were all grieving together. I don't know if I could have lasted without having to get up each morning and make sure they could get through the day."

"I'm sorry. I'm sorry."

"So what I came to ask you was this. I want to ask you if you'll let me see them from time to time. I'll move back to Boston if I have to. I've got Donnelly out there right now, fixing up Summerly. Just a few weeks, now and again. You don't even have to see me, if you don't want to. I'll send a car or something. I just can't imagine my life without—and I think they're attached to me, too—"

I reach out and take his hand. "Shep, I said no. I told her no."

He lifts his head and turns to me again. His eyes are wet. "What did you say?"

"I told her no. I would never take those kids away from you. They've suffered enough. I told her no."

"But she said—when I went to see her—"

"You saw her?"

He nods. "Yesterday. Fox made the arrangements. I begged her, I said—I told her—and you're saying you told her *no*?"

"Emphatically."

Shep stares at me. Beneath his tan, the blood has

drained from his cheeks. "Gosh," he says. "I don't know what to say."

"So you don't have to move back from California, after all. You can stay and marry that nice girl and carry on being a big happy family."

"But what about Aunt Olive? What about the— whatever it is, this exchange of spies?"

"Oh, I have every confidence in Mr. Fox. He'll find a way to pull it off, don't worry. Everything's going to be fine."

"I don't know. My aunt's pretty stubborn."

"Trust me," I said. "Fox has a way of getting what he wants."

Shep glances down at my hand, which still clasps his where it rests on the counter. I pull it away and grasp the stem of my glass instead. From some distant room— the lobby, maybe—comes the sound of a piano. Some familiar, sentimental piece of music, though I can't quite place it. The bartender's disappeared somewhere, the bar is empty except for the two of us. Shep's hand rests a few inches away. I can still feel the big knuckles imprinted on my palm.

"I wonder where my fish has got to," I say.

"Cricket," he says slowly, "I can't lie to you."

"No?"

"I mean I have to confess something."

"What's that?"

"The thing is. The *truth* is, I'm not really engaged. That is, we *were* engaged, until a couple of months ago. But we broke it off."

I select a broken peanut from the bowl and pop it into my mouth. "Well, that's just terrible. Why on earth?"

"A lot of little things, I guess." He lifts the martini and drains it. When he sets the glass down again, he turns to me. His eyes are still shiny, but a tiny, familiar dimple appears at the corner of his mouth. "But mostly because she couldn't sail."

Later, as we lie wrapped together in a bandage of sleek Mayflower linens, Shep asks me the question I've been dreading.

So why didn't you reply to that letter?

The room is dark. We have made love twice, like a pair of teenaged newlyweds. The sorrow of years has compressed to nothing. From the first kiss, when our lips came together as inevitably as the elevator doors that kissed shut beside us, we haven't said a word. Words intrude at a time like this, they part you. All we wanted was to connect. Against the wall, as soon as we reached my room. Then the stripping away of his clothes and mine, the tumble into bed, the slide into possession, the skin against skin, the brinksmanship, the final worship. Now a stupefied aftermath settles over us like a fog. My right hand clasps his left hand. Our fingers tangle luxuriously. Shep whispers his painful question. In such an intimate arrangement, you have to say the truth.

"Shep," I whisper. "I have a confession to make."

It takes some time for him to master his shock. He sits on the edge of the bed and tastes her name in his mouth.

Lizbit, he says. Lizbit.

We named her for the princess, I tell him. Well, she's the queen now. Either way, the name fits her.

Elizabeth. He puts his head in his hands.

I lay my hand on his shoulder. He shrugs it off.

I knot my hands together in my naked lap. "I didn't tell you because I was afraid. I was afraid your parents would try to take her away. I thought it was best for everybody if we made a clean break."

"You *thought*," he says.

"I thought you hated us. I thought you wouldn't even want to know."

He lifts his head. "My mother died without knowing she had a grandchild."

"Yes. I was wrong. I was young and terrified and I was wrong. And I'm sorry."

Shep climbs to his feet and bends to pick his clothes from the floor.

"Don't go," I say. "Please don't go."

"You expect me to stay? After what you just told me?"

"I want you to stay." I'm sitting on my knees, legs folded underneath me. I place my palms on my bare thighs and stare at my own fingers because I can't stand to look at him, putting his legs in his trousers. I whisper, "I need you to stay."

He stops with his hands on the fastening of his trousers. I have the feeling his eyes are closed. I rise to my knees and clamber to the edge of the bed, where I can just about reach his shoulders and pull him back against me. In his ear I whisper, "She needs you. She's the best kid in the world, and she needs you in her life."

"You never gave me a chance."

"I'm giving it to you now. I'm asking you now."

Shep grasps my hands and removes them from his shoulders. I guess he clears a lot of brush on that vineyard of his because his back is taut and tanned in the lamplight. He walks across the room to pluck his undershirt from the back of the chair and stick his head through the neck hole. One by one his arms thrust free. He casts around for his shirt and finds it next to the window. "You were born to break my heart, weren't you?" he says. "Over and over. It just doesn't stop."

I watch him button his shirt, fasten his cuffs. His hair sticks out from his head. His skin is flushed pink. I'm inside every pore of him, the way he's inside each pore of me.

"When you're done being mad at me, you should meet her. You'll love her to pieces."

Shep shrugs his jacket over his shoulders and sticks his necktie in his pocket. He stares at me on the bed, just sitting there naked as a worm with my hands in my lap. Though I may be a coward in some things, I won't flinch under his gaze. He has gained a few lines around his eyes. A couple of hollows under his cheekbones. I remember how he came home from the war a different man, and now he's changed again, and I have been robbed of all of it. All those minutes and hours I could have spent with him, the days and nights we would have shared, the kids we should have had. It seems to me his face softens, looking at me, but maybe that's because I want it so badly.

His hat's on the bedpost where I hung it. He reaches out his long arm and snags it.

"I'm sure I will," he says, and he turns and walks out of the room.

After he leaves, I put on the blue-striped pajamas and tunnel back into bed. The sheets smell like Shep, like what we did together. It's a comforting smell. I tell myself that it had to happen eventually, that he'd have found out soon enough and it's better that he finds out from my own confession rather than finding out by himself. I tell myself that he'll get over it. He won't stay away this time. He can't. He'll come back, because of Lizbit. Children have a way of bringing people together, even when they're mad at each other.

My eyes flash open. I startle upright and stare at the dark mass of curtains at the window.

The card is still in my pocketbook, thank God. With trembling fingers I dial the number, which goes to an answering service. I leave a message with the operator and sit in the chair at the beautiful writing desk, drumming my fingernails against the wood for what seems like an hour. The early May dawn starts to poke between the curtains. Finally the damn telephone rings back at me. I snatch up the receiver.

"Please hold for Mr. Fox," says the operator.

"Fox?" I yell. "Fox?"

"Miss Winthrop?"

"Where are you?"

He sighs. "I'm at the hospital."

"At the hospital! Is it the baby?"

"Any minute now," he says, "so this had better be an emergency, Miss Winthrop."

I draw in a deep breath. "I need to speak to Olive."

Olive is tired and triumphant. I don't think she's slept any more than I have, though for different reasons. She eyes the cigarette box greedily. I spring to my feet and hand her one, light it for her. My fingers shake. She closes her eyes and savors a long, opulent drag while I drop back into the chair and drum my fingernails against the table, much as I did against the Mayflower desk a couple of hours ago.

She opens her eyes. "You'll ruin your nails," she says.

"You did this on purpose, didn't you?"

"Did what on purpose?"

I wave my arm. "All of this. You don't want me to take those kids and raise them by myself. You know they're happy with Shep."

"Of course they're happy with him."

"This spy exchange."

"What do you want to know?"

"Whose idea was it?"

She smiles. "Well, it was Jurgis."

"*Your* Jurgis?"

"Do I know any other? He got a postcard through

to me a year or so ago, through some mutual friends in England. He survived the war in a labor camp. Discovered what had happened to me. Ever since, he's been trying to devise a way to get me out. That traitor Digby presented an opportunity at last." She holds up her hand and gestures to the room around us. "Here we are."

"So it was a bluff. This ultimatum of yours. You were never going to walk away from the exchange, were you?"

"No."

"Then why me? Why bring me into it?"

Olive reaches for the ashtray and smiles at me. Her eyelids are bruised, her skin pallid. Her gray curls spring in every direction. Even her gray dress is creased and exhausted. "My dear," she says, "you already know the answer to that, or you wouldn't be asking me these questions. You just want to know if your guess is correct."

"Because of Shep. Because you wanted to find a way to bring me back together with Shep."

She just gazes at me with her feline smile and smokes her cigarette.

"Why? I don't understand. Why the hell do you care?"

"Emilia. I've always cared. Haven't I said so from the beginning? I understand why you did these things.

Why you betrayed me. If our positions were reversed, our beliefs were reversed, I would have done the same thing. Denounced you to the authorities."

"I didn't *denounce* you—"

"Yes, you did. It amounts to the same thing. But you did what you thought was right. You denounced me according to your own principles. We must all strive to do that. We must all set aside our personal feelings and act according to the greater good." She angles her head and worries the cigarette with her thumb. "But you paid an awful price. It hurts me, what an awful price you paid. It keeps me awake at night."

"You mean leaving Winthrop and my family?"

Olive shakes her head. "I mean Nathaniel. I've always had a special feeling about Nathaniel. There's something *true* about him, isn't there? Something idealistic, like you and me."

"*Shep?* Shep isn't like you at all! He's kind and loyal. He cares about people, not ideas."

"Why, what do you mean? Not care about *people*?" Her voice is shocked. "Emilia, that's all I care about. I've fought my whole life for a more just economic order."

"For which you would willingly sacrifice human lives."

Olive stands up. The chair legs rattle behind her.

Her arm moves and for a second I imagine she's going to hit me, she's going to reach across this table and smack me on the side of my head. But she only lifts her hand to her mouth and smokes her cigarette in a hard, deep pull that makes the end flare like a match. I would say that her eyes glitter, except eyes don't really glitter, do they? Not by themselves. Requires an outside light. Still, I seem to have struck some type of fire behind the windows to Olive's soul, if you look closely. The hand trembles as she brings it back to rest on the table, cigarette burning between her two fingers. She pulls back the chair with her foot and sits down again. The act of sitting seems to calm her. When she speaks, she's found this warm, sympathetic voice that makes me want to scratch my own ears.

"Forgive me, Emilia. You reminded me of somebody, just now."

"Isn't that funny."

She misses the irony and carries on. "She was somebody I met in Moscow once, on a training program. Did you know I went to Moscow? It was before the war, when we were living in Switzerland. Sebastian was just a baby. It broke my heart to leave him behind, but it was my duty. And my God, it was exciting. It was thrilling to be needed, to be able to contribute to something so important. I made all these friends. We were desperately close. We cared for each other like brothers and sisters."

"Except for Jurgis," I point out. "He was a little more than brotherly."

Olive examines the stub of her cigarette, frowns, reaches to the box for another, which she lights with the end of the old one. "I shared an apartment with a woman named Tanya. She was from Leningrad. A pure, noble, beautiful soul. We used to take long walks together, coffee together, talking about the books we were reading, our training, the future to come. She had so much enthusiasm. We spoke in Russian so I could practice, even though her English was flawless. Her hair—I remember her hair, the color of hay when it's ready to be cut."

Olive turns her head and coughs. When she stops, her eyes are damp and shiny. I offer her a glass of water but she shakes her head.

"One day," she says, in a voice that has taken on a grainy edge, "I came back to the apartment and found Tanya crying on her bed. I asked her what was wrong. At first she wouldn't say. But I'm persistent, you know—"

"You don't say."

"—and at last she told me she'd learned an old friend of hers had been taken in for questioning and found guilty of subversion. He was executed shortly afterward. But she was certain he was innocent. And she simply couldn't accept it."

"I can't imagine why not."

"I think it provoked a crisis of faith with her. She told me how many of her friends and teachers had been arrested, people she admired, and I admit I was shocked. I had known a few myself. It was a terrible night. We couldn't sleep. All these terrible thoughts crowded in, fears, the kind of doubts that attack you in the middle of the night. At one point I fell asleep, and when I woke, it was morning and Tanya was dead."

"Dead!"

"She'd taken poison." Olive taps her cigarette into the ashtray. "I went into shock. Thank goodness for Jurgis. I think that without him near, I might have cracked. I might have gone the same way as Tanya. Nothing made any sense. Grief is such a terrible force, isn't it? It takes you over, it makes you doubt, it weakens your mind. But Jurgis was there. Jurgis gave me strength. I realized I was going to have Charlotte, that Tanya had been taken from me but now I had a new life. A new life given to me by a true love. And at that moment, that exact moment, I heard the old saying in my head."

She looks at me, eyebrows raised, like she's expecting me to prompt her. I can't think of a word to say. I haven't eaten since that sole meunière I shared at the bar with Shep, nor have I smoked or slept or drunk so much as a drop of precious coffee. *She's just playing with you,* I tell myself.

At my silence, Olive lets out a faint sigh. "You know. You must have heard it. *You can't make an omelet without breaking eggs.* Remember that, Emilia."

"People aren't eggs. And I don't see what this has to do with Shep."

"I'm only illustrating my point. You and Nathaniel, the two of you have what the Hindus call a *raj yotaka,* a royal yoke. I saw it from the moment you were in the room together. Do you remember? In the cottage at Summerly. It was as obvious as sunlight. It's what I shared with Jurgis."

The light overhead casts a brutal glow on her face. I guess mine as well. When I look at her eyes, the color seems to have washed out of them, but maybe that's because of the sodium quality of the light. In my head, I hear Fox's voice—*The Soviets play the game like a chess match, you see. Several moves ahead.*

"Shep came to see me at the hotel last night," I say.

"I thought he might. We exchange letters, you know, from time to time. He keeps me apprised of the children. When he got rid of that tiresome fiancée of his, I said to myself, *Aha. Here's our chance.*"

I set my elbows on the table and slide my fingers into my hair. In front of me, the long crumb of ash in the ashtray breaks apart and one half falls to the side.

Olive leans forward and rests her hand at the joint of my elbow. "Emilia, all I've ever wanted is to see you reach your potential. And I was right. You're flourishing at college. Every moment, every step brings you closer. Now I've brought Nathaniel back to you. You're living the life you were meant for, all because of me. One day you'll thank me for all I've done. One day you'll realize just how much you owe me, and you'll—"

I lift my head. "What did you say?"

"I've brought Nathaniel back to you," she says.

"No. After that. *All because of me.*"

She smiles. "Well, because it was. You would have spent your life on that island, if I hadn't done what needed to be done."

The room spins around the axis of Olive's sharp eyes. Slower and slower it goes, like a record player that has been unplugged.

"I don't understand. You can't mean you *wanted* me to turn you in. You can't mean you did that on purpose."

"Of course not. I mean your mother."

My tongue has gone dry. I can't seem to move my lips. "My mother?" I whisper.

"But darling. Don't say you never guessed."

"Oh my God," I say. "Oh my God."

Olive sets her cigarette stub carefully on the edge of the ashtray and takes my cold hands. Her thumbs rub against my finger joints to soothe me. Her expression is so kind, so motherly.

"Emilia, darling," she says. "It was the only way. It was the only way to set you free."

I n the years since, I have looked back on the events of that August night a thousand times. I've considered each possible course I might have taken, each choice I made, each action. I would like to think I couldn't have done anything to change the outcome, other than to have done nothing at all, but maybe that's just my own conscience trying to absolve me of any blame for what happened.

What I do know is this: I wanted to do the right thing.

Sumner Fox arrived at the house half an hour after I telephoned him. He cycled most of the way and left his bicycle in the shed by the old hayfield, carrying his equipment in a picnic basket. Very clever of him, I always thought. After all, writers are expected to do eccentric things. You see a fellow carrying a picnic basket across a hayfield and you shrug to yourself. *Oh, he's the writer, remember?*

June Lindstrom arrived soon after that, driving her

sunny Lincoln with the top down, trailing her scarf in the wind. Hiding in plain sight, I guess. She swept inside carrying a small brown suitcase and swept back out again with Susana in tow, bound for the Club where they were supposed to wait tables at dinner. By now it was almost five o'clock. I put on my hat and my old capacious raincoat—the afternoon had been warm and humid, and the usual thunderclouds were gathering to the west—and set out for the guest cottage to the distant, uneasy rumbling of the summer air.

As I cycled past the giant rhododendron, I couldn't help thinking of Shep. I'd tried to banish him from my mind until all this was over, but it was like trying to banish your desire to breathe or eat. The message I'd left at the USO waiting room at South Station had not been especially coherent. *Delayed by sickness at home, will catch later train and meet you in California, more soon,* I'd dictated to the telephone operator at the station, who hadn't seemed like she was all that interested in me and my little problems. I had heard the distinct smack of chewing gum down the line. But I knew better than to send a telegram from the post office. You might as well broadcast your message by shortwave radio, such was the discretion of Mrs. Collins's sister—Western Union confidentiality regulations be damned. I kept imagining his stunned face as he read this message, his confusion and hurt, all of which was nothing compared to what he would feel when he learned the truth.

I'll speak to him myself, Fox had said. You're doing the right thing.

Olive stood waiting for me on the front step, dressed to the nines in a blue evening gown and red lipstick. She must have put her hair in curlers or something, because the ripples were all smoothed out into luscious waves. I remembered there was some kind of themed party at the Club tonight. "Hooray for Hollywood," or something like that. Now that the war was over, nobody was holding back. It was like the twenties all over again, except with booze flowing in perfectly legal torrents—a delirious return to fun after years of depression and war. Olive's dress reached her ankles and on her feet she wore sandals with high, slender heels.

"I must run," she said, kissing my cheek. "They've been fed! I'll be back by nine!"

Sure you will, I thought. She hurried into her car and started the engine. I still recall how she waved at me as she reversed out of the drive. I waved back.

Inside the cottage, the kids lay on their stomachs on the living room floor, flipping through picture books. They scrambled up at the sight of me and flung their arms around my middle, all at once. I laughed and pulled away.

"Hold on a minute," I said. "I've got to take off my raincoat first."

"Why are you wearing a raincoat?" asked Charlotte, always sensible. "It isn't raining."

"It might rain, and then where would I be?"

"Indoors."

I hung my coat carefully on the hook. The sun still streamed through the windows, though the clouds gave off another ominous rumble. I felt a little dizzy and realized I hadn't eaten all day. Hadn't given nourishment a single thought, imagine that. I turned to face the shining, innocent faces of the Rainsford children. Matthew still clung to my left leg, babbling something about a train. I lifted him up and blew a raspberry into the tender spot of his round baby belly, where his shirt parted company with his short pants. He shrieked with joy and curled his legs to my chin.

If Olive went to prison, what would happen to them?

I set Matthew on his feet. "Let's go to the kitchen and see what your mother's got in the icebox," I said.

One thing about Olive, she believed in strict bedtimes. I guess this was mostly because she worked in the evenings, but she once said something about the housekeeper she'd hired in England, who insisted on a rigid household schedule to save electricity, and how the children thrived on it. At six o'clock precisely I ran their baths. By a quarter to seven they were dried and fragrant in their clean pajamas. They drank their warm milk while I read two stories, then Charlotte insisted on reading the third one herself. She displayed each picture solemnly to her brothers after reading the page. Then I tucked them into bed and kissed each soft cheek. For the last time, I thought.

I rose and flipped off the electric light at the switch by the door.

Good night, I said.

Good night, they chorused back. Except Matthew, who was late by half a beat.

I slipped out of the room and shut the door soundlessly behind me.

By now it was half past seven and the sun had dropped low in the sky. I stood in the middle of the living room for a moment and stared at the front door, almost as if I expected it to swing open. But Olive wouldn't be back for at least an hour. I thought it was funny she was going to a party at the Club tonight, but then I wasn't a spy. Really, who would suspect that a woman could carouse around the Winthrop Island

Club dressed as Lauren Bacall, and then go home to transmit secret information to the Soviet Union from a longwave radio in her attic? Nobody, that's who.

I walked to the hook on the wall and stuck my hand inside the gigantic pocket of the raincoat. When I pulled it back out, my fist contained a small, penlike object that, when pulled open, became a camera.

I could only hope that the kids were half asleep already and not paying attention to the groan of the attic stairs as I pulled them down in the hallway outside the bedroom. Olive had brought her wartime blackout curtains home from England and hung them over the bedroom windows. Plenty of exercise, warm milk before bed, and a nice properly dark room—that was her maxim. Knocks them right out. I set the bottom step gently against the floor and listened to the walls.

Not a whisper.

Upstairs, the light was pure gold. The dying sun hit the western window just right and for a moment I stood at the top of the stairs and watched the motes of dust dangle in the sunbeam that slanted across the room. Fox had explained a lot of things to me during the course of the afternoon. He said the radio transmission itself didn't take long—couldn't take long, because the longer the broadcast, the more risk of discovery. No, what kept Olive upstairs for hours was the cryptography. Every message had to be translated into code, using a cipher and a thing called a one-time pad, a Soviet innovation that encrypted each message in a second cipher that was unique to that particular communication.

You don't need to understand it, he said. Just understand that it's a laborious process. Requires tremendous power of concentration. That's what she's doing up there all that time. That's why she needs you to keep the children out of her way.

But she can't transmit all that information by radio, I said. All those scientific papers. She can't encode them all and then transmit the whole thing over the radio in ten minutes. It's impossible. It would take days.

That's true, he said. For a cache like this, she'll arrange for the material to be picked up by a courier.

We were sitting in my bedroom, which happened to have the clearest line between the house and the roof of the guest cottage, a hundred yards away. On my desk sat the brown suitcase June had carried over in the back seat of her Lincoln-Zephyr, now open to reveal a black Bakelite box decorated by several dials and meters that gave it the appearance of a grinning face. A wire ran from the bottom and out the corner of the window to a delicate antenna Fox had perilously stuck to the roof. A receiver, he told me, designed to intercept longwave transmissions such as those broadcast by a Soviet radio operator. Fox had settled a pair of earphones on his head and was fussing with the dials as he explained all this to me, but when he said the words *She'll arrange for the material to be picked up by a courier*, he'd turned and met my eyes, dead serious.

I thought of the night of the Peabodys' party, that disastrous party at the beginning of summer, and how Olive had emerged from the path in the beach roses, all by herself. How I'd never stopped to wonder what she was doing alone on the beach at the height of a swell party like that.

That's why she's here at Summerly, I said. The perfect location.

Fox had turned back to his radio and replied, Exactly.

Still, as I stood there in the dying light, keeping company with the dust and the immaculate surfaces of Olive's office, everything in its place, everything put away as conscientiously as a good spy should, I couldn't seem to move. I couldn't bear to disturb the barrier of her privacy. If I wanted to find something, I would have to hunt for it. I would have to discover where she'd hidden it. A line existed that I hadn't yet crossed, and I couldn't seem to stretch out my foot and step over to exist in that universe, in which I betrayed my friend.

But the world outside the attic did not stand still. The sun fell farther and the bar of gold light began to fade and disappear. Fox's stern voice intruded in my head.

Start with the bookcase, he had suggested.

I stepped forward and ran my eyes along the rows of titles. Most were in German, some in English. A couple in Russian. I drew out one of the Russian ones and fanned out the pages, but it was just a book. I stuck my fingers into the space it had occupied and found nothing except the back of the shelf. One by one I inspected the other books and discovered that Olive Rainsford did not hide any clandestine documents, or anything else, inside her bookcase.

I straightened and turned to take in the rest of the room. Fox had listed other possibilities—a false drawer in the desk, a false bottom on the typewriter, the underside of her chair. But it seemed to me that Olive wasn't going to resort to that kind of physical trickery. She would lock up her secrets in a straightforward way.

She would lock them up in the bureau, where she kept her radio transmitter.

The bureau stood at the opposite end of the attic, right where I had left it yesterday. My God, was it only yesterday? If I listened carefully, I could hear the dainty snick of the second hand making its way around the face of the clock. The sound reminded me that Olive would return in an hour, maybe less. She had work to do, she wasn't going to dance away the evening like all the other women, the idle summer wives. As soon as June and Susana and the other waitresses cleared the dessert, she would make her excuses and hurry back.

I started forward. I had taken off my shoes, so my feet made no sound on the wooden boards. When I reached the bureau, I looked around the back of the clock. There was the wire I had seen yesterday, snaking from a tiny hole at the back of the cabinet to scurry up the wall and outside through the corner of the window frame to the slanting roof. The antenna to which it connected would face east, on the opposite side of the entrance to the house, so you wouldn't even know it was there unless you were looking carefully, and even then you wouldn't think anything of it. You would figure it was just a regular antenna for an ordinary radio, such as most Americans kept in their living rooms and their kitchens for entertainment and for news of the world outside their doors.

I returned my attention to the bureau itself. As before, the door to the top cabinet swung down easily. I drew the wooden bracket out of its pocket to support the surface and ran my hand over the soft green felt. It seemed to me that the material bore a slight indentation, like something heavy had been regularly placed on it, but maybe that was my imagination. I opened the doors to the little drawers, going counterclockwise. Each one slid open under my fingers. The broken knobs gave me a little trouble. I had to wriggle the darn thing loose until I could fit my pinkie into the gap. But once emancipated, the rest of the drawer came right out. Each one was empty. The pristine paper linings looked as if they had never held anything at all. When I reached behind the drawers to investigate the space inside, my fingertips met nothing but the wooden slats at the back of the cabinet. I peered around the side to make sure the actual depth matched what my fingers perceived, that there wasn't some kind of secret recess. Everything Fox had instructed me in his brief, dense tutorial on the concealment of objects.

On top of the bureau, the solemn clock ticked. Twenty minutes past eight. I slid the wooden bracket back into place and swung the cabinet door back up into place.

But I had already known the top cabinet would be empty, hadn't I? Maybe Olive wasn't going to stash her precious documents inside hollowed-out books and secret compartments, but she wasn't going to leave them lying around in an unlocked cabinet, either.

I stepped back and contemplated the bottom cabinet. The pair of carved doors, locked shut.

I was back to where I was yesterday, wasn't I? I had to find the key that unlocked those doors. Of course, if Olive kept that key on her person, I didn't stand a chance. If she kept it elsewhere in the cottage—her bedroom, a kitchen drawer, behind a painting in the living room—I stood little more, at least in the time that remained to me.

But I didn't think she kept it elsewhere. She'd always gone straight upstairs, had simply pulled down the attic stairs and climbed to her office, no lollygagging around pulling keys out of hidey-holes. And she certainly didn't keep any keys in her pockets or around her neck or anything like that. I would have noticed that. So the key to that cabinet must be up here, somewhere in the attic.

Just use your head, Miss Winthrop, Fox had said. *You've got a sharp mind. Trust it.*

This is her office, I thought. She's on an island, she's inside a cottage on a private estate owned by her own brother-in-law. She's upstairs in an attic to which you can gain access only by a set of stairs that swings down from the hallway ceiling. She doesn't need to be clever about this. She just needs the key to be handy when she's ready to work. She'll hide it in plain sight.

My eyes climbed up the carved cabinet doors until they reached the polished wooden top and the old clock that rested there.

I had filled two tiny rolls of film in the Minox camera and started on the third when I caught the glare of headlights on the window glass. I looked at the clock—six minutes to nine. She was early.

I gathered the papers and stuffed them back in the brown envelope. The envelope had an elastic that slipped around the ends to hold them shut, and for some reason my fingers fumbled with this loop. I couldn't seem to stretch it far enough to fit over the top and bottom of the envelope. I was afraid the elastic itself might break. Outside, the soft rumble of the car engine drew close. I pictured Olive rolling to a stop in her usual place outside the front door. The engine idled and cut out. At last the elastic slipped into place. I shoved it back onto the shelf in the lower cabinet, next to the small black radio set, and set the earphones back on top of the envelope, exactly as I had found them. I shut the two doors and locked them with the small key and put the key back inside the glass door of the clock.

The car door slammed shut.

I switched off the desk lamp, grabbed the camera from the desk, and hurried to the stairs. In my haste, I stubbed my toe on the edge of the opening in the floor. I felt myself falling and caught the top stair just in time. For a second or two I hung there by my hands, swinging my legs until my foot found the steps.

The front door opened directly into the living room. Around the corner of the doorway, I heard the knob rattle and turn. Down the stairs I scurried like a crab. The front door creaked open. I lifted the bottom step and folded it back and heaved the stairs upward. The hinge groaned. The front door shut. Olive's tall sandals clicked on the wooden floor.

"Emilia!" she called. "Is that you?"

"In the kitchen!" I called back, breathless. I looked down at my toe and saw it was bleeding.

After I bandaged my toe, I sat down in the old chair in the living room to gather my wits. What next? Return to my own house, I guess. With Olive upstairs at her radio, the kids quiet in their beds, I could hurry back and deliver the rolls of film to Sumner Fox. I could deliver the film and wash my hands of the whole affair.

I stood and reached for my coat on the hook by the door.

The film rolls. I had left them in the attic.

Before I left, Fox gave me some elementary instructions in the fine art of taking a Minox photograph. I asked if that was legal, what with the Bill of Rights and all, and he said she invited you into her house, didn't she? Therefore you could snoop all you wanted. As I laid out the papers from the envelope under the light of the desk lamp, I had followed Fox's instructions to the letter. The Minox was tricky, he'd told me—difficult to focus, difficult to center the image properly because the camera had no viewfinder. And the subject had to be well lit. You had to keep your hands steady at a time when you were supremely nervous. There was a lot to remember! He'd had me practice a few times before I left the house, but taking photographs of recipe cards at the kitchen table wasn't the same as snapping shots of stolen scientific documents in the attic of a Soviet spy. I was sure that half the photos wouldn't turn out at all. Then Olive had arrived when I was only half-way through the stack, not even that, and I'd had to cover my tracks swiftly. They were tiny, those rolls of exposed film, each about the size and color of a large bug. No wonder I'd forgotten to scoop them up from the corner of the desk where I'd left them.

I sat there staring at the blank white wall, maneuvering my mind around the situation. Would she notice the film at all? Would she recognize what it was?

Of course she would. She'd probably filled hundreds of rolls of Minox film herself.

Had she already found the rolls? When I was in the bathroom, bandaging my foot?

I limped to the bottom of the attic stairs. My toe hurt even more now than when I'd stubbed it. The hallway light was switched off, so the glow from the lamp upstairs poured down the shaft. I could see the bookcase at the top of the stairs and the corner of the desk, but not Olive herself. Even when I angled myself to the extreme edge and stood on my tiptoes, I couldn't quite make out whether she was there in her desk chair, or whether she worked on the desk surface of the bureau cabinet. If I closed my eyes, I thought I could hear a series of faint, irregular clicks I recognized as Morse code.

It almost goes without saying, doesn't it, that I knew Morse code like I knew my own handwriting? In the first place, I'd grown up with boys. In the second place, I'd grown up by the sea. My father always said Morse code could save your life, if you were shipwrecked or your equipment was knocked out by a storm or something. Most radios could still transmit pings even when they didn't have enough power to broadcast voices. Not only that. You could communicate Morse code in flashes of light, in drumbeats, all kinds of ways. As soon as I knew my letters and words, Pop made me learn each combination of dots and dashes to which they corresponded. Shep and

I used to talk back and forth with our flashlights at night, when we were kids and supposed to be in bed.

I closed my eyes and listened for a moment or two. I couldn't make heads or tails of the clicking above my head, but then I wasn't supposed to. They were in cipher, after all. But it was enough to know she was transmitting this message from her radio set right now, right this moment. A hundred yards away, Fox would be listening through the earphones attached to his receiver. He would be recording what he heard. Why, they might not even need those two rolls of film, although the additional evidence might prove helpful if she managed to destroy the papers themselves before they could be gathered by investigators.

Either way, the Minox camera contained another half a roll of photographs.

There was no need to worry, really. I'd done it. I'd done the right thing, I had done the impossible. Nearly a year after the war was over, I had struck my blow for the world democratic order.

Now all I had to do was find Shep and explain everything, before he discovered for himself what I'd done.

As I opened my eyes and turned away from the stairs, I realized the clicking had stopped. I heard the scrape of a chair leg and hurried for the doorway to the living room. As I found the chair, Olive's voice floated down the attic stairs.

"Emilia, darling. Is that you?"

I limped back to the doorway and put my hand on the wall. My toe throbbed inside its bandage.

"Emilia?" she called again.

I gathered myself. Channeled my voice into just the right note of sleepy confusion.

"Olive? Is something wrong?"

"Would you mind coming upstairs for a moment? I need to speak to you."

I curled my fingers around the corner of the wall. "Of course."

As I stepped forward into the hallway, my toe hurt so badly I thought maybe I'd broken the bone. It wouldn't be the first time. I'd dropped a boat hook on my foot when I was ten—the blunt side, thank God, but I'd had to use crutches for three weeks. And there was that time I cut the ball of my foot on a broken shell. Boy, did that bleed. Now, maybe my toe didn't hurt quite as badly as the time I'd broken my foot with the boat hook, but the nature of the pain was the same. Each time I set down my foot—on the floor, on the first step, on the third one—an excruciating jolt flashed halfway up my leg. I had to bite my lip to keep from calling out.

I tried to place the middle of my foot on the step, but when I shifted my weight to lever myself upward, the pressure screamed in my nerves. I carried on. When I got to the top, I hoisted on my good foot and turned to face Olive, who stood next to the bureau wearing a toothy smile. The desktop was down and the black radio set sat on top of the green felt, in open view.

Olive's gaze traveled downward from my face to land at my foot. Her smile faded away.

"Oh, dear," she said. "Have you hurt yourself?"

For some reason, I followed her stare all the way down. Gingerly I held my foot on the floorboard next to the stair shaft. A bright red spot of blood had leaked onto the white gauze. On the floor next to my foot, where I had stubbed the toe, a few smears of blood had already begun to dry to a dull red brown.

I looked back up at the same instant Olive did. Our eyes met. I had the impression that she was surprised, that she hadn't seen those bloodstains before, that maybe I had miscalculated her intentions.

"Yes," I said. "I thought I heard a noise up here. A rodent or something. The light was off and I stubbed my toe."

Olive still wore her evening gown, though her red lipstick had faded to splotchy pink. As I said, she had put her hair in curlers for the occasion and it was funny how the silky, unfamiliar waves caressed the wide angles of her cheekbones and made her look like a different person, softer and more glamorous.

"You should be more careful, Emilia," she said. "This stairwell is much too dangerous. What if you'd fallen? Next time, bring a flashlight."

"I will."

"Well, then. Lesson learned, eh?" She smiled and reached for her pocketbook, which she had slung over the corner of the bureau. "You don't mind staying in the house for a bit, to watch over the kids? It's such a pleasant night, I feel like a nice smoke on the beach."

I remember I stood in the hallway for at least a minute after the door closed behind her. Maybe it was longer, I don't know. My heart was jolting so fast, my brain was whirling so madly, I lost all sense of time.

Run to Fox, I told myself. Run down the lane and get Fox, he'll know what to do.

But what if he arrived too late? What if her Soviet contact was already waiting for her on the beach right now, in some kind of motorboat, ready to speed off with those papers—that vital scientific information that could possibly help to build an atomic bomb? Her pocketbook wasn't large but I saw how it bulged. You could certainly have folded up those papers and fit them inside, if you shoved hard enough.

Telephone, I thought. Use the telephone, stupid.

I ran to the kitchen and lifted the receiver. When the switchboard operator answered (Winthrop was still on a manual exchange in those days), I asked her to connect me to my own house. The switchboard was at the post office and it was Mrs. Collins's loudmouth sister on duty, so within minutes the whole island would know something was up, but I didn't have a choice, did I?

"I'm sorry, honey. The line's busy," she told me.

"It's very important. Could you interrupt and say it's an emergency? Tell them—tell my father it's an emergency and he has to come to the beach, right away."

"What kind of emergency? Don't you want to tell him yourself?"

By now I was shouting. "It doesn't matter! Just tell him it's an emergency! I'm going down to the beach right now, I'll meet him there!"

"But—"

I slammed down the receiver and ran out the kitchen door, hoping to God the kids wouldn't wake up.

I don't remember running to the beach. I must have gone around the other side of Summerly, along the path that ran from cottage to beach, the one we'd taken that first day I had come to visit Olive and the kids. There wasn't much moon and the path cut through the newly trimmed boxwoods and then the beach roses, which explains the scratches I found on my arms the next day.

At first, when I reached the sand, I didn't see anything. As I said, the moon was just a sliver and my eyes weren't yet used to the dark. The Summerly lights twinkled to my right, from the library and possibly Mrs. Peabody's room upstairs—it was hard to tell from this angle. The air was heavy and smelled of brine.

"Olive!" I called out softly.

There was no answer. I called out a little louder and a voice called back to me, not far away, from the rocks at the edge of the Summerly lawn.

"Cricket? That you?"

The funny thing was, I knew the voice was familiar. I knew it belonged to a man of my acquaintance, but my brain was so paralyzed I couldn't quite place the voice to the man, if that makes sense.

"Who's there?" I said.

I saw his hair first, catching the light from the house. Then his face, his familiar shoulders. The tiny orange dot of a cigarette at the end of his hand.

"Cricket! What the devil are you doing out here? Shep's been ringing up the house all night. Wanted me to track you down and see if you were all right. Say, have you heard the news?"

"I can't—"

"We're getting married, Cricket! Susana and me! I spoke to Tippy tonight, she understands, no hard feelings. I think we've both known for a while that we made a mistake. So I'm free. I'm going to be a father, Cricket! I guess you know that already." Amory stopped before me without the slightest sign of embarrassment at the shocking details. As the light grew on his face I saw that what I had assumed was a kind of drunken daze was actually happiness. I remember thinking, *My God, he's in love with her.*

"Isn't it grand, Cricket?" he said.

"It's—it's wonderful, Amory. Wonderful news. But I—I can't—I'm looking for Olive—"

"So I went right over to Susana! At the Club! Cornered her after the dessert service! And she said yes! I guess it's going to be a hurried-up wedding, but at least we can count on you for bridesmaid, right?"

"Olive! Have you seen her?"

"Why, I guess so. At the Club, an hour or two ago."

"I mean here! On the beach!"

As the words left his mouth, I heard a noise behind me, at the far end of the beach, where the Summerly property ended in a narrow marsh cove. I turned and wallowed across the soft sand while bolts of agony shot up my leg from my toe.

"Cricket, what's going on? What's the matter?"

I reached the line of high tide and the sand became hard. My brain was white with pain. Ahead of me I saw a flash of light. Some pale, curving shapes gathered the trace of moonlight. Now voices—rough, male, foreign. Someone barked out a noise of warning. A flashlight found my face, blinding me.

"Olive!" I cried out.

"Emilia?"

Amory skidded up next to me. "What's going on? Who the hell are these men?"

The flashlight moved to Amory, and though a large black spot danced before my eyes, I could now make out the boat, the two men, Olive stock-still in her luminous evening gown. She yelled something to one of the men and he raised his hand. He must have held a gun.

I know this because Amory yelled out some profanity and lunged forward in front of me, and a loud noise broke the air apart just as the beach filled with running men.

Much of what happened afterward, I learned from Fox. I went into what the doctor called a state of shock, precipitated by the sight of Amory's body lying motionless on the sand, streaked by flashlights, so it comes back to me like a dream or a movie, or like something that happened to another person while I stood watching. Sometimes I think it was a dream. I'll be standing in front of a lecture hall, say, or standing in line at the butcher, and the memory will come back to me and I'll think, *Well, thank goodness that was just a dream.* Then I remember it wasn't a dream, that it was true.

I understand that I knelt down to check on Amory to make sure he was really dead, and once I saw there was no hope, that the life had whooshed out of him in a single bang, I apparently stood calmly and walked toward the Summerly lawn, without the slightest limp, while about a dozen FBI men tried in vain to swim out after the motorboat. The Soviets had their papers but they had left Olive behind. I remember Susana flying past me, before I could stop her, and you can imagine the screaming. I understand Pop had to take her away and Dr. Pradelli, once he was done attending to Amory's corpse, gave her some Nembutal to make her sleep. At some point during all this, I leaned over and vomited politely on a flowerbed. That was where the Peabodys found me. They were pretty sauced from their night at the Club, as you might guess, which was probably a blessing.

Don't go out there, I said to Mrs. Peabody, but she did anyway.

Sometimes I think that if only Shep had been there that night, everything would have been different. He would have been able to comfort his mother, to comfort me. He would have taken charge of the situation. He would have seen with his own eyes, and I would have been able to tell him what happened from my own mouth, before the details blurred in my head and the FBI took me away and Mrs. Peabody had her breakdown, and everything else followed from there.

But Shep was in Boston that night, waiting for me. He told me that he stayed all night in that USO waiting room, hoping I would turn up, frustrated and worried because the Winthrop Island telephone circuits were jammed, and that was why he only discovered what happened the next morning.

He told me this while we lay together in bed at the Mayflower Hotel, pouring our confessions into the skin of the other. Then he asked me why I hadn't replied to his letter, all those years ago, and I told him the truth.

I told him that his brother Amory was not gone altogether but had left something of himself inside the womb of my sister, a baby girl born at the start of the following spring and carried home to our little house in Wellesley, Massachusetts, where we raised her together and just about ruined her with love, such that the mere possibility of some Peabody arming his Harvard lawyers to take her away might well have destroyed us.

Epilogue

MAY 1956
Winthrop Island

At three o'clock in the morning, I type the last word on the page and roll the paper out of the cylinder. I read over the paragraph and discover an error—*teh* instead of *the*. I'm afraid it happens when I'm trying to type as fast as the words are flowing in my head. I correct the mistake with a swipe of my pen and lay the paper facedown on the stack next to the typewriter.

My office is on the third floor, a small room that used to belong to a maid, back in the days when maids were cheap. In the beginning, I tried to work in the study downstairs, but it was soon evident that I would be forced either to murder my family or to work elsewhere.

I think I made the right choice. I like it here. Through the little window (those thrifty Peabodys didn't waste glass on mere housemaids) you can gaze right out across the ocean, Long Island to your right and Rhode Island to your left. Block Island straight ahead. At three in the morning, the sky and the ocean merge into the same giant nothingness. The lights twinkle from the shore points. A faint moon quivers behind the thinning clouds. On nights like this when the world is small, when you can sigh and reach the far side of the earth, I feel her presence most keenly. She looks over my shoulder as I write and whispers in my ear. Reminding me to what I owe everything around me.

All because of me.

Of course Olive regretted the necessity of my mother's death. She made her regret clear, in that bare, windowless cube while the dawn broke unseen beyond the walls. I remember how tenderly she spoke of that last morning on the beach, how hard she tried to make sure Mama's final hours were happy ones. How she selected pentobarbital precisely because it was such an easy way to go, you just drifted off to sleep and that was that. In fact, she'd been trained in its application during her special course in Moscow before the war. She knew what dose to use, how to drop it into Mama's water while she and Susana sat with her at the kitchen table, waiting for me to change clothes. Easy as anything.

When she finished her account, I rose from my chair and went to the door. The guard stood outside and I told him he could take her away now. She stood and held out her arms for the handcuffs. I remember she sighed and said she supposed I would think she was a dreadful person.

I told her on the contrary, my opinion hadn't changed a bit.

The guard led her to the door, where she stopped. Over her shoulder, she said that once she was inside the Soviet Union, she would find a way to send word that she was safe. I told her I didn't care one way or the other, really.

But you will, she said. One day you'll understand. One day you'll thank me for all of this.

When she left, I remained in the room for some time. I smoked cigarette after cigarette with my shaking hand and called myself an idiot. Because I should have known all along.

Wasn't it Stalin himself who said it first? You can't make an omelet without breaking eggs.

From time to time I hear from Fox. He tells me the exchange went off without a hitch, though you wouldn't have read about it in any of the newspapers. Sasha Digby now lives in Montana somewhere, under a new name; the former Mrs. Digby has married somebody else and lives in England with their children and a new baby. As for Olive, Fox can't say exactly. His sources suggest she lives in a flat outside of Leningrad with her lover, that she makes regular trips to Moscow to instruct new KGB officers on various points of tradecraft. He asks if she has made any attempt to contact me. I tell him no.

In a couple of hours the sun will be up and so will the kids. Everyone will be delighted to hear I've finished the book. Apparently I can be difficult in the last stages of writing. That's what Charlotte says, anyway. She's at that age when she likes to challenge you. Cato would have cited Freud or somebody but I just think she's a teenager. I stretch my arms to the slanted ceiling and rise from the chair. I can't seem to find a paperweight so I place an empty coffee cup on top of the stack of pages. When I switch off the lamp, the world goes black and quiet. I hold still and think of the people fast asleep below my feet. The boys in their room and Charlotte in hers. The baby in the nursery next to our room.

At the thought of Eddy, I start for the door. The moon makes just enough light to illuminate the hall and the narrow staircase down to the second floor. I whisper down the corridor and crack open the nursery door. Not a sound from the crib by the wall. I hurry over and place my hand on her back, just to make sure she's breathing. Eddy's always been a sound sleeper, even when she was brand new. I would hand her to Shep after nursing and he would lay her against his chest and her eyes would roll back in delirious pleasure at the massive thump of his heart. He would settle her in the crib and the honest truth is I'd have to go in and wake her up myself because my breasts were about to burst, that's how well she slept. Everybody warns me that we'll pay for this peace with the next one.

You're probably not all that interested about my book, but I'll tell you anyway. It's really an expansion of my dissertation, "Colonial Folkways and the Great Snow of 1717," which I completed and defended a year ago last March, just after Edwina was born. I don't recommend getting married, giving birth, and preparing a doctoral thesis all at the same time, but it wasn't as if I had a choice—at least with the first two endeavors. I wish I could tell you how I managed it, but the fact is it's all a blur. What I do remember is that the head of the department took me aside afterward and recommended I turn this subject into a book for a popular audience, so maybe I've stumbled into some kind of alchemical creative process after all. Not that I have any plans to try it again. For one thing, I'm pretty satisfied with the husband I've already got.

Eddy's nursery used to be Mr. Peabody's dressing room, so once I've assured myself that my daughter is still alive, I slip through the door that interconnects with our bedroom. What moonlight exists falls directly on Shep, who sprawls across the bed on his stomach, shaggy hair half-hidden under a pillow. At present we are trying to conceive another baby and Shep approaches stud duties with all the discipline and perseverance you can imagine. For a moment I consider whether I should continue to the bathroom, wash and dress. After all, the sun will rise soon, and Susana and Lizbit and the little Harvey squirt will be arriving around noon for a couple of weeks' stay with their cousins and to get away from Harvey, though Susana doesn't exactly say so. I've got to make sure the beds are aired and the groceries ordered and all those thousand and one tasks that make up an ordinary day at Summerly. But there's something about the lure of my husband's body. I don't mean sex, either—I mean something more essential, primitive, belonging to caves and ritual. I make my way around to the other side of the bed and crawl in next to him. He doesn't wake, but in his sleep he knows I'm there. He grumbles, rustles, turns on his side and scoops me into his middle. He mutters something into my ear about hamburgers.

Oh, he was mad, after I told him about Lizbit. He was mad for *weeks*. But I was right. He came around. Well, he *had* to come around, once I explained to him that he was going to be a father, thanks to his *reckless passion* (those were the exact words I used, in my most indignant voice) that night at the Mayflower. He likes to joke about how I trapped him into marriage but you should have seen him when he met his daughter. The nurse had her swaddled up in a hygienic white blanket so only her little squashed red face peeked out. They have the exact same hazel eyes, it's a marvel. They looked at each other and fell in love. So now he wants another one. What a family man, Shep. Even in his sleep he wants to make another baby with me. His hands realize what they're holding. His belly stirs. Olive whispers in my head—*This lovely ripening sensation, you know, this miraculous creature growing inside you, planted there by someone you adore.* I turn in his arms and sling my leg over his hip.

I wake up alone in the middle of the morning, confounded. The bedroom's wracked with sunlight. I can't remember how I got here, what month it is. The old panic hits me. I don't belong here, I'm a burglar. A thief in the night. This bed, this room, this house— none of them mine.

Then I see the silver bell on the pillow next to me, the note underneath. *Ring for coffee.*

Our old joke. One night in the bleak midwinter I was up late writing my dissertation and fell stone-cold asleep around three in the morning. Shep stole early out of bed to get the children ready for school and left this bell and this note behind, and the tradition stuck.

I sink back on my pillow and finger the edge of the bell. The first time I returned to Summerly I was Shep's bride. We spent the month of August here as newly-weds. I remember he carried me over the threshold and told me the place was mine. He was giving Summerly to me as a wedding present, in my own name. He joked that he hoped I wouldn't mind letting him and the children stay there with me. At that point I was about nine weeks along with Eddy and sick as a dog most of the time, so I didn't find a lot of things funny. But I laughed at that. It was only later that I wandered through the rooms and up the stairs and down the corridors, and instead of triumph I felt shame. I felt somebody dogging my footsteps, stealing from behind to lay her fingers on my belly and tell me how I was ripening.

I pick up the silver bell and ring it savagely.

A few minutes later, Shep brings up a cup of coffee. It's a good thing I've slung on a dressing gown to cover my nakedness, because Matthew storms in with him. "I've brought the mail!" he announces. He dumps a couple of envelopes and a small brown parcel on my lap. "Shep says I can skip my tennis lesson and go to meet the ferry with him. Can I?"

I kiss his forehead and ruffle his hair. "Whatever Shep says, darling."

Matthew whoops in triumph and runs out of the room. Shep hands me the coffee and sits down next to me, on the edge of the bed. He's grinning ear to ear, as well he might. "That was something, last night," he says. "I guess you must have finished your book."

"I felt like celebrating. Where's Eddy?"

"Charlotte's playing with her. Sebastian's out sailing. I'm just sitting here, falling in love with my wife all over again."

How he grins. You haven't seen anything until you've seen Shep grin. It's like the sun rising on the first day of summer. It's the same smile he wore on his wedding day, the same smile he wore when he carried me into Summerly and spun me in circles on the living room floor. The same smile he wore when the nurse put his daughter in his arms for the first time. It's the kind of grin a man wears when all his burdens have been lifted, when he's happy as a young colt and he doesn't realize what his happiness is built on. So far as he understands, the only thing that remains of Olive is her offspring— her three children that are the joy of his life and mine, the center of our world, together with Lizbit and Eddy and this new baby to come, I'm sure of it now.

I set down the coffee and put my arms around his neck. "You're too good to be real, do you know that?"

He returns my kiss and tells me he's going downstairs to make me some imaginary toast.

After he's left the room I turn my attention to the brown parcel in my lap. It's small and oblong, about eight inches in length, held together with old-fashioned twine instead of adhesive tape. I assume it's from Lizbit—she's recently taken up a habit of sending me objects in the mail, like an odd-shaped stone she found in the backyard or a ceramic rhinoceros she made in school—but the return address seems to be missing and the postmark, when I examine it more closely, indicates a town somewhere in England.

I set aside the coffee and the envelopes and rise to sit on the edge of the bed and turn the parcel over in my hands. I suppose I'm looking for some way to tear apart the thick brown paper, but it's all wrapped tight by some sorcery of twine. Eventually I resort to the sewing scissors I keep in one of the drawers of the dressing room. The final knot falls away. I unwrap the paper and open the cardboard box. Inside is a packet of about twenty typewritten pages of extremely thin paper, folded and bound by another length of twine. I snip the twine and unfold the pages. They are crisp, almost brittle, and the lines are typed close. I smooth them out on top of the chest of drawers. By now my heart is hammering against my ribs. At the top of the first page, the packet's title runs across in block letters:

ON THE CULT OF PERSONALITY AND ITS CONSEQUENCES
(SPEECH GIVEN BY NIKITA KHRUSHCHEV AT 20TH COMMUNIST PARTY CONGRESS, MOSCOW 25TH FEBRUARY, TRANSL FROM RUSSIAN ORIGINAL)

Shep's voice floats up the stairs. "Cricket, honey, toast is ready!"

I fold up the papers and stuff them back in the box. I set the box in the top drawer and cover it with socks. The paper and twine I gather up to put in the box next to the fireplace.

"Coming," I call down.

Author's Note

As I complete the final revisions to this novel, the news of Russian atrocities streams out of Ukraine. Anyone who has done even the most superficial research on Soviet tactics during the Second World War and its aftermath, let alone enforcing its own internal security, will share my own sense of historical echo. Because German war crimes were themselves so horrific, because the Soviets were our allies, because Soviet totalitarianism was so often excused and even ignored by its contemporary apologists in a way that Nazi totalitarianism was not, we have forgotten what a Faustian bargain Western liberal democracy struck with Stalin in order to defeat Hitler. The Cold War was its consequence, and Vladimir Putin is its natural heir.

While the history of the Second World War is by

now familiar to most readers, the subsequent struggle between the Communist East and the capitalist West is relatively undiscovered territory. Open warfare was conducted by proxy and morally complicated. Direct operations were sporadic, cloaked in secrecy, and rarely reported to the public. The histrionic McCarthy hearings—echoing, with an irony no doubt lost on the senator and his allies, the show trials of 1930s Moscow—cast a paranoid light on the genuine problem of Soviet agents within Western centers of power that colors historical perceptions to this day. Even as the Cold War shaped the childhoods and adult lives of those of us born between 1940 and 1980, we didn't know a fraction of what was really going on. (I am frequently approached at book talks and on the internet by people who only recently discovered that a father or mother wasn't really a reporter for *Time* magazine in Vienna, after all, but a CIA officer operating under cover.) But as archives are opened and documents declassified, a wealth of information is finally making its way into the public domain to deepen our understanding of this almost insurmountably complex conflict.

The Beach at Summerly is based on no single person or incident during the Cold War, but rather a range of them. While the character of Olive Rainsford arises from my own imagination, her history of involvement in Soviet espionage is loosely modeled on that of Ursula Kuczynski, whose career with the GRU (the Soviet military intelligence service) reached its apex when she facilitated the transfer to Moscow of top secret information from Klaus Fuchs, one of the leading physicists on the atomic bomb project and a devoted Communist, the arrest of whom precipitated her defection to East Germany in 1950. Ben Macintyre's engrossing account of her life and espionage career, *Agent Sonya*, gave me invaluable insight into the nuts and bolts of a Soviet intelligence agent's activities, to say nothing of the intellectual jujitsu required to continue risking your life in support of a regime that has imprisoned or executed so many of your friends and Communist fellow travelers.

While the other resources I consulted are too numerous to list here, I'd like to point out a few for those interested in further research on Cold War spies and spycraft. To learn more about Richard Sorge and the vast network of Soviet intelligence agents active both before and during the Second World War, I highly recommend *An Impeccable Spy*, by Owen Matthews. Allen Dulles's *The Craft of Intelligence* is a classic for understanding the development of a permanent, professional intelligence service in the United States, and *In the Enemy's House*, by Howard Blum, engagingly recounts the story of the VENONA decryption project that broke open both the Rosenberg case and the Cambridge spy ring, among others.

Of course, *The Beach at Summerly* is really a story about people, and how the grand historical forces of geopolitical conflict transform the lives of ordinary citizens. In the course of my research, I came across the narrative of an English teenager whose life was upended when the nice lady who moved in down the street and befriended both her and her mother turned out to be a Soviet radio operator. When I revisited a map of Long Island Sound, it occurred to me that the location of Winthrop Island—a fictional enclave I introduced in my earlier novel *The Summer Wives*, inspired by the real-life Fishers Island, a summer retreat for a certain type of discreetly well-heeled Easterner—at the sound's eastern edge might just be an ideal place for a Soviet spy to operate under the most secure of covers.

As always, thanks are due to a large and varied supporting crew, starting with my all-star literary agent, Alexandra Machinist of ICM, and my editor, Rachel Kahan at William Morrow, for encouraging me to turn a summer novel into a Cold War spy drama . . . or is it the other way around? I'm also deeply in debt to publicist extraordinaire Brittani Hilles and marketing maven Tavia Kowalchuk of William Morrow, who have worked so hard over the years to send my novels into the world with all the fanfare.

I owe so much to my dearest friends Lauren Willig and Karen White—so dear, in fact, we also write novels together—who buck up my spirits and bring me coffee, dark chocolate, and the occasional cocktail to keep body and soul together, and without whom I might have given up this gig many books ago. My husband, children, and wider family are always there with love and humor to remind me what really matters.

To the marvelous community of booksellers, book bloggers, and book pushers, you are my heroes. To my readers, both old and new, I am more grateful than I can say for all your support—your messages, your posts, your reviews, your book purchases, your enthusiasm that keeps me writing on, book after book. Thank you.

About the Author

BEATRIZ WILLIAMS is the author of fifteen novels, including *The Summer Wives*, *A Hundred Summers*, and *Our Woman in Moscow*. A native of Seattle, she graduated from Stanford University and earned an MBA in finance from Columbia University. She lives with her husband and four children near the Connecticut shore, where she divides her time between writing and laundry.

Discover great authors, exclusive offers, and more at hc.com.

HARPER LARGE PRINT

We hope you enjoyed reading
our new, comfortable print size and found it
an experience you would like to repeat.

Well – you're in luck!

Harper Large Print offers the finest in
fiction and nonfiction books in this same larger
print size and paperback format. Light and easy to read,
Harper Large Print paperbacks are for the book lovers
who want to see what they are reading without strain.

For a full listing of titles and
new releases to come, please visit our website:
www.hc.com

HARPER LARGE PRINT